Blackout. December 8, 1941. Pearl Harbor bombed only hours before and Manila on bombing alert. The streets of the city still quaked from the day's frenetic pounding of traffic—rushing civilians, heavy rattling carabao carts, weaving horse-drawn calesas, honking cars and trucks in near collision; and pedestrians yelling in a cacophony of Tagalog, English, Spanish, Chinese, merging with other tongues.

The outer Manila bore the face of order and cooperation; the inner Manila had become a spy, turned inward to secret hiding places, where she listened to shortwave radio broadcasts, kept guns, and horded food, money and jewels for the day when the Americans would return. There was that certainty: They would return. Everyone in the city felt it, pro-American or not, the people sensed the occupation was temporary, if they managed to live through it. But how long would the liberation take? And how many would live through it? That was the question that weighed in the air of the city, a once-proud Asian queen, now a prisoner in fading robes; but a fierce defender of a heritage that she refused to surrender.

The beggar woman rose, hobbled over, and stood behind Vida's shoulder, her body turned away as she whispered, "If you have anything for me, go to the fish stall on the left and drop it in the drain ditch. Come back in ten minutes. There will be something for you. Bless you."

Sarita, Pia and two guerrillas, *known as "Aguila" and "Cocodrilo"—one named for the power of an eagle; the other for the stealth of a crocodile—were hunkered in a shadowy rice field. A convoy of Japanese trucks rumbled by on the narrow road to Malolos. One of the vehicles pulled to a noisy stop fifty meters away from the four figures who hid, flat on their stomachs, between the thick rows of rice.*

All eyes focused on the gate, outside of which three Japanese soldiers stood, their faces lit by fire, the barrels of their guns moving, as they poked at the heavy padlock, which they had placed there months before. One of them stopped, lifted a nambu *woodpecker machine gun and was about to shoot off the lock, when another soldier pointed to the flames eating the back of the Kellers' house. At that instant, a throaty order was called to them from the street. Shots cracked into the air. The three soldiers turned, answered the fire and bolted away. A clatter of wooden* bakias *echoed sharply. Desperate screams split the fiery night. Ripping machine gun fire followed. Then silence, except for the roar of the avalanching flames.*

Other books by Doreen Gandy Wiley

Sing the Day (1972) Miracle Publications, LaGrande, Oregon (o.p.)

Poems for Twelve Moods (1979) Dragon's Teeth Press, Georgetown, California

A New Leafing, A Journey from Grief (1985) Celilo Publications, Portland, Oregon

FIRES OF SURVIVAL

a novel

by DOREEN GANDY WILEY

Introduction by Jean M. Auel

Strawberry Hill Press

Strawberry Hill Press
3848 S.E. Division Street
Portland, Oregon 97202

Cover by Ku, Fu-sheng
Typeset and designed by Wordwrights, Portland, Oregon
Water color sketch and maps by the author
Proofread by L. Ann Porter

Manufactured in the United States of America

Library of Congress Cataloging-in-Publication Data

Wiley, Doreen Gandy, 1927-
    Fires of survival : a novel / by Doreen Gandy Wiley ;
  introduction by Jean M. Auel
        p.   cm.
    Includes bibliographical references (p.).
    ISBN 0-89407-114-9 : $10.95
    1. World War, 1939-1945—Philippines—Fiction. I. Title.
PS3557.A49F57 1994
813'.54—dc20   94-32708
                             CIP

ACKNOWLEDGMENTS

My deepest thanks to:

My husband Joe for his day-by-day caring and tireless ear!

Members of my family; and colleague friends—Ruth Robertson and Marlene Howard—for their pre-publication reading of the manuscript and for their clear insight.

Jean M. Auel and Donald Staight for their much valued written comments.

Marcia and Buck Clark for helpful resource material.

And last, but never least, to Jean-Louis Brindamour for his professional guidance; and to Ku, Fu-sheng for his creative artwork on the cover of the book.

DEDICATION

For my cherished family and friends, and for all who experienced World War II in the Philippines—those of you who survived, and those of you who lost your lives. Your struggles are reflected in these pages, your courage is commemorated.

Publication of this book has been made possible, in part, by a grant from Donald C. Staight, Certified Jungian Analyst, who is a member of the C.G. Jung Institute of San Francisco.

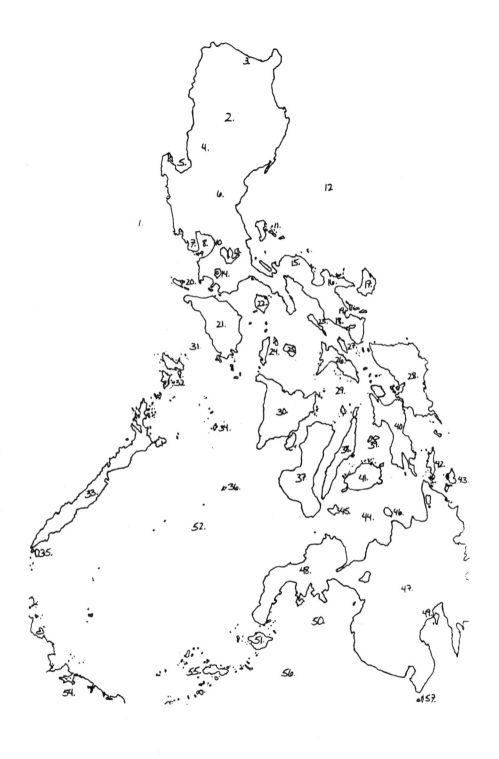

PHILIPPINE ISLANDS

(Map drawn by Elena for her tutor)

1. South China Sea
2. Luzon
3. Aparri
4. Baguio
5. Lingayen Gulf
6. Cabanatuan
7. Bataan Peninsula
8. Manila Bay
9. Corregidor
10. Manila
11. Polillo Islands
12. Pacific Ocean
13. Laguna Bay
14. Lake Taal & Volcano
15. Camarines Norte Province
16. Camarines Sur Province
17. Cataduanes Island
18. Albay Province
19. Legaspi
20. Lubang Island
21. Mindoro Province (Island)
22. Marinduque
23. Burias Island
24. Romblon Province (Island)
25. Sibuyan Island
26. Masbate Province (Island)
27. Ticao Island
28. Samar
29. Visayan Sea
30. Panay
31. Mindoro Strait
32. Calamian Group
33. Palawan
34. Cuyo Islands
35. Bugsuk Island
36. Cagayan Islands
37. Negros
38. Cebu
39. Camotes Islands
40. Leyte
41. Bohol
42. Dinagat Island
43. Siargao Island
44. Mindanao Sea
45. Siquijor Province (Island)
46. Camiguin Island
47. Mindanao
48. Zamboanga Province
49. Davao
50. Moro Gulf
51. Basilan Island
52. Sulu Sea
53. Cagayan Sulu Islands
54. Borneo
55. Sulu Province (Islands)
56. Celebes Sea
57. Saragani Islands

INTRODUCTION

Fires of Survival takes us back to World War II, and the takeover of the Philippines by the Japanese military shortly after the bombing of Pearl Harbor.

But this exciting drama is not so much a war story as it is a moving evocation of life during the occupation, seen through the eyes of a girl growing into womanhood.

Born of an American father and a Spanish mother, whose second husband is Swiss, Elena Neville typifies in her own existence the mixed heritage of Manila.

Through Elena's story, Doreen Gandy Wiley portrays with convincing detail and subtle conviction the frustrations of trying to maintain a semblance of normal life under difficult and dangerous conditions. The underlying fear and the courage it took to face each day with only a dream of hope, and the dramatic conclusion when the Americans finally return to liberate Manila, depicts with stunning clarity the brutality of war to a vulnerable civilian population.

Though the setting is the forties, **Fires of Survival** is a timely and poignant parable for the nineties.

Jean M. Auel
1994

DISCLAIMER

All characters in **Fires of Survival**, with the exception of public figures, are fictitious. As they walk across the stage of history, their reality, though imaginary, is based on the collective human experience forged by war. It is the story of their grim confrontation with death and their fierce will to live—an inner strength born from the fires of survival that burn from within.

Table of Contents

Chapter One

The First Bombs

Blackout. December 8, 1941. Pearl Harbor bombed only hours before and Manila on bombing alert. The streets of the city still quaked from the day's frenetic pounding of traffic—rushing civilians, heavy rattling carabao carts, weaving horse-drawn *calesas*, honking cars and trucks in near collision; and pedestrians yelling in a cacophony of Tagalog, English, Spanish, Chinese, merging with other tongues. A Tower of Babel!

Eight p.m. and dark as a cave except for a few fireflies sparking in random bushes, and the rumble of U. S. Army trucks, their headlights filtered to a light-obscuring blue glow.

Elena Neville sat cross-legged on the long, wide ledge of her Spanish-styled bedroom window. She pressed her nose hard against the screen and felt the cold pressure of iron bars that framed the six-foot tall window casing in which she could freely stand.

Elena toyed with the translucent *capiz* shell shutters, sliding them back and forth nervously, then resettled herself back on the ledge. She clicked on the weak light of a flashlight, opened a lined notebook and began to write in her journal.

"*December 8, 1941,*" she wrote, then stopped to take a deep breath, filling her lungs with a night air that was sultry with moisture and the scent of *kalachuchi* blossoms—a sweet, seductive variety of frangipani—although she knew it was a night that was anything but sweet and seductive.

"*I must tell this slowly, step by step,*" she wrote, "*as it happened, because I'm still totally stunned by today's unreal events. So much has gone on, I feel like I'm a hundred years old instead of fifteen-and-a-half!*

"*As planned, our family gathered for Uncle Ben and Magdalena's wedding at the San Marcelino Church. It was to be such an affair, with all twenty-six members of the Fernandez clan there. I can still see Belana's proud face...*"

Elena set the pen down as the day replayed itself on the screen of her mind. She found herself back on the steps of the ornate church looking up at her grandmother, Sofía Fernandez—always "Belana" to Elena—as she shepherded the family through the massive carved double doors of old San Marcelino.

How regal she is, Elena thought, observing Sofía's floor-length gown made of tawny satin, which her grandmother designed and sewed herself. And it was true, Sofía Fernandez had the air of a queen mother. For a moment Elena was carried back to one of her favorite stories—her grandmother's ocean voyage in 1898 from Spain to Manila to meet her new husband Lorencio. She'd arrived just in time to be caught in the historic events of Admiral Dewey's seizure of Manila Bay. Forty-three years ago. Now the Philippines were on the threshold of another war! This time with Japan.

Spotting Elena, Sofía summoned her to stand beside her by the door. "*Aquí*, Elena!"

Elena ran up the steps. "Belana," she said, patting her grandmother's hand, roughened by the hard work of raising seven children by herself. Not easy being a dressmaker after being brought up in Spanish drawing rooms. Lorencio died at forty-eight after losing his fortune in a tobacco business. His family was left penniless.

Sofía patted Elena's arm. "*Muy bonita estás, querida*," she said, admiring her granddaughter's organdy dress. Elena smiled, though she was uncomfortable in the tight bodice securely fastened by thirty mother-of-pearl buttons. The bodice was attached to a flaring circle-skirt that revealed her long bare legs.

They watched the family arrive: Elena's mother, Milagros—Mila—and her husband, Carl Keller; followed by Elena's younger brothers, Dan and Tim. Next, Agustín Fernandez, known as Tino, Sofía's oldest son and his family, plus Josefina, second oldest, and her husband Carlos. Younger daughters, Neva and Luisa and their families trailed behind. Twenty-four had arrived. "They are all here," Sofía sighed.

"Not quite," Elena pointed. "Here comes Constancia with Tony and little Ian."

Daughter Constancia, fourth in line, wore a bright fuchsia and blue print dress. "We're late!" she called to her mother. Sofía waved her on. "Don't worry, nothing will begin until Padre Moyerin gives the signal." Then she added, "Now we are all here," as she leaned over to rescue a small grandchild who had started down the steep steps.

"*Oye*—listen!" she pointed to the bell tower, "There is the signal."

Bong, bong, bong, clanged the church bell. "*Hijas, hijos*," Sofía called out, "Padre Moyerin said, 'listen for the bell.'"

Elena drifted back to walk with her mother Mila, her stepfather Carl and her brothers.

How clearly she remembered feeling overcome by incense as she walked into the church. Her imagination took hold once more as she continued to write in her diary.

"*Like brightly colored birds finding their perches, the Fernandez flock filled the pews. We could not help being noisy. 'Shh,' someone hissed behind me as I tried not to stumble over Tim, 'here she comes.'*"

"*All our heads swiveled at once. The women wore flowered or feathered hats; some wore ribbons. The men's heads were all bare. You could hear breathy 'oh's—ah's' as the bridal procession floated by like magic to the strains of a most moving wedding march played on a sixteenth century pipe organ. The organ vibrated from its raised platform. The organist played with gusto. I could tell his blue-black hair was dyed. Murals of saints and angels looked down on Magdalena as she moved in her white tulle. There was a tiny curved smile on her oval face, which I could see through her veil. She was on her father's arm. He coughed several times trying to conceal his tears. He's quite fat and his face got very red. He concentrated on looking at the saints. I have seen these saints before and know they are very old. They were brought over by the Spaniards during their 300-year rule over the islands.*

"*My eyes were glued to the bride and groom. I caught every movement and expression as they joined together at the altar. How grand they were! I couldn't tell whether Magdalena was actually crying, but she probably was because her cheeks were very pink. Uncle Ben looked older than twenty-four. Although he was elegant in his white tuxedo, his receding hairline made him seem at least thirty. But I've always loved his brown eyes. They are big just like the rest of the family's. I heard Mom whisper to Carl that Ben looked just like her father. Usually he is such a clown and is considered the baby of the family, but today he was so serious, almost as if he sensed what was coming next.*

"*The mass was far too long. Stand. Kneel. Pray. The wedding vows went quickly. In sing-song Latin, Father Moyerin tied it all together in his bass Irish voice. At that point, the whole church was sniffling, including me.*

"*Then something unbelievable happened. Just before the benediction, a whisper started at the back of the church. It grew louder and louder as it traveled from pew to pew. Its impact left us with open mouths. When it reached the front pew, it stopped, as if it had collided with an invisible line just before Father M. heard it. 'In the name of...' Father's jet black brows arched like church steeples. He sensed the urgency in the air around him. His eyes darted from pew to pew. We knew something he didn't know! He made a quick sign of the cross. Heads bobbed up everywhere. The organ boomed out a final chord. Talk exploded. This was it! Pearl Harbor bombed...a few hours ago...bombs on Davao...Japanese double-cross...Baguio bombed...Manila next...war!...hurry to your homes!*

"*The news itself fell like a bomb. I saw my mother's face turn to stone. Carl frowned. Belana was already saying goodbye to Ben and Magdalena when we joined the fast exit out of the church. I've never seen such an exit.*

"*Father Moyerin was yelling. 'Quiet! Quiet down. Let me talk. Please,' he cried, trying to sound calm, but the high pitch of his voice gave him away. His voice trembled when he went on. 'The Japanese...the Japanese have bombed Pearl Harbor. Last night—early Sunday morning for Pearl—caught them all by surprise. Devastated planes, ships. They have bombed Baguio today—Camp John Hay Army Base to the north. To the south of us, they have bombed Davao in Mindanao. We are next! Stay calm. Hurry home. Listen to your radios. I will pray for us all.'*

"But I can tell you that no one stayed calm. Not even Father, who started praying so fast no one could understand him. Everyone was babbling as well. I heard Carl yell to Uncle Tino, 'Did you hear? I just talked to someone who said nine people were killed or wounded in Baguio. One woman lost her leg. At least that's the rumor.'

"Uncle Tino stared at Carl. 'Didn't Elena just get back from Baguio?'

"Carl glanced back at me and nodded. 'Just in time.'

"I gulped at that.

"'Thank God,' Uncle said and put an arm around Aunt Dale. Then he pulled cousins Debra and Rosie close.

"At that point I couldn't even talk. Three days ago I went to Baguio with our girls' basketball team. The whole school took the train up. We played an all-girl team there that beat us. Could I have been killed?"

Elena stopped writing. Her brain felt overloaded. Her legs were stiff from sitting cross-legged on the ledge. She thought through what transpired next, needing to relive the succession of incidents before she could write. The details were all there, in her mind...

She recalled that as slowly as the wedding group had filed into the church, they now quickly dispersed. Purses were gathered, wedding gifts were scooped up, and children were loaded into cars. Wedding guests either bypassed the broken reception line or gave the bride and groom fragmented wishes, "*Salud. Felicidades.*" Father Moyerin waved everyone ahead. "Go. Don't linger. Ben and Magdalena are going home. No photographs today. Sorry."

The bridal pair stood alone and watched their wedding celebration fall apart.

"Please stop crying," Ben said to his bride.

But Magdalena was inconsolable. "Our wedding...our honeymoon... oh, Benjamín!"

"We'll make it up later, *queridísima.*" Ben squeezed her hand. It was cold as ice despite the 80-degree heat.

Mila and Carl stopped on their way to the car. Elena, Dan and Tim hurried behind them. "We're so sorry, Ben. *Pobre* Magdalena," Mila said. "But we must get home. The news is bad. They say eighty Japanese transports have been sighted off our own island of Luzon—in fact, on the coast of Aparri, and in Lingayen Gulf. There are ships off Vigan and Ilocos Sur," she said. She repeated news she had heard in bits and pieces as it flew from mouth-to-mouth in the church exodus.

"*Dios!*" exclaimed Magdalena and started to weep again. How could the Japanese approach all those islands so fast? Elena wondered. Was this all real? It must be a nightmare.

As Elena piled into the 1939 Oldsmobile, she spotted her grandmother and gave her a quick wave.

Carl had trouble driving home. Manila, where tales were known to begin at breakfast in one part of the city and spread to the other side of town by noon, was electric with rumors and panicked people. Pedestrians wandered aimlessly. One man crossed the street, ran back and crossed it again. Horns blared. Army trucks warred with horse-drawn *carromatas*, *carretelas*, and carts pulled by stubborn *carabaos*—water buffalo that much preferred to be in the rice fields.

Drivers swore—*"Putanginamo!"* Traffic crawled a few yards at a time. Angry horns and cursing drivers plugged the streets.

Elena leaned over the front seat. "Do you think we are at war already?" she asked, her voice elevated by excitement. She knew the situation should be abhorrent to her. Something as serious as war shouldn't excite her. But it did. Her parents stared ahead, faces set.

Carl, who was Swiss, prided himself in his sense of logic. "Yes," he nodded, "war, though I question the accuracy of everything we heard in that church madhouse..."

"We'll go home and get ourselves together," Mila added. "We'll listen to news. Cook extra food...Vida has probably started preparing things." She cleared her throat.

She's really nervous, Elena thought, hearing her mother's familiar habit of clearing her throat when she was anxious.

Her pen poised in mid-air, Elena recalled those moments and quickly filled in the sequence of events. Referring to her mother's nervous habit, she wrote, *"Ever since I was little, Mom has had that 'ahem, ahem' that tells me she is upset. It never fails.*

"What a ride home," she continued, holding the pen less tightly to ease the writer's cramp. *"On top of everything, Tim's face suddenly got chalk white. He was perspiring. 'My head hurts,' he said, almost crying. He looked like six instead of twelve.*

"Mom reached back and felt his forehead. 'Fever,' she said. She smoothed his hair back like she always does when we're sick. Her hand always feels so good.

"'Hold on, Tim,' Carl told him, but Tim began throwing up like a spigot —all over his white shirt and dress pants. Dan held his nose and so did I. The smell was terrible.

"Thank God, a few moments later we reached our outer driveway. It seemed to take Carl forever to unlock the inner gate.

"I've never been so glad to have Max and Sheba jump all over us. Vida and Marcelina ran up and wanted to know all about everything. Vida told us she had already made the dinner. She is so good about running the kitchen. I assured Marcelina that everything will be o.k. I don't think it will be, but she looked so scared I had to say something. She's only a year older than I am.

"By tonight, Tim had a high fever. He's coughing. Mom fixed an ice pack for his head and gave him aspirin. He did not eat much dinner, though the rest of us were starved. In the meantime, Vida had made several extra meals.

She's a wonderful cook, though I will always remember her best as my amah. She told such great stories. Anyway, we'll have chicken stew, Spanish adobo, mongo beans, and vegetables to pour over rice. It felt comforting to smell that food.

"Carl, Mom, Dan and I listened to the news. Timmy was on the couch, still white as death. Radio Manila said to expect a bombing any time.

"After the news, we got together to plan what we'd do when the air raid came. 'O.K.,' Carl said, 'we don't have an air-raid shelter, so we'll go to the backyard and stand against the stone wall by the bamboo clump. We should have some protection there.'

"I hope he's right. I wonder how close the bombs will come.

"Mom seemed to read my mind. 'The bombs may get close. If they do,' she said, 'we'll fall to the ground and press against the wall as close as we can.'

"Marcelina looked like she wanted to cry. We all waited for the next word. 'Don't worry,' Mom told us, 'we're as safe as anyone else in Manila. We're not that close to Nichols Field to worry about direct hits.' She waved a yellow pencil in the air and went on. 'Don't forget to open your mouths and put a pencil between your teeth if the bombs get close.'

"I wonder if that will really help. We'll all look crazy with pencils in our mouths!

"Mom handed out pencils. 'These will prevent concussion.'

"Tim was bleary with fever, but he was listening. 'What is concussion?' he asked.

"'That's when the pressure from explosions pushes on your eardrums. It can make you deaf,' Mom explained.

"At that point Carl said, 'O.K., everyone go to bed.' He unbuttoned his sports shirt. 'My God, it's hot tonight. I need to walk around in the garden for awhile.'

"I wonder what he was thinking when he left us so suddenly. All I know is that I am through writing for tonight. I better try to sleep before the bombs come."

She closed the notebook and prepared for bed.

Elena could not have imagined Carl's thoughts when he announced he wanted to walk in the garden. He knew he had to get away. He averted his eyes from them. The pit of his stomach felt like a rock. Muscles on his neck were taut. Veins stood out. Carl was afraid. Fear was not an emotion he acknowledged easily. He could not deny fear, standing there in front of his family. Get yourself together! he told himself. You must be responsible, trustworthy. Head of the family. Don't let them down. Be in charge! He bit his lip, then straightened himself.

When he looked up, Mila's eyes caught him, and drew him in like a current. She knew! Her intuition told her in a language of feeling that she and Carl shared. On his own, Carl was guided by reason. Raised in a strict Swiss-German household, he was forged by clear-thinking parents into a predictable human being. By few words and much action, his mother and father schooled him. Think. Be sensible. Don't trust what you cannot prove. Subsequently, Carl turned his back on emotion. In school he concentrated on science and mathematics. He liked the accuracy of numbers. Choosing accounting as a career became a natural goal.

He and Mila were compatible. What one lacked, the other provided. Two halves. Held in the assurance of her gaze as he faced the family, he felt the blood warming his tense muscles. The dark brown of her eyes was gentle, diffused. He loved that look. It stirred childhood memories of long hikes in lush alpine meadows among soft-eyed cows grazing in the white daisy grass. The bells around their necks clanged notes that echoed in the pure mountain air.

A sense of trust returned. Carl swallowed. His jaw relaxed. Begin by doing something, his old philosophy said. Fear faded. "We need a plan," he announced. He faced the family squarely, then turned and walked down the steps to the garden.

When Elena crawled into bed through the opening in her mosquito net and tied the flaps down, she felt more disoriented than she had at church. What was she doing in her own bed waiting for an air raid? Was it possible that just this morning she had stood in front of her tall, white armoire getting ready for the wedding? She had been excited about wearing a new green organdy dress. Now, lying in bed, remembering, she saw herself looking into the armoire mirror, her deep-set, gray-green eyes reflecting the color of her dress. Ash-blonde hair framed her high cheek-bones and dropped to her shoulders. Wispy hair, she had always called it. Despite a light curl made by the paper curlers she had tightened into her scalp, her hair hung thinly. She wore no make-up, and her face had an ivory cast to it. Habitually, she bit her lips to force color into them. Upbraiding her image that morning, she talked to her reflection. "What a pale creature you are—like an anemic turnip! You need lipstick. Rouge! Too bad your mother and Carl won't let you. The other girls in ninth grade do, but you—you have to be retarded. And your big *tetas* don't help a thing!" She tried to flatten her breasts by pressing them down with her palms, but she couldn't control the bulge. "¡Ay," she exclaimed, "must be your fault, Belana. Mom doesn't have this problem." She'd let out her breath and turned from the mirror, giving her image a final sour look.

Elena had been anxious to see how everyone would look at the wedding. Her thoughts took her back to early Sunday morning when she entered her mother's room. She knocked on the door. "Mom, are you ready?" she asked.

Sitting in front of her round vanity mirror, Mila addressed her daughter's reflection in the glass. "Almost," she said, smoothing her dark eyebrows and studying her deep brown eyes—eyes as dark as Elena's were light. Her hair, not quite black, was enhanced by the light blue chiffon dress she wore. She was not only different from Elena, but she appeared too young to be her mother.

She was young, for she had married blond Stuart Neville, an Englishman, when she was only nineteen. Educated in a convent through her freshman year in high school,when she had gone to work to supplement the family income, Mila's background was different from Stu's. They had problems from the beginning. Spanish and English cultures warred. After four years and three children, the marriage broke up. Mila had struggled through divorce, not wanting it; and almost broke down with the nervous strain of raising three children—Elena, three-and-a-half; Daniel, one-and-a-half; and Tim, six months.

Her life had changed when she married Carl. There was no trace of pain now in her shining eyes as she looked into the mirror. She's beautiful, Elena thought, like a real-life portrait.

"How does this look?" Mila turned away from the mirror and faced her daughter.

"*Elegante*," Elena said in Spanish. "*Muy elegante.*"

Mila looked pleased. At that moment Carl entered the room. He wore a starched dress shirt and white trousers. "Perfect," he said, "you look perfect." He eyed his wife for longer than Elena thought it should take to make an appraisal. Mila smiled, recognizing his indulgence. Elena waited for her turn. Carl slowly turned to look at her. It was a teasing look. "You, too," he smiled.

She shrugged her shoulders and looked back at him. Carl was ruggedly handsome. His teeth were too long for his face, Elena thought, but that seemed to add to his looks. There was a hint of autumn color about him. His skin was bronze, and his hair, a curly copper-brown. Years of swimming in the tropical seas of Manila Bay had developed a strong torso and muscular legs. Elena had marveled at how the color of his eyes and hair were a perfect match. She sought her stepfather's approval, partly because he had raised her since she was seven years old; partly because her determined nature was stimulated by the strength of his character. They had sparred often, but both had a basic trust and admiration for the other.

Carl was not one to wait around. As soon as everyone was dressed for the wedding, he walked out to call Dan and Tim.

Could all that have happened just this morning? Elena asked herself, turning over in her bed. She had to get to sleep, but her brain wanted to process. Questions hung in her mind without answers. She felt uneasy, in turmoil about many things—this terrible day that fit together like a jumbled jigsaw; and worse, the way she had been feeling about herself lately. Her hidden self; not the Elena the family knew—mostly agreeable and compliant—but an angry rebellious person who mentally challenged everything. She had even challenged the solemn prospect of the Philippines at war. Exciting—she had found the idea exciting! The rest of the family seemed genuinely horrified. Why was she so out of step? After all, she came from a large family that offered a nest of security. Each member of the Fernandez clan blended as part of the family personality.

Elena acted her role on the family stage; inwardly she questioned her lack of loyalty. She didn't feel totally committed. She wasn't totally anything, beginning with the fact that she was not even pure Spanish, only half. Going down a long list, she doubted her commitment to the Catholic faith, and yet was bound by it. She was torn by sexual feelings— base thoughts, strange surges. What was happening to her? These conflicts couldn't be normal. Now, added to everything else, the imminence of war! She was not ready for any of it.

A mosquito dive-bombed her ear and interrupted her reverie. It was useless to swat at it in the dark. She slipped her hand under the mosquito net and switched on the night-table lamp. For seconds, she followed the persistent whine of the insect. It buzzed in all directions. Then when it was within sight, just above her nose, she swatted hard and crushed it between her flat palms. The insect's tiny bloody wings lay still. Elena grimaced. She got out of bed, holding her hands high, and went into the bathroom to wash, looking away when the dead insect went down the drain. She held her hands under the water for almost a minute.

Back in bed, she reflected on the life of the mosquito. You monster, you killed it! Then the analogy came. Would war be in charge of her fate as she had been of the mosquito's? When they were bombed, who would protect her from being killed? God? Where was God when random acts of nature obliterated entire cities and killed thousands, in floods, famines, earthquakes and typhoons? Why did God lose control? The church claimed sin was at the bottom of it—humanity's big original sin. This answer did not satisfy Elena. The warm pillow on which she lay made her neck perspire. She sat up, gave a sigh and picked up the familiar rosary. In an irony she was unaware of, she lay down again and began to pray. As she turned each cold round bead in her fingers, the words came by rote, sending her into a hypnotic drift. The clock in the living room chimed—11 p.m. Finally, she slept.

In the meantime, Carl and Mila lay awake in their bedroom at the far side of the house. They, too, heard the clock chime. Carl reached for his wife's hand. "Asleep?" he whispered, sensing she was as awake as he. Mila answered by facing him and pressing her body against his. He reached down and gently rubbed her back up and down. Then slid his hand to her warm thigh, massaging her skin over the green silk nightgown. Slowly her arms crept up behind his neck. "I'm frightened," she said.

He pressed her tight. "You were brave today," he murmured, for a moment recalling his own fear.

She stroked his hair and his ear, rubbing the lobe between her fingers. "Was I?"

"Very."

"Sure?"

He could feel her eyes in the dark. "I can't say don't be afraid," he kissed her cheek, then her mouth. He felt her lips tremble.

For a moment she said nothing, then, "What can you say?"

"Just...I love you," he said.

Bombs began to rain on Manila at 3:30 a.m., December 9. Jolted out of their beds by the rumble of bombers blasting Nichols Field three miles to the south, the Kellers flew to the safety of the back wall, robes and slippers forgotten. Wave after wave, the bombers droned above them. The sky was filled with them as huge American searchlights crisscrossed over the formations. The planes concentrated on the military airfield. Some of the bombs fell nearby. The ground shook. Elena put her fingers in her ears, forgetting about the pencil. She glanced at her brothers. Both were entranced—eyes fixed skyward.

The night became a fiery stage. Flares shot up and skyrocketed into the dark like giant firecrackers. Combined with the deafening shatter of bombs, Manila—a city already pulsing with fear—exploded in flashes of searing light.

As the bombs thudded closer, Elena's heart tripped with fear and excitement. She felt the impact of the explosions inwardly, almost as if each detonation originated from her chest. She saw her mother shoot Carl a look of fear. Carl raised his eyebrows in return. He motioned for everyone to get closer to the wall. No one moved, for they were as close as they could be.

The Kellers blended like druids under the graceful sway of the bamboo canes above them. Bombs cracked like thunder, leaving an unearthly silence in their wake.

Teeth chattering, Tim broke the silence. "I'm cold," he complained, winding himself in a sheet Mila threw around him.

"You look like a ghost," Dan said. Coming out of the shadows in white pajamas he had outgrown, Dan looked like a ghost himself.

"He's still burning with fever," Mila told Carl. She suspected Tim had *dengue* fever, common enough that it hit several of them each year. Symptoms of fever, chills and severe back pain usually lasted four or five days.

"It'll have to run its course," Carl said. "Let's get back to bed. Thank God, this raid is over."

Carl picked Tim up. Moving like phantoms, the Kellers filed past the thick, forty-foot *bonga betel* palm that darkened the stairs by the house. Elena imagined the betel palm as a perfect shelter. The thick fronds created a cave-like sanctuary for insects, birds and lizards. If only it were possible to climb in through the forbidding foliage and hide. Twenty-four hours ago she never would have thought of the old palm in this way.

She caught the aroma of *sampaguita* as she went up the front steps. Ironic that it should smell so sweet on such a night—a night beginning to lighten into a silent dawn.

Next morning, the Kellers heard that flares had been set by saboteurs hidden around Nichols Field, signalling the target area for Japanese bombers. "Bastards," Carl said. The airbase suffered heavy damage.

Schools closed, including the American School attended by Elena, Dan and Tim, which was located right behind the Kellers' stone wall. The city concentrated on survival. People dug trenches for shelter. A day after the bombing, the Kellers began to dig a trench by the stone wall. Eventually Carl planned to build a covered shelter. He drew a model of it. The shelter would be constructed using four-by-four posts set in a five-foot deep trench. It would be roofed with sandbags, topped with layers of earth on which they would plant *camote* vines for camouflage. The Philippine sweet potato vine had thick dark leaves, ideal for this purpose. They could also eat the *camote*.

For now, a long trench would have to do. The family took turns digging the fifteen-foot trench, which was shaped like an L—three feet long at the short end—twelve feet of which would eventually be covered. There would be an emergency opening at the head of the long end. Carl felt good about his plan.

The ground was packed and digging was slow. They worked each morning and put their shovels down at noon. Elena's job was to pack dirt around the edge of the trench so sandbags would have a secure base. Dirt caked under her fingernails and split them. She hated the work, but liked being a part of the effort. At noon they cleaned up and ate. After four days, the trench was completed. It became a familiar refuge as Japanese planes returned again and again.

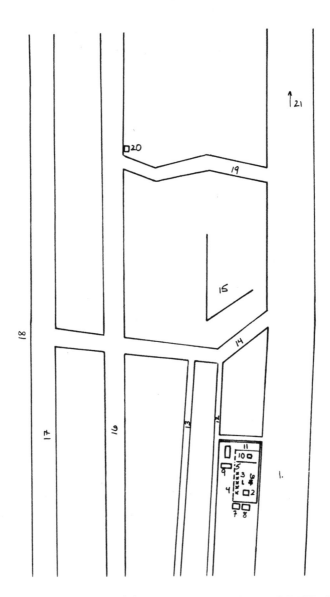

ELENA'S MAP OF THE KELLERS' HOME AND
SURROUNDING NEIGHBORHOOD

1. Taft Ave. (aka Daitoa Ave.)
2. Kellers' house
3. Air raid shelter
4. Stone wall
5. Large bamboo clump
6. Bonga palm
7. Chews' apartment house
8. Kamikaze apartment house
9. Japanese military compound
10. Neighbor
11. Menlo
12. Donada
13. Leveriza
14. Vito Cruz
15. Rizal Stadium
16. F.B. Harrison
17. Dewey Blvd. (aka Heiwa Blvd.)
18. Manila Bay
19. San Andreas
20. Ben's house
21. Downtown Manila

Chapter Two

Jerry's Visit

One afternoon during the week of the first bombing, an American Army truck lumbered outside the fence and stopped by the eight-foot, iron-barred Keller gate. Four soldiers in fatigues piled out of the truck. Their faces were red with perspiration, and their clothes and boots were wet and caked with drying mud. The oldest and tallest of the soldiers clanged the bolt on the outside gate. Carl ran down the driveway and let them in; first, through the iron gate and then through the smaller wooden gate that separated the Keller property from the house next to them. The tall soldier stepped forward as the leader of the group.

"Excuse me, sir, I'm Second Lieutenant Chuck Ross. We've just driven one hundred and fifty miles northwest of Manila from the air base at Iba, Zambales. We're looking for our commanding officer's house. We'd like to rest for a few minutes."

"Come in. Come in," Carl said. "I'm Carl Keller and this is my family—my wife, Mila, and my children." He gestured toward Mila, Elena and Dan who had followed him to the gate.

Carl glanced at the rest of the men. They were muddy and had scratches on their arms and faces. Chuck Ross explained. "The Japs hit our airfield at Iba a few hours ago. They surprised dozens of P-40's refueling. About 80 Jap bombers, dive bombers and fighters had a field day. They wiped us out. Guys blown up everywhere. I understand they did the same to Clark Field. I'm afraid they got the grounded B-17's there."

"My God," exclaimed Carl. "Please. Please come in and wash up. We'll give you something to eat."

"Thank you, sir—Mr. Keller," the lieutenant said, trying to brush away some of the mud that clung to the seat of his pants. "We hoped we could get a shower somewhere and sit in the shade for a few minutes."

Another one of the men stepped forward. "We're so filthy we can wash up under a faucet somewhere." Blond and blue-eyed, he seemed the youngest of the four. "I'm Jerry Merrill," he said, extending his hand. Seeing how dirty it was, he pulled it back and nodded instead.

He immediately caught Elena's eye. She tried not to stare at him. His voice seems too deep for his young face, she thought.

"Oh, I'm sorry. Damned impolite of me," interjected the lieutenant. "These are my men. Corporal Jerry Merrill, Private Joe Banks, and Sergeant Tom Maloney, otherwise known as 'the New Yorker.' He's Irish but speaks like Brooklyn," he said with a broad grin.

"Pleased to meet you all," Carl shook their hands; Mila, Elena and Dan nodded and smiled. "Don't worry about coming into the house for showers. We'll just spread some newspapers for you to put your wet things on."

Carl motioned to the house and the soldiers followed him. Elena hung back and watched them. Jerry Merrill looked at her as he walked past. He grinned.

My, Elena thought, his eyes are blue, and he smiles with his whole face.

As the soldiers cleaned up, Mila and Elena worked in the kitchen and made sandwiches and *calamansi* lemonade, while Vida continued to prepare the evening meal. As she spread mayonnaise on thinly sliced bread, Elena's eyes wandered to the door of the bathroom. "I'm glad we can help them," she said. Excitement elevated her voice. "I hope they can stay awhile." She felt her ears redden.

Mila pretended not to notice. "Hurry, so the food will be ready when they come out. I'll take a sandwich to Tim. His fever broke this morning. He'll be fine in a day or two." *Dengue* usually lasted several days, leaving its victim weak, recovering from fever and severe muscle and back pains.

Elena quickly set the trays of food on the black *narra* table in the dining room. Jerry was the first to come out. He wiped away a trickle of water that ran down his temple. "It's strange to have to put on these filthy clothes again. But it sure feels better."

Elena met his eyes and then looked away. "At least you got to cool off a bit," she managed to say before lowering her eyes. Then looking up, she hesitated, "Was it terrible at Iba?" Could he tell her heart was beating so fast she could hardly breathe?

"Well, I didn't have time to think about it, really. Just ran like he... heck...into the open fields and joined the *carabaos* taking their siestas in the mud holes."

Elena laughed as she imagined the scene, then shifted her gaze away from him. He must think I'm a fool, she thought. But Jerry went on talking. "Yep," he said, "shared a mud bath with the black water buffalo."

Drawn back into the conversation, Elena said, "Normally, *carabaos* don't like strangers, especially whites." She felt good about adding something she thought was significant.

"Not these fellows," Jerry said. "The bombs made us pardners." His eyes crinkled when he laughed.

Elena watched his Adam's apple bob up and down as he talked. His lips were wide. She noticed his hands as he described the Iba bombing. They were square and tanned. Suddenly, she realized he had stopped talking. "Oh," she said and added hastily, "where are you going now?"

"Don't know. Things are such a mess. We have to get orders from our C.O."

"Oh," Elena said again, nodded and began to busy herself with the food.

The others finished their showers and joined them. The food and *calamansi* lemonade, made from small tropical limes, disappeared as quickly as it was served. "Would you like some more?" Mila offered.

"No, thank you, ma'am. We should be going," Lieutenant Ross said.

They picked up their doughboy helmets, rifles and gun belts and headed for their truck. As they were climbing into the truck, Jerry yelled back, "If I'm around this area, I'll come by to say 'Hello.'" He looked straight at Elena.

"Please do!" Carl called back. "All of you come back, anytime."

Yes, Elena thought, please do!

In between bombings, the trench got deeper and wider. At the end of the second week, it was finished. By Christmas, Carl had also dug in the supporting posts, built a floor and retaining walls to keep the dirt from falling in, and had started the roof. The Japanese made successful landings north at Aparri, northwest at Vigan and Lingayen; and southeast at Legaspi, in a multidirectional thrust on Luzon. Filipino-American defense, without an air force, with insufficient weapons and limited transportation, could not resist the Japanese drive toward Manila.

Filipino-American defense forces—the First Philippine Division, the Forty-fifth Infantry, Regiment of Philippine Scouts; the 91st, 71st, 31st, 21st, 11th and Twenty-sixth Cavalry—withdrew in stages. They struck the superior Japanese invaders wherever they could throughout the island of Luzon, but by Christmas Eve, it was obvious to Manilans that the Army planned to evacuate the city and retreat to an area outside Manila for final defense.

"The Army is leaving the city," Carl told the family as they watched hundreds of trucks and commercial vehicles, which had been converted to military use, lumber past their house, covered headlights dimmed, shining an eerie blue in the blackout.

"What will we do?" Mila asked. "Should we stay here?"

Elena envisioned the family trapped in their home as the Japanese invaders swarmed the city; but Carl was ready with a secure answer. "I've just talked to the Swiss Consulate. Manila is being declared an open city. I understand Swiss families plan to gather at the Swiss Club for protection when the Japs occupy Manila."

Mila frowned. "What about our house?"

"We'll just have to secure everything and nail up the case of corned beef we bought. We'll bury it near the shelter, and we'll take as many valuables as we can with us," Carl said. His eyes looked tired.

Mila was glad they had a plan. "I'll take our first aid kit, and we'll pack only essential clothing," she added.

Carl nodded. Elena went to her room and set aside a few items of clothing. In the room next to hers, her brothers did the same thing. Later that evening, she was drawn to the bathroom window that faced the street by the rumble of trucks evacuating the city. She rested her chin on the sill and counted the blue headlights as they passed. On and on they passed—fifty-nine, sixty... Her mind wandered. Where was Jerry Merrill? She had hoped he would return.

The sun came up early the next morning. It shone on the ripening mangos in the umbrella-like tree that grew at the upper end of the driveway near the house. Dan was out walking Sheba, the fox terrier. Elena was in her bedroom combing her hair. She heard Dan's voice from the gate. "Jerry's here!"

Straightening the red and white sailor blouse she wore, Elena ran down the stairs, her heart racing. The rest of the family followed.

Jerry, assigned to a rest camp a mile away, had returned as he promised. The Kellers were delighted, and Elena couldn't hide her excitement. She and her brothers set up folding chairs by the *bonga* palm and visited with the soldier, while Mila prepared snacks. Carl paused on his way to the office. "See you later," he said. He rode his bicycle to the insurance company, where he was comptroller, several times a week to check on office matters. Although the company was closed during the emergency, Carl felt it was important to supervise things there.

Jerry gave him a wave, then turned to the kids. He told them he was a ground crew radio man for the Army Air Corps. "See," he patted the patch on his arm. He entertained Elena, Dan and Tim by taking coded messages from the radio. He scribbled letters and phrases with his left hand.

Elena leaned over his shoulder. "What does that say?" She smelled the sun in his hair and a scent that was uniquely his. She couldn't identify it, but something inside her sensed an intimacy, and she drew away as if she had come in contact with fire. "I c-can't read it," she stammered.

"You can't read it because it's all abbreviated, Elena."

"E-le-na." How nice my name sounds when he says it, she thought, still keeping her distance.

After taking several coded messages, he entertained them by drawing cartoon-like sketches of people, animals and scenes reminiscent of his home in Colorado.

"Those are amusing," Elena giggled, forgetting herself. "I like the one with the skunk following the old man on skis."

"Sit still, Elena. Let me draw your profile," Jerry said, holding up his pencil.

She shook her head. "Just for fun," he coaxed. Elena sat and turned her head as he indicated. While he drew, Dan sensed the attraction between them. She's getting all the attention, he thought. "Me next!" he announced.

"Sure," Jerry assured him and kept on drawing Elena's profile—the soft hairline, deepset eyes that had a hint of sadness in them, the slightly upturned nose, and a mouth that drooped into a small pout.

Impatient, Dan said, "You look like a statue, Elena. Smile!"

But Elena was so self-conscious she couldn't smile. She felt each line Jerry drew was actually being drawn on her face, as if the pencil strokes were a direct touch from him. She wanted the sensation to last forever, but she hated being watched, especially by Dan. Jerry put the pencil down. "Done," he announced.

She examined the sketch. "Does my mouth droop like that?" she asked.

"A little," he answered, "but it's becoming."

"Mmm," Elena mused.

Jerry drew Dan's profile, then Tim's. Elena watched. When he finished, Elena said, "Jerry?"

"Hmm?" His eyes focused on hers.

Ignoring the combination of pleasure and discomfort she felt when he spoke, she asked, "How old are you?"

"Twenty-three—an old man," he laughed.

"No, you're not. I'll be sixteen next April."

"Just old enough to be my sister."

"You don't have a sister?"

"No, just two brothers. Both younger. Sure would like to see them."

"Why did you join the Army?" Elena asked, gaining more and more confidence in herself.

His voice was low and steady when he answered. "I'm asking myself that question now. Just a stupid need for change," he explained. "Things had gotten a little tense for me with my folks." He paused, remembering. "I guess I wanted to prove I was grown up, independent. I was pretty hard-headed then—sure I was right about everything. I felt they didn't understand me."

Perhaps he had felt as she felt now, challenging the values of parents and society. "I can understand how you felt," she said.

"Yes," he lowered his eyes thoughtfully, "but I found out one small decision can sure change a man's life." For a moment he looked as if he had forgotten she was there.

"Say, got to draw another masterpiece," Jerry said, picking up the pencil again. He tried to sound light-hearted, but Elena sensed the regret in his voice.

"Don't worry," she said. "Carl says President Roosevelt says help is coming. When the Americans send reinforcements, we'll beat the Japanese."

"Yeah!" Dan exclaimed.

Without looking up from the pad, Jerry said, "Hope so." Then in a surprise move, he put the pencil down again. "That's all for now." He smiled at them. Then looking at Elena, he commented, "You sure have the greenest eyes."

He made her blush. There was that tingling sensation again. "Only when I'm happy," she said, shifting her glance away from him. "My mother says they turn grey when I'm angry, and blue when I'm sleepy."

"Green when you're happy?" he smiled. "I'm glad you're happy now."

"Who cares?" Dan said. "Yeah, who cares?" Tim echoed.

At that point Mila came with refreshments. She sat with them while they enjoyed the snacks. When Carl returned in the late afternoon, he joined the family until it was time for dinner. They ate chicken *adobo*, a spicy Filipino dish made of chicken marinated in vinegar and served with vegetables and rice. After the meal Jerry stayed as long as he could. Finally, he said, "I'm due back in a few minutes."

Just before he left, Jerry shook hands with everyone in the family, including Vida and Marcelina. "Thanks for everything you've done for me, folks. I'll never forget it. Elena, Dan, Tim, you've been great company...and the food, everything! Thanks, all of you."

Elena felt her eyes sting. I can't let him see me cry, she told herself. He's feeling bad enough. "Jerry," she stepped forward, "ah, we'll be thinking about you..."

"Thanks, little one." The familiar twinkle came back into his eyes. "That's worth a lot."

"I'll be thinking about you, for sure," Dan piped. "We'll have a good time after the war."

After the war? The reality hit Elena—it would be a long time, she told herself.

Jerry picked up his gear and headed for the driveway. The Kellers trailed behind him to the gate. "Goodbye," he said. Elena called after him, "Goodbye, Jerry."

Jerry turned back and waved, his face bright in the setting sun. The gate clanged shut behind him.

He did not visit them again. Later, the Kellers would find out he joined the final Filipino-American defense on the Bataan Peninsula, some eighty to ninety miles over the Calumpit swamp detour, and only forty miles east, in a direct line across Manila Bay. Bataan was a steaming jungle full of impassable roads, dense overgrowth and malaria mosquitos.

Christmas came and went. It was like an ordinary day. No tree. No gifts. The Kellers concentrated on preparations to leave their house and go to the Swiss Club. As Elena packed a small suitcase, she stopped and took down a picture of Betsy Ross holding the American flag and hid it under the paper lining on one of her armoire shelves. She knew she was only supposed to take essential clothing, but she took a small wooden music box from under her pillow and hid it at the bottom of her suitcase. Belana had given it to her on her seventh birthday. Her grandmother had had the music box since she was a girl. A black Cuban soldier had given it to her at a parade when her family lived in Cuba. Sofía's father had been a career military man in the Spanish Army. Elena thought about her grandmother and her other relatives. They had not seen one another since the wedding, but had phoned to let one another know they were all right. Most of them were going to stay in their homes; some were going to the Spanish Club for safety.

Stuart Neville called to say he had closed up his house and had joined the Army as a civilian agent. "I've been back and forth to Corregidor," he told his children. "I'll be leaving again tonight. This time, probably to help defend the rock." Corregidor was called "the rock" because it sat like a tiny island fortress at the opening of horseshoe-shaped Manila Bay.

When Elena got on the telephone, her father said, "Elena, dear, I just want to say 'Goodbye.'" His familiar British accent came through. Even when he was saying "Goodbye" there was little emotion in his voice. He sounded in control. She wondered what he was like when he was sad, or when he was frightened. She had never lived with him long enough to know. Early memories of him brought only recollections of being held on his shoulders.

"I hope you'll be safe, Daddy," Elena said, her own voice distant.

"I hope so. I just wanted to tell you to take care of yourself. And don't lose faith, no matter what happens. We'll win this war. One other message, dear: Santiago says to send you all his regards. He's just joined the Philippine Army as a cook." Santiago was Stu's cook. He had always been kind when Elena and her brothers visited their father for the day, making special coconut candy for them.

"But he's too old to fight," Elena exclaimed, remembering the old man who had been in the Neville family for over a decade, first for her father's parents, then for Stu.

"You're never too old to serve your country, dear. He won't be fighting, but they can use him as a cook," said Stu.

Her father's voice slowed. "Just one more thing, dear, remember, I..." he stopped, and she could hear his breath on the line, "love you," he finished quickly.

He had never told her that. Elena's voice constricted, "Daddy," she started to say, but her father had already hung up. For a few minutes she hunched over the receiver. Then she wiped her eyes and dialed her best friend. "Trish?"

"Elena, hi. What are you doing? I've been worried." Trish's voice was higher than usual. She and Elena had been friends since the third grade. Now, in ninth grade, their worlds were being pulled apart.

"I just talked to my dad. He's going to Corregidor."

"Corregidor!" exclaimed her friend. "That's bad. My father says the fighting is going be terrible." Trish had a slight lisp, which Elena often tried to imitate.

"I know," she said. Trish seemed to read her mind. "I am worried about him," Elena agreed. It's going to be bad."

"I hope he'll be o.k, Elena." Then her voice picked up. "We're going crazy here—packing, hiding things, wondering what to do with our dog. We're going to our friends the Hagers on the Ermita. A bunch of other Americans are getting together there. Safety in numbers."

"When are you going?" Elena wished she could be with her.

"Tomorrow. Dad says all the British and Americans will be rounded up. At least we'll all be together."

"I hate this!" Elena blurted. Tears halted her words.

"Please don't cry. You're making me cry, too!" Trish said, her own voice hesitating. "Are you leaving your house, Elena? You could join us, you know."

"No, we can't. Carl says we're going to the Swiss Club, where we'll be safe with other neutrals," Elena explained.

"But you're not Swiss. Aren't you American?"

It's so mixed up Elena thought,but she tried to explain. "Yes, I am American because my father is a naturalized American through his father; but my brothers and I are in my mother's custody. She and Carl are both Swiss citizens." It had never been important before.

Trish didn't quite understand. "But isn't your mother Spanish, Elena?"

Elena sighed. "Yes, but through marriage, she's Swiss. I know it's a mess. But that's why we're going to the Swiss Club!"

"You're lucky," Trish said.

Elena felt her throat tighten again. "I don't feel lucky. I've got to go now, Trish. I'll call again later."

Elena's shoulders dropped. She felt as if she had deserted her friend. She felt she should be with other Americans, yet was confused about her mixed background. A heritage of many ingredients, she was of Spanish/English blood; she had been raised in that culture, with Swiss, American and Filipino added. And she was a U.S. citizen, which was now the most important thing in her mind. But should she declare she was the child of an American, when her father was going in secret to Corregidor? What a mess! she thought. Running to her room, she locked the door. She picked up her rosary. Prayer stuck in her throat. Flinging herself on the bed, she remembered—I forgot to tell Trish about Jerry!

Still in a foul mood, she went out to the yard to the heavy rope swing that hung from an old mango tree that grew near the bamboo clump. Dan was swinging leisurely. She sat at the foot of the smooth trunk and watched the rope go back and forth. Dan shinnied up the rope. "What's the matter? You look awful," he said.

Elena kicked off her sandals and dug her toes in the dirt. "I hate saying goodbye. First, Jerry; then Dad and Santiago; now Trish." She didn't look up.

Dan slid down the rope and sat down beside her. Though younger by two years, he was taller than she, but his voice hadn't changed yet. At thirteen-and-a-half, he was rangy. His feet were disproportionately large. Elena was glad he was there. "I'll never see Jerry again," she said.

"How do you know?" He pulled a up a piece of new grass. Putting it between his lips, he chewed on the tender end. "I just have a feeling," Elena said, brushing her cheek with her hand and unknowingly spreading a smudge of dirt on her face.

"I think you've fallen in love with him." Dan leveled his eyes at her. "That's what Mom thinks, too."

Elena frowned. "Did she say that?"

He nodded. "She says it's 'puppy love.'"

Elena's face fell. "Puppy love!" she exclaimed, and lifting herself onto the rope, she pushed into a wide swing off the ground, leaving Danny staring after her. "What's wrong with you?" he cried.

When she didn't answer, he shrugged his shoulders, turned and left her swinging on the rope.

Elena went back and forth on the swing until her legs were tired. She had been so excited about the war. Now she hated it. What would the Swiss Club be like? she wondered. How would the Japanese soldiers act? Would her family be harmed; would people in the city be killed? Raped?

Chapter Three

Manila—Open City

The feet of the enemy march like thunder. Swift as lightning, they deliver overwhelming change. The familiar is transformed into something strange, threatening. They surround what is real with the unreal—a nightmare. This is not real. This is not real. As in a bad dream, the dreamer asks, "When will it end?" When will it end? A litany in the mass mind of a conquered people.

Elena wrote in the diary she began after the first bombing of Manila: *"January 2: The Japanese are here. No bombs. No shells. They just marched in and took over the city without firing a single shot. They came on foot, on bicycles, in tanks and trucks. Everywhere one looks, they are there, their short bodies striding and their gruff voices commanding Manila.*

"We watched them arrive from the windows of the Swiss Club. It was terrible to see them, wave after wave. They act like they own our city. I guess they do. I can't get used to it. Carl says we have to keep our feelings to ourselves. No one knows how they will act. If they kill and rape like they did in China, we are finished.

"We won't be going home for another day or so, until we are sure it's safe. We couldn't sleep at all last night. New Year's night. Imagine, celebrating it with dozens of strange women and children sprawled on the floor, their bags and clothes spread everywhere.

"The fire that started in the Pandacan oil district has spread. All night, little drops of oil came through the windows and landed like fireflies, except they hurt when they fell on our bare arms.

"I talked to Lise Muller, a Swiss girl from my old class at school. We became much better friends. I told her about Jerry. She understands how I feel about him. She doesn't think he's too old for me, even if Mom thinks it's only puppy love.

"I hope Belana and the rest of the family are all right. Belana moved in with Uncle Ben and Aunt Magdalena just before Christmas to the new house they are renting about a mile or so from us on Taft Avenue. I can't believe their wedding was only a few weeks ago.

"Danny was sick all night. It must be the dengue *Tim had a few weeks*

ago. I wonder if I'll get it. I feel nauseated. It's so awful here. I hope we can go back home soon, provided we still have a home. Some of the people at the Swiss Club say the Japanese might confiscate our houses if they need them.

"I must put this away now. They are calling us for dinner. I hope it's not tough stew again."

A day later, Japanese soldiers came to the Swiss Club and interviewed the leaders of the Swiss community. Weighted down by ammunition belts, canteens and rifles, they moved heavily in their baggy uniforms. Officious, barely polite, the officers urged the people at the club to return to their homes as soon as they inspected their papers.

Mila and Carl showed their passports to one of the officers. He scowled at the pages, turning them slowly, backwards and forwards. Raising his helmeted face, he wiped his hand across his mustache and pointed at Elena, Dan and Tim, saying, "Children?"

"Yes," said Carl, "our children."

Elena stared at the star centered on his helmet, then at his eyes, which looked half-closed. Her heart pounded. He looks like General Homma, head of the occupation Army, she thought, recalling a leaflet she had seen. She looked away and stared down at her hands, which she was holding together so tightly her fingertips were turning blue.

The officer jerked his chin forward. "Go!" he commanded, and the five of them pitched forward and walked quickly and silently to their car. Out of breath, Carl said, "Hurry, get in. Let's get out of here!"

Nearly out of gas, their car made very slow progress. They moved with hundreds of troops that trafficked the streets and sidewalks. Japanese civilians emerged from their homes and places of business, where they had been prisoners of war short hours before. Their faces raised in jubilation, they shouted, "Banzai! Banzai!" The soldiers grinned back at them.

Putting her hands over her eyes, Elena heard her mother whisper, "Stay down, children. Don't be conspicuous."

Although they were not stopped before they got home, they were slowed down as they approached their driveway by Japanese civilians from the business compound across the street from their houses, who, in an elated chant, waved flags, greeting the troops. The red ball of the Japanese flag grew as the Kellers drove closer. Elena shut her eyes, but she could still see it in her mind's eye, becoming larger and larger, until it was the size of a giant beach ball. It was a great relief to hear Carl say, "We're here!"

Vida and Marcelina ran to greet them. "We thank *Dios* you are home!" Vida raised her arms to Mila. They embraced. "*¡Ay, yes, gracias a Dios!*" Mila sighed. "You are all right?"

"Yes," declared Vida, "we are afraid, but we are fine." Marcelina put her arm through Vida's.

The house had not been disturbed. Peace. Quiet. The first they had had since they had left a few days before. Only the dogs were noisy, barking and jumping up at them repeatedly.

Stark contrasts marked the days that followed. After the troops rolled in, they posted guards at every street corner. Loud, guttural cries that sounded like "Koo-raa, koo-raa," cracked into the air. Trucks rolled in by the hundreds, bringing supplies and more soldiers. The Japanese gave the order that all private cars were to be garaged. "No gas, except for the military," the order read. The open city became a captured city. The wires and bars of a prison camp were absent, but the guards were there—their watchful eyes and strident voices. Manila, untouched by street fighting, had been emotionally raped and was being held prisoner.

The Kellers did not move from their island of fenced-in security, or at least what they hoped was security. They finished the shelter, planting the dark green *camote* vines to camouflage the sandbagged trench. Mila kept the suitcases packed and the first aid kit handy. Several days passed. Carl became restless. "I've got to get in touch with Joe Garza at the office. We've got to get money for food, buy vegetables and meat," he said.

"Please, Carl," Mila cried, "don't go out just yet. The radio says by next week, everyone will be registered. We can get formal passes then. It will be much safer."

"I'll use the temporary pass they gave me at the Swiss Club," Carl insisted. "If I don't return by dinner, call this number at the Club."

"The phone's not working," Elena said. "I tried Trish's number a few minutes ago and it's dead."

"Oh, no," Mila said. Despite the danger, she knew Carl would go. I hope he's doing the right thing, Elena thought, hearing the strain in her mother's voice.

"Never mind. I'll be back. I've just got to go, "Carl told them. "Dan, get my bicycle; I'll get my wallet. Damn it, we're out of money."

They stood in silence and watched him go. Two hours went by. Elena stayed close to Mila. "He'll be back, Mom. He'll be careful," she tried to assure her mother, though she was not convinced by her own words.

Another hour went by. The two o'clock sun beat down without mercy. It was the siesta hour, not a good time to be in the streets. Finally, they heard the gate. "He's home!" Mila exclaimed.

Carl's tanned face dripped with perspiration. His white shirt clung to his skin. As the sweat dripped from his forehead into his eyes, he breathed hard. "I went directly to the Swiss Club," he explained, "for a new pass. Apparently, civilians can move around in the city, provided they aren't what they call 'enemy aliens,' which means Americans, British, Dutch, Canadians, Australians, and so on."

"So we're safe?" she asked.

"I hope so...temporarily. We have to register the children as Americans in Santo Tomás."

"Santo Tomás? You mean the university?" Mila was puzzled.

"All Americans and British have been interned at the university, which they have turned into a concentration camp."

Elena recoiled. "Concentration camp! Trish!" she cried.

"Don't worry," Carl said, "from what I hear, no one's been hurt. They slapped a few people around when they registered, but no one has been really hurt—yet."

"Yet!" snapped Elena.

Mila's mind turned to her sisters, Neva and Luisa, who were married to American citizens. "I suppose they've picked up Neva and Luisa and their families," she said, concern riding in her voice.

"Yes. I have news of the family," Carl sighed as fatigue from the long ride set in. "I stopped by Ben and Magdalena's on the way home. Ben told me Luisa, John and Carla are already in Santo Tomás, and Neva, Brian and their David and Miranda have been summoned."

"What about Constancia and Tony?" asked Mila.

Carl paused a moment. "Ben said that they finally decided to separate. Tony has gone into Santo Tomás, but Constancia and Ian are with Ben and Magdalena. You remember, Constancia kept her Spanish citizenship when she married Tony."

"I can't believe it," Mila shook her head. "I know Tony has been drinking again and Constancia talked about separation, but to do it now?"

Carl shrugged. "Maybe they felt now was the time to do it. At least Constancia and Ian aren't in the camp like Neva, Brian, Luisa, John and their kids."

"I don't understand them," Mila said. "I guess a crisis can bring things to a head."

Carl had more news. "The word is that Stuart Neville has also been rounded up and put in camp. I understand he made it back from Corregidor. There are rumors he's still involved with the American Army," Carl continued. His face remained expressionless.

Elena listened and did not say anything. She knew Carl strongly disliked her father. In fact, he never mentioned him except under unusual circumstances. The news was received in silence by her mother and brothers also. Though Elena said nothing, she was relieved to have news of her father. "That's it," Carl told them as he wheeled his bicycle toward the garage. "Oh," he stopped, "look here. I bought these seeds—beans, *talinum*, chard, tomatoes. We're going to plant a garden." He showed them the packets of seed.

Dan and Tim beamed. "Do we get to help dig it?" Tim asked.

Carl chuckled. "Sure. And how about you, Elena? You are a million miles away."

"Uh?" Elena mumbled. Her mind had been occupied with thoughts of Trish, her relatives in camp, and of Jerry. Jerry. Where was he? How was he? "Yes, I'll help," she said, her words barely audible. *Talinum*! Who wants to eat *talinum*?. It's so much like spinach, she thought.

"What's the matter with you?" Dan looked at his sister.

Mila intervened, "Come on, Dan. Your sister is rightfully worried."

Elena disliked being the focus of attention, especially when she was being criticized. Her mother's comments in her defense only made it worse.

Carl stepped in and made light of the situation. "Come on Elena, don't be so moody. Things aren't all that black," he said, patting her on the shoulder.

Pulling away, Elena did not respond, but her mind was busy answering back. How do you know? How do you know how bad it is for them —you aren't there! She walked back to the house behind the rest. They seemed together; she, apart.

A third of the half-acre on which the Kellers' house stood was turned into a vegetable garden. They planted twelve rows of vegetables, carefully watering the seed several times a day with a large tin watering can. Carl bought some banana suckers and ringed the vegetable garden with them. The bananas would produce a large Honduran variety of the fruit, provided they survived the rainy season.

In the first month of the Japanese occupation, the Kellers also built two chicken coops for six white leghorns and a half dozen Rhode Island Red layers. Dan and Tim brought some ducklings home one day from the market to add to the farmyard. They made pets of the baby ducks. Two of the three ducklings survived—Wobbles and Donalda.

Also in those first weeks, Carl and Mila took Elena, Dan and Tim to Santo Tomás to register them as American minors. Riding in a horse-drawn *carretela*, they were able to see the Japanese sentries waiting at the fortified gates of the concentration camp. Elena pressed her hands together tightly as the *carretela* got closer and closer to the sentries. Telling the family to walk behind him, Carl approached the sentries. They stared at him and did not move or say anything. "I want to talk to the commandant," Carl said. The sentries continued to stare ahead. Elena stepped closer to her mother.

"Who are you?" a voice asked. A Japanese officer walked toward them.

"My name is Carl Keller. I am here to register my step-children," he said. Elena marveled at the even tone of his voice.

"You, American?" the officer asked, showing uneven front teeth.

"No, Swiss." Carl showed his papers.

The officer looked at them and nodded. "Why children American?" He scrutinized Elena, Dan and Tim. Elena looked away. The officer snapped, "See the commandant." He led them to the official building.

As they walked behind him, they saw several of the internees on the way. They watched and remained silent as the Kellers walked by. Elena strained to see a familiar face among them, but she saw none.

The Japanese head of the camp waited at a large wooden desk that appeared to be too big for him. "Yes?" he looked at Carl steadily. Thank God, he speaks English, thought Elena. Carl explained the situation. The commandant did not seem to think anything was unusual. "Children must register as American minors in custody of you—Swiss, and you—mother—Swiss," he pointed to Mila. "They must wear red armbands to show they are American citizens. Papers will tell about situation. You, you and you must report to Santo Tomás when pass says to make renewal. That is all." He waved them away. An hour later, Elena, Dan and Tim had their passes and wore the red armbands that announced in dark Japanese characters that they were Americans out on passes. "I feel like I've been branded," Dan said.

Elena was too choked to speak. As the *carretela* pulled away, she fixed her eyes on the formidable walls and barbed wire that turned the old university into a prison fortress. Was Trish really within its walls, a prisoner of the Japanese? She concentrated on the reality of the clip-clop of the horse's hoofs as they made their way back through the city and across the Pasig River—home.

What the Kellers saw was not the old Manila. The former activity of cars, buses and busy citizens had been slowed to the movement of a few people riding in *carretelas* and *carromatas*, small, more elite horse-drawn buggies; and here and there, vendors and serious-faced people walking around. There were sentries posted on sidewalks of major streets. They wore impenetrable masks, but they observed every move around them. Manila had lost its bustle, the excitement of trade, the chatter of its citizens—its freedom. On the street corner of the Escolta, which was usually so crowded one often had to walk on the street rather than the sidewalk, Elena observed a small huddle of Filipinos whispering. Eyes downcast, a mother tucked a crying baby under her arm and hurried off.

The outer Manila bore the face of order and cooperation; the inner Manila had become a spy, turned inward to secret hiding places, where she listened to shortwave radio broadcasts, kept guns, and horded food, money and jewels for the day when the Americans would return. There was that certainty: They would return. Everyone in the city felt it, pro-American or not, the people sensed the occupation was temporary, if they managed to live through it. But how long would the liberation take? And how many would live through it? That was the question that weighed in the air of the city, a once-proud Asian queen, now a prisoner in fading robes; but a fierce defender of a heritage that she refused to surrender.

It was dangerous to listen to New Delhi news broadcasts, but it was like opium to an oppressed existence. The Kellers hid their shortwave radio in the dark walk-in closet of Mila and Carl's bedroom. Once a day Carl cloistered himself in the closet, Mila's dresses brushing familiarly against his face, and listened to what was happening on the Bataan Peninsula, where the remnants of the Filipino-American forces fought to retain the last bit of the island of Luzon. The news was not good. Japanese forces, with a flow of reinforcements, battered at the diminishing force of

Filipino-American defenders. When Carl was through, he would gather the family and whisper the news.

January crawled by, then February. In mid-February, 1942, the Japanese cracked down on theft by making pitiful examples of ordinary citizens who had stolen from them. A Filipino laborer, about thirty years old, stole a package of cigarettes from the *bodega* at the American School. The warehouse, located right behind the Kellers' stone wall, was stocked with canned goods, paper products and cartons of cigarettes, which were getting harder and harder to find on the open market.

The thief was caught by the vigilant Japanese guards, beaten with a wet rope and left on the sidewalk to die as an example to passersby. His dying screams rose from the street outside the Kellers' house, keeping them awake in a shared agony. At dawn, the eerie wails faded to guttural moans and then stopped altogether. The hot sun beat on the man's body; flies gathered on the corpse.

Elena refused to eat breakfast. Dan ate little. He hurried back out to see the tortured body. He and Tim ran in and out of the yard all morning. Elena brooded in her room and wrote in her diary. At noon, Dan rushed to announce that the corpse was being dragged away. "Come and see him. His face is bloated twice its usual size. He looks hideous—like a monster."

Elena pursed her lips hard. "What's the matter with you? Who wants to see something so horrible?" she snapped.

Mila put her hand on her son's shoulder. "Danny, I didn't know you were out watching like that. You shouldn't have. It will make you sick."

They heard the sudden screeching of truck brakes as the Japanese soldiers stopped to pick up the corpse and carry it away. "I guess he's gone now," Dan commented, as the engine started up again. "I heard the Japs hate thieves worse than anything. Even in Japan, they kill them."

Disgust still in her voice, Elena said, "How come you know so much about them?"

"I heard it from Ramón, our garbage man. He goes all over the city and he knows." Dan lowered his voice, "He told me he is a *guerrilla*."

Carl, who had not been listening carefully, picked up on Dan's last comment and frowned. "Hey, that's dangerous talk, Dan, even if it's true," he said.

I think Dan is right, Elena told herself, for she had overheard Vida tell Marcelina that Ramón was involved in spying on the Japanese. A *guerrilla*! How exciting, Elena thought. She wondered what he did when he was not collecting garbage.

The day after the thief was killed, Elena and her mother were caught in an experience that was part of a crackdown on theft. Another break-in occurred. This time the thieves entered a big warehouse on Vito Cruz Street.

The *bodega* was located in front of Rizal Stadium, a huge athletic field, which the Japanese had converted into a military post, and which was a few blocks from the Kellers'.

Everyone who passed the intersection at Vito Cruz was searched, and in an unexpected act of reprisal, the Japanese guards enforced an order for all pedestrians to bow to the sentry on guard. The order was scrawled in Japanese characters, and there was no visible sentry, only a group of disheveled soldiers who stood at ease or sat sprawled on wooden chairs placed on the sidewalk under the sign. They talked in loud and fragmented Japanese, phrases exploding from their mouths. When unwary pedestrians passed, they were stopped by shouts—searched, shoved and ordered to bow. The people who were stopped, mostly Filipinos, did not understand Japanese. Frightened, they stood mutely, while the soldiers ranted, slapped them and spat at them. Other Filipinos watched from across the street, and finally one would shout bravely, "Bow, they want you to bow!"

The *carretela* Elena and Mila rode passed the unruly post at Vito Cruz. They were immediately shouted down. One of the Japanese soldiers hung on to the bridle and forced the horse to a sudden stop, pitching the passengers forward on the wooden benches. Two soldiers, the flaps of their canvas hats bobbing furiously, ran and hauled the four passengers and the frightened driver off the rig. The soldiers pushed the two Filipino passengers to one side and concentrated on Mila and Elena, who stood stiff as statues, frozen in place. One of the Filipinos who was watching across the street shouted, "Bow to them! Bow to them!"

Like wound-up dolls, Mila and Elena began to bow automatically. Up, down. Up, down. The soldiers shoved them until they stood trembling in front of the other Japanese who were gathered under the sign. Mother and daughter held on to each other's shaking hands. Kicking over a frame chair on which he had been sprawled, one of the soldiers sauntered up to them. His narrow eyes looked yellow—"like a lizard's"— Elena later described in her diary. Jawing a mouthful of spit, he drew in his cheeks and blew out a glob at Mila's feet. The spit dribbled down into her sandal. Pretending not to see it, Mila continued to bow. Another soldier pulled off Elena's red armband. He raised his hand to strike her, when he was stopped by a command from a Japanese officer who had come from the Rizal Stadium. He picked up the red armband, looked at it and said, "Papers!"

Elena winced. She had her pass in the pocket of her dress and jerked it out. The officer looked at it and ordered them to leave. "Go. Now. Go!"

Clinging to each other, the two women ran unsteadily down the street to the *carretela* which had been waiting for them. The driver hailed them, "Get in, quick!" He extended his hand and pulled them in up onto the seats. "Thank you, *cochero*," Mila cried, "thank you!"

They were still shaking when they got home. When Carl heard what had happened, he got red in the face and yelled, "Those goddamn monkey bastards. I would have killed them!"

Dark circles ringed Elena's eyes. Her face was drained of color. "They would have killed you first," she said. Then startled by her own remark, she held her breath.

"She's right," Mila said. "They are insane."

Carl said no more, but put his arms around the two women.

It was several weeks before either Elena or Mila ventured into the streets, and then it was only for a quick trip to the open market to buy meat, rice or vegetables.

In the middle of March, the "Voice of Freedom" broadcast from Corregidor announced that the Filipino-American forces were losing ground on Bataan. MacArthur escaped to Australia in a PT boat and left the command to General Wainwright, whose approximately 75,000 starving and exhausted troops relied on an Air Force and Navy consisting of four PT boats, three mine sweepers, and four P-40s. The P-40s didn't last long. After a successful raid on Mariveles, a few miles from Corregidor, three crash-landed, leaving only one plane. Against this small force, about a quarter of a million Japanese had moved forward unopposed on Bataan, fresh for battle, with the support of heavy artillery and bombers.

By the end of March, the Japanese increased their tonnage of bombs on Bataan. A barrage of continuous shelling from Cavite Navy Base echoed back on Manila. The Bataan defenders under General King fought like tigers, often in hand-to-hand combat with bayonets. By the first of April, overwhelmed, they had to surrender. The First and Second Corps had become a straggle of men overcome by malaria and dysentery. Sick and hungry, they had fought until their weakened ranks were forced back. Even a flank of two thousand *guerrillas*, who had supported them valiantly, had lost its strength.

The men of Bataan had survived on everything, from tough *carabao* meat to horses from the Twenty-Sixth Cavalry. No supplies could come through. The Japanese blockade kept all ships and supplies at bay. Fresh reinforcements could not get through. Bataan could not go on. On April 9, 1942, General King surrendered to the Japanese. From the rock at Corregidor, General Wainwright planned for the final defense of the Philippines.

On April 8, the night before the Philippine-American surrender of Bataan, an earthquake shook the island of Luzon. Following the earthquake, Bataan capitulated.

Elena wrote in her diary: *"It was as if the earth protested the surrender of our brave forces on Bataan. I caught knick-knacks as they flew off the buffet in the dining room. The worst thing about earthquakes is they rumble like bombs, coming closer and closer, in a frightening tide of destruction. Three plates broke. Luckily that was all. Belana has described some of the earthquakes she has experienced in her lifetime here, and fortunately this one wasn't as severe as some.*

"The earthquake is a symbol of the fall of Bataan. The earth shook like

our spirits. Now, there is emptiness. Only Corregidor is left. It's just a matter of time until we are totally under the Japanese.

"I can't understand how life goes on, but it does. I am now being tutored by a Philippine-trained high school teacher, Mary Canda, who is excellent in all subjects. She is teaching me algebra, history and English. We're reading Matthew Arnold's 'Sohrab and Rustum,' a dramatic poem I like very much. I find the history dull, mostly review.

"I don't know how long we'll have money to pay Mary for tutoring all three of us. Carl is still working at the insurance company, but the money doesn't seem to go far enough. Japanese money, called 'Mickey Mouse' pesos, are not buying as much as regular pesos used to. Carl calls it inflation. Beef is disappearing from the market. I can't get my mind off Bataan. I search the black-and-white newspaper pictures for Jerry's face. All I see is groups of gaunt and tattered soldiers, whose ghost-like faces blur, one into the other. All I can do is pray."

Elena closed the diary and hid it where she had hidden other treasured possessions—the pencil Jerry had used to draw her picture, the red ribbon she wore that day, the picture of Betsy Ross, plus the piece of sheet she had fashioned into an American flag. Elena had used crayons to color the stripes red, alternating with the white of the sheet, and a field of blue to represent the background for the stars. Sadly, there were no stars.

As she put the articles away, she thought of MacArthur's last words— "I shall return." The words had been broadcast by a Philippine patriot, Salvador P. Lopez, in a USAFFE (U.S. Armed Forces in the Far East) newscast from beleaguered Bataan. It was a promise and it reached Elena as it had reached every Filipino on Luzon. "I shall return," Elena said aloud. It had to be true.

Several days after the fall of Bataan, Mila was out watering orchids that hung from baskets on several palm trees growing toward the back of the garden, where the outer fence cornered into an inner side fence. It was a warm day. Mila, dressed in flowered culottes she wore in the garden, let the watering can dribble on the thirsty dark earth. She had to stand on her toes to reach some of the baskets, which were made from tough reeds and hung like vases secured to the thick fibrous growth on the trunks of the old palms. Each orchid seemed like a treasure to her— white satin petals, with dark purple throats that gleamed in the sun. So absorbed was she in the orchids that she did not hear her name called from the other side of the outer fence. "Mila!" Then, "Mila!" again. She heard the high whisper and turned toward it. At first, all she saw was a shadowy figure behind bougainvillea that draped the fence. A female figure emerged from a maze of red blooms. Mila couldn't see the face because it was hidden under a large straw hat. The woman wore an old silk blouse and a faded blue sarong skirt. As the woman lifted her face to the sun, Mila recognized her before she said, "It's Angela!"

"Angela!" Mila cried. "Come in, *mi amiga*, come in!"

The two women walked quickly on either side of the fence to the gate. Mila opened the gate and they fell into a long embrace. "I've thought about you, Angela. You don't look the same," Mila said, studying her friend's face. She looked older, thinner, and her face was burned to a dark brown. Also, she wasn't in her familiar nurse's uniform.

"I know," Angela said, "the last time we saw each other was at the reunion at Santa Inez, a couple of years ago now." She paused and shifted the basket of fruit on her right arm. "It's a long story," she continued. "When the Fil-American forces began their retreat, I decided to leave the hospital in Pampanga and join the Army as a nurse. I wanted desperately to help. It was so futile...the retreat...then Bataan..."

Mila looked into Angela's large black eyes and waited for her to continue.

"I managed to get away and run into the hills in Bulacan, where we're in hiding: A group of us, soldiers, nurses, civilians—all wanted by the Japanese."

"You're in hiding!" cried Mila, moderating her voice to a loud whisper. She looked out into the street, but no one was there. "Angela, you're in terrible danger!"

"Yes," Angela said, the weariness heavy in her voice, "but we must go on. We need medicine, food, money. I'm here to make a contact."

Mila nodded. "What can I do?"

"Nothing, right now. *Gracias.* I just stopped to say 'Hello' and see that you are all right. *Los niños?*" she questioned.

"*Bien,* the children are fine," she answered in a mix of English and Spanish common to those of mixed culture.

"*Bueno,*" Angela smiled for the first time. "How do you like my costume? I look like a *dalaga* who has gone to market? Huh?" She laughed— the same old infectious laugh.

It was good to hear her friend laugh. Mila joined in the humor. "A housewife going to market? To those who don't know you, perhaps." Mila thought back quickly to the days in the convent. She had known Angela for over a decade, and her friend, who was orphaned early in life, had always had an indomitable nature. It seemed fitting that she should be doing something courageous now. "Angela," Mila's expression turned serious, "are you with the *guerrillas?*"

Angela, too, looked sober again. "Ah...ah, I can say nothing about that now." She looked out into the street. "I must go. It's getting very late. Good-bye, *cariño.*" She squeezed her cheek against Mila's and hurried through the open gate into the street, where she blended well with other passersby.

Mila stood in place, watching her friend walk away. She will be back, Mila told herself. I know Angela. "Mom?" Mila jumped. "Sorry, I saw you standing here. Who was that?" Elena asked. She had been feeding the ducks in the pens under the house and had seen her mother and Angela.

"Nothing for you to worry about," Mila said hurriedly. "That was my old friend Angela." She cleared her throat.

"Why are you nervous?" her daughter asked. "Is she in trouble?"

"Yes. But it's secret. You're not to pry about it,"

"You mean she might be a—a *guerrilla*?" whispered Elena.

Again her mother cleared her throat. "Not exactly."

"Then what?" Elena persisted.

"Just that she is in hiding. That's all. I can't talk about it." Mila smoothed her hands on her thighs, picked up the watering can and headed for the orchids.

Elena did not follow right away. She stood thinking about the drama she had witnessed between Mila and Angela. Her imagination took over from there. That's what Angela was—a *guerrillera*. Ramón, now Angela. How exciting, she thought, to be doing something so brave and secret for the cause of freedom. I wish I could be involved in the movement in some way, she told herself. From that day on she vowed she would not miss the opportunity should it offer itself to her.

As she returned to the duck pens, she passed her mother. Mila's back was turned toward her as she reached for an orchid with the spout of the watering can. Elena observed her tense shoulders and the clenched white fingers around the rusty can. She's scared. My mother is scared. Strange to see her in this way, Elena thought. From the time she was a little girl, her mother had seemed almost fearless. Elena took a step toward Mila; then stepped back. What could she say? Eyes lowered, she walked to the duck pens.

In her next diary entry, Elena was careful not to mention details of Angela's visit. She knew it would incriminate both Angela and her mother. Instead, she wrote about a lesson her tutor had given her on the origin of the Philippine Islands.

"Mary Canda knows so much. Makes me think I'll never be as smart as she is. So much of what I learn from her is interesting, but today she had to harp on me so I would understand how the Philippines was formed 50 million years ago. I lost interest in all the geographic details of how the islands rose from the sea through volcanic eruptions; layer by layer of lava built new land. Also how the continent of Asia became part of the drama because, supposedly, it drifted southward, which caused its edges to crumple and submerge. The depression made by the inundated land brought the S. China Sea into being. I still don't quite understand how the buckling in the submerged land formed folds which now make the eastern crests of high mountains that run north to south in most of the big islands. Mary said all of our islands originated from that great volcanic upheaval in the earth 50 million years ago!

"I do believe she is right about the volcanoes, because Belana told me that Taal Volcano, just a few hours ride away from here, erupted in the early 1900's, when she, my grandfather and family lived in a little house in old Manila. She said a lot of ash and hot pieces of pumice landed on the roof.

"I sometimes wonder why what happened 50 million years ago is so darned important for me to know! Mary got pretty annoyed when my mind clogged up and drifted off, and she had to repeat the whole thing. Finally, she asked for a pan of water. 'What for?' I asked. 'You'll see!' she said, and we marched to the driveway and collected some gravel. She dumped the gravel in the water, making a muddy mess. She worked the gravel into piles—Asia, the Philippines (little peaked piles) and the South China Sea between them. She patted down the gravel where the Asian continent drifted away. Then she pointed to the little piles and said, 'Here is where the earth's crust buckled and folded up. It's where the big volcanoes formed and made our islands.'

"As the water cleared, so did my mind. I really understand most of it. Mary ended the lesson by saying that a most important fact is that before the Great Ice Age, the South China Sea was so shallow it made land bridges from Asia, Malay, Borneo, the Celebes, and some others I can't remember, connecting these lands to the Philippines. Lots of trading went on, and some of the traders settled here.

"Then when the ice melted, the land bridges flooded a full fifty meters and cut our islands off. Traders still came in boats, even Arabs and merchants from India looking for gold. No wonder the Philippines are such a mix.

"Mary was smiling when she left. Guess she was pleased with herself. I could go on and on, but must get to sleep. One more thing. Today Mom had a visit from an old friend."

Chapter Four

Fortuna

Fortuna was the Kellers' *lavandera*. She arrived at sunrise, five days a week, via *calesa* from a poor *barrio* in northeast Manila. Each morning she could be heard washing a load of clothes in a shallow, fluted tin tub, three to four feet in diameter—as wide as she was tall. Her short roughened hands were no larger than a child's; but they were tendoned and strong and worked like fury over the dirty clothes—scrubbing with harsh coconut soap, pounding and flipping each garment until it looked as if it would shred apart. On stained items, Fortuna used a smooth rock brought from the Chico River near her hut in Bontoc, located in the high country of Luzon's Mountain Province. Fortuna's hill people belonged to one of the most fierce Igorot headhunting tribes. Neither the Spaniards nor the Americans had been able to alter the primitive ways of these independent folk, whose origins were still a mystery, and whose wondrous stonewalled rice terraces, layering mountains from ground level to summit, staggered the senses. If laid end to end, it was said these ancient terraces would run 1,000 miles!

Fortuna's daily ritual began with the smoky lighting of a *panatela* cigar, which she steadied in the wrinkled O of her mouth. All her front teeth were missing, and the teeth she had were stained blood red from the betel nut she chewed—a mild stimulant that put her in a singing mood.

No one knew the Bontoc woman's age, exactly where she lived in Manila, nor why she had left her Mountain Province to work in the city. Not even Vida, who was in charge of work schedules, knew. Fortuna spoke no English and very little Tagalog. She infuriated Vida by gesturing, pointing back and forth from her mouth to an imaginary bowl of rice. If Vida pressed her too hard, she broke into rapid Bontoc dialect, which made the younger woman roll her eyes and walk away. The two women had little to do with each other, which was much to the *lavandera's* liking. She did her work at her own pace and chewed as much betel nut, which she wrapped in leaves and sprinkled with lime, as she desired. The shadowy wash area under the house was often blurred by a cloud of *panatela* smoke.

When Fortuna hunkered down to do the wash, she tucked her navy wrap-around skirt, made of tough *ramie* grass fiber, under her thighs. She looked mythological—a wizened doll. She wore a red headband decorated with seeds to keep a cascade of floor-length hair wound tight around her head. Mysterious tattoos decorated her dark arms, from her wrists to her shoulders, mostly linear designs—a sign of prestige among her people. There were marks on her arms and legs from brass armlets and leglets. Dan was sure he had seen her in a market stall on several weekends, wearing a traditional multi-colored *lepanto* costume, complete with leglets and armlets. Averting her eyes as she handled carved wooden Igorot figures, she pretended she did not know him.

When she became frustrated at laundry that didn't come clean, even when left for hours spread on the grass to bleach in a blinding sun, she chanted mysteriously, before giving up and returning the garments to the washtub.

Fortuna took a fancy to Dan and Tim. She teased and flirted with them, often reaching out to touch their arms, then laughing outrageously at their white skin. She brought them treats, usually sticky sweets made from *camote* and rice.

Most of all, she took advantage of the fear most people had of head-hunters. With measured alacrity she pointed to the boys and slashed her leathery finger across her neck, then stamped her feet gleefully when they laughed at her antics.

Elena's relationship with the *lavandera* was not as congenial. Remembering days in Baguio's outdoor market, where puppies were fattened in cages until they resembled furry toads, then were sold by Igorots as specialty eating fare, Elena shuddered when Fortuna joked about eating the two fox terriers. The dogs hated her, barking and snapping at her when she delivered stacks of clothes, still warm from the heat of the heavy coal iron—the *plancha*.

Fortuna's presence added a lively delinquent flavor to the Keller family's anxious days during the dreary months of the Japanese occupation.

One sweltering afternoon, Dan and Tim sat hidden in a nest of branches in the mango tree. A shady retreat, it was a secret place where they could talk, eat mangos and share the silence of sultry afternoons.

Not wishing to be heard, they spoke in whispered sentence fragments. Dan reached up and plucked a ripe mango, a huge golden oval oozing droplets of amber syrup through its taut skin. It hung so close to his nose, he could smell its tangy-sweet perfume. He salivated as he peeled the fruit with the small worn blade of a yellowed bone-handled pen knife given to him on his eighth birthday by Carl.

"Hurry up!" hissed Tim, sucking up his drool.

A glint in his eye, Dan took his time. Expertly cutting off a long wedge, he handed it to Tim. In a prolonged ritual, the boys ate, yellow juice syruping down their chins.

From their high perch, they could view the length of the driveway. "Hey," Tim pointed, his mouth still full of mango, "there's Maxie and Sheba." He paused. "They're going to do it again."

They watched as the fox terriers came under the tree, prancing toward each other, then darting away, in a heightened mating dance. Caught in an irrevocable magnetism, the dogs drew closer and closer with each pass, the male pushing, and the female inviting, then rejecting his attentions, until he became so frenzied, he began to lunge at her. He was able to mount her finally, his forepaws so tight around her miniature waist, she could not have gotten away if she had wanted to. The brown markings on her inflamed pink underside looked like tiny dark islands as she succumbed to the male's rhythmic thrusts.

The boys were glued to the scene, their senses fully aroused. The mango pit, still warm and juicy in Dan's hand, slipped away and fell with an audible plop on the ground below.

Neither one had heard Fortuna pattering up the driveway with her daily mid-afternoon pile of laundry. She held the cloth-wrapped bundle on her head. It was balanced there by a multi-colored head ring that she bore like a proud crown. Wide as Fortuna's shoulders, the tall hefty bundle did not shift as she glided under the tree, her hips swaying imperceptibly.

The fruit pit fell a mere two feet from the *lavandera's* path. Her eyes darted up the tree like a raven's and flashed a split second on the boys, as they peered down like frightened nestlings, not sure whether or not she had seen them.

Eyes straight ahead, she walked by smoothly. A deep throaty chuckle escaped from her throat when she was out of earshot.

In the meantime, other eyes had observed the scene. Hidden behind the *capiz* shell shutters of her bedroom window, Elena also watched.

Panting, the fox terriers separated, dragged themselves to the cool grass, and lay down, their pink tongues dribbling, their eyes now blank.

"All clear!" Dan said. The boys quickly shimmied down the mango tree, bare feet soundless on the broad trunk.

Tim spotted Elena standing in the frame of the window. He grimaced as she prissed up to her full height and sputtered, "How scurrilous!"

Dead in his tracks, Dan looked up at her. "Scurrilous?" he questioned, eyes a wide innocent blue.

Tim stuck out his chin. "She means that's what the dogs did," he said disdainfully. "She thinks she knows everything!"

"Yeah," Dan echoed, but at the same time looked down guiltily. "Let's go."

The two hurried to the chicken coop, where they knew they could work out some of their discomfort by concentrating on their chores.

In the house, Fortuna laid out the crisp-smelling ironing on armoire and closet shelves. She was still chuckling.

Chapter Five

Corregidor Falls

The Japanese assault on Corregidor was relentless. From Cavite and Bataan, a few miles away, they hit the rock fortress night and day with 500-pound bombs and heavy shells. After the fall of Bataan, hope of an American counter-attack faded. The eleven thousand defenders of the tiny island lasted for another twenty-seven days against impossible odds of some two hundred fifty thousand Japanese.

Malinta Tunnel was jammed with thousands wounded, many of them casualties from Bataan. Supplies were precariously low; the main water source which came from deep well pumps had had its main electrical current cut repeatedly, and several tanks that served as reservoirs had been destroyed. Corregidor had become a last-ditch stand.

By the first of May, 1942, the forty-eight field guns they had started out with to defend the fortress had been knocked out; two remained. By the fifth of May it was easy for General Homma to land on North Point, a strategic spot on the northeast tip of the island, where the rock was thinnest, like the tail of a tadpole to which its shape was often compared. Bombardment from the Naval base at Cavite and Bataan never let up. The four main districts—Topside, approximately 500 hundred feet above sea level; Middleside, about half that; Bottomside, appropriately named because it was just above the water line; and the Malinta Tunnel were bombed and shelled mercilessly. Because barracks, warehouses, machine shops, power plants and other vital buildings had been demolished, what was left of the defense of the island moved into the Malinta Tunnel.

When the enemy force was several hundred yards from Malinta Tunnel, the Voice of Freedom made its final broadcast. *"Message to General Homma...For military reasons which General Wainwright considers sufficient, and to put a stop to further sacrifice of human life, the commanding general will surrender to Your Excellency today the four fortified islands at the entrance to Manila Bay together with all military and naval personnel and all existing stores and equipment."*

The broadcast delivered its dark message: *"At 12 noon, local daylight saving time, May 6, 1942, a white flag will be displayed in a prominent position on Corregidor..."*

His expression drawn, his eyes blank, Carl emerged from the closet where he heard the last broadcast from the Voice of Freedom. His face revealed the news. Mila put her arms around his neck. He pressed his lips hard on her forehead. "Let's not tell the children until after lunch," she said.

By evening, Japanese radios on Luzon were triumphant with news of the surrender. Pictures of the gaunt Wainwright with the wooden-faced General Homma appeared on every newspaper for days after the fact.

A heavy pall lowered over Manila. For the next few days, the Kellers spoke to one another in monosyllables. Mary Canda cancelled tutoring; Elena retreated to the duck pen underneath the house and wrote in her diary, reminiscing about Jerry and Trish. In this retreat, she felt less touched by the reality of the surrender—they were now under total Japanese control, prisoners, whether in concentration camps or not.

Wobbles nesting in the corner of the pen became an unexpected comfort. For hours, Elena knelt by her white-feathered Royal duck. Wobbles, a name that had suited her as a duckling, no longer fit. The mature duck had grown a bright red crest and was a mean defender of her eggs. "Let's see your eggs, Wobbles," Elena cajoled, and Wobbles noisily pecked at her intruding hand. "Not, yet...maybe tomorrow."

Following a full, humid moon, the next day dawned heavily. Not a good day for hatching. Wobbles waited on her nest like a stone. The crest over her beak was pale.

Faint peckings began at dawn after a night that had not cooled. Mosquitoes hung on the crossed slats of the pen. They would hang there all day. A blue-black horsefly buzzed sluggishly over the soft-feathered nest.

Dankness rose from the packed dirt floor. The odor hit Elena when she came to kneel by the nest. She stroked Wobbles' smooth white neck. The duck barely responded, pecking disinterestedly at her hand. She didn't turn her head to give Elena her familiar glare—a crystal blue eye that asked, "Who do you think you are?" A look that made Elena smile.

Something is wrong, Elena thought, as she put her hand under Wobbles' heavy warm breast to check the four eggs. The duck spread her feathers in protest. "Oh!" Elena cried, seeing that one duckling had hatched and was dead, its feathers wet and sticky, its eyes glazed. She picked it up and gazed at the lifeless form, which hadn't fully developed. The yolk that normally nurtures the duckling while it is forming had not been absorbed. Balloon-like, it protruded from the duckling's lower underside. Elena could see it was abnormally attached, mixed up with internal organs. Growth had suddenly gone awry.

"It wasn't right, Wobbles," Elena said, laying the dead duckling near the rocks surrounding the pen's enclosure, where she would bury it later. She reached over and stroked the curve of the mother duck's white wing feathers.

Three eggs remained. The second never opened; the third produced a malformation like the first. It lived just minutes, gasped a few breaths and stilled. Elena laid it gently by the first duckling. What went wrong? The grotesque bulges, dirty yellow and red-veined, blood oozing from ruptured membranes, did not answer the bigger question. A perfect God created such an abnormality? A punishment? Elena dared not think there might not be a God in charge at all.

A horsefly buzzed over the dead ducklings like a vulture. "Get out!" Elena swatted at it, but in seconds it was back. She turned away. Nothing to do now but wait for the final egg to hatch.

Knock. Knock. Knock. A snub flat beak appeared through the cave in the egg. Wobbles took new interest, picked at the shell, causing jagged pieces to break away. Quite suddenly, the pecking stopped. A button-eyed baby duck shouldered itself through the hole and rolled out, small webbed feet paddling the air. Wobbles trilled at it and immediately began to groom the wet feathers. As she did so the crest on her beak grew redder and fleshier. Sun waffled through the slats, drying the yellow down. Within minutes the baby duck wobbled on perfectly formed flat feet, its yellow fuzz puffed like a dandelion. Elena shook her head. A miracle. A perfect miracle. Had the fourth duckling not lived, Elena could not have prayed with any conviction that night. Thank you for the miracle, God. She did not mention the deformities, the deaths. It might mean accusing God.

The next morning Elena shared her experience with her mother. Mila smoothed her daughter's tangled hair. It had not been combed since she had gotten up. She noticed the dark circles under her eyes. Seconds passed. Neither woman said anything. Then Mila put her arms around Elena. "Life is a puzzle, isn't it?" Mila said. "It's so fragile...yet such a miracle."

Nothing she could have told her daughter would have equalled the experience she had had. Just turned sixteen, my daughter has come up against the puzzle of existence, she thought, about which there are no absolute answers.

In the weeks that followed, the hope of liberation drove deeper underground. It fed on rumors. It fed on the activities of Philippine *guerrillas*, and on the bravery of common citizens who risked their lives. One of these fighters against Japanese rule was Angela. Hiding in the deep mountainous valleys of the province of Bulacan, she nursed her fellow *guerrillas* and POW comrades in hiding.

One day in late May, Angela showed up again at the Keller house. She appeared so unexpectedly, Mila was once again shocked to see her old friend. Thinner yet, eyes so intense they dominated her face, Angela looked desperate. "I know you're surprised to see me," she said, embracing Mila.

Mila stepped back and looked at her. "You are so thin, *amiga*, so thin...and look at your beautiful hair. You had it cut off. *Dios mío!*"

Angela's long black hair had been cut into a sharp bob. Her dress hung loosely. Her hands were tanned and rough. "I've lost about twenty pounds, I think," she explained. "Rations are very slim. We live mostly on rice, and fruit from the trees around us; once in a while we catch fish, or someone steals a pig from the village."

"Come in," Mila said. "I'll give you some food. I can't stand to see you this way, Angela."

But Angela would not go into the house. She stood behind the big mango tree so she could not be seen from the street. "We...we...need money, Mila," she hesitated, eyes downcast. "We can't go on without money to buy supplies." She reached into her dress pocket and pulled out a hand-rolled black cigarette. Lighting it against the cup of her trembling hand, she raised her eyes to Mila, who had not moved and whose gaze was riveted on her.

"Stay here!" Mila cried. "I'll be back in a minute."

She ran up the front steps into the living room. Opening the top drawer of her engraved Chinese desk, she drew out an envelope with several bills. At that moment Elena appeared. "What are you doing, Mom?" she asked.

Mila rushed by her. "I can't explain now. Don't follow me." The screen door slammed behind her as she ran down the steps and back to Angela.

Elena watched them through the screen door. Mila handed Angela the money and gave her a quick hug. Angela returned the hug, tucked the money down into the front of her dress and hurried out. When Mila came back into the house, she was out of breath. Face flushed, she explained to Elena why Angela had come. "She's there in those back hills nursing wounded men who would now be in the prison camps at Tarlac and Cabanatuan."

As her mother talked, Elena thought of the Bataan Death March...the endless miles the bedraggled Filipino-American prisoners had walked in the merciless sun. Sick with dysentery and malaria. Starved. Beaten by guards who drove them without rest to hovels that were to become their places to live in concentration camps. "She's a heroine," Elena exclaimed. "Angela is a heroine," she repeated.

Tears made their way down Mila's face. "Yes. A brave, brave woman. Her name is no longer Angela," she said. "It is Carmen Cruz. She's a *guerrillera*. No one must know who she is or reveal where she is hiding. She's trusting us, Elena," Mila said, lowering her voice.

Elena nodded and put her hand to her heart. "I'd die first," she said. "I want to help. I have a little bit of money in my savings."

Her mother nodded. "When she comes again, you can help."

Before dinner that evening, Mila and Carl called the family together. "We've all had feelings and ideas about what we can do to help ourselves during this time of occupation," Carl shared his views with them. "We're all worried about staying alive. About food. Clothing. About everything, I guess," he paused. He had a habit of squinting his eyes when he was concentrating on something. He squinted now. "The first thing we have to do to help ourselves is to stick together. That means we help one another in every way we can. We'll work harder than we used to. Vida and Marcelina, we'll be working with you more in the house. We'll also all work harder in the garden to produce our vegetables. We'll relieve one another so no one has too much to do." He stopped again. His squint became more pronounced, his nose sharper. "Another thing," he continued, "we will keep our mouths shut. Whatever you hear that could get someone in trouble—keep it quiet. Don't repeat it."

"And watch out for rumors," Dan piped in.

He broke the tension and they all laughed. "Yes," Carl joined him, "watch out for rumors."

"And watch out for the Japanese," Tim added. This time no one laughed.

"Shh!" Vida breathed.

The next day, still reacting to Carmen Cruz's visit, Mila listened to Elena playing the piano and was soothed by it. Making her way softly through a Chopin nocturne, Elena was obviously engrossed in feeling. Mila, who had always wanted to play the piano herself, but never learned because of the many demands in her large family—seven brothers and sisters, all needing to be fed and clothed by a widowed mother—found deep pleasure in Elena's musical expression. True, her daughter had struggled through lessons that had started when she was ten. Elena enjoyed musical interpretation and was especially successful at playing sonatas, nocturnes, waltzes, and even fugues. She was not good at strictly technical aspects of piano, such as solfeggios. She disliked long hours of practice, reading new music, counting beats. Mother and daughter often locked horns over whether she had met the two hours of practice required by the piano teacher, Sarita Reyes. Sarita despaired over Elena's lack of technical perfection at the keyboard. "If you didn't have such feeling, you would be a failure as a musician, Elena," she told her. And Elena, always polite, continued to be the way she was. The more Sarita drove her, the better Elena's interpretation. The rest stayed the same.

Sarita had studied under Dr. Friedman in Manila's music academy. Friedman was a Jew from Austria, who had taken refuge in the Philippines after being tortured in a German concentration camp. His fingers had been frozen and were partly paralyzed. He could no longer play the piano, so he concentrated on becoming a first class conductor. "I must be near music," he was often heard to say.

When Sarita arrived to give Elena her lesson that afternoon, Mila said, "Elena, tell Sarita I won't be seeing her today. I am very tired..."

Sarita arrived in a flourish. She wore a print dress of large fuchsia flowers on an electric blue background. Short and pigeon-breasted, her stark white face was pointed like a bird's. A tall mound of hair stood like a pagoda on her head. She flounced in the door and went straight for the black piano stool, which creaked as it bore her weight. "Solfeggio first; then the waltz," she announced.

"No," Elena sighed, moving in restlessly beside her.

"Yes!" Sarita said, louder than before.

Elena clenched her hands, opened them and hit the keys: Quarter note, half note, two eighth notes—one, two; one, two; three, four. 'Speed it up!' One, two...Elena counted the beats, Sarita breathing down her neck, booming when she missed a beat. "No, no, no! Do it again!"

When the exercises were finished, they were both perspiring profusely. Sarita's floral perfume smelled acrid. Elena said, "Let's rest, okay?" It was a relief to stand up and stretch her legs, and to get away from Sarita's warmth. "I'd love some *calamansi* juice," Sarita said, before Elena offered it.

When Elena returned with the iced juice, Sarita arranged her wide skirt over her knees. "Thank you, *cariño*. It's delicious." She sipped at the edge of the thin glass.

Elena was suddenly eager to talk. "Sarita, have I ever told you about Jerry?"

"Jerry?" Sarita's dark lashes fluttered over her dark round Spanish eyes. She was all ears.

Remembering Carl's counsel, Elena hesitated. Then trusting her intuition, she told Sarita about Jerry. Sarita listened intently as Elena expressed her feeling about Jerry. Her eyes turned luminous and softened. "I have a friend also," she ducked her head and continued in a whisper, "a lieutenant. I don't know where he is either."

Feeling the bond between them, Elena grew excited. "Oh, Sarita, if we could only find them. Suppose they're alive!"

"Maybe we can find them," Sarita said, her eyes secretive. "I know someone in the underground."

"You do?"

"Yes. I've been thinking about doing something to find my lieutenant."

"Is something happening through the underground to help the POWs?"

"Yes, but it's very secret. A lot of people could be killed," Sarita pursed her lips. "Later, when I find out more, I can tell you. I trust you, Elena."

Suddenly Elena found her eyes stinging with tears. "I trust you too!" she exclaimed. Emotionally overcome by the idea of finding and communicating with Jerry, Elena squeezed Sarita's hand. "Thank you," she said, "oh, thank you!"

When Sarita came for subsequent lessons, she never said anymore about their conversation. Elena waited. It would be June of 1943, a year later, before the subject would come up again.

In the meantime, the Kellers continued to live day by day under the shroud of occupation. When the rainy season came, the air-raid shelter filled with three feet of water. To keep wood rot from setting in, they bailed out the water each day. "When we need it again," Carl said, "we want it to be in good shape." But they knew it would be a long time before they would use the shelter again. Liberation! Even the wish for it seemed a long way off. It became like a dream, a whispering shadow that urged them on to act as if some day in the future it would be a reality. Hope. That's really what it was.

The vegetable garden thrived and provided them with tomatoes, carrots and greens, which they were less able to find or to afford at the open-air market. The price of all food was going up. Rice and fresh meat went first to the Japanese Army and Navy; what was left was sold at inflated prices. *Carabao* meat became a weekly item on the Kellers' menu. It was tougher than beef and gamy in flavor, but it made good stew when the gravy was seasoned and hid the fact that it was not beef.

Families all over the city shared new ways of cooking, as old staples were substituted. Mila shared recipes with her mother and sisters. They cooked with coconut milk, cassava root—basically like a sweet pota-to—and they used rice flour. Lard replaced butter or margarine. Mongo beans became one of the main sources of protein. Like round lentils or tiny olive-green peas, the mongo bean went a long way in completing a meal, especially when it was cooked to a porridge-like consistency and poured over rice.

The women of the Fernandez clan visited each other often. They gossiped, spread rumors among themselves and shared recipes, as they awaited a new birth in the family: The birth of Magdalena and Ben's baby, due in September of 1942. It was a time for involvement and celebration—a positive note in an otherwise oppressive year. The baby's layette included hand-crocheted and hand-knitted booties, caps, sweaters, soakers and blankets. The women fashioned shirts and little dresses from used tablecloths and lightweight curtains. Everything was embroidered as if it had been made of the most expensive linen. Sofía and her daughters made some lace from very fine string. "Remember my layette for Elena?" Mila said one day as her mother, her sister, Constancia, and Magdalena worked over the baby's clothes.

"*Sí. Claro,*" Sofía sighed. "I remember. I also remember how I made clothes for you children after your father died. Make-overs, they were, from worn, cutdown pants and dresses. Remember the hand-me-down shoes?"

"Do I remember!" Mila exclaimed. "How Josefina's high heels pinched my feet!"

Sofía's eyes looked far away. "Yes. You weren't ready for heels."

"*Hola!*" Elena suddenly appeared in the living room where they were sewing. The three women all looked up at her, and Elena blushed. They chuckled. Elena picked up a ball of string and began to wind it into several smaller balls. "Did you know it's raining?" she commented.

"When isn't it raining?" grumbled Constancia, who usually did more listening than talking when there were several members of the family together. She was smaller than Mila and more buxom, but both women had lively dark eyes. Constancia's nose was sharper than her sister's, which was shorter, wider and slightly upturned, a characteristic Elena had inherited. But by contrast, Elena's fair complexion seemed pale, even wan next to her mother and aunt's.

"How is Ian?" Elena asked her aunt, who doted over her only child.

Constancia caught a stitch with her needle. "He's fine," she answered, looking up intently. "I'm hoping you will consider tutoring him. We talked about that a few weeks ago. Remember?"

Elena glanced at Mila. "Mom and I discussed it," she said, "and I can do it. We just let my tutor, Mary, go. We're now looking for a tutor who will charge less. If you can pay me a little, it will help me start my own lessons again."

"*Está bien,*" Constancia nodded. "That will work out well. When Neva comes out of Santo Tomás next month, she'll have David and Miranda with her. She has been given a medical pass to remain out of camp until the dysentery they caught clears up. They're all very weak." Constancia cleared her throat, a habit she shared with Mila, which revealed she was tense. "Anyway, David will need tutoring. Could you do both?"

Elena didn't hesitate. "Yes," she answered.

Sofía looked especially pleased. "Come here and sit by me," she said to Elena.

Constancia glanced at Mila and said, "*La favorita!*" referring to Sofía's partiality to her oldest grandchild. Mila nodded and shrugged her shoulders.

Elena sat by her grandmother and continued to wind the balls of string. She sensed the bond between them, smelled the light cologne Sofía splashed on her arms, neck and hair. She noticed the skin on the older woman's arms was still smooth by contrast to her rough, large-knuckled hands, which testified to a life of hard work. Like the skin on her arms, Sofía's complexion bore few wrinkles except for a few spidery lines around her eyes and two frown lines. Her eyes, dark and very deep— almost haunting—bore a watchful expression; they carefully guarded the scars of inner pain. She had pinned a rose carved of ivory above the first button of her pale peach cotton blouse. The only other piece of jewelry she wore was a black onyx ring on the third finger of her right hand. Two heavy gray braids were wound around her head like a crown. How Elena envied that hair. Her own fine hair, bunched into a handful, only equalled half of one of her grandmother's braids.

Elena's mind drifted back to when she was nine or ten when she spent entire days visiting with her grandmother. At that time Sofía lived in a rented house on Mabini Street with four of her unmarried children. She took in sewing and her grown children all contributed their salaries to living expenses.

Elena could still envision Sofía's old green tongue-in-groove kitchen walls. Now remembering, she was back in that kitchen for a hair-washing ritual: Camomile brewed on Sofía's converted wood-to-gas stove, sending a storm of vapors into the kitchen. There was no escaping the sickish herbal odor. Her grandmother waited until something in the alchemy told her it was just right for pouring over her granddaughter's head. "*Rubias* always should keep their color," she would say, as if Elena's fine blonde hair was the stamp of royalty born of English genes.

"*Rubita*," she called Elena as she led her through the suffocating fumes to the pot cooling in the sink. Then invariably she would pronounce the brew as still too hot. The green-gold liquid looked ominous as it cooled.

As they waited, Elena asked Sofía to retell a favorite family story. Her grandmother seemed to enjoy going over the family lore as much as Elena liked hearing it. In a mix of Spanish and English, her grandmother took Elena back over the oceans to Spain. Elena could picture the house over the bay in Huelva, where Sofía was born after her military father was transferred there. She could smell the oranges, see the ships; even imagine Columbus sailing to America. It was easy for her to envision the three famous ships in historic Huelva Harbor.

"Elena?" it was her grandmother's voice, bringing her back. "*Cariño*, you have finished winding that ball of string."

"Oh!" Elena exclaimed and looked around at her mother, Constancia and Magdalena whose heads were bowed over their work. Her grandmother smiled and handed her some more string to wind.

Suddenly Magdalena gave a cry. "*¡Ay, mosca!*" With a stiff reed fan, she swatted at a large fly and killed it. The women laughed in chorus. Still chuckling, Sofía said, "Ay, Magdalena, you're a wonder—so sweet, so patient with everyone—but deadly with a fly!"

Her daughter-in-law grinned broadly. The drape of her green rayon skirt slid over her tight round abdomen. She placed her hands on the sides of her stomach as if she were holding a large beachball. "It's moving again. What an acrobat!"

"Good!" Sofía said. "A baby should move—move a lot." She knew, for years ago she had had a stillborn. Mila and Constancia nodded. They had heard their mother say this before.

Ben's tall figure appeared at the door. "*Oye, niñas*," he said, "it's time to stop. *Merienda*."

"*Merienda*," his wife repeated and got up. One by one, the women went into the kitchen to fix afternoon tea.

In the weeks that followed, Elena taught Ian and David elementary arithmetic and English. The lessons went well, even though she found herself having to give individual attention to each of them. Her aunt Neva went to live with Ben, who seemed not to mind having extra relatives in the house—five adults and three children, one on the way.

With the money Neva and Constancia paid her to tutor her cousins, Elena was able to resume her own lessons under a new tutor, an Austrian Jewish refugee named Hilda Grossman. Hilda, who was a little over four feet tall and whose spine was so curved she looked like a dwarf, was a genius at math. Elena learned geometry as if the formulas were transmitted to her by osmosis. Everything Hilda showed her made sense. In several weeks, she was well into the course, and Hilda told her she had earned several days vacation.

Elena spent the days reading, playing the piano and cleaning out the duck pen, which had grown to a populous brood of eight ducks and ducklings. She wrote in her diary each day. Sometimes she had to push herself because there didn't seem to be much to write about. But on September 20, Magdalena's baby girl was born and Elena was elated.

"Aunt Magdalena gave birth to a seven-pound baby girl at three o'clock this morning. She had been in labor for only six hours and had an easy time. Uncle Ben worried he wasn't going to get her to the hospital on time. He is so happy! The baby is beautiful. She has dark curly hair like her mother and very white skin. They will call her Paz. What better name in time of war— Peace."

Then it was Christmas again—the second Christmas of war. Like the first, they did not celebrate, except for a small exchange of gifts. It was as if they were saving the holiday for a time in the future when they hoped the old spirit would return. Elena knitted a pair of string socks for Mila, and Mila gave her a sapphire pin that had been a present from Stuart. Carl and the boys exchanged old tools. Vida and Marcelina each received glass bead rosaries. In return, they presented the family with six tapered candles, which they burned Christmas night. Fortuna arrived late for the modest festivities, in full Igorot dress. From a basket strapped to her back, she drew a bundle of aromatic rice cakes and laid them on the Christmas table with a flourish.

Carl reminded them they should be grateful that the marines in the Solomons had put up a real fight against the Japanese. "I think the tide is turning," he said. "After the Battle of Midway, anything can happen."

Chapter Six

A Visitor from Santo Tomás

Nineteen forty-three was a new year. The only thing different in the dreary rules and routines that characterized life under the Japanese occupation—do's and don't's regarding traffic, rice rationing, water usage, curfews—was the staunch severity, with which they had controlled Manila in 1942, had let up a little. Sick "enemy aliens"—Neva and her children were a case in point—could live in specially cleared residences with relatives and in guarded convalescent homes outside Santo Tomás. People in the camp were allowed to receive packages and visitors, and occasionally some of the women and children got temporary passes to visit outside. Censored notes were allowed back and forth into the camp—everything very guarded and controlled, but it meant some communication was possible.

General Sigemori Kuroda, who replaced tough General Homma, was given credit for the noticeable letting-down on the part of the Japanese. Kuroda wanted to teach the Filipino people Japanese ideology. The spirit of Asian co-prosperity was the subject of daily news propaganda. Under this mantle of Japanese "brotherhood," the secret forces of the military Kempetai worked as deviously as ever. Neighborhood associations were formed. Several houses on a block were tied together by a chairman who orchestrated all activities. He was responsible for the workers in community truck gardens. He snitched on individuals who were suspected of being anti-Japanese collaborators. For the first few months the chairman in the Kellers' neighborhood was too busy with initial organization to get all the neighbors involved. Carl was ready with a plan when his turn to be interviewed came.

Mila received a note from her sister Luisa telling her that they were "all well" in Santo Tomás. Elena was encouraged by this and tried to contact Trish to see how she was. A few days after she wrote to her old friend, she received a note from her. The next step for Elena was to try to get a visitor's pass for Trish to visit.

"Please, let's get Trish to come," she pleaded with her parents. "Lise Muller was able to get Mary Sorenson to visit her for a few days. Listen to what Trish says in her letter: *'I was thrilled, excited, happy and everything else to receive your letter. This morning, Mary Sorenson, Jane Little (British from Hongkong—you don't know her), Jill Wier and I were waiting at the gate for some friends who were coming in to visit,'"* Elena paused to catch her breath, *"'when who should walk in but Lise Muller. We managed to sneak over and talk to her. I wish it had been you. I want to see you so bad!'"* Elena finished and folded the letter. She stared at Carl and Mila, waiting for an answer.

"We'll try," Carl said.

After some delays in paperwork, he was able to arrange for a pass through the Swiss Consulate.

Elena cleaned her room and waxed the floor to a shine with the *lampaso*. She used halves of the coconut shell—*"bunút"*—first. Putting the shell halves, one under each foot, she "danced" over the waxed floor until it shone like a topaz mirror. Holding the shell husks under her bare feet was not easy, but she had practiced enough with Vida and Marcelina that she was able to work up to a graceful dance, keeping her rhythm across the floor of her room. She finished the routine, called *"lampaso,"* by taking a wad of rags and buffing over the floor in a final polish. The result was beautiful but disastrous, for everything slid so easily over the waxed surface that accidents could happen. Elena slid onto her behind as she rushed to gather all the cleaning items and hurry on to something else. Trish's visit was all she could think about.

Part of the preparation included setting up a folding cot for herself so that Trish could sleep on her bed. Mending mosquito nets and sewing on new ties took time. The nets were getting worn out, and tears had to be darned because no new nets were available. The final touch was to set up a vase of orchids on a clean dresser doily, and to splash cologne on Trish's pillow!

Trish arrived under escort by two Japanese guards and a member of the camp committee. Her blue eyes darted excitedly over the Kellers' familiar gate. She spotted Elena and was ready to jump from the high step of the Army truck on which she had come, when suddenly the camp committee member held her by the shoulder. "Remember," he warned, "you're absolutely forbidden to leave these premises, and you must be waiting right here at this spot in three days at fourteen hundred hours, on the dot!"

Her eyes still fixed on Elena's eager face, Trish jumped from the truck, promising, "I will! I will!"

Like lost relatives, the girls embraced. Eyes closed and breath held, they froze in each other's arms. "Here, here," laughed Carl, putting a hand on each of their shoulders, "you've got three whole days. Come in and say 'Hello' to everyone."

Trish gave him a smile. She had grown three inches taller than Elena and was thinner. Her face, tan from working in the prison camp garden, was accented by the same bright eyes that had changed, only in that they seemed more guarded, more aware—an alertness that approached vigilance.

She wore shorts and a washed-out blue blouse Elena remembered having bought with her after school almost two years ago. Stitched over many times, the holes in her tennis shoes had been patched by hand.

Trish talked for hours, often without stopping.

Santo Tomás was fun, she told Elena, because school and her friends were there. "Plus, she added, "hundreds of kids I never knew from Baguio and some of the other islands." They all went to school together and had social activities including dances which were held twice a week.

"Dances?" Elena asked, enviously.

"Oh, yes. If we weren't behind a fence with soldiers guarding us with bayonets, it would be like being at a school camp," Trish explained. "Except there are other awful things—the food is terrible. It's mostly rice and sometimes a little meat or fish, covered over with a thin vegetable broth. We have no hot water, even for showers, and you have to wait in line for everything, even the bathroom." Trish paused a moment, then continued. "Sometimes it's hard to sleep with thirty other people in the room, snoring and carrying on."

Elena cocked her head, listening to every word. "If we could only combine your life and mine," she said, "we could have it perfect—at least as perfect as it can be under the Japs."

"Wouldn't that be something," Trish commented, shifting her position on the front steps on which they sat. Then studying Elena's face, she said, "You really are lonely, aren't you?"

"Yes," Elena nodded, her eyes filling with tears. "I miss you all so much, and I feel like a traitor—disloyal. I don't know what I am— Spanish, Swiss, English or American. You know, I've told you before..."

"It is complicated with you, isn't it?" Trish's eyes clouded over. "But no one blames you, Elena, for being out of camp. They just envy you."

Then Elena posed the question that had weighed heavily on her mind. "Do you resent my being out?" When Trish didn't answer right away, she continued, "I think I'd resent it if it was the other way around."

"Really? Oh, don't listen to anyone who says you're a traitor, or anything like that. They're just jealous!" Trish cried.

"Has anyone said anything?" Elena persisted.

"What I mean is, if anyone should say anything, don't pay any attention. No, no one has."

"Thanks, Trish," Elena said, reaching out and touching her friend's hand, but inside she was not convinced. The dilemma of her identity would continue to plague her.

Three days went by too quickly for the two teenagers. They talked about the old times they had shared. They talked about the present—the war, the differences in their lives, and about boys. Trish's life fascinated Elena. By contrast, her own life was without social excitement. All she had to offer was her feelings about Jerry and her hope that she would be able to find him.

"Boys!" Trish went on, the second evening after they had had a special meat dinner with chocolate pudding for dessert, "Boys all over the place. And there are so many romances, you wouldn't believe it!"

Elena's green eyes widened, "Tell me—who?"

"Oh, you know," Trish slowed down, "Sally and Billy and Jill and Bobby—Jill and Bobby, they even..."

"They even—what?" Elena whispered.

"Well, they even kissed," Trish sighed, then gave a slight laugh.

Elena was transfixed. "Oh!" she said, "did Jill tell you what it was like?"

"You mean kissing?"

"Yes."

"Oh, it's neat. You know."

But Elena didn't know, and there was no way Trish could explain more to her, except to say, "Kissing isn't everything. Everyone holds hands and dances, too. That's great fun."

Elena grew silent. "What's the matter?" Trish asked.

"I just wish I were in camp with you," Elena said.

"I wish you were, too," Trish said, putting her arm around her friend's drooping shoulders.

When Trish returned to Santo Tomás, her arms were loaded. The Kellers had filled two large paper bags with items they felt she and her parents would be able to use. Mila gave some of the bitter chocolate with which she had made the pudding Trish liked. Dan and Tim climbed the mango tree and picked six ripe mangos, which they had to wrap separately because they were dripping with sweet juice. Carl placed a bunch of ripening bananas in the bag, which he picked from one of the trees he had planted. Elena's gift was not one Trish could eat. She gave her half of the precious bottle of cologne she had splashed on her friend's pillow. Vida and Marcelina made some coconut candy and ran up just as Trish was leaving. "Good-bye!" they cried, handing her the carefully wrapped package as the *carretela* pulled away. Trish was crying so hard she could barely see the expressions on their sad faces.

They watched the *carretela* until it blended with the rest of the traffic. In silence, except for Elena's sobs, they returned to the house and to their routines.

Depression rode Elena's mood for the following week. The excitement of Trish's visit over, she felt more lonely than she had before her friend came. She went to see Lise Muller, but talking to Lise didn't make her feel much better. Lise showed her some of her movie star albums, pictures of favorite actors and actresses they both admired.

Elena barely looked at them. "Come, on, Elena," Lise tried to console her, "you'll see Trish again."

But they both knew that was not certain. "I feel so low," Elena sighed, "like nothing will ever be the same again. I'm not sure who I am anymore. You...you seem so sure of yourself, Lise," she paused. "At least you know you are Swiss."

"Swiss," Lise responded, "but what difference does that make, except I often wish I were American and in the camp with them!"

"That's just it," Elena cried, "you're not confused about it like I am. I feel a bit of everything..."

"Like a calico cat!" Lise interrupted. "You're all colors in one!"

To Elena, the allusion was not amusing. It sounded ominous. "Sure. Like a calico, a stray mix that can't call itself anything," she pouted.

Lise would not be dampened. "Oh, Elena. Don't be so serious. You may be a 'calico,' but remember they're said to be a sign of good luck."

"Good luck?" mumbled Elena. "Where did you hear that?"

Not long after, Elena went home, feeling disgruntled. Lise had only added to her misery. The only thing that came out of the visit was Lise's new nickname for her—"Calico."

A week later, the subject was still on Elena's mind. When Sofía invited her to go on a walk in the boulevard after mass, which they attended at La Salle College because it was located between their houses on Taft Avenue, she went, hoping she would be distracted from her mood.

Sensing something was on her granddaughter's mind, Sofía said, "You seem quiet, *querida*. Is something bothering you?"

At first Elena looked away. Then she said, "Oh, nothing. I'm just feeling depressed because my classmates are all in camp. I feel different, out of place."

"How do you feel different?" Sofía's look drew back Elena's eyes like a magnet.

They turned a corner, and as their pace quickened, Elena explained, "I feel, as an American citizen, I should be in camp. I'm neither Spanish, English, Swiss or American—I'm nothing!"

They had reached the long line of palms in the boulevard. "Oh, that's it!" Sofía gently pulled Elena's hand into hers. "Nothing? *Qué tonta*—silly. Nothing, ha? Why, you're a blend of several of the greatest cultures in the world—Spanish, English, Swiss, American. Look at you, *eres linda*—beautiful! You have the face of an English noblewoman, with my eyes of course, and the heart of a Spanish poet. American citizenship is just a piece of paper. It's what you feel inside that means something, and you feel loyal to everyone—to your family and to America and its cause. I'm not American—no—but I feel that way just the same."

Tears Elena had held inside since Trish left were released and ran down her cheeks. "You see things so clearly and poetically, Belana. I guess I am a crazy blend of everything...As you say, it is what I feel inside that counts, isn't it?"

Sofía stopped walking. "Flow like the water, *cariño*," she said. "Blend with your surroundings. You can travel in a freer atmosphere that way. Find your true self, *corazón*. People are basically the same the world over.

I believe cultures differ, and we get along most happily with those who are like us, but people deep down are the same."

As they started to walk again, Elena forgot herself and concentrated on Sofía's words. "Cultures are different," she said, thoughtfully, "especially in war, don't you think?"

"People's attitudes are different in war. War seems to bring out the best and worst in people."

Several Japanese soldiers passed them, and Elena felt her grandmother's grip tighten on her arm. "What I mean is that the regular people in Japan must be different from these rough soldiers we have here," Elena explained.

Sofía nodded. "We see their military culture here. They're doing some bad things." Sofía lowered her voice. "But you know, I remember some unruly Americans in my time. This very bay you see," she pointed to the deep blue water glittering on the other side of the sea wall lining the park-like boulevard, "was filled with sunken Spanish ships, and the Americans were the enemy then. In fact, your grandfather Lorencio was a civilian guard on this sea wall."

"Really?" Elena said. "But I can't imagine anyone being as bad as the Japanese."

"*Verdad*, but it was a frightening time just the same. Sofía bit her lower lip, remembering. "There was killing. There was shortage of food. But in spite of that, there were good memories, too," her grandmother added.

"Like what?" Elena asked, interested in what Sofía was telling her. It was a story she hadn't heard before.

"Well...I met an American major called Bob Thompson. Your grandfather thought he was sweet on me. I just thought he was friendly, though he did come around a lot. He brought us all kinds of food and put us in touch with his fellow officers who looked after us." Sofía smiled faintly.

"I wonder where he is now," Elena commented, thinking about Jerry.

"That was forty-five years ago—the Spanish-American war. He did write. The last letter was ten years ago now."

Sofía reached into her purse, took out an embroidered handkerchief and patted at the perspiration on her brow. "His wife was ill, and he was being re-stationed in Texas as a brigadier general."

"Do you think you'll ever hear from him or see him again?" Elena asked. She could envision the major and her grandmother, distinguished and in their sixties, meeting romantically.

Sofía shook her head. "I don't think so. I've known so many people in my life, Elena. I'll never see a lot of them again—Americans, Englishmen, Spaniards, Filipinos..."

Realizing they had walked the length of the boulevard, they turned. "I suppose I should be glad I'm a blend, Belana," Elena said. "You've had many friends from many countries."

"They've influenced my life, made me strong."

Suddenly, the nickname "Calico" didn't seem so bad. She would have to tell Lise.

Elena had her seventeenth birthday in April. In June Sarita's promise to tell her more about contacting prisoners of war materialized. As Elena stumbled over the unfamiliar chords of a Beethoven sonata, she waited for Sarita to call a recess. Just when her fingers started to cramp, Sarita announced, "Time for iced tea."

Stretching her fingers, Elena said, "Thank you. I don't think I can play another note." She sighed and raised her eyes to the ceiling of Sarita's spacious piano room. The piano teacher had so many students now it was easier for them to come to her house than for her to go to theirs.

In a few moments Sarita returned with the tea. As she passed the large wall mirror in the room, she looked at herself and swept a strand of hair back into her high pompadour. "You just get too tight, Elena. Relax. Let the fingers curl lightly," she stopped, then added, "Just a minute, let me get more ice for the tea. When I come back I have something to show you."

Intrigued, Elena watched her swish out of the room for the ice. She sat on the edge of the piano bench, but when Sarita returned and clinked the ice into the glasses, she kept her in suspense and said nothing. Breaking the silence, Elena said, "I hate reading notes."

"I know. I know, but it's the notes that make music!" Sarita threw up her hands, then laughed. Elena joined her. Suddenly their laughter stopped. "Sit still," Sarita said in a whisper. She rose, went to the mirror, pulled it away from the wall and slipped her hand behind it. Carefully she drew out a folded piece of lined paper. "It's from my lieutenant," she said softly.

Elena's hands flew to her face, stifling a loud, "Oh!" as Sarita put the note in her hand. The paper was folded over several times, with the ends tucked into the final fold, making it slightly over two inches square.

"What's this name on the outside?" she asked, seeing the name Stephan Gaines written on the outside of the note.

"That's my code name," explained Sarita. "Read it."

Fingers trembling, Elena opened the letter and read it. John Knowland, Sarita's "lieutenant," thanked her for money she had sent him at the Cabanatuan POW camp in Nueva Ecija, located northeast of Manila, a day's ride away. He told her of his battle with dysentery, the long days of work in the hot sun. His weight had dropped to one hundred and thirty pounds. Food was scarce and he appreciated the money, which he used to buy food and other items from priest-escorted vendor carts that were allowed into the camp occasionally.

When she was finished, Elena folded the letter back carefully and looked up at Sarita with tears in her eyes. "How wonderful," she said huskily.

"I think we can find your Jerry Merrill," Sarita confided.

It sounded too good to be true. "Do you really think so?"

"All you have to do is trust me," Sarita said. "There is me, someone in the middle, and the actual person who delivers the notes to the camps— Cabanatuan, O'Donnell, Bilibid." She paused, curled her fingers together and continued. "After they find him—that is, if he's still alive—you can write to him by using a code name."

Wide-eyed, Elena asked, "What if one of us gets caught?"

"Don't think about that. The underground network is smooth and informed. There are people in every *barrio* on Luzon involved."

"How do they manage to get the letters in?"

"They deliver them to the camps through priests and vegetable vendors who take produce in to the prisoners. Old wooden carts loaded with *camote* and fruit make an ideal hiding place."

Her eyes turning a lucid green, Elena exclaimed, "I'll do it."

Sarita stepped forward and gave her a great hug.

July passed. August. No word from Jerry. The letter Elena wrote under her code name "Michael Greene," went unanswered. Finally, on August 25, 1943, a folded note arrived. Printed clearly was the code name Michael Greene.

When Sarita went to the mirror to get it, Elena sensed there was something for her. "Oh, my God!" she cried.

Sarita pressed the note hard into her hand. "I am so thrilled for you!" she said.

Elena clutched the note and closed her eyes before she opened it. Fold by fold, she worked the letter open. Then almost afraid to look at the penciled lines, she lowered her eyes very slowly and began to read Jerry's message. When she finished, she could not speak. Sarita waited, hands on her lap. "Listen," Elena said, her voice wavering. "It begins, *'Dear Elena, I don't know of any way to start, except that I am about the happiest man on earth now. I have been counting the days until I could look you up and find out that you are all coming through all right.'"

Clearing her throat, Elena continued, "*Elena, I could not forget you, and I often prayed that our horrible host had not pulled any of their torture on any of you.*

"*I have had many close experiences. Last year, I caught malaria and was expected to die, but I outwitted the old man with a scythe. Then I contracted dysentery and was moved to a place where a fellow had to be a pretty good man to come out walking. Now, I'm in as good condition as a person can be on a diet of rice three meals a day for the past twenty months. We work awful hard, long hours in the sun every day and sleep on rough bamboo slats at night. But no matter how tough they make it for me, I'm going to grit my teeth and pray that it will not be too long before I can once again think for myself and not have one of these little fellows standing over me with a club.*"

Sarita sighed, "Such suffering..."

Elena continued: *"I have saved up an awful lot of things to tell you in these long months and I assure you I will be a very good correspondent. Keep your chin up, and I am always anxious to hear from you. Yours, Jerry. P.S. Please excuse the paper and penmanship."*

Elena's voice gave way as she finished. "Sarita, thanks to you!" she managed to say, holding up the letter. Both women were in tears.

"Thanks to you, too, Elena, you were willing to take the risk to help the cause."

"I'll do anything for him," Elena said, the tears gone now from her voice. Sarita recognized the energy, the conviction in her pupil's statement. It was how she felt also.

"I feel like Mata Hari," Elena joked as she tucked Jerry's note into her brassiere, picked up her music and headed for the door.

"Don't laugh. You are a Mata Hari."

"I guess...if they catch me..." Elena didn't finish, but waved and shut the door behind her.

She waited on the sidewalk for a *carretela*. Her face was flushed, her arms protective against her body. Relax, she told herself, make your face go slack. Don't let your fear show. She took a deep breath and hailed a *carretela*. In her hurry to climb onto the narrow pedal and hoist herself up to the wooden bench, she lost her footing. She didn't fall, but her music went flying. *"Dios!"* she cried, arms crossed on her bosom. A young Filipino leaped out of the *carretela* and helped her pick up the scattered sheets. As he handed her the music, he noticed Elena's awkward pose and asked, "Are you in pain?"

"No!" Elena said, letting her arms drop to her side. "I'm fine. Thank you. Thanks so much!"

As he helped her onto the bench, the young man smiled. He looks like a student, Elena thought, and she smiled back. Thank God, she said to herself, settling back against the railing. She looked at the other passengers—a young mother and a child, about ten. Their eyes were focused on the passing traffic.

When Elena arrived home, she showed the letter to her mother and Carl. "Your wish has come true, Elena," Mila said. "I'm glad. I'm afraid, but I'm glad."

Carl remained silent for several minutes. "I know how important this is to you. I'm also glad for you, for Jerry, but you must be terribly careful. If you—we—should get caught..." He paused. "I have my doubts about this involvement," he said, the familiar squint in his eyes.

"Yes. I know. Sarita has warned me. But it's done."

"True," Carl said.

Elena slipped Jerry's letter into a dictionary and put it on top of the desk in her room. Later, she said to herself, later I'll hide it better. She shared the letter with her brothers, and by evening she had read it four times herself, committing most of it to memory. The lines turned to live scenes in her mind. She visualized Jerry, sick and gaunt, working with a shovel in the blistering noon sun. She saw him spooning a sickish broth into his mouth. Saw him writing to her, a slight smile on his face, his eyes as blue as she remembered... She could almost touch him—he seemed so close.

The next day the letter was still in the dictionary. Elena was not ready to put it away in a safer place. After dinner, a sunset sky blazed deep purple, orange and pink, before turning leaden gray. There was an unexpected clanging at the gate. A Japanese officer stood and waited for someone to let him in. Dan started to run to the gate to open it. Carl shouted, "Let me!"

"Elena, the Japs are here!" Dan yelled to his sister, who held the dictionary in her hands. "Put it down!" Dan cried. "You can't do anything about it now!"

Elena dropped the book back on the shelf. She looked as if she had been struck by lightning.

"For God's sake, get away from there!" yelled Dan.

Quickly Mila walked to Elena and pulled her by the waist to where she and the rest of the family stood, inside the front door. "Stay calm. He's an officer," she told her daughter. "And, thank God, I think he's speaking to Carl in English." She peered through the screen door as Carl and the officer approached the stairs.

The Japanese officer, dressed in a dark green uniform, was almost as tall as Carl. He chatted as if he were on an evening stroll. "I am Captain Watanabe," he bowed. He gave a straight smile, revealing an even row of teeth. They bowed back. "May I sit down?" he asked.

Carl pulled extra chairs into the living room. The officer sat on the flowered cushions of the rattan sofa.

"Yes," he said, "I came for a visit." He looked at his carefully manicured fingernails. "Just for a visit," he repeated, noting the serious looks around him. "I am new at headquarters," he said, waving in the direction of the school.

Carl was scowling. Mila spoke first. "Would you like some tea?" Her words were measured.

"No, thank you. Just tell me a few things. You are a Swiss family, I understand."

"Swiss," Carl nodded, appearing less tense.

"Your children?" Watanabe pointed to Elena, Dan and Tim, who sat in straight chairs across from him. Carl nodded.

"Ah!" exclaimed the captain, enthusiasm building in his voice. He reached into the pocket of his trousers and pulled out a series of small paper frames, folded in accordion fashion. Pointing methodically to each black and white snapshot, he named his wife and three children. "My wife, Fumiko; my oldest boy, Kijuri; second child, Yukiko; third, Fumiko, the baby girl, two years old.

He took each picture out of its frame and passed it around. He watched their faces as the pictures went from one to the other. After all the snapshots had made the rounds, with the appropriate nods and smiles from the Kellers, Watanabe looked pleased. They heard a little hiss in his smile.

Elena's breath came more easily. She could not take her eyes off Watanabe. He was different from what she had expected. He looks as if he belongs in a garden with cherry blossoms, she analyzed. And his family—they look so gentle! Then she caught herself. Mustn't trust him!

Putting the pictures back in his pocket, the officer rose. "May I please see the house?"

Elena's heart sank as he went from room to room—dining room, master bedroom, Dan and Tim's room, and, finally, after seeing the kitchen and bathroom, he said, "I did not see that bedroom. He pointed to Elena's room.

The Kellers, who had processioned through the house with him, trailed into Elena's room, while she prayed. Don't let him search my desk, please God.

Captain Watanabe took his time. He stopped to admire a reproduction of a painting by Amorsolo that hung in Elena's room. The delicate scene was of a Philippine rice field in early morning. "Very beautiful," he breathed. Then he leaned against Elena's desk and played with the dictionary, fingering the pages without looking at them. "I studied English —four years—at Harvard."

"Have you been to Japan?" he asked Carl, as he pushed the large dictionary so it was flush on the desktop edge.

Carl shook his head; the rest of them did likewise.

"It's very beautiful," Watanabe repeated.

Slowly he moved out of the room, studying the walls and furniture. Noting its narrow mirror, he paused at Elena's white dresser, which Carl had made for her on her twelfth birthday. He said to Elena, "Nice room for you." Then added, "I must leave now. Thank you," he bowed. He hurried down the stairs and was gone.

Elena ran to get Jerry's letter and shoved it down her brassiere. "What are you going to do with it?" Tim asked.

"I'll sleep with my bra on." She gave him a hard stare. "Tomorrow, I'll hide it near my diary in the duck pen."

The following day she hid the letter in a pillbox and concealed it under a flat rock near one of the duck nests.

Chapter Seven

"Via S - c/o MU"

Elena wrote to Jerry again, addressing the letter by code. Although she didn't understand its significance, she printed the letters with care: Jerry Merrill, Via S - c/o MU. Who was S? Who was MU? Would she ever know?

Her letter related incidents in her daily life. She did not mention her feelings about him, except to say, "I think of you so often. You are always in my prayers, Jerry. God Bless you." She ended the letter as he had hers, "Yours," and then signed her name with her best signature.

Before she folded the letter, she approached her mother, Carl and the boys and asked if they would like to add something. Surprisingly, Carl, who felt encouraged by the way the first communication had been handled, added a note. "I know it's still a big risk, but I'm also going to enclose thirty pesos for Jerry. He needs it. I wish it could be more, but it'll help him buy something from the vendors."

Mila, Dan and Tim wrote their notes, and Elena folded the pages and the money together into a tidy square, following the pattern she had first seen in John Knowland's note to Sarita.

On September 18, another letter arrived from Jerry through Sarita's underground connection. Elena was elated. She studied the familiar writing, penciled on lined notebook paper. Holding the letter to her nose, she breathed in its unique scent—a mixture of sun and tropical dampness. Jerry had had the same pieces of paper in his hand, had folded them into the creases she traced with her finger. As she settled herself in one of Sarita's highback chairs, she felt as happy as she thought she could ever feel.

"*Dear Elena,*" he wrote, "*I hope I've not kept you waiting too long. I had a talk with a fellow about mail, and even if I do go on a new detail, we can correspond, as my mail will be forwarded to my new location. The only difference is that it may take a little longer time.*" Elena paused. The thought of losing contact with him made her shudder. "*Now for a little history,*" the letter continued. "*When I first came to O'Donnell, the first camp I was in (we marched from Bataan), I started working in a kitchen. While many men were profiteering, I was helping out some fellows from my squadron and asked no returns. One week after my coming here, I was doing several men's work in the rain on top of a huge rice vat. I passed out. Next, we came to Cabanatuan, where we had to sit out in the sun, and I came near going out again. I tried to work here, but malaria had me and I could not go on. The day before going to the hospital, I begged a cup of blood from a carabao that was being butchered. I stuffed this down.*"

"*Carabao* blood!" Elena exclaimed. "I can hardly stand *carabao* meat."

At the piano Sarita took no note she had heard her. Elena went on reading. "*I was afraid of the hospital, and no one expected me to return. I finally received a little quinine from the Medical Corps here (good people). Then I came down with dysentery and was moved to a shack with my commanding officer, an awful place. Almost every morning I would awake and try to awaken the guy on the bamboo beside me. No use.*"

Elena was totally drawn into the scene Jerry described. The thought of touching a dead person was more than she could bear, even in her imagination. Oh, Jerry, how hard this has been on you.

"*Next,*" she read on, "*the officers and the medics received a little pay, and they were eating good food, but that did not help me. I started catching rats to earn tobacco, which I traded to buy a few necessities, salt and a few eggs. Thank goodness I do not smoke. Well, I ran out of rats (what a business), and now I'm going out on the farm, barefoot, from the break of day until dark.*"

Looking up, Elena cried, "Rats?"

"*I hope I've not bored you with this dull letter. Elena, dear, I must write fast, as I must collect my rags and get ready for a very early take-off from here, Sunday, sooner than I expected when I started this letter yesterday.*

"*I'll pray connections are not broken. If they are, I'll come to see you the first chance I get.*"

The letter was signed, "*As ever yours, Jerry.*"

There was a note to Carl, Mila and the boys, which Elena also read. "*Hello, Carl, Mila, and the boys, I'm heading I don't know where, but the going will probably be tough. At least I'm not leaving the islands, and the tougher these fellows get, the more they will receive later.*

"*I should give you a growl for trying to help me. You seem like my own parents, and your gift of letters and money has made life worth living again. KEEP 'EM FLYING, Jerry.*"

Her heart sinking, Elena knew Jerry was telling them that they may be losing contact with him. "Sarita," she said as she joined her teacher at the piano. She did not have to wait to get her attention.

Sarita looked up immediately from the music. "You look awful. What did he say?"

"They are moving him to another camp," Elena clasped her hands together tightly. "Will we lose track of him?"

Sarita's answer was sober. "Can't tell. The network is good, but it's difficult to re-establish connections with another camp. It's like trying to relocate him all over again. If he moves often, it'll be impossible to trace his whereabouts. I don't know, Elena. I just don't know."

"That's what I was afraid of," Elena said. She picked up her music. Sarita walked with her to the door. "Elena, remember how much the contact has meant so far. That's what counts," Sarita said. She put her arm around her dejected friend.

In a voice that was barely audible, Elena replied, "I know, but the more you write, the more attached you get. I care so much about him."

Sarita's eyes watered. "When you love someone, it's worth the pain. Even if I never see my lieutenant again, I'll always love him, and he feels the same way."

Shaking her head, Elena said, "I can't accept how unfair life is. Why should Jerry and John—all of them—suffer so? They've served their country. Now they are prisoners of war. Jerry is sick, hungry...I know the letters help, but that seems so little..." She couldn't finish.

A frown creased Sarita's high white forehead. "That's where you are wrong. Our contact means everything to them. Can't you sense it, even beyond what they say?"

Elena nodded slightly. "I guess so. I know the letters mean everything to me. My mother may call it 'puppy love,' but I know it's much more. My feelings are so..." She extended her arms.

"Sure it's more. You're willing to risk the danger of getting caught for what you're doing, aren't you?"

"Yes, but I try not to think about that," Elena said.

"Good!" Sarita's smile was wide. "Go home and try not to worry. A little prayer helps."

"I hope!" exclaimed Elena as she went out the front door, down the wooden steps and onto the street. "Bye," she waved to Sarita, who stood in the doorway, her brilliant red dress blowing in the breeze, exposing her sturdy legs.

When she got home, she gave Mila Jerry's letters. After reading them, her mother said, "I'm glad he got the money. Our letters seem to have lifted his spirits, *pobre*—poor guy. Carl will be glad and so will the boys."

"I think we'll lose contact with him," Elena said, feeling depressed again.

"The underground will do everything to help us keep in touch. Beyond that, you can't do more. He wouldn't want you to risk your life, or ours, more than we have," Mila consoled her.

Elena followed her mother into the yard. "It helps to keep busy," Mila said, picking up the familiar watering can. "Keeps your mind off your worries."

"Seems I worry even when I'm busy."

Mila raised her eyebrows. "You're just a worry wart."

Elena shrugged. Turning toward the duck pens, she said, "The ducks are laying eggs like crazy."

Mila brightened. "Vida said there are more than enough for cooking. You've done a good job of taking care of them."

"The turkey hens Dan bought in the market last week are already laying also. We'll have so many eggs we can start to sell them," Elena said, her mood lifting.

"Yes, or salt them to save for later," her mother added, referring to a process whereby eggs were boiled, set into barrels of brine, and cured for weeks. Firm and salty, they were a treat for the famiy. Often as part of the process, they were tinted a deep rosy pink to distinguish them from regular eggs.

"Mmm," murmured Elena as she went off to the duck pens.

Night sounds drifted in through Elena's screened window—the crickets' croon, the familiar clop of horses' hoofs, slowed after a long day of pulling *carretelas* and *carromatas*; the annoying whine of ever-present mosquitoes, and the call of the gecko. "Gek-ko, gek-ko." Sometimes one call, sometimes nine. Vida told Elena the call held a key to the future. "Make a wish before you go to bed. When the gecko calls, count the number of times it says 'gek-ko.' That will tell how many years it will take your wish to come true."

"What if he doesn't call at all?"

Vida's eyes gleamed. "Then the wish will not come true."

"Ever?"

"I don't know. You can wish it again and again, until you hear the gecko." Vida's smile was slightly sly.

Elena knew the story was based on myth. Still, it had an authenticity about it. Surely, Elena convinced herself, someone had tested it. She set logic aside and chose to believe the story. No one had disproved it, had they? Anyway, it gave her something to look forward to, even if it proved to be only a game she played.

For now, the gecko had power. Hiding in the thickest of leaves, the reptile worked his camouflage well, so well Elena had never seen the elusive lizard, which made it and its call that much more mysterious.

The day after she received Jerry's second letter, she decided to wish on the gecko. As soon as night fell she made her wish and waited for the call. "I wish that I could see Jerry again," she said, eyes squinted shut.

She lay on her bed, enshrouded by the white mosquito net. More than an hour passed. She was close to sleep when "Gek-ko!" broke through the night air. Startled, she heard it three times—"gek-ko, gek-ko, gek-ko." Three years? That can't be right! I'll wish it again tomorrow.

The next day, she pondered over the gecko. What did the reptile really look like? Was it just an ordinary lizard? Vida told her the gecko had magic sticking pads on its toes; and that when it jumped from limb to limb it could stick on any surface, even on human skin. "If the gecko lands on you—look out! Nothing can unstick it except a mirror."

"A mirror?"

Vida nodded. "When it sees its reflection, it jumps at it. It thinks it's another gecko."

Elena decided she would see the gecko for herself. At sundown the following evening she went to the thick bamboo clump where Vida was sure the gecko lived. Would he be as magical as his call, with red eyes and a prehistoric tail? Would she see his adhesive feet?

Standing by the bamboo, she waited. Imagining the gecko hiding over her head, she challenged him. "Come out!" she stuck her chin out. "I want to see you, you magical creature—you!" A warm breeze played on the back of her neck. She raised the collar of her blouse. Geckos can drop down on you and stick to you, she reminded herself. And she had forgotten to bring a mirror!

Several seconds passed; then one, two minutes. She was sure she was close to the gecko. It was so deadly silent.

"Come on, gecko, show me where you are," she said out loud. Stepping forward, Elena reached forward into the thick foliage and pushed at a shadowy green clump of bamboo suckers that rose like thin seaweed, and smelled cool and fresh.

Still no movement. She peered into the dark maze of leaves and shoots. In that intuitive way that the senses know what the mind does not, Elena raised her eyes. She felt something very close, staring at her. Looking up furtively, she met a pair of shining eyes that gleamed like dark diamonds. The gecko! Elena and the lizard both froze. Then like a streak of black lightning, the gecko flew over her head and landed into a nest of dried bamboo leaves, crackling its way back into the clump and disappearing into it. Elena saw no more of its form than its four outstretched padded feet and its regal tail. It measured about five or six inches from head to tail. The reptile moved so fast, Elena's mouth gaped open. Her heart thumped in her throat. Adrenalin flooded through her body, and suddenly, she sprinted from the spot, shrieking all the way up the front steps, and running into Vida, who was coming the other way.

"¿Qué pasa?" Vida exclaimed, holding on to Elena as she flew by.

"Gecko!"

"Gecko?"

"Yes!"

"You saw him?"

"I did!"

"Oh!" Vida's braids shook. "Not so good. Not good to see the gecko. You saw him well?"

"No, barely. He almost got me."

"You did not see him well. Good." Her look was somber.

Vida's words were little consolation for Elena, whose skin still prickled from the experience. Vida placed her hand on the back of Elena's neck. Her fingers felt warm, and her voice, soft. "Do not worry, Elena," she said. And Elena felt suddenly quieted, as she had when she was little and Vida soothed away a bump or a bruise.

"I'm through with superstitions," Elena said, patting Vida's hand and slowly moving away from her.

Vida smiled, a smile that was more polite than reassuring. Elena could see she didn't believe her.

Lying in bed that night, Elena found herself waiting for the gecko to call. She could still feel its physical presence. She had come so close in contact with it, she shivered again at the thought. When the gecko finally came, it no longer seemed like the far-off mysterious call of the past. But she found she had a new respect for the reptile—its speed, its energy, its sense of survival. "Gek-ko. Gek-ko. Gek-ko." Each call broke into the darkness like a shot.

Although it was too hot for a cover, Elena pulled the sheet up to her chin. She did not make a wish.

Not far from the house, Vida lay awake in the servants' quarters next to the garage. She stared out a screenless window and looked for her favorite evening star; but Venus had already set. Then she heard the gecko and smiled to herself, recalling Elena's dramatic encounter with the mysterious lizard. Elena—such a child yet, Vida thought. At her age I was grown up and ready to leave home. Leaning forward she cupped her chin on the sill. As her eyes fixed on the luminous milky way, her mind slid back to the rice field and to the *nipa* shack in Batangas Province, where she was born to her tenant farmer parents, Sergio and Andrea Guzman. She was the sixth in a family of eleven, eight of whom lived through infancy.

Batangas—how green it appeared in her mind's eye! It was a rich rice basket, as well as a lush garden of fruits and vegetables. Several hours south of Manila, the province was bordered by the South China Sea. Ocean breezes fanned rice fields, which were blessed by dark volcanic loam from Taal Volcano's eruptions over the centuries. Taal's cones rose as an island from Lake Taal, several hours away by *carabao*.

Heartened by Vida's lusty cries at birth, her mother and father looked forward to the time when their daughter could work in the rice fields, which they farmed for a rich rice baron, a Chinese-Filipino called Su Chung. In good years, when the monsoons blessed the crop with rain, when drought was a bad memory and typhoons did not rip up the tender shoots, the Guzman's could count on filling their stomachs.

At six, Vida had a daily job of carrying pails of drinking water from the well to the family workers in the rice paddy. Guzman farmed twelve hectares of land for Su Chung, already so rich his house in Manila was filled with antiques from leisure trips to Hong Kong.

Vida shifted her position at the window and thought back on a typical hot noon when she carried two water-laden pails to her family. The smooth handles had cut a calloused line into each palm. It seemed she walked miles to reach the hairpin figures of her family bent over young rows of rice, their feet immersed in a shallow lake of water so necessary if the thin seedlings were to survive.

The little girl looked over the mirroring water, which held the broken reflections of her family—her mother, father, numerous aunts, uncles and cousins—as they tended the precious rows of rice, thinning out stalks, replanting weak or broken plants and pulling out weeds that threatened to overtake the fledgling rice.

A floppy weathered sun hat made of woven grass poked its dried loose strands and prickled the nape of Vida's neck. She set the pails down, careful not to let the water from the rice field flood over the tops of the containers into the drinking water. Then she took off her hat and held it between her sturdy knees. The loose hem of her dress hung behind her as she bent over and dipped her hands in the water. How cool it felt! She cupped up hurried handfuls and splashed them around her tired arms, hot face and ears, dousing her sore neck and hair. When she finished, a tiny waterfall of water trickled down the single dark braid that hung down her back. Drop by drop, the water rained from her hair into the shallow lake to join a shimmering dance of green blades of rice.

When she finally looked up, she saw her mother, Andrea, still a miniature figure a half hectare away, stand up and stare directly at her. Vida winced. "¡Ay!" she exclaimed, recognizing her mother's reproachful look, "I'm late again."

Picking up the water pails, she double-stepped into the field. Gradually, she, too, was drawn in by the wide stage of the paddy, until she became a tiny doll approaching the converging line of thirsty relatives. Cupping their hands into ladles, they flocked around one another like so many birds at a birdbath, as they took turns dipping into the pails. Minutes later, only inches of dirty water remained.

The work for the day finished before dark. The rice lake became tinged with sunset, spreading wider and wider with vibrant hues of yellow and orange, until it looked like a giant golden gong about to signal the dark curtain of the coming night.

The Guzmans, after a filling meal of boiled rice and dried shark and bean sprout soup, prepared their *petate*, sleeping mats. By dark their palm thatched windows must be closed to keep out the night spirits.

Andrea reached for the pale blue glass rosary which hung from a nail, in line with a *machete* Sergio had forged to cut tangles of tall *cogon* grass. The sharp blade reflected a candlelit shrine of the Sacred Heart of Jesus, which was arranged on a shelf next to the rosary.

Soon the drone of *aves* filled the one-room *nipa* shack, blending with a chorus of twilight song. Birds chirped in the coconut palms and rustled in the tall *kalachuchi* trees, whose trunks resembled melting candles.

Vida's prayers were recited by rote. The drone of words hypnotized her and added to her reflective mood. Her senses torched by a bleeding sunset, she fantasized she was on a flight above the coco palms and the

giant stands of bamboo to where her father's out-riggered *banca* lay in tall
rushes, waiting for the next fishing trip to the ocean.

The sky flamed orange, then carnival pink, and finally washed to a
deep indigo shade of purple. All the while, she imagined herself in her
father's *banca* heading for the glossy expanse of Manila Bay.

And so Vida remembered how her daydreams became part of her
evening prayers. As she grew older, she vowed she would not be like her
mother, whose breasts hung like dried figs under her *bata*, shriveled from
too many nursing babies. Nor would she wring her hands over several
small white crosses in the church cemetery, chanting anguished prayers.

Still at the window, she saw a star shoot down into the horizon, its
trail fading instantly. How long ago it seemed since she had left home—
ten years! She realized her dream when she left Batangas at seventeen. I
thought I was so smart, she recalled, when I waited until the night of the
harvest celebration to tell my parents. I felt the news would go over more
easily after the festivities. What did I know?

She remembered that night vividly. The main event after the religious
procession through the *barrio* was the traditional harvest dance, done to
the tune of ukuleles, guitars and several exotic *bandurrias*, stringed
instruments that sounded like dreamy mandolins.

Choruses of happy voices rang with song to accompany the dance of
the young women—*dalagas*—dressed in *terno* style. Their low-necked,
stand-up, butterfly sleeve blouses were made of sheer pineapple fiber,
which gave them an air of delicate elegance. Scarflike embroidered
pañuelos, often worn over the blouses, added to the effect. Long silky
skirts with colorful trains, hitched up for dancing, completed the
costumes.

Memory of the rice dance was clear and nostalgic. Two long hollow
bamboo poles were held at each end by young men in *barong Tagalog*
dress—cool white trousers and *piña* fiber long-sleeved, embroidered
overshirts, so airy their *camisetas* showed underneath. As the pole holders
moved the poles sideways, apart, and together again at a faster and faster
tempo, the *dalagas*, who sometimes danced alone and sometimes in a line,
would step in and out of the poles, jumping away when the bamboo
collided. Hollow detonations from the poles sounded more and more
intense as the beat of the dance accelerated. The women wove in and out
to escape getting their feet caught. Giddy with excitement, the spectators
cheered wildly and sang louder.

Because the dance symbolized the actual process of the rice harvest,
the motions had real significance. When the dervish subsided, and one or
two *dalagas* were left, jumping in between the poles, the spectators
cheered feverishly, anxious for the finale. *Dalagas* who survived the dance
were received like heroines of the festivities.

That night, a decade ago, Vida defied the bamboo poles. To the end, her
smooth brown feet and strong calves eluded the hollow clashing of the

bamboo. Expertly, she danced in and out of the moving maze, sometimes jumping in backwards as if she were skipping rope. The crowds hushed. They were captivated by Vida's form. She was taller and more graceful than the other *dalagas*. Goddess-like, she held her head high and did not smile until the dance ended; and, amidst their wild cheering, the people of her *barrio* threw flowers at her. Her mother and father's eyes shone with pride as their daughter fell in next to them, and they were led to the banquet. She was sure the time to tell them she was leaving had come.

Tuba flowed. Its unique flavor and elixir came from the fermented flower stalk sap of the coconut palm and roused the celebrants further. Over a huge earthen pit, a suckling pig—*lechón*—dripped aromatic juices as it turned on a spit. Varieties of farm-grown vegetables and sweet fruit weighted low bamboo tables surrounding the *lechón*. There were steaming dishes of *pancit* noodles and golden fried *lumpia* alongside tomatoes, papayas, mangos, *lanzones* and other fruits and vegetables. Desserts were set on a separate table.

"*Masaráp*"—delicious—was heard again and again, as men women and children ate with their hands, sucking their greasy fingers as they finished pieces of savory *lechón*. They would not eat like this until the next good harvest. When the eating, drinking, talking and laughter ended, Vida went past the dying wood embers of the *lechón* fire. The air still smelled of rich roasted pork, sweet *bibingka* dessert and fermented fumes of *tuba*. She took a deep breath and blurted out the news of her departure. "I am so sorry to tell you this. I must leave to find my future in Manila, I will be leaving when the sun comes up."

Sergio and Andrea received the news in silence. Minutes later, as they climbed the open ladder to their *nipa* hut, her father looked down from the top step at his daughter and said, "We, your *Iná* and I, always knew you would want to leave some day." He paused then added, "You know how to work. Go. Find your way. We will be here."

In tears, Vida could not speak. She looked at her mother. "*Iná*," she began, reaching for her hand, but her mother looked away.

At sunup the next day, Vida found a knotted white handkerchief she recognized as Andrea's. Rolled up in it were a twenty peso bill and a few coins. Her parents had gone to the *barrio* market and were not in the hut.

By mid-morning, Vida was riding atop sacks of rice, in a cart pulled by a large *carabao*. Her uncle Paulo was taking the cart to a Manila market. She smiled to herself, remembering her romantic notion of going to the big city via the enchanted waters of Manila Bay in her father's *banca*.

Roused now from her memories, Vida leaned away from the window. Her arm had gone to sleep. Here she was, ten years later, in the middle of a war, working for the Keller family. She had gone to work as an *amah* for the three children after spending a couple of years working for a *meztizo*—Spanish-Filipino—family. She had done well. Now earning 30 pesos a month as the Kellers' cook, she managed the domestic help and the market budget. Although she felt she had become part of the family, she still yearned to be truly independent. Perhaps after the war...perhaps after the war she could have her own *sari-sari* store and sell convenience items in a small neighborhood. Then she could send more money home. It was a dream, but like her dream to escape the captive life of tenant farming, she vowed to pursue it. At the same time, she felt as her cultural belief dictated: *"Bahala na"*—"What will be, will be."

Chapter Eight

High Water

"We're getting to be a regular farm," Mila said to Carl as he mounted his bike to go to the office. "Vegetables, banana orchard, ducks, turkeys, chickens..." she trailed off. "Mmm," he responded, adjusting papers in his pack and finishing a cup of coffee, a bitter mix of chickory and other grains blended with a small amount of pure coffee. He handed her his cup.

Mila went on. "And let's not forget Sheba, Maxie, and the four pigeons, for which Dan and Tim bartered in exchange for *talinum*, okra, tomatoes and five bunches of bananas."

Carl gave her a kiss. "I'll be home early," he said. "Not much going on today. Insurance is taking a beating these days."

After eating a breakfast of bananas and cracked wheat cereal drenched in coconut milk and brown sugar to hide its rancid flavor, Elena and Tim joined their parents. Tim wiped his mouth with the back of his hand; Elena said, "Bye."

"Tell Dan to cut the *penca* of bananas on the tree nearest the house. It's ready," Carl said. "Oh, there he is now." Carl met Dan at the gate, gave him the message and rode off.

Carrying a sack of corn, Dan walked up to the family. Wearing a pair of khaki cutoffs, he appeared taller, lankier these days. His voice had changed. He took his job of trading in the open air market seriously. In charge of the chickens and pigeons, he made sure they got their rations of corn each day. Tim was his assistant. Mila offered Dan breakfast. "Later, Mom, I'm too tired to eat." He dug into his pocket. "I have something important..."

No one moved as he pulled out a folded note. "I met Ramón outside the gate. He was taking out the garbage in one of those huge cans he carries on his back. I didn't expect him to stop. He hailed me and gave me this."

Mila took the extended note. "It's from Carmen Cruz," she said. Lips pursed, she read Carmen's message with its plea for more money for the *guerrilla* cause.

"How are we going to help her?" questioned Elena. Dan stepped in. "Through Ramón, the *basurero*. His code name is Marco."

"Wow!" cried Tim.

Mila held up her hand. "Not a word of this! We're in this together, just like we are with letters to Jerry."

"Everything fits," Dan said. "About a month ago, Ramón told me he had contact with others who sabotage Jap activities. They operate from hiding places all over Luzon. It all ties together."

Mila frowned. "It may all fit, but suppose he's a spy for the enemy? Carmen wants money. She's working with *guerrillas* who are operating an underground radio station. I have the frequency number here. She wants us to listen."

"O.K.," Dan said, clapping his hands with a snap. "Tonight we'll listen. If Carl can tune us in, it means the message is real."

"What if it isn't real?" piped Tim.

"We have to take that risk. Carl will help us decide." When Carl returned, he agreed to try to find the station. Cloistered in the closet, he played with the dial until he located the frequency. Faint and interrupted by static, the station came through. It's message was clear: "This is the voice of the free people of Luzon. Today, a Jap truck convoy from Manila was attacked by a raid carried out by our brave *guerrilleros...*" The broadcast faded and was cut off by loud beeping.

"Interference," growled Carl and switched it off. He met the family outside the airless closet. "Let's get some air," he said, leading them to the giant *bonga* in the garden. There they decided to work through Ramón to continue to help Carmen Cruz.

A slow dusk fell and the cicadas started to sing. The air was sweet with *sampaguita*. No one said anything for a few moments. Carl broke the silence. "It's a risk, but let's trust this one. When Ramón—er, Marco—comes, give him fifty pesos. No notes. If he's caught, there's no trace."

"But I want to write a special message to Carmen, so she'll know the money is from us," Mila broke in. "I don't think they will be able to trace back what I plan to say. Only she will understand."

Carl looked puzzled. "What do you want to write?"

"Just this: 'Good luck, Love, Sister Segundina.'"

He raised his eyebrows in question, "Sister Segundina?"

"I know!" Elena cried. "Sister Segundina is from the convent. She was the good nun, right, Mom?"

"Right," Mila grinned. "She was an angel—our favorite nun when we were in eighth grade. Carmen will know in an instant. Segundina spared us from a lot of punishment."

"It's probably safe," Carl said, showing some amusement.

Before dawn the following day, Dan put fifty pesos and Mila's note into Ramón's calloused brown hand. In the gray light Dan could see harsh lines on his face had softened. He was pleased. "*Salamat po,*" he said in Tagalog, thanking Dan. "It will be delivered tonight."

Dan wanted to ask Marco where he was going, but he knew better.

"*Salamat po*," was all he said. He watched as Marco pushed the money and note into a secret pocket hidden under his belt, picked up the large dented garbage can, and, without a sound, turned to go. "I'll be back with more," he stated as he headed for the fence and jumped it, avoiding its spiked iron bars.

In the half-light of dawn, Dan saw the deep scars on his legs; his tough dirty feet had hit the gravel as if it were soft sand. He's like a big jungle cat, Dan thought. I am glad he's on our side.

At breakfast, he told the family about his contact with Marco. "He's authentic. I'm sure of it. I saw the scars on his legs. He told me earlier they are from Jap torture. He was tortured in the prison camp at O'Donnell; but he managed to escape. He was in the Philippine Scouts. I believe his story," Dan assured them. "I believe it more than ever now."

"I hope so," Mila commented, passing tepid *carabao* milk to her son. "There's a lot at stake."

"I'll say," Elena added. "You know, that's where Jerry was at first— O'Donnell."

"That's all you think about," Tim joined in. "Jerry, Jerry, Jerry!"

"Enough!" Carl boomed from his end of the table, where he had eaten in silence until that moment. "We're under enough strain without picking on each other. Tim..."

The *basurero* continued to collect the garbage as if nothing were different. A few days after Dan gave him the money for Carmen Cruz, Marco brought a note for Mila, thanking them for the money. She signed it "*C.C. Segundina.*"

Mila was convinced that Marco was a *guerrillero*. Before he jumped the fence that morning, he also told Dan that he was spying against the Japanese to get information for the free radio broadcasts. "I can tell you this," he said, "because you and your family are part of us: Secrecy or death. Do you understand?"

Marco's eyes turned a deep hazy green-brown. The image of the large cat crossed Dan's mind again. "Uh, sure, Marco," he managed to say. "On my honor."

Several weeks went by and no more word came from Carmen. At the same time, Elena waited for news from Jerry. None came. Sarita's fear that the Japanese were moving him from camp to camp, making it impossible to keep track of him, appeared to be well-founded.

By November, 1943, it was obvious that, for the time being, they would have no more news from Jerry. A warm rain fell incessantly. It rained every day—heavy gray drops that soaked the ground but did not cool. As she stared out the barred, cloud-darkened window of her room one afternoon, Elena felt like a prisoner. Her dreams had lost substance. For the last six months she had based her life on Jerry's letters. They had enriched her dreams, given her hope in the future, provided excitement. Writing in her diary, reading Shakespeare—a favorite of Mrs. Grossman's—playing the piano, doing chores—nothing could compare to the contact she had made with Jerry.

Something inside me is drying up, Elena told herself. She stared into the mirror of her armoire. How much I've changed since this all started the day of Ben and Magdalena's wedding. I look older than seventeen-and-a-half. I'm getting fat. Too much rice and mongo. Look at my hips, and these, these *tetas*...ugly!

She looked into the reflection of her face. A pair of sober gray eyes stared back at her. Hollow! she thought. You have concentration camp eyes. And your face—pale, always pale. She turned in front of the mirror —this way and that. "Still," she said aloud, "not a bad figure." Her body, in fact, was now the body of a woman. It pulsed with the energy of young blood, no matter how low her spirits sank. And she felt the sexual surgings regularly. They were a problem she had to confess to Father Kiley every few weeks. "Bad thoughts, Father," she would say.

"So what good is your figure when you are dead inside?" she asked her reflection, turning away from it in disgust.

Fear of the Japanese soldiers made Elena hide her looks as much as she could. When she went to her music lessons, to visit her grandmother, or to church, she cinched her brassiere to the tightest hook. She wore her only skirt—a floral green dirndl she and Mila had sewn from the living room curtains. The skirt hid her shape under its gathers. Its large white flowers were distracting. With the same fabric, they had covered a torn umbrella and fashioned a sun parasol to match the skirt. Elena's dark blonde head was hidden under it. She wore *bakias*—wooden-soled, wedged sandals that clomped on the hard sidewalk. To avoid attraction to herself she walked on the black-topped street. Her stride was purposeful. Don't act afraid, she told herself.

Lise Muller had given Elena some red nail polish—an unusual gift, for cosmetics had all but disappeared from stores. Occasionally, she wore the polish at home, but never for long.

Before the war she would have given anything to be allowed to wear lipstick. Now she didn't dare. Ironically, Mila had given her a lipstick on her seventeenth birthday The case was metallic gold; it clicked open with a special catch. In the past, Elena would have been proud to show it off. Now, she only brought it out in the privacy of her room and put it on, usually at *siesta* time when she spent an hour or two by herself, resting or doing what she wanted.

The *siesta* was a two-hour stretch, beginning at noon, when the tropical world fought the enervating heat by retreating from it.

Elena seldom napped. She would do whatever struck her fancy—put on lipstick, write in her diary, or just lie on the tight sheet over her mattress, and, half-naked, daydream to her heart's content.

Able to look at herself without restraint, her daydreams easily turned to sex. As she fanned herself with the *pay-pay*, she dwelled on the shapely contour of her legs, the soft rise of her breasts, pink-tipped; her flat stomach, which rose rhythmically as she breathed.

One *siesta*, as she fanned herself, she spread her arms and legs to cool the prickly heat rash brought on by the sweltering temperature. It was ninety degrees and the humidity was very high. Her wet back stuck to the sheet. The rash, which flourished under her breasts and inside her thighs, itched. As she scratched herself to relieve the prickling itch, the heel of her hand rested on her pubic bone. She pressed down and felt a surge of intense pleasure that radiated over the entire lower part of her body. Making a circle with the heel of her hand, she felt the shock again; this time the sensation traveled up to her breasts. She touched her nipples and felt them hardening. Fascinated and captive to the feeling, she repeated the movements over and over.

She flipped over on her stomach, half-determined to control the tide of pleasure mounting in her, but she could not keep her hand away from the burning area between her legs. A growing pulse under her hand compelled her to pull her underpants off completely and to thrust her finger deep into the channel inside herself, and over the sensitive spot at its opening.

She rode on the crest of a wave so powerful, so natural, she was lost as a part of its design. Electrified, churning in a lightning glare of speed, she rode to the highest peak. There, like a sea creature released from the deep, she was flung onto the white shore, her entire body contracting, her breath in short gasps, her eyes closed.

Curled like a small circular shell, she lay inert, folded in on herself. Her breathing deepened slowly. Lost in a drift of sleep, a nuance of a fleeting dream...

Then suddenly she was wide awake, the shock of what she had done facing her. "¡Ay, Dios!" she cried, swinging her bare legs over the bed and standing straight up, all in one motion. "What have I done to myself?" Cupping her hand against her mouth and closing her eyes in horror, she didn't move. Her thoughts were racing. What would she tell Father Kiley? She had touched herself before, but never like this. Had she injured herself? Did it show in her eyes? Insane! That was it. She was surely losing her mind!

She went into the bathroom and took a long shower, using lots of soap and cool water to wash herself. Then after drying herself thoroughly and putting on clean shorts and a loose shirt, she went to the duck pen. Taking out her diary from its hiding place near the duck's nest, she tried to write. Nothing came. All she could think about was her sin. How would she tell Father Kiley? By necessity he was her confident, for she certainly couldn't talk to her mother! Lise? No. Trish, perhaps, but that was impossible. Father Kiley was the only one to whom she could turn. Didn't he say all was forgiven at confession? He must have dealt with such sinners before, she told herself, taking some consolation in the thought.

At the dinner table that evening, Elena was quiet, almost sullen. Her mouth turned down at the corners and her eyes downcast, she barely touched her food. It was *carabao* stew again, and the smell of the boiled meat sickened her.

"Elena?" Mila reached over and touched her daughter's arm. "Are you sick?"

Elena looked up but did not answer. Instead, she played with her fork.

Carl shifted in his chair. "Elena, your mother asked you a question."

"No, I'm not sick," she finally said.

"Must be Jerry again," volunteered Tim.

"Shut your mouth, Tim!" Elena cried, flinging her fork on the plate and leaving the table.

"Elena!" Carl shouted. "Excuse yourself!" He half-rose from his chair.

Fierce tears in her eyes, Elena turned and said, "Excuse me!" She fled to her room.

Mila stood up, "I hope she's all right. She has been moody lately, but not like this."

Carl softened. "It's her age. But it's no excuse to behave that way," he said. Then looking at Tim, who had had his head buried in his plate, he said, "Your remark didn't help, Tim. I want you to stop talking out of turn like that. You understand?"

"I'm sorry," Tim said. "It's just that I get so sick of her and her silly ways."

"You're just as silly sometimes. Now finish your food," Mila said.

The remainder of the meal was spent in silence. Mila's thoughts were about Elena. Perhaps it was her monthly. But it couldn't be that because Elena always asked for fresh rags just before she was due. Each month both women would replace old rags that had rotted to shreds from repeated scrubbings. No, it wasn't her monthly. Could it be the strain of the occupation was affecting her more as the months went on? Yes, probably that, as well as her age.

The confession was torture. Elena pulled aside the purple velvet curtain and knelt gingerly on the wooden kneeling board. Crossing herself, she leaned forward, her face inches away from a tight screen made of reed caning that separated her from the priest. When he pulled open the door to his side of the screen, it creaked. Elena could feel his breath against her face. Suddenly she felt as if she was entombed in the small dark and musty confines of the confessional. Her heart jumped in her chest. I've got to get out of here, she thought. But the father had her captive. "Are you there, child?" he breathed into the screen. She could see the outline of his head and heavily frocked torso.

Feeling faint, Elena, steadied her head against the screen. "Bless me, Father, for I have sinned..." she whispered hoarsely.

She blurted it out. All of it—the touching, the pleasure, the orgasm, which she simply described as "I went into terrible spasm and felt faint," because she didn't know what she had experienced. The important thing, she was sure, was to tell the priest that she had sinned greatly.

Once she had relieved herself of her guilt, Elena fell back against the side of the confessional. The priest gave her one more "Our Father," and one more "Hail Mary." That was all? Her usual penance was three of each. Had he heard?

She could hear his voice, the haunting song of Latin, exonerating her. She was free! She was forgiven—at least for now. Elena charged out of the confessional. She genuflected hurriedly in front of the altar—down, up; down, up.

A cool breeze hit her perspiring face as she ran down the aisle; the statues on either side became a moving blur. Just before she reached the main steps, she stopped dead. She suddenly realized, Why, that wasn't Father Kiley! Some other priest had given her confession! Never mind. That was good enough. She vowed she would never have to explain that sin again.

In mid-November, 1943, there was a flood in Manila. It began with one of the worst typhoons the city had ever experienced. Against the relentless breath of black clouds, the wind cut a flashing rapier through the trees, turning everything silver. Wind and rain brewed a tempest that blew at a velocity of 100 miles an hour. *Nipa* shacks were lifted off their stilts and tossed like toys into the gale. Roofs flew like box lids all over the city. They crashed in the thunderous wind, crumpling whatever they struck.

The Kellers' house was sturdy, built of strong wood foundation posts that rose seven feet from cement blocks to support the main floor. A galvanized tin roof topped the structure. It proved to be an effective shield against the driving wind and rain, and it withstood the storm's full punishment.

It rained enough to float the city; after the wind subsided, it continued to rain. Gutters that had not been properly cleaned or repaired since the occupation began, filled to overflowing and backed up. Sewers also overflowed. The Pasig River, its brown mud boiling, swelled over its banks. The city flooded: first, one foot; then three; four, and finally, five feet. The water line barely stayed under the top step of the Kellers' house.

The streets of Manila became rivers. They carried everything that would float—people, who seemed to swim aimlessly, makeshift *bancas* that were so full they were close to sinking; uprooted trees, and amputated roofs. Dead dogs, cats, horses, all in various stages of decay, created a stench that threatened to overcome the entire metropolis.

The Kellers turned their house into a Noah's Ark. All the animals were moved indoors. Temporary coops were made of strung chicken wire on the barred and screened window ledges. Three feet in depth, the ledges were deep enough to hold a half dozen ducks and chickens apiece. The turkeys were housed in the bathroom. They did not stop gobbling until a perch was made for them that ran from the shower to the wash basin. The mess they made was hosed twice daily.

On the third day of the flood, Elena came out of the bathroom laughing. "Come in and see this dumb turkey. She's laying her egg from the perch onto the tile floor!"

Dan and Tim put down the pan of corn they were feeding the chickens and rushed in to see. It was just as Elena described. The turkey, whom they had named Lilliput, was laying her egg from the perch, four feet above the tile floor. As they watched, the egg splattered on the tile.

"My gosh," said Tim, "what a waste!" Running into his room, he returned with an old straw hat. "Here, put this under her. When she lays her egg tomorrow, we'll catch it!"

All three of them laughed. The next day they held the hat under the turkey and caught the egg. A day later, they rescued another egg. "Let's let her hatch these," Dan said. "We'll remember how the chicks were laid!"

The turkeys and chickens all survived, but several ducks drowned or swam away. After floating in the flooded garden, they chilled and weakened. With their usual resting ground under water, they had no place to rest. After hours in the water, their feet turned pale and limp. Two of them collapsed in the water and drowned before they could be rescued by Elena, Dan and Tim, who spent hours taking turns swimming in the murky water after them. They kept their shoes on and walked in places where the flood waters were less deep. They kept their heads above the polluted water.

At one point Elena saw her favorite duck Wobbles. She had been in the water for hours. Her red crest had turned a pale pink and her movement through the water was very slow. "Help me, Dan, I'm going after Wobbles. You head her off up ahead."

When Elena caught up with Wobbles, the duck didn't make a sound. Holding her up, well above the water, Elena tried to swim with one arm. The flood waters were above her head. "Dan," she called out, "hurry. I can't hold her and swim at the same time."

Dan laughed as he reached his sister. "You'll manage to drown Wobbles for sure that way!" He grabbed the duck, held her up to the level of his chin and pushed through the water.

Elena swam after them, still not tall enough to stand until they got close to the house. Drenched, they carried the dripping duck inside, dried her off and offered her some food. Wobbles refused to eat, but in a few minutes, the red returned to her crest, and Elena knew she was regaining her energy and would be all right.

In a few days the flood waters receded. Many were left homeless. Others became ill from water polluted by raw sewage. There were cases of typhoid fever and dysentery. The emergency reminded the city once again of what could happen when disaster struck.

The Kellers managed to get through the flood with enough food. They had provisions in a small storeroom off the kitchen to last several weeks—rice, mongo beans, cassava flour, brown sugar and ripening bananas, along with other necessities, including enough coconut oil to light three lamps when the electricity was cut off. "The only thing we need to get busy on," Carl said after the water had receded and things were getting back to normal, "is a well. If we lost our water, we couldn't survive for very long."

Being close to the ocean, they dug six feet and found water. Close to the vegetable garden, they decided they would use the well water and mix it with water from the hose to water the vegetables. The water was still too salty, and they found they could not use it on the vegetables. The next step was to get a filter. The filter, designed for drinking water, was a simple vat with an inner funnel made of a hardened, porous, claylike material that removed the salt as the water filtered through it. It held several gallons. They fashioned a bamboo pump with which to pump the water from the well, and found it did not take long to fill the filter. Though the water still tasted salty, it was safe to drink after it was boiled.

Knowing they might not be able to rely on a stove if gas were cut off, Carl bought a large native cooker made of red clay called a *kalan* that burned either wood or coal.

In a few weeks, Lilliput hatched the two eggs saved during the flood. The baby turkeys were called Rosie and Winnie, after Roosevelt and Winston Churchill. Although they peeped a lot and were thin and leggy, they thrived. In fact, the Kellers had a virtual farmyard. At dawn, a green and russet cock virgorously crowed the hours until sunup. His name was MacArthur, mostly because he crowed in a clear, three-syllable pattern, with an accent on the middle syllable: Mac-ARTH-ur!

Choosing these names was also a way of reaffirming loyalty to the Allied cause. Hope for a liberation seemed closer. By Christmas, news from the shortwave radio announced that the landings made by the Americans in November were taking their toll of the Japanese. The news on all fronts was good. MacArthur's offensive in New Guinea had widened; in Europe, Naples and Genoa had fallen to the Allies. There were rumors of a bigger invasion...

Before the war, Baguio Christmas trees were shipped to Manila from the Mountain Province. As with so many other traditions, the occupation forced changes, and the Christmas tree became a symbol of better days. The Kellers brought out their decorations, went to the large bamboo clump, cut several graceful stalks, planted them in a pot and fashioned a Christmas tree. They used only the lightest ornaments. It was the most ethereal tree they had ever had!

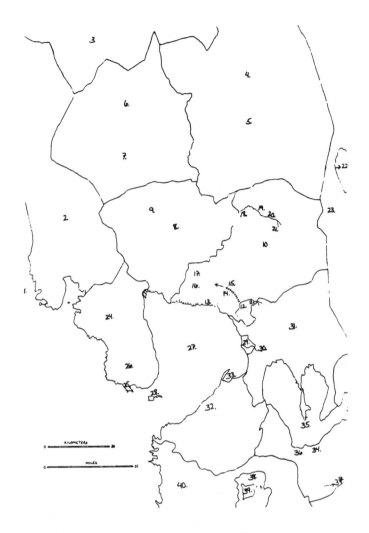

ELENA'S MAP SHOWING SARITA'S ESCAPE
ON AN HISTORIC ROUTE

1. South China Sea
2. Zambales Province
3. Pangasinan
4. Nueva Ecija
5. Cabanatuan POW
   Camp
6. Tarlac Province
7. O'Donnell POW
   Camp
8. Pampanga Province
9. Clark Air Force Base
10. Bulacan Province
11. Marilao River
12. Marilao

13. Swamps
14. Balagtas
15. Railroad
16. Malolos
17. Plaridel
18. San Miguel
19. San Miguel River
20. Biak-na-bato
21. Mt. Lumot
22. Pacific Ocean
23. Tayabas Province
24. Bataan Peninsula
25. Mariveles
26. Mt. Mariveles

27. Manila Bay
28. Corregidor
29. Manila
30. Pasig River
31. Rizal Province
32. Cavite Province
33. Cavite Naval Base
34. Laguna Province
35. Laguna De Bay
36. Los Banos POW Camp
37. Mt. Banahaw
38. Lake Taal
39. Taal Volcano
40. Batangas Province

Chapter Nine

Fort Santiago

"They're beginning to round up members of the underground," Sarita told Elena during a music lesson.

"That's because the news from all fronts is bad for them," Elena commented. She had been practicing on Chopin's Waltz in C-Sharp Minor, polishing it up to play it after Easter at a recital at the academy. Her fingers aching, she welcomed Sarita's interruption. She leaned forward on the bench. "Sarita, you're dangerously involved in the POW letters."

"Too involved." Fear sharpened Sarita's voice. "I'm getting very nervous about it. Just a few days ago one of our leaders was caught distributing POW letters. That can involve everyone down the line. Fort Santiago can make you talk!"

Elena gripped the edge of the bench. "Oh, God, I hope whoever it is doesn't talk. Santiago is worse than hell! Most anyone can be made to talk."

"Worse than hell..." Sarita's voice trailed. Elena could see she was thinking about agonizing stories they had both heard. The Kempetai practiced hideous torture on their prisoners. Housed in the bowels of the sixteenth century Spanish prison within the fortress of Intramuros, they beat and starved their prisoners mercilessly.

Few came out of its dank, thick walls alive. Those that did bore unspeakable scars. Since the days of Spanish rule, the prison had been a symbol of torture. Originally, it held Filipino political prisoners. Then as now, the nightmare of torture and starvation was made insufferable by the presence of poisonous insects, monstrous rats and disease-bearing bacteria. Under the Japanese military police, Fort Santiago's image of horror inflated; its mere reference made people cringe.

Elena felt her stomach turn. She thought of a recent story Vida had told the family about a cousin who had been a Philippine Scout and was caught with some *guerrillas*. Thrown in Fort Santiago, he was grilled mercilessly for seven days. Starved, he was hung by his thumbs in a dark narrow cell. Vida was sure he had been killed.

The thought of Sarita in Fort Santiago was too much for Elena to face. "W-what are you going to do," she asked.

Sarita sighed. Her large breasts rose under a sheer pink blouse. "I'm just going to act normal—carry on with my music, play in the recital. What can I do?"

Elena reached for her hand and squeezed it. Sarita went on talking. "You know, my mother isn't well. I can't burden her with this."

"I'm involved, too," Elena said. "If they discover you, I'm in trouble." She tried to sound matter-of-fact.

Sarita's laugh was sardonic. "I'll only talk if they pull out my fingernails," she huffed.

"Don't say that!" Elena's eyes opened wide.

"Anyway, *cariño*," Sarita's voice calmed, "there hasn't been recent correspondence with Jerry. We still don't know where he is."

Biting her lip, Elena lowered her voice. Sarita could hear a sadness in it. "Yes, I know."

Sarita shrugged. "We can't afford to despair now, Elena. Both of us— all of us involved—have to keep our spirits up."

Elena managed a smile. "Yes. I better get back to Chopin or I'll ruin the recital."

When Elena got home after her lesson, Mila waited with more bad news. The Kempetai were making raids everywhere. "Carmen's radio station has gone dead," she announced. Elena could see her eyes were red from crying. "Marco told Dan she's been caught and brought down from Bulacan to Fort Santiago."

"Oh, Mom!" Elena cried. Putting her arms around Mila, she said, "She is such a friend. I'm so sorry."

"Since the convent—my friend..." Mila wept.

Elena could find nothing to say. She held her mother, all the while fighting images of Fort Santiago. Finally, she asked, "What can we do?"

Mila's tears subsided. "Nothing. Lie low. That's the word that's out now," she said. "Hide Jerry's letters well, and your diary, too. Put them in a place, Elena, where you can get rid of them quickly."

"I already have. The letters are hidden in a toilet roll in the bathroom. If the Japs search, I'll flush them down. My diary is buried under a rock in the duck pen."

The next morning, Marco didn't show up to collect the garbage. "He told me he might head for the foothills if things got too hot," Dan explained. "He left this note stuck under the lid of the garbage can. It's for you, Mom. From Carmen."

"From Carmen!" Mila cried. They gathered around her. The note was written in faint pencil. "Mi amiga, *Segundina, my eternal thanks. They may have my body, but you, who love me, have my spirit. Carmen Cruz.*"

Mila bit her lips, but did not cry. Carl put his arm around her and Elena held her hand. Dan and Tim stood close by. Dan tried to console her. "I have faith in Marco, Mom. He'll be in touch, I know. He told everyone in the *guerrillas* knows exactly what is happening when one of them gets caught. Somehow they manage to keep in touch."

Mila looked at her son. "Thanks, Danny. I don't have much hope..."
No one said anything more.

Numbed by grief and worry, Mila barely spoke to anyone. She took
solace in her plants. Watering the orchids, the lush Easter lilies and the
scarlet bougainvilla, and digging around the roots of these plants so
moisture would penetrate, made her feel in touch with the survival forces
of nature. Somehow, her contact with growing things energized her belief
in life, and strengthened her prayers for Carmen.

Elena turned to her diary. The entry on Easter Sunday, 1944, read:
*"Got up at seven. Went to communion at La Salle Chapel with Belana. Aunt
Constancia and Ian met us there. Ian is getting so tall, but he looks thin and
is quiet. Couldn't find words to pray for Carmen, but was consoled by the
service. The altar was all in white lace, and the organ music was soothing.
When we got home from church, I made cassava waffles with rich brown
sugar syrup. Ian especially gorged himself! Aunt Constancia tried to talk to
Mom, but nothing seems to be able to pull her out of her worry about
Carmen. I was especially glad because Aunt Josefina and Uncle Carlos
dropped by later after visiting with Uncle Ben, Aunt Magdalena and little
Paz. We don't get a chance to see them much anymore, as going across town
gets more and more dangerous.*

*"Tonight I feel depressed. I'm obsessed by what Carmen must be suffering
in Fort Santiago. Her bravery unites with the symbol of Bataan, which fell
April 9, two years ago. Yesterday was the anniversary of that date. It stands
as the spirit of hope in this captured land. Like Bataan, Carmen had
sacrificed herself, but she's not dead. I seem to sense that. We have to hold on
to that hope.*

*"Then Jerry...he haunts me. He's alive, too, I know that! But where is he?
What is he suffering? I hope he doesn't write now, no matter how much I
want to hear from him. As Sarita says, and I'm worried sick about her also,
the Japs are on to the POW underground, and it's vital to lie low. Outside,
the night seems as dark as my terror.*

*"There's no one I can turn to about my personal problems with myself
except the priests. My battle with sin is bigger than ever. Seems I go to Father
Kiley with the same recital of transgressions every few weeks. I feel relief after
my penance, but then the temptation returns and wins me over! Perhaps if
I lose my mind, it will end it!"*

On a more hopeful note, she continued. *"Carl says time is our greatest
ally in this war. The sooner the Americans push upward from New Guinea,
the more chance we'll have of being liberated. They'd better hurry because as
the Japs keep on losing, they will get tougher here—if that's possible, after what
has just happened to Carmen.*

*"Heard that Santo Tomás will be under military control again soon. Had
word from someone who saw Dad recently that he is all right. I'm sure he
doesn't write because he doesn't want to get us in trouble if his activities on
Corregidor are ever dicovered. The word from camp is no more visitors will*

*be allowed out, and no more notes can be written back and forth either. The
Japanese civilian administration of the camp this last year will be taken over
by the Japanese Imperial Army. That means, under the dreaded Kempetai,
communications with those inside will end. God knows what it will mean
for the internees...I haven't heard from Trish in several months."*

Finishing the entry, Elena wrapped the diary in a canvas cover she
had stitched and returned it to its burial spot in the loose dirt under the
rock by the duck's nest.

A few days after Easter, Marco suddenly showed up with another
note from Carmen. Dressed in black, he knocked on the frame of the
kitchen door. In the gray light preceding dawn, Vida saw him from the
window in her room, adjacent to the garage. "Marco!" she hissed at him.
"No one is up yet. What do you want?"

She was out the door, gathering her long sleeping *bata* around herself.
Marco's shadowy form wavered in front of her. His voice was gruff. "No
time to lose! Here!" He pressed a folded piece of paper into her hand.
"From Carmen."

"Stop!" Vida cried, reaching for him. But he was moving so fast, she
barely touched his shirt. "Marco!"

Then suddenly she touched his fingers. A sudden erotic charge fired
through her. His hand in mid-air, Marco felt as if he had been torched,
overcome by an overpowering surge of feeling. They froze. Then he
grabbed Vida's arm and pulled her to him. He slipped his right hand
down her loose *dagmay bata* and pressed her naked back. Holding her so
she could hardly breathe, he pressed his chest tight against her breasts,
bare under her gown, as another thrill pulsed through them.

Moments hung in the cool dawn; the two locked, their brains
numbed by passion. An Atlas moth flew out of the shadowy *mabolo* tree
and hovered over their heads, its pale brown wings marked with dramatic
gray and black. It trembled as if it were caught in the field of their sensual
energy. Seconds, and then it wafted back into the shadows, its wing span
a full nine inches.

"*Hindî*—no!" Vida cried, awakening from her trance. She jerked
herself away from his hard grip. He pulled back as if he had touched a
live wire. Astounded, he stared at her, then turned quickly, the muscles
of his legs flexed as he ran for the fence.

Vida's breath came in panicked gasps. Her hands shook as she
remembered the precious note. It was still clutched in her right hand. She
watched the *guerrillero* as he ran. "*Locos!*" she breathed, sure they had
gone crazy.

As Marco leaped over the fence, his black, agile form appearing more
cat-like than ever, the last thing he said was, "I've got to get out of here!"

Placing her fingers on her temples, Vida whispered, "*Waláng hijâ!*"
Marco? What was this insane feeling for Marco—the *basurero*—someone
she barely knew? She did not realize it then, but Marco had become a

symbol—an embodiment of courage, intrigue, excitement. In her mind he
had turned into an archetype for Philippine freedom, the quest for liberty
that had burned in patriots during three centuries of Spanish rule; over
the domination of the Americans since 1898, and now under the bitter
fight against the Japanese. She, Vida, was a fellow torchbearer with
Marco, for she had drawn from his fire. For a few moments they had
glowed together in a common flame. By evening Marco would be well on
his way to Mt. Banahaw, a *guerrilla* headquarters in Laguna Province, east
of Manila. In two days, riding in farmers' carts and walking, he would
reach the mountain hideout, cross the same paths that survivors of action
against Spain in 1841 had crossed. He would pass the Cave of God the
Father, "*Kuweba ng Dios Ama,*" hunkering over slippery gullies and
enormous boulders. Pitong Lihim would rise above him, a monolithic
rock. Then he would pass the place called "where twisted trees knelt," a
grove of low-lying, leaning trees. One more day and he would reach the
hideout, one of many in the eastern mountains of Luzon.

Unsteady on her feet, Vida stared into the quiet street. The sun was
rising—a clear band of light stark against the hem of night. Move! she
ordered herself and sprinted forward up the stairs. She was met by Dan,
who always slept with an ear out for Marco. He reached for the note, but
Vida said, "No. I must give this to your mother. Marco said..."

Dan rushed after her and together they awoke Mila. She came out of
her room dressed in a thin pink negligee, rubbing sleep from her eyes.
Taking the note to the light of the dining room window, she looked up
with triumph in her eyes. "She has escaped! *Dios!* Carmen has escaped!"

Elena and Tim joined in the excitement. "How?" Elena asked. "How
did she escape?"

Carl appeared, shaking his head in disbelief. "I've got to hear this!"

Her voice shaking, Mila told them, measuring each word as if what
it implied was a gift. "She says she was in a grave-digging work party
yesterday, and managed to hide in a garbage heap. The prisoners were
outside the prison digging their own graves! She was ready to be
executed!" Mila stopped for breath. "Somehow the *guerrilleros* knew, and
were nearby with a garbage cart when Carmen buried herself in the trash
pile. I'm filling in the details, obviously, but it sounds as if the *guerrilleros*
picked her up with the garbage. It's not exactly clear, but we'll know
eventually." Mila paused. "The most important thing," she continued, "is
what she says next: '*Segundina, please meet me at the Pasay market by the
fish stalls this afternoon at four o'clock. I will be dressed as a beggar. Do not
show you recognize me. Hold up your hand as if you are ready to bargain
with the fish woman. I will come up behind you and you will know what to
do. If you cannot come, send someone we trust. We need help.*'"

Mila was so stunned at Carmen's request, she didn't know what to
say. Carl put his arm around her shoulders. "We'll help, Mom," Elena
stepped forward. Dan, Tim and Vida chorused their support.

"Fine," Carl said, taking charge. "Look, this is very dangerous business for us. I'm sure the Kempetai has had their eye on Marco. They know which houses he's serviced in his garbage route. You can bet they know more than we are aware of. It's too dangerous for you to go, dear," he told his wife.

Hearing Carl's purposeful tone, Mila revived. "Oh, no. I'm going!" she cried. "Carmen needs more money. She has to know we aren't letting her down!"

"That's true, she needs our help," Carl reasoned, "but as whites, you know too well we're very obvious, especially if the Kempetai are watching. They are everywhere."

"That's true, Mom," Dan chimed in. "You know, there are a hundred Filipinos to one white person in the market."

"Then I...I will go!" Vida stepped forward. Her jaw was set firmly, her eyes revealed her terror.

They all cried out together, "No!"

Vida had her mind set. Finally, they agreed it was better for her go than it was for anyone else. Mila gave her one hundred pesos, which she rolled up in brown paper. She realized it might be the last time they could help Carmen's *guerrilla* efforts. And Marco's.

Just before Vida left for the market, Mila gave her a tiny white box to put into her *supot*, the bag they took to the market regularly. "Please give this to Carmen," Mila said. She squeezed Vida's hand. "You're very brave!" she exclaimed.

Vida's velvet skin had paled to a light bronze. "I am not brave. I am doing this for Carmen, for us, and for my dead cousin. He...he was brave!"

The market was two miles away. As Vida set out, the mid-afternoon sun glared down. Perspiration gathered in small droplets on her temples and slid down the sides of her face. Her *bakias* raised dust on the sidewalk. *Carretela* wheels rolled by; trucks filled with Japanese soldiers roared dangerously close. A chill went through Vida. "God spare me!" she prayed.

As she approached the market, she imagined soldiers everywhere, waiting for her. The stench reached her, blocks before she arrived. Coming from the stalls, it was worse in the afternoon. Dead carcasses that had not been sold—chickens, fish, beef—decayed in the heat. Swarms of flies covered everything, including mounds of limp vegetables.

The market was filled with poor. They waited for the afternoon throw-aways. There were beggars around every stall. They would stay until sundown when the vendors would heave their discards.

Vida took a deep breath. Spotting a woman who had unusually fresh beans, she walked up to her stall. "*Magkano?*" she asked. When the woman told her the price, Vida nodded her head, pointing to a bunch of beans. "*Sitaw*," she said. The vendor wrapped the beans in newspaper and Vida put them in her *supot*. Suddenly, she felt someone nudging her shoulder. It was a Japanese soldier! He reached toward her bag. Quickly,

Vida took out the package of beans. "*Sitaw?*" she questioned. He grinned, seeing she was frightened, enjoying it. He pointed to the wrapped package. Vida held her breath. Slowly she opened it, revealing the *sitaw* for him to examine. He looked at the beans, lifted them to his nose and grinned again. Then he waved her away and turned to the stall.

Painstakingly, with half an eye on the soldier, Vida made her way to the fish stalls. She spotted a beggar woman sitting close to one of the overhangs. Her hand was out. She passed her without looking at her. "*Patawarin,*" she said, "sorry." That couldn't be Carmen Cruz, Vida told herself. She had streaks of white in her hair and her dark arms were bruised under the makeshift sleeves of a tattered brown drape she had wrapped around herself.

Following what Carmen's note had instructed her to do, Vida started to bargain with the fish vendor. She raised her hand and held it up for a few seconds, all the while bartering for the fish.

The beggar woman rose, hobbled over, and stood behind Vida's shoulder, her body turned away as she whispered, "If you have anything for me, go to the fish stall on the left and drop it in the drain ditch. Come back in ten minutes. There will be something for you. Bless you."

Vida did not turn around. When she was sure Carmen had limped away, she shook her head at the fish vendor and walked to the other stall. She heard the vendor curse her. The drain ditch by the fish stalls was dry. There were still pieces of fish entrails from that morning's cleaning drying in the ditch. Pretending to scuff her *bakia*, Vida bent over to adjust her foot under the leather strap. As she did so, she dropped the tight money roll and the box. Her heart pounded in her head as she leaned over. I am going to faint, she said to herself. I can't! I must act natural! She steadied herself, rearranged the *supot* on her arm and walked slowly to a fruit stand on the other side of the square. Ten minutes! Carmen had told her to wait ten minutes! She looked around as she fingered some *lanzones*, turning the shiny yellow-green fruit in her hand. No soldiers. Good, she thought. The fruit vendor stared at her. Vida reached into the *supot* for her coin purse. "*Isá,*" she said. "One?" cried the vendor. "Yes, for myself," Vida nodded. The woman's expression changed. "Ah!" she said and gave her two for the price of one. "*Salamat,*" Vida smiled, thanking her. The vendor chuckled. "It tastes good this time of day."

The two women fell into a conversation, and the ten minutes passed. Relieved, Vida told her goodbye and returned to the drain ditch. Yes! There was a note from Carmen. Quickly, she picked it up and held it in her hand until she walked out of the market square. A Japanese soldier strolled by. He did not look at her. Her pace quickened. Home, she told herself, I've got to get home.

She arrived home in half the time it would have normally taken her. The Kellers were all waiting for her. Breathless and pale, all Vida could say was, "*¡Ay!*"

Mila embraced her. "It's all right, Vida. You are safe now."

Vida sighed. She gave her Carmen's long note, in which she explained in greater detail what had happened to her. As Mila read aloud, each of them envisioned the dreaded Fort Santiago—its grim, massive, moss-covered walls; its foul-smelling, dark narrow cells; the screams of the tortured. They could imagine Carmen as the Kempetai beat her black and blue, smashed her fingernails and kicked her in the kidneys. Remembering her limp, Vida winced.

The story of her escape held them entranced. *"This is the hardest time I have ever experienced in my life. I still cannot believe I got away from the Japs. I am in hiding tonight and can write in safety. Just this morning, I was scheduled to be executed. A truckload of us were taken to a field outside Santiago, where we were to dig our own graves. Thank God for Marco and the* guerrillas. *The underground had kept in touch. They knew everything!*

"I knew what I was to do. The truck stopped by a large pile of garbage, which our friends had hauled there. There was mass confusion as we got off the truck. The guards pushed and kicked us as we gathered our picks and shovels. Part of the group went ahead, while the rest of us straggled on the other side of the truck. Suddenly, a garbage cart with three of our friends rolled by noisily and stopped.

"The two soldiers who were guarding us ran forward, waving their rifles, shouting. The garbage pile was right behind me. In that instant, when the guards were completely distracted, I rolled into the pile of garbage. It took me a few seconds to push myself into the muck. The guards came back in less than a minute. They yelled out their orders, as the work party pushed on down the road to join the others, who were already digging their graves, about a hundred yards away.

"I made a breathing hole by clawing through the filth. The stench of putrid garbage was so horrible, I vomited. It was only bile, for I hadn't had any food for several days, only a little water. I was buried in slime! I prayed for God to give me the courage not to cry out. He had given me strength I never thought I had. As much as they tortured me, I never gave away our secrets!

"Then the most sickening thing happened. I heard the cries of my fellow prisoners as the guards beat them as they dug their graves. I fainted. I don't know how much later it was, but I heard voices above me, and suddenly I was scooped up and thrown into the garbage cart that was waiting to rescue me. In just seconds, we rolled away. I fainted again. Somewhere outside the city, the cart was dumped. I was so numb, I didn't feel anything in the shuffle. Marco, blessed Marco, pulled me out of the muck!"

Dan interrupted Mila, "See, Mom! Marco—he was the one! I knew it!"

Mila wiped her eyes, nodded, and finished the letter, which described how Carmen disguised herself, streaked her hair white, and got together some rags to drape over herself. *"I didn't have to do much. I already looked like a beggar. Now, it is time, my dearest friends, to say goodbye to you until after we are liberated. Never doubt—we will be liberated. Thank you from the bottom of my heart for the money you're giving us. Every centavo counts. If I should perish in this fight for freedom, my spirit will surround you with the love I feel for you, Segundina, and all of you. Forever yours, Carmen Cruz.*"

They were all in tears. Carl, usually stoical, was red-eyed. "What a miracle!" Mila cried. She reached for Dan and Elena, who were standing by her. They in turn, reached out, until they formed a tight circle.

After several minutes, Mila broke the spell of silence. "I have to share with you...I gave Carmen a silver medal of Jesus, one I have had since the convent. It was given to me by Ang—I mean Carmen—when I was twelve."

"Oh!" Vida cried. "That was what was in the box. She will be so happy."

"She got that box because of you, Vida. Thank you," Carl said.

Not long after Carmen's escape, the recital at the academy of music took place. Wearing their best clothes, faded and patched, but clean and starched, the students, under Dr. Friedman, performed to an audience of family and friends.

Her fingers riding over the keyboard, Elena played the Chopin waltz she had practiced, with an energy fed by nerves. She had not slept well since Carmen's escape, and the fear that Sarita might also be picked up plagued her.

Just before it was Sarita's turn to play, she signaled Elena, who was sitting next to several members of her family. As casually as she could, Elena got up and went backstage. "What is it?" she asked Sarita, who waited for her, and immediately drew her aside.

"I'm to be investigated tonight. After the recital. They came to the house about two hours ago. Said they'd be back at 9 o'clock tonight!" Sarita's eyes bore in at Elena. She was short of breath.

Elena shut her eyes. Shaking her head, she cried, "What can I do?"

"Nothing. I just wanted to tell you. I've done everything I can— burned every trace I ever had with the underground, including all my letters from John."

"Oh, no, Sarita!" Elena exclaimed. She reached for her friend's hand. "You know I'm with you all the way. Tell me, how will you let me know where you are?"

Sarita took a step back and stared at Elena. When she spoke a few seconds later, fear sapped her voice. "You will know," she said, then paused to clarify her thoughts. "You know your Philippine history?"

"Sure," Elena shrugged. "It's what Mary Canda concentrated most on —that and geography."

A sudden glint of light shone in Sarita's eyes. "That's it, then! I'll let you know through symbols—historic symbols. For now, just know that we'll be heading..." She ducked her head and whispered, "north!"

Giving Elena a fierce hug, she slipped backstage.

The hall in the academy was not acoustically built for a grand piano. A few moments later, Sarita's small hard fingers worked through the "Appassionata," by Beethoven. The notes burst through the walls of the room, carried far beyond the provisions of the hall and reached the audience, full of force and feeling. Her face, white as a cameo, her dark hair, swept up higher than usual, Sarita held everyone spellbound. Elena could not take her eyes off her determined friend. Her heart welled up and she began to cry. Sarita's emerald green dress became a blur; the music took over and transported Elena to a world of dreams, where nothing mattered but the music. For a few minutes, she was able to forget the madness of her world. Then as the sonata played to a close, she prayed for Sarita as hard as she had ever prayed before.

For two days, there was no word from or about Sarita. On the third afternoon, Elena received a message from her. It read: *"Don't worry. I am safe. I am with my mother. Do not try to contact me. I will stay in hiding.*

"Remember Baltazar's poetry. He struck a fire in the heart of the Leader who searched for truth in the caves that are dark with mystery, filled with bats and misty springs. He dreamed of a free land, rich with cotton and tender rice fields, for the good of his people."

The message ended with *"God bless us all."* It was not signed, evidence that the *guerrilla* communication network had used extreme caution.

Elena pondered Sarita's message for hours. After thumbing through her Philippine history book, she began to decipher some of the symbols: Francisco Baltazar, born in Bulacan Province, must be the poet mentioned, for his birthplace was Balagtas, northwest of Manila, along the narrow gauge railroad. The next piece of the puzzle fit into place. The "Leader" could be none other than Emilio Aguinaldo, Filipino patriot who was enshrined in Bulacan, one of the key provinces where the quest for Philippine independence flourished. Mary Canda's praise of Aguinaldo remained, verbatim, in Elena's memory: "He was a simple farmer's son, a man small in stature but tall as a giant in leadership."

So far so good, Elena told herself, but what did the caves, the bats, the misty springs signify? She went back to the history book and studied an historic map of Bulacan. There it was—the answer, in Mary Canda's pencil outline of Aguinaldo's brave journeys from Balagtas to Malolos, where he authored the first Philippine Republic. Forced to travel northward during the war with Spain, he hid his headquarters in Biak-na-Bato in the remote area of Bahay Paniqui Caves. The caves were known as the Bat Caves, home to hordes of bats that seemed to fly from the depths of hell each evening at sundown. The "misty springs" referred to the mysterious underground springs in the caves.

"Thank you, Mary Canda," Elena wrote in her diary after breaking Sarita's coded message. *"All the symbols refer to places in Bulacan—the caves, the bats, the springs, even the cotton and rice fields! Believe it or not, 'bulak' means cotton, and that's where most of the cotton on Luzon is grown—in Bulacan."*

Elena finished the entry without mentioning Sarita's name, fearful as always that the Japanese might one day discover her diary.

She flicked off the nightstand lamp and found herself imagining where Sarita might be at that moment. She shuddered as she envisioned her friend hiding in some jungle path, huddling against the elements, weakened by thirst and hunger.

Elena was not far off in her imaginings: Two *guerrillas* had led Sarita and her mother Pia on a midnight escape from Manila. They headed northwest through swampy deltas and dense crisscross paths studded with marshes to reach the Marilao River in Bulacan. Now they were bypassing Malolos en route northward to the mountainous country of the Bat Caves. The four had traveled a circuitous fifty kilometers to avoid discovery.

Sarita, Pia and two *guerrillas*, known as "Aguila" and "Cocodrilo"— one named for the power of an eagle; the other for the stealth of a crocodile—were hunkered in a shadowy rice field. A convoy of Japanese trucks rumbled by on the narrow road to Malolos. One of the vehicles pulled to a noisy stop fifty meters away from the four figures who hid, flat on their stomachs, between the thick rows of rice.

Fear bolted in Sarita's throat as a Japanese soldier walked into the field and stood in place a mere twenty paces away. He must know I am here, she thought. At any moment he will jump me. A deep terror uncoiled from the pit of her stomach. She drew in a breath and held it until she felt she would burst. Then a sudden swoosh of water streamed in an arc from the soldier's black silhouette. Sarita trembled, then exhaled her tortured breath. Acid fumes rose from the steamy vapor and rankled in her nose.

The soldier buttoned himself and ran back to the truck. Within seconds the vehicle lumbered away into the star-filled night.

Hours later the four fugitive travelers tapped on the thatched door of a *nipa* hut, a shelter known as a designated *guerrilla* hideout, one of many in a network of sympathizers.

In the dark, a woman greeted them; she gave them handfuls of cold rice. Later, Sarita and Pia were led to petate mats on the floor while the two *guerrillas* kept a vigil from the corner of the hut nearest the door. They spoke in barely audible voices. Sarita strained to listen, trying to keep awake.

"Another week and we'll be at the caves."

"We will travel jungle paths east of the main road. No damn Japs there just now."

"Others will join us when we get to the San Miguel River. Then on to the caves..." Cocodrilo's voice trailed.

An old man lying on a sleeping mat close to the *guerrillas* sat up, lit a cheroot and blew haloes of smoke around himself.

"What do you say, grandfather?" Aguila said, peering through the dark at the wizened figure.

Up on his bony haunches now, the old man puffed again. Phlegm cracked in his throat when he spoke. "Almost fifty rice harvests ago, I fought two enemies—here, right in this spot. First, España, then America."

The younger men listened as they would to a revered elder. Although they could not make out his face, they both sensed the old man's eyes fixated on them. "War does not change things. We are still not free."

The elderly patriot had served as an insurgent in Aguinaldo's Philippine Revolutionary Army in 1896. He had lost one brother to the Spanish torture chamber at Fort Santiago, another to a bullet fired by a "Yanco" captain during the Philippine-American War in 1898.

Cocodrilo saw the irony. "We are fighting a new enemy with an old enemy," he said.

In a dreamy monotone the insurgent went on. He quoted lines from Aguinaldo's last speech, given June 12, 1899, before he surrendered to the Americans. *"We have never hidden our hopes; we have announced before all nations, calling the Almighty Creator and ruler of the universe to witness that we want nothing more than our independence, and in seeking that we do not waver one moment.*

"We desire nothing more than our independence..."

On those words, Sarita was drawn into a heavy sleep. Five hours later, the four took to a back road in a farm cart and headed northward toward the town of Plaridel. A peach-pale sky outlined their silhouettes on the creaking cart as they disappeared into a narrow brushy trail.

For the next seven days they followed a chain of *guerrilla* hideouts, kilometer by kilometer. At night they would stop, be given food by network sympathizers—cold rice, and now and then, a juicy yellow mango or an *atis*, thick with sweet pulp and pitch black seeds. They always had a place to sleep.

When Japanese troops were in the area, the four often slept during the day and took lengthy detours in the dead quiet of night.

Sometimes they were lucky and made it to a river hideout, as they did when they arrived at the San Miguel River. Sarita and Pia undressed in the bushes, bathed in the cool jade green water and scrubbed their sweaty, torn clothes on the river rocks. Within an hour their clothes would dry under a blistering sun. While they waited, Sarita wrapped the raw spots on her feet with damp banana leaves. Then she did the same to soothe her mother's sore feet.

Both women had lost weight. Sarita's firm bosom and broad thighs looked deflated. Her once proud pompadour had wilted to a humble bun at the nape of her neck. Without make-up, her eyes were tar-black against her snowy face.

Pia's short wiry frame had shrunk to ninety pounds. She looked like a *provinciana* in her faded skirt and blouse. Unlike her daughter, Pia had a deep olive complexion. Her skin was as smooth as a girl's. Not yet forty, she had borne Sarita when she was barely seventeen. She suffered from bouts with malaria.

The two women were close. They shared a camaraderie that was evident as they chatted while bathing and doing their laundry. "When we finally reach our destination," Sarita joked, "I think we will turn right around and walk back to Manila. Surely the war will be over by then!"

With a laugh, Pia added, "We can sneak past all our old friends. Who will recognize two bedraggled witches?"

Standing naked in the river, Sarita quipped, "Not even the Japanese, ha?" Then catching a flash movement in the brush, she exclaimed, "Ay, no!"

Pia drew back, sending a tail of long wet hair whipping on her bare shoulders. "*¿Qué?*" she cried, crouching over and covering her breasts with crossed arms.

"There—look!" pointed Sarita at a jungle embankment, where the growth was so thick it looked like one large entanglement.

"Japanese?"

"Japanese who speak Tagalog!" Sarita said, stepping into the water and crouching in it up to her chin.

Quickly, Pia followed her daughter back into the river. From the tangle of jungle growth, three armed Filipinos, a woman and two men, came out onto the bank. They all had grins on their faces as they waved to Sarita and Pia before heading down the path to join Aguila and Cocodrilo.

Then suddenly out of the brush, a miniature Igorot woman emerged, trailing behind her comrades. She wore the *lepanto* dress of her northern province. Her arms had visible tattoos. As she passed Sarita and Pia, she gave them a toothless, betel-stained grin. It was none other than Fortuna who had taken leave of the Kellers to "help" her family in Bontoc Province.

The two women gave her a hearty wave. Now there would be eight traveling the final stretch of the journey to the Bat Caves, through Biak-na-Bato and up to the foot of Mt. Lumot, where they would take refuge in the main *guerrilla* hideout. In one hundred and fifty meandering kilometers, Sarita and Pia would arrive safely.

The night of their escape, the Kempetai searched Sarita's house, ripping open mattresses, breaking the mirror behind which the POW letters had been hidden. They bent the strings inside the beloved piano. They found nothing. Enraged, they would surely hunt for her.

The hills and mountains of Luzon were crawling with *guerrillas* and resident Filipino sympathizers—a powerful underground that Elena was certain would lead Sarita and her mother to safety. Knowing her determined friend, she was sure she would remain in hiding until it was safe—probably until after the war was over.

For Elena, it meant the end of her music lessons; more than that, it ended her hopes of hearing from Jerry. She felt helpless as a puppet whose strings had been pulled too many times. Her life suddenly went slack. For days, she withdrew, spending hours in the duck pen, talking to the ducks, who liked to be held in her lap and stroked. She wrote pages in her diary, releasing her emotions, getting her thoughts organized. She could carry on, she knew that, but the spice had been taken out of her life. It was as if there was nothing left to do but concentrate on survival.

In fact, the total population devoted its energy to staying alive. A war within a war, the battle for food raged. Black market activites and hoarding were rampant. Lack of clothing, scarcity of housing and limited transportation were minor compared to the basic need for food. The Philippine puppet government organized cooperative efforts among the neighborhoods; but they were authoritative in their approach, and many balked at their orders. The neighborhood associations that were formed earlier turned into compulsory work groups. Vegetable gardens, individual or communal, became mandatory. As the months passed, the entries in Elena's diary reflected the crisis. On May 18, 1944, she wrote, *"Let me quote the newspaper: 'Compulsory labor groups in Manila are now a daily routine for the ordinary citizen. Work is going on in all districts everyday. Draftees may be seen everywhere in the city, busy with rakes, picks and shovels on certain sections along Heiwa Boulevard.'*

"I can't get over calling Dewey Boulevard 'Heiwa.' It seems so foreign. What the article says is true. We saw working parties this morning on the way home from visiting Belana. Later, we found out that our neighborhood association has been told by the Japanese that we all have to go and work on the boulevard. Sure enough, our neighborhood association representatives came by to pick us up. Carl met them at the gate and brought them in to see our huge vegetable garden. The Japanese guards with them said we didn't have to go because we have our own large garden. Thank God! But now we have to share our vegetables with the neighborhood families. We plan to share mostly with Uncle Ben and the family, who are just a walk away from us. That is neighborhood enough! Also there is a lovely Chinese-Filipino couple living next door we will share with. Carl has planned that all along! Better than forced labor."

She added another comment. *"Instead of concentrating on public vegetable gardens, the city officials should take care of cleaning up the sidewalks of Manila. They are unfit to walk on. Every two or three blocks one comes upon a week-old garbage heap that is sickening—dead dogs, pigs, anything imaginable is mixed with the rotting food. In some cases, garbage heaps are used as public toilets! Beggars hang around the worst piles and fish out papaya skins and rotten camotes."*

Occasionally the entries in the diary told of incidents that, in a wry sort of way, were humorous. Nowadays, Elena felt, there wasn't much to laugh about, but she found irony in some of these occurrences. Then as her writing skills developed, she enjoyed embellishing on what she saw, read about or heard. *"A certain widow was the laughing stock of Manila,"* she wrote. *"She was walking along the boulevard with two gentlemen companions one night when she stopped to remove her shoes because they pinched her feet. She told her two companions to walk ahead. 'I'm tired,' she said, 'I want to rest on this bench awhile. Don't bother about me, I'll catch up with you.'*

"So the two men walked on and forgot their lady friend until one of them said, 'Doesn't it seem an awful long time since we left her? We'd better go back to see if anything is the matter.'

"No sooner did they turn around than they saw a white flutter approaching them. In tears, the widow came running in nothing but her petticoat! She told them a man had suddenly come behind her as she rested on the bench, clamped his hand over her mouth and made her take off her clothes. The thief ran off into the night with her dress and her purse. The twist to this story," Elena concluded, with a flare, *"is he didn't steal her shoes, which were hidden under the bench!"*

Once in awhile, Elena saw Lise Muller and two of Lise's girlfriends—Isabel and Chiquita—who also became her friends. Lise gave her a box of fragrant face powder for her eighteenth birthday. Her card read: *"Happy birthday, Calico. Hope that next year we'll be celebrating it in style."*

The nickname didn't bother her as it once had. In fact, Elena secretly liked the name. Since her talk with her grandmother, she'd begun to see her mixed heritage as a positive element in her life. How would she have been able to get in touch with Jerry otherwise? Or be part of the family's effort to help Carmen Cruz?

Elena also felt better about her role in the family. Boring as they sometimes were, her chores were a significant contribution to their daily lives. She often had to do things that were distasteful, as did everyone else. They learned to save and re-use items that in pre-war days would have been thrown away.

By mid-year, 1944, the family found Carl's paycheck could no longer cover their expenses. They spent 600 pesos a month on food; he made 900. Mila started to sell her jewelry. A jade ring brought two hundred pesos. A diamond pin was sold for three hundred. Elena offered a turquoise pin given to her by Aunt Josefina. Mila refused it. "Keep it. We can't get much for it." Then she gave Elena a ring she had saved for her. "Elena," she said, taking the ring from an old velvet box, "I've had this many years. It was given to me in Spain by an old aunt. It's been a lucky ring for me. I can't sell it. It's yours."

Elena was stunned by the beauty of the delicate ring, shaped like a rosette of textured platinum studded with diamonds and sapphires. Around the outer edge of the rosette was an exquisite circle of sapphires. Elena held the ring to the light. Its brilliance felt magical. "Put it on, *cariño,*" her mother urged.

The ring fit perfectly on the third finger of her right hand. "I'll never take it off," Elena breathed. At a loss for words, she gave Mila a hug.

A true treasure, the ring also became a special symbol. Her mother had given her something very personal—a ring that otherwise would have been sold for food! No telling what they would need to do to make ends meet in the days ahead, but for now the family could keep a few of its valued possessions.

One day in late June, Mila called Vida and Marcelina and told them they could no longer afford to pay them. "You are welcome to stay and live with us, go on doing some work, but we can't give you a salary. I am really so sorry."

Mila could tell by Vida's eyes that she had known this day would come. "Marcelina is ready to return to her family in the province," Vida said, "as Fortuna did. As for me, I will stay. I am part of this family."

Mila shut her eyes, squeezing back tears. "*Maraming salamat*," she said, putting her arms around them both.

Major Hiroku was revered by the military compound behind the Kellers' for his ability to speak Tagalog and English. Known as "the translator," he had rescued his enlisted men from many crises in communications. No telling when he would be summoned, night or day.

On a particular morning in July, he rose to reveille and joined his outfit on the exercise field. When he left the field, perspiration beaded on his bald head, and fog steamed his rimless glasses. He rushed for the steam bath. "Ahh," he sighed, letting the scalding steam envelope him. Hot vapor sang on his hairless legs. He felt cleaned and polished as brass. But not for long. Pounding on the door startled him. Not another crisis in communications! Yes. Hurry. Over the wall. A robbery from the Kellers' yard access to the compound. Two new truck tires stolen! Footprints, tire marks by the Kellers' fence. Evidence! The Keller family was already assembled for questioning.

The major cursed, dressed quickly. He could have taken a shortcut and jumped the stone wall to the Kellers' backyard, but he chose to walk formally onto the street and to the Kellers' gate, where he was met by an enraged enlisted man. A brief salute. A bow. A torrent of accusations. "They did it. Footprints by the iron fence. They are guilty!" the younger Japanese shouted, pointing to the fence along the street side of the property.

"So?" Major Hiroku put his hand on his hip, his fingers touching his holster. He barely glanced at the evidence—two footprints clearly visible in the dirt by the fence. He shook his head. It was the usual problem. Communication. He joined the tight circle of Japanese interrogators standing on the Kellers' front steps. They shot gutteral phrases at Carl, Mila, Elena, Dan, Tim and Vida. The two fox terriers barked furiously.

Carl's face was livid. Furious, he drew back his lips and yelled, "Do you think we'd leave footprints if we had stolen your damned tires? Do you think we would be that stupid?"

Mila tried to hold Carl's gesturing arm. "Dear, listen, dear..." But she couldn't get his attention. Carl persisted, even as the interrogators flashed their guns at him.

When Hiroku sauntered up the stairs, Carl was swearing. "Goddamn fools, you goddam fools," he said over and over. The loaded guns waved as the Japanese shouted back. Major Hiroku could not hide the smile that played on his lips. His talk was sauve. "What seems to be the trouble here?" he asked, lips pursed.

He shoved his face under Carl's chin. Carl backed up. The swearing stopped. Hiroku, once again, had found his podium. English poured out of his mouth, spoken with Japanese inflections. He let it out, like a bolt of silk unraveling, knowing he could be smooth, take his time.

The other interrogators backed up. Hiroku was in charge. "We must review this situation, this crime against the Japanese Imperial Forces. Two tires were stolen last night. It is evident the thieves came through your yard, jumped the wall and raided our compound. Yes, raided our compound. Stole our tires. You would agree that this is a fact. Yes? Yes. Guilt points to you. I must say, if it was not you, then who perpetrated this crime?"

Hiroku took his time. His words flowed, his eyes tantalized, holding Carl captive. But Carl managed to regain control, though his own eyes still burned. At least this fool can speak English! he told himself.

When the Major finally slowed down, Carl pushed his way in. "Look. Look. We know nothing about this. Nothing. Obviously, the thieves came in over our fence. Footprints are there..." He paused a moment, then aimed his logic. "Notice the footprints are of bare feet and not at all like mine. I wear shoes."

Again, a faint smile crept up Hiroku's face. He stood there, nodding; then, like thunder, he roared. "Show me!"

Elena, who was so terrified she could not swallow, uttered a sound that never left her throat. She fell against Vida, who had her hands over her own face.

The other Japanese started to shout as if on cue. Carl shouted back, as Mila tried to hold on to his waving arm again. "You bet I'll show you!" he yelled.

In seconds the entire group was reassembled around the footprints. Carl took off his shoes and placed both feet by the prints. They did not match. Carl's footprints were shorter, his toes closer together. Hiroku waved him away. "Not you!" he barked. He pointed to Dan and Tim. Both boys removed their shoes. Dan's foot, now as big as Carl's, did not match either. He stared at the large footprint.

The toes were rangy, the heel well-developed. Suddenly, a light of recognition flashed through Dan's mind—Marco! Who else but Marco could have come over the fence like that? Who else but Marco would have left such a calling card?

His face blank, Dan looked up and stepped away. "Never mind you!" the Major grunted at Tim. In a voice grown weary, he said to the women, "Not you either!" Then in a final explosion, "Go! All of you, get out!"

Shoulders lowered in relief, Mila quickly herded everyone back into the house. The group of interrogators huddled in conference. More shouting, pointing. Then they broke up and charged out the gate.

Several hours later, another group of soldiers came and put up a wire fence around the footprints. Still later that day, Hiroku showed up again. No longer loquacious, he told Carl briefly they would return the next day to construct a more secure fence. "We will add barbed wire, up to eight feet, on the existing fence. We will give you a lock to put on your gate. There will be no more stealing. This property will be under surveillance."

No one in the family seemed surprised when he told them what the Japanese planned to do. "Hope that's all," Mila commented, her expression marked by worry. "We'll really have to watch our step now. The idea that they are watching us is frightening. We must be extra careful."

In the meantime, Elena knew what she must do. Every trace of evidence linking them to Jerry had to be destroyed. She took the letters from inside a roll of toilet paper, which she had hidden in a space between a facade of tile and the main wall. Then sitting on the floor of the bathroom, she put her head against the toilet bowl and wept. She held the letters in her hands, touched them up to her cheek. Tracing every word with her finger, she read each one of them again. Carefully spreading them onto the water, she watched—wooden—as the paper became soaked, the penciled words blurred. In one sweeping move, she rose and flushed them down. Slamming the lid on the toilet, she ran to her room and threw herself on the bed, holding a pillow to her face so her cries would not be heard.

But Jerry's words were fixed in Elena's memory. Line by line, she could recite every letter he had written. Here and there, in the days that followed, she wrote some of the lines on scraps of paper, disjointed, so only she could recall his letters, should she begin to forget them.

Though the family did not hear from Marco, they knew it was he who had stolen the tires. On the black market, the tires would have brought a good price—money for the underground. "I'm glad Marco stole the tires," Dan commented, "but I'd like to tell him he almost got us killed!"

"That's the truth!" echoed Tim.

Chapter Ten

Jerry

Dan and Tim went to the open air market several times a week to pick up bargains for the farmyard. They traded vegetables for corn. Dan bought young roosters and groomed them for the cock fights. He could sell them at a top price and use the money for the chickens, ducks, turkeys and pigeons. As the market prices skyrocketed, the Kellers began to eat their own fowl.

Turning a young rooster into a fighting cock was an art. The bird had to be well-fed but kept lean and feisty. It had to be exercised. Its comb had to be cut off so as not to get in the way during a fight. The cock fights were vicious. Often in just a few minutes, one of the birds would be mortally wounded by the sharp knives attached to its opponent's spurs.

Dan developed a detached attitude toward the birds. It was a business, he told himself. Then Napoleon came along. A speckled, black and white rooster, he was majestic in his stance. Dan groomed him carefully, becoming more and more attached. When the day came for him to crop Napoleon's rich red comb, Dan had second thoughts. As he crouched over the rooster, stroking its wings, he said aloud, "Napoleon, how can I do this?"

Napoleon looked up at him with a fiery eye. "No," said Dan, "you wouldn't be good with the hens. Not now. You'll end up in the pot. That would be worse!" He paused. Stroking the bird's underside, he continued, "There's no choice, Napoleon. You are a fighter."

He got the things he needed for the operation—the knife, the sharpener, the coals for the fire, the clean cloths. He prepared the knife, sharpening it until the blade thinned and gleamed in the sun. He built a small fire, letting the coals burn down to ashes, all the while holding Napoleon. Then gently securing the bird between his legs, he held the head in one hand and the knife in the other. With learned skill, he sliced the comb down to a quarter inch, reached for the hot ashes, which burned his hand as he scooped them up, and seared the bleeding gash on Napoleon's head. "Hold on, Napoleon, hold on," he said, clamping his hand hard on the wound to numb it from the pain. While Napoleon struggled and squawked, Dan rocked him back and forth. He did not realize he was crying, until the tears blinded him. "I won't sell you. I'll be your manager."

Napoleon won his first fight a week after the operation. Dan brought home a bag of corn and twenty-five pesos. He won three fights after that. The ring of gamblers, dressed in colorful Philippine shirts on a Saturday night, whooped and shouted as the cocks fought.

Napoleon's dark sleek feathers were a dramatic contrast to the more common russet and green feathers of his opponents. Plumage flashed, spurs flew upward in the din that rose from the gamblers. It was all over when, in the flash of a knife, a mortal wound was dealt. The dying cock flapped a few times, and lay down to die. When a wounding took place, the story was different—the killing became a torture.

Napoleon's wins brought over five hundred pesos. On the seventh fight, a tall white rooster killed him in one fast stroke.

Dan vowed he would never groom another fighting cock. He continued to go to the market and devote himself to caring for the fowl, staying as unattached as he could, because he knew they could not be kept as pets.

On many of his long walks on Daitoa Avenue, formerly Taft Avenue, on his way to the market, he saw truckloads of American POWs being hauled to and from work sites. Always, he would strain to see if he recognized Jerry among them. Routinely, Elena asked him if he if he had spotted him. She sat on a garden chair behind the high barbed wire fence for an hour every afternoon, hoping to see Jerry in one of the trucks transporting POWs. Both she and Dan could imagine him among the prisoners that went by.

One afternoon Dan came running in from the street.

"Elena," he called out, "I've got some good news!"

He met his sister hurrying down the stairs. "Jerry?" she asked, waiting intently.

"Yes. I was down at Uncle Carlos's. He's helping me fix my bike. A group of POWs is working by the river close to Uncle's house."

"B-but, did you..." Elena tried to interrupt.

"Wait," cried Dan, "let me tell you. As I was passing them on the way home, several of them were close to the street, getting ready to get into the trucks." He paused a moment. Wide-eyed, Elena hung on his every word. "This one blond guy had his back to me, but when he turned around, he stared at me like he knew me!"

"Jerry!" breathed Elena, clasping her hands together tightly.

"Jerry! It really was! I didn't recognize him at first. Elena, he looks terrible—skinny, his clothes are a wreck. But he smiled and I knew it was Jerry!" Dan himself was smiling and shaking his head. "It was like I had seen him just yesterday."

"Oh, Dan," Elena cried, twisting her hands. "I've got to see him!"

"That's just it," his voice grew deeper. "Uncle says about fifty POWs have been working on a retaining wall that supports a shaky walkway to a loading dock on the river."

Elena could not contain herself. "Let's go tomorrow!" she cried.

"I plan to," her brother grinned. "We'll go together. Auntie and Uncle are already expecting us. We'll probably get a chance to see Jerry up close."

"How do you mean?"

"The guys come up after they work and hose off in their backyard."

Elena bit her lower lip and turned away.

"Are you crying, Elena?" Dan asked.

"No, I'm thanking God," she said.

The next morning, the two of them took a *carretela* to their aunt and uncle's house, which was across town on the Pasig River. Elena took her time getting ready. She washed her hair and dried it vigorously, until it was light and feathery on her shoulders. She rubbed some rouge on her cheeks, just enough to hide her pallor. Then she put on her dirndl skirt, pressing down the starched gathers. She had two white blouses, both mended. She chose the one that had a little lace around the collar. Slipping on her *bakias*, she was ready. As she put coins into her small cloth purse, she felt her hands shaking. What a day this will be! she told herself.

Josefina and Carlos's place had always been special. With no children of their own, they spoiled their nieces and nephews. Elena had always noticed special touches—favorite food, carefully matched place settings; and most important, a personal interest in what each of them was doing.

When they arrived, Josefina greeted them, chucking both of them under the chin, as she had when they were little. "*¡Hola!*" she smiled. Her eyes sparkled and her teeth, though large for her narrow face, were straight and white. She wore her black hair off her face in a loose bun. Taller than her sisters, her walk was as regal. Arm-in-arm she led Dan and Elena into the house.

The large *sala*, or living room, was furnished with dark rattan furniture. Delicate patterns of lavender and pale yellow flowers decorated the large pillows. A huge round brass tray with intricate oriental designs sat on a teak stand and served as a coffee table. As a child, Elena had banged on it, taking pleasure in the musical sounds she could play by hitting different areas of the tray.

Today, she was not interested in lingering in the living room. One thought dominated her mind—Jerry. Her aunt sensed this and ushered her out to the back porch which overlooked the river. Elena pushed aside a line of drying dish towels and peered through the screen. She heard voices coming from the riverbank. "Not there," Josefina said. "Come. I'll show you where they are."

They walked down the porch steps to the side of the house. The bank of the river rose and fanned out into a small spit. About twenty yards away, a group of American prisoners of war worked on the muddy bank. With boards, hammers, picks and shovels they were rebuilding the retaining wall that supported a dilapidated wooden walkway to a small loading dock. Several of the men carried heavy crossbeams. Surrounding the workers stood Japanese guards, their rifles ready.

At first, Elena saw them as a group, like a black-and-white picture of slaves she had seen in history books. Black-and-white, because there was no color in the scene. The faces of the prisoners looked gray, a blend of their pallor and river mud. Their clothes were made of bleached rags, remnants of tattered army uniforms. Most of them were barefoot. Emaciated by disease and starvation, their skin close to their bones, there was a sameness about them. They were like ghosts. Hollow-eyed, they moved slowly; but they moved, for the guards would not let them rest, and they knew this.

In a trance, Elena continued walking toward them. "Don't go further," her aunt cried, holding on to her wrist. "The guards will suspect us."

The guards! Elena snapped out of her trance. She hadn't paid attention to the guards; but they were there, six of them straight ahead, patrolling back and forth. Occasionally, a gruff command burst from them as they gave their orders. But they did not seem to be paying attention to Elena and Josefina.

Dan and Carlos joined them. "Step back, Josefina," Carlos said. "You're too close." He put his arm around his wife's waist. He was shorter than she was, bald, with an animated face; laugh lines played around his deep dark eyes. "Let's take a look at the river."

He led them away from the prisoners to the riverbank close to their house. They pretended to gaze out at the water, talking softly to one another. Dan could not contain himself. "Elena," he said in a hoarse voice, "look slowly to your right. One of the guys is wearing an old rag around his forehead. Not the one who has shoes on, the other one. He's closest to the river."

At first Elena couldn't spot the prisoner her brother was sure was Jerry. There were two men with rags wound around their heads. Yes. One had boots on. The other one? He had a headband also. Jerry? That could not be Jerry! He didn't look like Jerry at all. Wait. There's something. Something about the way he walks, holds his head. And the grin. He's smiling, and he's looking straight at us!

Elena reached for Dan's hand. "It's Jerry!" she cried.

Dan steadied her. "Pretend you don't recognize Jerry or anyone; there's a guard staring at us," her brother warned.

"Let's go back to the house," Carlos said, turning from the bank and casually walking back.

As she turned, Elena could not resist another look at Jerry. Bending over to pick something up, he was still looking their way. Elena lifted her hand slightly, then dropped it back to her side. Simultaneously, Jerry's head went down in a slight nod.

Her legs were trembling as she followed the others back to the house. The image of Jerry burned in her mind. How could anyone have changed so much? she asked herself. He must be thirty or forty pounds lighter than he was. Not only thin, he looked so drawn! Her heart seemed to stop as his image fixed itself forever in her mind. Fate had carved its deep and fearful initials on someone she loved. He would never be the same. Neither would she.

"Sit down here, *cariño*," Josefina said, leading her niece to one of the flowered rattan chairs in the sala. "Dan, go in the kitchen and ask Rosa for some water." Then turning back to Elena, "You're white as a sheet, *querida!*" she exclaimed. "Here, lean back. Dan's bringing you some water."

Elena leaned back on the cushion and closed her eyes. A nightmare, she thought, none of this is real. Then as the image of Jerry came forward again, she drew energy from it. Something fierce grew in her. He has survived, she said to herself. I can't pity him! I'll fight for him. I have to let him know that! And suddenly, she was sitting straight up. "Dan," she called to her brother, who was on his way back to her with the water, "Dan, when can we see him again?"

Dan looked puzzled. "Hey," he said, pushing her shoulder back, "get back there. You've had a heck of a shock. I told you he looked awful."

He handed her the glass. "I don't want it," she said. "Drink," he ordered, and she lifted the glass to her lips. Then returning it quickly, she said, "That's enough. I'm fine."

"Good. We can see them all again when they come up this afternoon around four o'clock to use the hose."

"*Ven a comer*," Josefina called, announcing lunch.

They sat around an oval *narra* table in the dining room. Elegant chairs and a mirrored buffet matched perfectly. Placemats made of Philippine *piña* cloth, a pineapple fiber, were at each place. Green and white china gleamed.

There was a tight knot in Elena's stomach, but she forced herself to eat. Her aunt had prepared a *talinum* salad with bits of egg and tomato in it. There was hot homemade cassava bread, with guava jelly and *café con leche*. Josefina had saved several cans of milk. Having coffee with milk was the ultimate treat. "*Gracias*, Auntie," Elena said, "you are always so good to us."

Josefina smiled. "Why not? You're my favorites!"

The afternoon crawled by. The heat of mid-day had warmed the back porch so it felt like an oven to Elena, who had not moved from the screen, through which she could see the POWs. Too far away to make out their faces, she kept her eye on Jerry, identifying him by his headband and bare feet. While he worked, carrying crossbeams, nailing boards, shoveling mud, he would look occasionally toward the house.

Each time he did, Elena's heart leaped. Though he could not see her, it was as if there was a telepathic line between them, a feeling she had that he was right there next to her.

Josefina brought out a chair. "Sit down. It's too hot to stand out here!" She put her arm around Elena. "I know how it is, *cariño.*"

"You do?"

"Oh, yes! *El amor es poderoso.*"

"*El amor es poderoso,*" Elena repeated. "Love is powerful." Perched on one leg, she braced herself up on the stool. Seconds telescoped into minutes, minutes into hours. Her vigil became a reverie of imaginative scenes. Jerry talked to her, told her how much he had missed her. She held his hand, offered him food. Together they sat by the river. No longer muddy, the waters of the Pasig were clear and rippling. The war was over...

Dan burst into the porch. His head hit the line of dish towels. They danced up and down; one or two fell on the floor. "It's time. They are getting ready to clean up."

The tempo of movement among the prisoners began to pick up. They stacked picks and shovels into a pile, threw boards together, collected hand tools, while the guards stood by and watched. When they were finished, one of the guards pointed to the trucks and gave a command. It sounded like a blend of harsh consonants, "Koora! Koora!"

The men moved, avoiding the rifle butts used to prod them on. Jerry was one of the first to carry a load to the trucks. He lifted it up to the waiting hands of a fellow prisoner. Back and forth the POWs went, sweat pouring from their gaunt bodies, bony chests heaving in the hot sun.

Elena could hardly bear the sight. Yet, she knew when they were finished they would come up to the garden hose, just feet away from the back porch. "Oh, hurry, Jerry. Hurry!" she said. She had picked up a dish towel and was twisting it in her hands.

One by one, the POWs gathered around the faucet. As each one came closer, Elena's heart beat harder. Color, which had not been visible from afar, suddenly became evident. Under the dirt and sweat, she saw a red beard here, curly brown hair there, green eyes over here; blue eyes next to them. And their tattered clothes had faded color in them also—light blues, green, tans. Scars were clear in the bright sun, some still oozing from arms, legs, feet and faces. Then she focused on the face she had waited so long to see—Jerry's. He had spotted her and stared so hard she knew he was trying not to blink. Tears stung her eyes. Fiercely, she wiped them away with the twisted dish towel. Don't cry now! she told herself. You'll miss seeing Jerry right in front of you! Instead, she struggled to put a smile on her face. It crept in tremulously, as Jerry watched, his own face breaking into a full grin. His blue eyes crinkled, his teeth were shiny and white. He stood straight and proud. They stared at each other for seconds, minutes.

"Drinks first!" one of the men shouted, as the group pushed to get at the hose. The guards stood aside. "I was first, buddy," another said. "Wait your turn!"

Someone else laughed. They shoved, almost as if they were playing. Then suddenly, a whisper started among them.

"Look at her!" cried the one with the dark curly beard.

Elena took a step back away from the screen, her eyes still glued on Jerry, who had not moved. "Hey, Jerry," the man standing behind him said, "Better drink up, if we're all going to have time with the hose." He stared at Elena. Slowly Jerry picked up the hose, turned the gush of water over his head, his eyes still on Elena. Her smile broadened as she saw the water rushing down his face, over his body, cleaning off the mud. Then he drank deeply, standing there as long as he could. As he drank, she felt the water as if it were cooling her own throat. His image became hers. For those few moments, she sensed her being blending with his.

Sunlight caught his wet hair. It shone like gold. The faded rag he had worn around his head lay on the ground. She saw a deep scar above his elbow. As she watched him, he formed a word with his lips—bea-u-ti-ful! And she knew that he saw her as a woman now, not the fifteen-and-a-half-year-old he had first met almost three years ago.

The guards, who had stood apart, talking, began herding them to the trucks. Engines roared. The prisoners climbed in. Jerry stood apart for as long as he could. Feelings continued to pulse between them. He raised two fingers and pressed them to his lips. Then his eyes rested on Dan, who had moved up and was standing next to his sister.

Turning the same two fingers downward, Jerry formed an upside down V. "V for Victory," Dan whispered. He did not have a chance to return the sign. Elena was transfixed, the two fingers she had held up, still pressed against her lips. It was the last thing Jerry saw before he joined the others in the truck.

He stood toward the tailgate, and kept looking back, the smile never leaving his face. Elena watched him until the truck was down the street. Jerry's face blurred, but still he stood, looking in her direction. The sun blazed down on his head. He looks like an archangel! she thought.

When she could no longer see him, she leaned back against her brother. Tears would not come. Her whole world seemed to have gone dry.

"Well, that's it," Dan said. "Their job is done. They won't be back tomorrow."

"They won't be back tomorrow," echoed in Elena's ear. "They won't be back."

Chapter Eleven

First by Air

Early in September, Mrs. Grossman stopped tutoring Elena. Dan and Tim had also been taking lessons from her. "I have not been feeling well," she told them. Mila had given the tutor lessons in Spanish in exchange for instruction in math, history and English. A few days after the last lessons, the Kellers heard that she was in Fort Santiago, accused of being a collaborator. When the news came, Mila was stunned. "I had no idea! Poor Mrs. Grossman, she is such a good human being."

"The Japs don't care about 'good human beings,'" said Dan. He shot a look at Elena, who was silent, tears slowly reddening her eyes.

"Just hope to God that she gets out of that hell hole," Carl added. He shook his head. "I'm going out to move that sickly banana tree from the back fence. It isn't getting enough sun." He started for the door, then turned around. "How do you feel about not having any more tutoring?" he asked the three of them.

Dan volunteered first. "I have so much to do with the animals, it's fine with me."

Tim, who disliked anything to do with school, gave a wry smile. Though still inches shorter than his brother, he was beginning to look as if he would soon be fifteen.

"I'm very busy, too. I plan to buy a pig. It will be good to have a pig in reserve."

"Not another animal to feed!" Mila exclaimed.

"That's just it," Tim said, "a pig will eat anything. I'll take care of it."

Carl smiled. "O.K., Tim. But whatever we can't eat, as food gets more scarce, we will sell."

Elena remained silent. "I don't care whether I have any more lessons or not," she said in a flat voice.

Mila looked at her daughter. She has become such a daydreamer, she said to herself. She has been so down. Ever since she saw Jerry... "Elena," she said, keeping a conscious lift in her voice, "I heard that there is a group of nuns at Santa Scholástica's who are teaching classes in bookkeeping and shorthand. Would you like to go there?"

Without looking up, Elena answered, "I don't care."

"Let me see about it," her mother said. "It's not far and I don't think they charge too much."

A few minutes later, Elena sat on the top step of the kitchen stairs, cleaning rice. She liked the ritual. It gave her time to think while doing a chore. Her head level with the thick green leaves of a *mabolo* tree and its plump, fuzzy, red-gold fruit, which paradoxically looked like a giant peach, but smelled of sulphur, she nurtured her dreams. Still obsessed with Jerry, she imagined herself being rescued successfully with him: The enemy pursued them, but they made their way safely to the *guerrillas*. As they worked in the underground, taking life-and-death chances, their love grew. Then the liberation—bombing, shelling, fire, the dead lying everywhere...

Her fantasies never ended with the two of them riding away into the sunset. However, united, they shared the fight for freedom. She did not visualize them in a scene beyond that, as she had in earlier fantasies. She could not bear to think one or both of them might perish. But the fear persisted, grew in the back of her mind and shouted to be recognized. She began to behave compulsively. *"Step on a crack and break your mother's back."* If I do everything right, her inner self seemed to tell her, nothing bad will happen. Death will not touch me. The more she feared death for herself and for those she loved, the more the superstitious rituals grew— *"Don't step on a crack and you won't break your mother's back."*

At night before going to bed, she knelt in prayer by a little night table altar, where statues of Jesus and Mary stood, surrounded by a tiny vase of freshly picked flowers. A rosary, a prayerbook, and a collection of holy pictures lay neatly around the statues. Prayers could no longer quell her fears. She prayed at least an hour each night. Before getting into bed, she would check her room—her dresser, her desk, her clothing, shoes —all in order! If the least item were out of place, she would rearrange it. Unhappily, her anxiety followed a circular pattern. Compelled to repeat ritualistic actions to ward off "bad thoughts," she tried to control the fears that drove her mind: Scenes of destruction—Manila, an inferno of dead and wounded; Manila, once known as the "Pearl of the Orient," a mass of rubble, shelled, scorched, stinking of gungpowder and rotting flesh. In that Manila, she was helplessly consumed by fire, and perished in an agony of burning bodies. She saw those she loved perish with her.

During the day, she kept busy, moving from chore to another, forcing herself to concentrate on what she was doing, holding the fantasies and the rituals aside, as much as she was able.

Cleaning rice was orderly. As Elena tossed the rice, her thoughts alternated between scenes of chaos and control. Thrown from a flat grass-mat tray, the grains rose, geyser-like, loosing their fragrant scent in a fine white cloud. Cascading in a musical shower, they fell, until the last grain clicked down on a full tray.

Elena's fast hands, with her thumb and index fingers acting like a beak, routinely picked out the fat white worms and black pebbles, flinging them high in the air, letting them fall on the ground twelve feet below, where they landed on the overripe, foul-smelling, golden *mabolos* that had dropped, forming a ring around the tree. Each worm and pebble flung out, like the intruding elements that invaded her thoughts. Ironically, no matter how many times she tossed the rice, there remained a scattered worm or pebble that was cooked inadvertantly, and was eaten.

Eyes far away, her lips pursed downward, Elena set the trayful of clean rice aside. In the pens below, her brothers took care of the fowl. Tim yelled something about getting more feed, and started up the kitchen steps. The look on his sister's face stopped him. He paused for just a moment and then said, "Hey, come down and see the new baby pigeons. They just hatched."

He turned and went back down the stairs. Elena lagged behind him, but when she saw the pigeons, bug-eyed and almost featherless, she gave a small laugh. "Aren't they ugly?" Tim said.

Elena didn't say anything right away. She kept watching the pink-skinned chicks, mouths wide open, calling for anything their anxious mother would feed them. "It's hard to believe they will be so beautiful in a few weeks," she said, stroking a trembling little neck with the back of her fingers.

"They are strong little critters," Tim laughed.

When Elena and Tim walked out of the pigeon's pen, Mila was waiting on the landing of the kitchen steps. She watched her son and daughter. How they have grown! she thought. She heard Dan moving around as he worked with the chickens. My children are no longer children. Yet, they aren't adults either. Where has their childhood gone? She answered her own question. It has been swallowed up by war and occupation! She was proud of them. But she hurt for them.

"It's Saturday, Elena," she told her daughter. "You've cleaned the rice and done your chores. Why don't you visit Lise this afternoon?"

Elena shook her head.

"*Sí!*" Mila cried, "you need to get out; enjoy yourself a little. Boys," she added, as Dan joined them, "you, too, take the afternoon off. *Basta!* Enough work!"

Tim livened up. "O.K., I'll go buy my pig!" he announced, cocking his head and waiting for his mother's response.

"*¡Ay!*" Mila slapped her side. "Your pig! Go buy your pig. But remember, no food except scraps."

So they took the afternoon off. Elena went by *carretela* to see Lise in the Ermita. Isabel and Chiquita were there. The four girls decided to go to Madame Rahbi, a fortune teller, whose reputation had grown in Manila.

Card readings gave those who felt uncertain about their futures some predictions to ponder. "I don't really believe what she says is true, do you?" Lise said. "But it's fun going. It's exciting."

Isabel, the light of anticipation shining in her clear brown eyes, squeezed her hands together. "I'm going to ask her when she thinks the Americans will get here," she said. "I also want to know if we'll leave the Philippines like my father plans."

"I'm not sure yet what I'll ask about," Chiquita grinned, her chubby face dimpling.

Madame Rahbi lived with her blind teenage son in an old house in need of paint. It was surrounded entirely by a dilapidated veranda. She greeted the four girls on the creaking steps of the veranda. Wearing a wide black skirt and a white blouse that did not hide her fleshy bosom, she waved them in. Elena noticed her skin was yellowish; a large black mole on her heavy chin accented her coal-black eyes and slightly hooked nose.

Madame Rahbi did not pretend to know the future—she knew it. "Cut the cards," she told Lise, when they were all seated around a shaky card table in her garlic-scented kitchen. The blind boy hung by the door, listening. Lise giggled as she separated the well-worn cards. "You will take a long trip across the ocean soon," she said, peering thoughtfully at the cards she had laid out.

Lise was excited. "Yes, you're right! After the war we are going back home to Switzerland."

Madame Rahbi's son slowly moved into the kitchen and leaned against the green tongue-in-groove wall.

The fortune teller's eyes narrowed to dark slits, "You will survive the battle for Manila, but you will be enveloped by fire, shelling, bombs... There will be flames everywhere before you get away. You will be hungry."

"I'll escape?" Lise asked, her voice tightening.

"Yes."

Four pairs of eyes concentrated on Madame Rahbi's heavily browed face. They were drawn by every word. "Me, do me next," begged Isabel after she told Lise a few more things about her future.

When she finished with Lise, she started to read Isabel's cards. "You are a very nervous person," she said, studying the young girl's finely boned face. "You are looking ahead to the day when your family can live as they used to before the war," she continued. "Your father was wealthy." Madame Rahbi's fingers knotted over the cards.

Isabel's eyes were brilliant. "Yes. Yes, my father was in copra, but now..." she explained.

"He will be rich again. But you...you be careful, my dear. When the fighting begins, hide. Don't move around."

Her eyes dilating, Isabel leaned forward. "What to you see, Madame Rahbi?"

The seer gazed at the cards. Her words measured, she said, "Fire... guns...starvation. Yes, I see this everywhere. But..." her tone changed; she looked up and went on, "I see a loving family. You are very close to them; they to you. Correct?"

"Yes," Isabel breathed, "we are very close. But the fire...the..."

"Just be very careful child. God be with you."

Madame Rahbi finished Isabel's reading quickly and turned to Elena. "Now, you," she nodded.

Visibly shaken, Isabel sat next to Lise, who put her arm around her. "It's just a card reading," whispered Lise.

Elena looked very serious as the fortune teller began.

"You are a very sensitive person—too sensitive." She stared into Elena's intense gray-green eyes, observed the golden rings around her pupils. "Do you see into the future? Some of the things I have been saying? Fire, bombs, dead in Manila?"

"Y-yes." Elena answered softly. "I have strange daydreams where I see the city in...in ruins."

"You are clairvoyant," Madame Rahbi pronounced, and a ripple of excitement went around the table.

A faint smile crept into Madame Rahbi's face. "Ruins. Yes. But don't let these visions frighten you. They only warn you of coming danger. Like a sixth sense, they protect you. Be aware. You can help yourself by knowing."

She stopped, visibly tired now. "You will also be enveloped by flames. Like a great oven. Manila will burn and burn. You will live." She paused again, frowning down at a card, touching it with the long nail of her index finger. "This is a bad card—the queen of spades." She pointed to a card next to it. "Someone dear to you will die by drowning."

"Drowning?" Elena gasped. The others echoed her fear. "Oh no!" Isabel exclaimed. Chiquita gasped.

Ignoring them, the fortune teller continued. "Have you had a premonition about this?" she asked.

"In a way, I have," Elena answered. Tentative, but caught by the impact of her words, she said, "I have a horrible feeling Jerry will die. But not by water. I always see him engulfed by flames."

The flesh on Madame Rahbi's arms shook as she shuffled the cards for Chiquita. "It will be a death by water for someone dear," she repeated. "Many will die at that time. I am sorry. Nothing anyone can do," she finished.

Chiquita's reading also told of a terrible battle for the city. She described Chiquita's house destroyed by fire, but told her she would survive the war.

As the four girls walked away from Madame Rahbi's house, they saw the figure of the fortune teller's son leaning over the veranda, his blind eyes turned to them as if he could see.

Elena was still shaken when she told Mila about the readings. "That was all you needed, Elena, to get more upset than you are. *Tonta!* Foolish! What does she know? Why depress yourself with that nonsense?"

"I'm not so sure it's nonsense, Mom," Elena said. "In a way, she made me feel better. I thought I was the only one who has these nightmare scenes."

Her mother's voice softened. "I don't have 'visions,' but, of course, I—all of us—fear what could happen when the Americans return. We imagine the worst sometimes. But I don't let myself get obssessed by it. You have to stay busy, *cariño*. Just don't think about it too much."

"I try. I just wish I didn't feel the closeness of the fire, the loss of Jerry, I feel death all around me. I can't help it."

Her voice firm again, Mila said, "Yes, and if you dwell on it, it will get worse. I really think you should go to Santa Scholástica. You need to connect your mind to something that will occupy it, take the place of these thoughts you have. What do you say?"

"I'll go," she said. The next day she was enrolled.

Shortly before Elena became a pupil at the school, the Japanese began air defense exercises. The paper put out a complex list of instructions concerning two defense orders which closed certain streets in Manila when the air-raid alert sirens sounded. Defense Order #1 closed only specific streets. Defense Order #2 closed all main streets and restricted traffic during an air raid.

On September 7, the local paper reported American air raids on Davao and warned of possible raids on Manila, telling all residents to be prepared for such an event.

A few days later, the radio announced that an American task force had been sighted off southern Mindanao. Planes in groups of up to eighty raided Leyte, Cebu and Negros Islands in the Philippines. As a result, the alert signal and Defense Order #1 were in effect in Manila several times that week.

On September 11, Elena wrote in her diary: *"The all-clear signal was sounded at 10:30 this morning, but traffic suspension still continues in certain areas of the city. There is a tremendous sense of excitement. We all feel it's just a matter of time before we are bombed. I never realized when we went to Madame Rahbi that we might be under attack so soon! I keep thinking about her words that I might be clairvoyant. If that's so, then perhaps I'm not so strange! Somehow, I feel a little better.*

"Prices at the market are out of sight. Rice ranges at 120 pesos a ganta, scarcely two meals! People are hoarding. Tension about food is felt every-where. After the alert was lifted, we went to see if we could buy meat and vegetables at the Libertad Market, and we sure couldn't find anything but a little fish. It had already started to smell! Beggars were all over the market. I gave an old woman a peso, but I don't know what she could buy with it except maybe a small piece of fruit. The children of the beggars look so starved. They don't even cry. They just look at you.

"At almost every meal we are eating rice from the sack and-a-half we have on reserve. There is no meat. Mongo beans give us protein, as well as

eggs from the ducks and chickens, plus we have vegetables from the garden. The problem now is how to get enough corn for the ducks and chickens...Carl says we will have to start eating them. I can't imagine eating Winnie, Rosie, or MacArthur. I can't even think of eating my Wobbles. I would die of starvation first!

"We had word from Uncle Tino," Elena's entry continued. *"He, Aunt Dale and the girls are being evicted from their house by the Japanese military, who say they need it for security reasons. They didn't say what 'security reasons.' Poor Uncle Tino and his family have no place to live now.*

"We must make room for them here. Auntie Josefina and Uncle Carlos offered their place, but now Aunt Neva and the kids are living there because they were overcrowded at Uncle Ben's. They are all doubled up, and now it's our turn. I will have to move in with Mom and Carl, so all four of them can squeeze into my room. They'll be coming at the end of this week. I hope I can help take care of Debra and Rosie. Debra is very lively and bright. Rosie is quiet, but so cute. She's only four and still doesn't talk a lot.

"If this emergency continues, we can sell some of the animals rather than eat them. Even that will be hard to face, although I'd rather sell Wobbles than eat her. The rats are hungry, too. They have their eyes on the chickens and pigeons now. Last night the boys used their slingshots on an enormous rice rat that had attacked the baby pigeons and ate four of them. There was blood everywhere in the pen. Dan was so furious he wanted to find the rats' hideout and kill them all!

"The dogs are getting very thin. Eating our small rice and mongo leftovers is not enough food for them. I am starting to hate writing in this diary. I don't have much to say that is positive. The only good thing I can say tonight is that I am caught up with my bookkeeping lessons at school. I wish I knew Tagalog better. I could be better friends with the Filipina girls. Anyway, we giggle together.

"Lise, Isabel, Chiquita and I can't see each other now because of the air alerts. Traffic is so restricted, and tension is high in Manila. The Japanese seem more gruff than ever. It's a wonder I am caught up with my work because I am having a terrible time concentrating. What's the use? I ask myself. Who knows if any of us will survive what's ahead. What is ahead? That's the trouble, no one knows.

"Heavy feelings about what's coming persist. At confession last week I told Father I had a premonition we are all going to die. He warned me that thinking that way is a sin! Only God knows when one is suppposed to die. He also said fortune tellers are heretics. If my visions are true, I must be one, too! I can't sleep, worrying about everything!"

She concluded. *"Refugees are coming into Manila dragging their pushcarts and carrying bundles. Some carry their old sick relatives on makeshift bamboo stretchers. It's terrible to see the grief on their faces. The children cry as they trudge along. The little ones walk alone because their parents' arms are so full. No one knows where they are going. They have left their homes for many reasons. The Japanese have taken over whole areas for defense. Rice is more and more scarce. They don't want to starve. There is no more food or housing left for refugees in Manila. They will only find it is useless for them to leave the provinces looking for food and shelter here."*

A few days later, Tino and his family arrived at the Kellers'. They carried two suitcases packed with clothes. They brought their beds and mattresses. That was all. They were forced to leave everything else behind.

Tino was unshaved, Dale's face was strained, and the girls seemed lost. Rosie hung on to her mother and Debra stood back, her brown eyes saucer-like. They waited like refugees, their belongings strewn on the driveway.

Mila ran to them, arms outstretched. Carl called out from the front door, "Hello! Come on in!"

He took the stairs two at a time, followed by Elena, Dan, and Tim. Vida heard the commotion and hurried down the kitchen stairs.

Dale managed a smile when Mila hugged her. Tino extended a stiff hand to Carl. Debra tried to duck behind her mother, but Elena reached out and gave her a hug. "Come, I'll show you your room."

They trooped into the house, lugging their bags into Elena's room, where they would squeeze in, dormitory-style. Within an hour, they were set up, beds crammed against the walls, mosquito net hooks already in place. Elena's armoire was so full the doors would not close.

Debra sat on her narrow cot coloring a picture of two cats Elena had outlined for her. "I'll color the mother cat brown and the father cat black," she said. Her small fingers curled tightly around the crayons.

Elena nodded, glad she was feeling more at home. By lunchtime, Debra was talking so much her mother told her to quiet down. The Keller table had both extensions out, and odd chairs were added to seat the four extra family members.

Debra sat next to Elena, and for the next two days she followed her older cousin everywhere. Elena became engrossed in the little girl's play. Together they collected leaves from the garden, identified the flowers and made up stories. For the first time in weeks, Elena forgot herself and concentrated on the simple, direct and trusting spirit of her young cousin. Occasionally, Rosie would join them, making their relationship that much more absorbing.

Though Tino could not contribute money to the household, he and Dale had brought a sack of rice, another of mongo beans and a bag of cracked wheat to add to the reserves in the storage room, where Carl set large steel traps to catch vociferous rats that had invaded their house, as they had every house in the city.

A few days after Tino's family arrived, one of the rats got into their room. Rosie was asleep in her crib. Debra was coloring on some wrapping paper. Cat-sized, the rat got up on its hind feet and pushed its probing nose between the slats of the crib. Debra looked up and saw it. She clutched her crayon, too terrified to scream. The rat had its front claws on the mattress. Debra shrieked. It was a high thin cry of horror. When the family began to hurry into the room, Debra was jumping up and down, her long coffee-colored hair bouncing on her shoulders. "Mommy, Daddy, hurry, hurry, a rat is trying to eat Rosie!"

Intent on rescue, the family crowded into the room. The rodent dove under the crib and crouched into a corner, its pointed teeth bared, its black fur draped like a cloak.

Tino burst through the door. Vida followed on his heels. She swished a stick broom. Maxie and Sheba yipped behind her, slipping and sliding on the slick floor as they dove under the crib. Dan and Tim each carried slingshots. They aimed at the rodent as Vida got ready with the sharp broom. Tino and Carl moved the beds back to clear the way.

The rat didn't have a chance. Dan aimed at its head and shot a small rock that hit between the animal's black beady eyes, knocking it on its hairy side. Sheba raced for it and tossed it into the air, Maxie right behind her. The rat was dead before Vida swung at it with the broom.

In the meantime, Debra threw a pillow into the middle of the commotion, hitting her father on the head. Rosie screamed at the top of her lungs, while her mother grabbed her small arms and lifted her out of the crib.

Elena stood clutching the doorknob. She began to laugh at the scene. The sound of her laughter rose above the screams, the barking, and the general chaos.

With a quick flick of the broom, Vida lifted the dead rat high in the air like a hunting trophy. Its eyes stared like black stones. Vida's laughter rang out, blending with Elena's. One by one, they all started to laugh. But it was not the laughter of merriment so much as it was the laughter of nervous release—shrill and intense and contagious.

In the battle for survival, one rat had become a target of vengeance. For the family it became a symbolic incident in a fight to stay alive. Killing the rat revealed a paranoia in them—a paranoia that was spreading in Manila, a city anticipating destruction and death.

That evening Tino put his hand on Dan's shoulder. He paused a moment before saying, "Thanks, Dan. That rat could have really hurt Rosie."

Dan smiled faintly in response. He was thinking about the pigeon's bloodied nest, the slaughtered baby birds. The rat was small revenge.

On September 21, 1944, Elena rode a *carretela* to school. It was a short ride to the front door of the college. Routines were observed. Prayers. Roll call. Assignments. At nine o'clock sharp, the bookkeeping lessons began. Elena looked over the neat ledger she had set up. Sister Felicia went over the entries as each student checked her work. The large clock over the blackboard ticked. Elena glanced over at Anastasia, a bright-faced classmate who sat in the row next to her. Stasia looked up and raised her eyebrows at her. After the lesson they would meet for a break in the hallway, and in a mix of English and Tagalog, share bits of conversation. The air raid siren suddenly wailed. The students sat up in their seats. Another practice. They heard the drone of planes, faintly at first, then directly overhead. A plane dove low; another roared behind it. Heavy machine-gun fire exploded, followed by a volley of anti-aircraft shells. Before Sister Felicia spoke, her eyes told the class that the raid was not practice. "Air raid, girls. Air raid. Hurry to the hall. Hurry. Stay calm!"

The classroom emptied in seconds. Students lined up in the hall and followed Sister Felicia to a corner of the building where they crouched down. Mother Superior rushed down the polished hallway and spread her arms, the palms of her hands up in a motion of supplication, "Pray, Sister Felicia, pray!"

As the Mother Superior hurried off to other groups of students taking shelter in the hallway, Sister Felicia turned to her class. The young women were crouched as low as they could be without lying down. Elena had been pushed into the farthest part of the corner, where several pots of cactus were grouped together. Anastasia crouched next to her. "Don't be frightened, girls. Pray. God will take care of us," Sister Felicia said, her voice quavering, her hands working her rosary. "We will begin a rosary."

Crouched down in front of her, twenty students writhed to get into their pockets for their rosaries. Elena had forgotten hers. As the prayers droned, the dogfight above them raged. "Pencils!" the Sister yelled, interrupting a Hail Mary.

All eyes were turned upward as the students searched for pencils to put between their teeth. The glass in the windows trembled. Shells detonated overhead. Heavy bombs were thundering around them now. No one was answering the Hail Marys. Sister was praying by herself.

A bomb exploded so close, Elena felt her ears were bursting. A window of colored glass crashed down into the hallway, a dozen feet away. Some of the girls began to scream. Sister Felicia stopped praying. "Shh-shh...God is with us," she breathed. "Holy Mary, Mother of God..."

Elena struggled against the cactus plants. She had been pushed so far against the pots that the low-growing spines stuck her in the back. "Ouch!" she cried, and tried to shoulder herself forward unsuccessfully. She crouched lower and leaned into the girl in front of her. There was a shattered hole where the window had been, through which a square of sky was visible. Elena stared at it, as the spray of machine-gun fire continued, punctuated by the rhythmic thud of bombs. Suddenly, two planes filled the square of sky above her. They dove at each other, glinting in the morning sun. My God, one of them must be American! she said to herself. Her heart tripped, as a sense of pure joy overwhelmed her. "Americans!" she exclaimed. Amidst the rattle of gunfire, the bombs and the loud prayers, no one heard her.

People from the street began to come in to take shelter in the halls of the school. They were all chattering loudly, announcing details of the air raid. "There are hundreds of American bombers and fighters over us!" one man said. "They are coming in waves—wave after wave!"

He was right. The second and third waves were stronger than the first. Despite the ear-splitting explosions and the shattering of windows, there was more joy than fear in the halls of Santa Scholástica. The air raid was the beginning of liberation for those who took shelter there. The halls vibrated with the energy of people who had waited three years to hear the drone of American planes.

The bombers kept coming every ten or fifteen minutes. Elena saw six of them through the broken window. They look like silver angels, she thought. Fighters and dive bombers appeared as on a movie screen, zig-zagging under the bombers.

Concussion from another bomb close by rocked the buildings of the school. The students fell dizzily against one another, their perspiring faces looked doll-like. The blast blew out another cathedral glass window and sent it shattering, just feet from the students with whom Elena huddled. Glass splintered like colored ice, spraying the walls, the hallway and the students. Elena felt a sharp prick in her forearm. She clutched the sore spot and found it hurt more. Must be glass, she told herself, and ducked her head down until her forehead touched the cool tile of the floor.

Anastasia was crying. Elena looked over at her friend and saw that her cheek was bleeding. Quickly, she reached in the pocket of her dress and pulled out a handkerchief. She pressed it against Stasia's cheek. "Press," she said, "I can see the glass is out."

Elena looked down at her own arm. It was bleeding. She wiped the blood away with her hand and stared at the tiny sliver of blue cathedral class embedded under her skin. It's pretty, she thought, and it doesn't hurt very much. She decided to leave it alone until she got home. Home? Get home? It was the first time she had thought of home. How was her family? She had heard one man comment that the bombers concentrated on Nichols Field, just a few miles south of her house. I hope they're all right, she thought.

As quickly as the American planes had blanketed Manila skies, they now left. The heavy hum of the bombers slowly lessened. Machine-gun fire from the fighters stopped. Finally, the anti-aircraft guns were silent.

"It's over!" a Filipino businessman sighed. His words were followed by the blast of the all-clear siren. The voices of the people in the hallway rose to a crescendo. Sister Felicia raised her voice to her students. It was no longer quavering, but sounded strong and assured. "My dear girls, it is over! You may all go home now. Go back to the classroom and gather your books, but don't set out by yourselves. The streets will be closed to traffic. One of us will walk you home."

Elena grabbed Anastasia's arm and gently shoved her toward Sister Felicia. "Sister," Elena said, "Anastasia is hurt."

The nun's snappy dark eyes changed expression. "Oh, my!" she cried. "You are hurt! Come, we'll give you first aid right away. Elena, call the Mother Superior."

Elena ran down the hall. "Where is Mother Superior?" she asked one of the students who was coming the other way. The young woman frowned. "She is outside the door helping with an injured child," she said.

Pulling open the ornate wooden door of the front hall, Elena felt a cool rush of air hit her perspiring face. She stepped back with alarm when she saw the huddle of people in front of her. Mother Superior was dressing the bloody leg of a child who was no more than five. The girl's mother was sobbing as she held her daughter's foot up while the Sister wrapped the bandages. Blood was already leaking from the clean dressing. "Take her immediately to the hospital!" she instructed the mother. Someone cried, "But there are no *carretelas*. The streets are closed."

"Then you must carry her. Quickly, she can't loose more blood," the Mother Superior warned.

Three or four strangers from the crowd lifted the girl and formed a stretcher with their arms. "Oh!" Elena cried aloud, observing the child's chalk-white face, closed eyes and open mouth. Her arms hung limply.

Mother Superior put her hand on the child's weeping mother. "Take heart. God go with you," she murmured, patting the woman's arm.

"Mother, can you help us?" Elena whispered, touching the nun's black-caped shoulder. "One of our classmates has been injured."

The nun watched the human stretcher descend the steps. Then she turned to Elena. "Yes, my child. Show me."

They rushed back to where Sister Felicia was waiting with Anastasia. Mother Superior took one look at the cut on the young woman's cheek and said, "It's not bad at all. The glass is out. The bleeding has stopped. Good job, Sister," she said, turning to Sister Felicia.

Sister Felicia shook her head. "I didn't do anything. Someone gave her a handkerchief and she must have applied pressure. It's a nasty cut."

Anastasia reached for Elena's hand. "She helped me," she announced. "God be praised!" Sister Felicia exclaimed. The Mother Superior smiled. Elena looked down, but inside she felt pleased.

"Come. Come, Sister," the older nun said, "let's get these girls home to safety. Each of us will walk six or seven of them home. No telling what the mood of the military is after this air raid!"

Sister Felicia, a full head shorter than Elena, marched down the hall and out the door with her six charges. The air in the streets was still thick with the smell of dust and the smoke of fires that had started as a result of the bombing. Pieces of jagged metal from exploded shells lay on the ground. Wounded were sitting on the sidewalks awaiting assistance. Doctors and nurses had appeared on the scene. There were emergencies everywhere.

Sister Felicia escorted the students past the heavily guarded street near Rizal Stadium, several blocks away from the school. Then she turned back up Taft Avenue and dropped off two more. "Don't stare back at the guards," she warned them. "Just walk normally. I don't think we will be bothered. The Japanese have too much too worry about to pay attention to us."

They arrived at the Japanese compound next to the Kellers'; several soldiers shouted orders to civilians to clear the street for a convoy of trucks. The trucks were loaded with guns being transported to another part of the city. Sister Felicia and Elena crossed the street and waited for the trucks to stop for inspection at the compound. Gingerly, civilians began to walk away from the scene. The Japanese guards were fully absorbed with the convoy. Several inspected the bullet-riddled hood of a truck. "Hurry!" the Sister told Elena, and they fairly ran the last block to the Kellers' gate. "Thank you so much, Sister Felicia," Elena said, giving the nun a hug.

"God Bless you, child, you're welcome." She turned and rushed off.

Mila heard the gate and came running down to greet Elena. "Thank God, it's you!" she cried, squeezing her hard. "You are safe! We've worried about you so much!" she said, adding, "Dan just came home, too —from the market."

"Mom!" Elena exclaimed. "Isn't is wonderful! The Americans are coming back!"

"Yes," Mila exclaimed, "wonderful and..." she hesitated, "terrible."

Together they hurried up the driveway and up the stairs. On the first step, Mila paused and pointed to the mango tree. "Look at that big branch, it's down. Shrapnel," she said. "That's not all, Tim got a bullet in his mattress! Dan had to duck into a ditch at the market. He was covered with fish entrails!"

Elena cupped her mouth with her hand. "¡Ay!" was all she could say.

"That's not all. More. Our electricity is out. We'll have to heat the *kalan* or eat cold mongo beans tonight."

Somehow eating cold beans struck Elena as funny and she started to giggle. Mila joined in. Together they walked up the stairs, giggling all the way into the house.

Everyone was so tired that evening, they decided not to heat the mongo. Nothing mattered except the elation they felt after their first air raid. Carl told them the shortwave radio verified the news that the American carriers were close enough to infict real damage to the Japanese in the Philippines. "This raid is only the beginning," he assured them. It was exactly what they wanted to hear.

"Yay!" shouted Debra, who had chattered through dinner.

"Shh," hissed Tim. "We can't get too loud about how we feel."

"He's right," Tino nodded, looking at his daughter and then at Elena, who sat next to her. "Hey," he said, "I see you have a cut on your arm. Did you get hurt today?"

Elena had forgotten the glass sliver that had embedded itself in her arm. "Ah..." she said, touching the sore spot, "it's a piece of cathedral glass from a window that crashed."

"Let me see," Mila said, getting up and leaning over to look at her daughter's arm. "It's a sliver all right. Get the tweezers, please Carl. We've got to get this out."

"No," Elena shook her head.

Mila leveled her eyes at her. "No?"

"No," Elena repeated. "It's nothing. Maybe I want to keep it."

"*Dios mío!*" cried Mila, "Keep it?"

"I know," volunteered Debra, "you want to keep it to remind you."

Mila laughed. "A *recuerdo*, ha?" she said.

Soon they were all laughing. "Oh, get it out!" Elena said. "I was joking!" and she joined in with them.

The coconut lamps on the table flickered. Merriment warmed the air. They felt safe. None of them imagined they would be bombed again the next day.

Chapter Twelve

Landings on Leyte and Luzon

On September 22, 1944, Elena wrote abut the second air raid: *"American planes returned from their carriers and bombed us again. They hit the air fields, the Port Area's piers and warehouses, and the Japanese embassy. An anti-aircraft shell fragment ripped into our kitchen! It cut connections to the fuse box and left us without electricity again. By tonight, the Japanese had declared martial law in Manila. No more school for me! We're all staying close to home.*

"I feel so excited, but I am very frightened to think what is ahead when the liberation really begins to take place. As Carl said, 'This is only the beginning.' The Japs are going to get really tough as the Americans close in on the islands.

"Last night I dreamed about the air raid. Somehow, Jerry appeared in a crowd of people who were rushing by me. I kept yelling his name, but he never heard me. Sometimes I feel so filled with emotion I think I am going to burst."

In the next few days, the imminent threat of war tightened around Manila. Each person found the circle of individual life closing in as the city slowed to a near stop, reserving its energy for defense.

When one was still fortunate to have a home, it became the center of one's world; everything emanated to and from this place of security. More then that, the home represented the final corner in which one would seek shelter and protection—it symbolized the essence of survival. In the Kellers' case, they had groomed their house and their air raid shelter as their final corner of security. When the final action came, however, it was to the shelter where they planned to go for their safety.

The shelter's fifteen-foot length and two-and-a-half-foot width became a storage place for pillows, blankets, and, most important, a clay stove, the *kalan*, which sat on a simple charcoal-burning oven base. A supply of rice, mongo beans, and an extra ceramic filter for well water stood hidden inside the emergency exit of the shelter, where a stool was placed to serve as a lookout point. The family had practice drills, where all possible routines they might experience in an actual battle for the city were exercised. Each of the ten family members knew what to do. Even little Rosie knew where she would sit in the crowded confines of the shelter.

After September 22, the Kellers were disappointed no more American air raids occurred until October 15, when carrier-based planes thundered over the city again and unloaded their bombs. Raids continued all through the week.

Several of the raids lasted all day long, with long intervals between bombings. The Kellers found they were having their meals in the shelter, rushing into the house only to relieve themselves. Dan and Tim simply went behind the bamboo clump.

Elena sang *"Three Blind Mice"* to the girls, teaching them to join in the multiple chorus. Mila often volunteered to sit on the lookout stool, where she prayed for the safety of the family. When the ack-ack guns fired too closely overhead, she joined the others in the sour-smelling shelter. Deodorants had been unavailable for a long time, and showers in the tropical heat lasted only for a few hours before the acrid odor of sweat rose above scented soap. But more insufferable than the smell of sweaty bodies were the irritable moods that took over as hours in the shelter grew. Rosie cried, while Debra demanded to be entertained. Tim, hearing "Three Blind Mice" for the sixth time in a row during one of the raids, stood up and smashed his head on the beams of the shelter. "Shut up!" he sputtered, holding his head. Dead silence followed. Someone stifled a giggle. "Here, Tim, let me see that," Tino turned the beam of his flashlight on his newphew's head. "Aw, it's nothing!" Tim cried. "I just can't stand all that singing!"

"If you want to know, it's driving me crazy, too!" Tino agreed. "Elena, can't you teach them something else?" Elena shrugged. "Give me some ideas."

Vida offered a suggestion. "Teach them something in Tagalog. How about '*Bahay Kubo*'? That's a nice one—about a little *nipa* shack."

"I know," Elena said. "You teach them. You know the words better than I do."

They heard *"Bahay Kubo"* for the next three hours, until the all-clear siren told them they could return to the house. By that time it was already dark and they had had a dinner of cold rice in the shelter, afraid to light the *kalan* for fear it might violate the blackout rules.

The bombings of the week of October 15 went hand-in-hand with the first American landing on the island of Leyte on October 20. Leyte—actually in the Philippines. The news seeped into Manila: "MacArthur has returned!"

The city, already burning with liberation fever, waited for a landing on Luzon; but no more landings took place, except for a landing on Mindoro Island, which put the returning forces that much closer to Luzon.

The week after the landing on Leyte, the air raid sirens continued to wail, though no more heavy bombings occurred. No one slept well. Runs to the air raid shelter in the middle of the night interrupted sleep, so that no one felt rested. Elena found she had frequent dreams. Sometimes, half-awake, waiting for the siren to go off, she would have a nightmare that was so real, she was sure it was actually happening.

One night, after the news of the Leyte landings, she had a dream that was like a vision, with colors so intense and feelings so real it felt as if it were coming to her from some mysterious place outside herself. In the dream, she stood overlooking a field of golden-yellow wheat. The wheat was undulating like waves in the ocean, blending with a burst of light from a sunrise horizon. She saw a form draped in purple, lying slightly suspended over the stalks of wheat in the middle of the field. She was drawn in by the scene—the peaceful body, its folded hands, its youthful blond head. Suddenly she screamed, "Jerry!" There was no doubt it was Jerry, lying motionless in the field. "Jerry!" she called out again, but he did not move. "He's dead!" she cried, waking herself, her heart jolting so hard she could scarcely breathe.

"Mom!" she yelled, sitting up and throwing herself onto her feet.

Mila, who slept lightly, was up in an instant and beside her daughter, who had slumped back onto her bed and was shaking uncontrollably. "Tell me, Elena! A bad dream? What's the matter?"

Awakened by Elena's cry, Carl got up on his elbows. He and Mila listened while Elena related the dream. Between sobs, she described the scene. "I know he's dead," she said. Suddenly, her voice was steady. "I know he's dead," she repeated. In the dim light of the window, her face glowed white.

"Shh," Mila soothed. "It's just a dream, *querida*. Just a dream."

Elena shook her head. "No, no, it's not just a dream."

"All right, all right," Mila said, "we can talk more about it in the morning. Let me get you some water."

"I don't want water," Elena said. "I don't want anything. I just want you to believe me."

"I believe you," her mother said, pushing Elena's head gently back onto the pillow. She brought the sheet up over her daughter's huddled form, and then returned to her bed, shaking her head. Carl reached over and held her hand. "Don't worry. She'll be all right," he said.

Mila cleared her throat and sighed. They lay in the dark, listening to Elena's sobs from the bed against the far wall of their room.

"How are we going to get through this war?" Mila whispered.

Carl hesitated, "We'll make it."

The next morning Mila suggested they visit Ben's to see how the rest of the family was doing. "Come with us, Elena. You need a change of scene."

It was just a short walk to Ben and Magdalena's house. Carl walked ahead of the two women to offer some protection against the confusion on the street—people hurrying to the market for the first time in days, Japanese trucks and soldiers trafficking back and forth. Some of the poor raked through garbage piles with their fingers.

The visit at Ben and Magdalena's did not go well. After she returned home, Elena wrote in her diary, *"I've never seen such a mess—Aunt Constancia and Aunt Neva aren't speaking. Earlier this week they got into a terrible fight and started hitting each other with a couple of high-heeled shoes. Belana got in the middle of them and got whacked a couple of times! What a disgrace. The entire clan over there is having clashes. All we are going through is so nerve-wracking that everyone gets on everyone else's nerves. Tensions are building here, too, but we're trying hard not to let them get to us. I, personally, barely made it today without breaking into tears. The dream I had last night is having a heavy effect on me,"* she concluded.

Later that evening, a lone B-24 flew over the city. Japanese search-lights tracked it over the skies until they had it flying into its bright beams. The big, silver four-engine bomber was flooded with light. It flew smoothly over the ack-ack that exploded around it. The Japanese fired anti-aircraft weapons called "flying onions" at the giant bombers. But the aircraft flew too high for the shells to touch it. It droned over the city, serenely, and with a confidence that said the skies belonged to it. It seemed to have no other mission.

When Elena put her diary away for the night, the last sentence she entered was, *"A terrible day ended with a beautiful sight."*

Though she was tired, she found she couldn't settle down and go to sleep. She prayed the rosary, but her words were rote; her thoughts kept pulling her attention away from the beads. The dream she had had about Jerry kept coming back. She found herself envisioning every detail. Something about the symbolism kept nagging her. The waves of wheat, she said to herself, why? Then as if a bright light had suddenly shone in her brain, she knew. "Madame Rahbi!" she cried out. "She told me about the sea—'someone will drown!' she predicted. The waves of wheat must be the ocean!" But how could Jerry be on the ocean? she wondered. She had heard that the Japanese had been taking POWs to Japan. Could that be it? Was Jerry one of them? She could only wonder.

Activites in the underground had become very covert. Under martial law everything was more suspect than it had ever been. Even news from Santo Tomás was difficult to get. Only the grapevine, with its active rumor mill, carried bits of information that were reliable. Dan would often hear rumors circulating in the market. When he told the family what he had heard, they matched the information with whatever else others had heard, stripping all the exaggerations from what seemed to be the kernels of truth. The rule of thumb became, "If you hear a rumor at least three times, there must be something to it."

The fact that prisoners in Santo Tomás were starving became known through individuals who visited the gate, asking for visitor's passes knowing none were available, just to get a quick look at some of the internees who wandered the grounds. "The internees are living on thin gruel. No food is reaching them from the outside. They are starving!" reports cried out and became grist for the rumor mill.

The Kellers found out from Ben, who had gone to the camp to see if he could get some food to Luisa, that the internees he saw through the gate were emaciated. He persisted with questions to the guards about his sister's well-being, until one of the officers was summoned. The officer looked over a long list, raised his eyes and said, "She and her family are not on the list of deceased."

The news so depressed the family that when they got together they expressed concern about it. "The Americans better hurry," Ben told everyone. "Starvation is going to wipe out everyone in the camp. There's not much food on the outside either. Food on reserve won't last much longer."

The first week of November brought an emergency to the Kellers'. They were running out of feed for the ducks, chickens and pigeons. A decision was made to eat the fowl that were not producing. Ducks and chickens that were growing old were to be eaten first.

Two days later, a pot of chicken stew appeared on the table. Everyone knew the fowl had not come from the market. They hadn't had chicken in months. Slowly the pot went from plate to plate. Dan put a small spoonful on his dish and stared down at it. Tim did likewise. When it came to Elena's turn, she turned her head. "No thank you. I'll have some rice."

No one said anything. Carl and Tino ate as usual. Mila kept glancing at her children, while she ate a small portion of the stew.

When the meal was over, Dan went down to the pens and sat with the birds. Tim joined him. "You know who that was, don't you?" Dan said. "Yeah, I know," his brother answered. "It was MacArthur. I guess we won't hear him crow anymore."

Tim went to his pig and stroked her. "You better keep eating scraps, Salome, old girl. We're not eating you!"

The pig grunted and nuzzled its wet nose into Tim's hand. Dan came over and hunkered down by his brother. "I feel sorry for Elena," he said. "Wobbles may be next on the list. She's not laying well anymore."

"Carl said we'd sell what we don't eat," Tim added. The two brothers got up and began their check of the pens before nightfall.

In the meantime, Elena dried the dishes with Vida in the kitchen. Mila carried in the last of the plates from the table. She stopped and looked at Elena. "I know it was hard tonight, but we have to face the reality that we can't afford to feed all our fowl. We have to have food for..."

Elena didn't let her finish. "I know. I know. But I don't have to eat what I don't want to eat!"

"No, you don't!" her mother raised her voice. "I just want you to understand."

"I understand." Her voice had a hard edge.

As Mila left the kitchen, she said, "I've talked to Carl about selling Wobbles."

Tears stung Elena's eyes. She didn't look up at Mila.

That same week Wobbles was bought by a friend of the Kellers, who came across town carrying a wicker basket. She took Wobbles and three old hens.

From the window of the bedroom, Elena saw her leave. The fowl squawked, as if they knew they were going to slaughter. Bitter tears clouded her view. In rage and frustration, she ripped the sheets off her bed and threw her pillows across the room. Then she sat on the floor and wept.

Moments later, there was a knock on the bedroom door. "Elena, open the door, please." It was Carl.

When she didn't respond, he called out more firmly. "I said, please open the door, Elena."

"Get away! I hate you!" Elena yelled.

Carl pushed open the door, strode in and grabbed his stepdaughter by the shoulders. "You stop that talk! You hear me? You're acting liked a spoiled kid!"

"Get away from me!" Elena struggled to free herself from his grip.

Carl shook her and flung her onto her mattress. "When you come back to your senses, I want to talk to you!" he cried, leaving the room and slamming the door behind him.

Elena spent the rest of the afternoon and evening in the bedroom. She did not come out for dinner. No one else tried to talk to her. By bedtime, when Carl and Mila came in to sleep, she had her face to the wall. Her eyes were open and dry now, the tears having stopped hours ago.

For the next two days, Elena spoke to no one except Debra and Rosie. She and Carl glared at each other across the table during meals, each expecting the other to thaw. Mila gave up on them and simply looked away when their eyes clashed. Elena recognized her stepfather's familiar squint, which revealed his stress over the conflict that had occurred in their relationship. Knowing this about Carl gave her a sense of satisfaction. At least he had some feeling about what happened, she told herself.

It was Dan who was finally able to talk to her. On the third day after the confrontation, Elena was working in the chicken pens. She scrubbed furiously at the crusted droppings that covered the wooden cubicles for the laying hens.

Dan, who had been feeding the fowl in silence, walked up to her and stood beside her. "Thanks for your help, Elena. I was going to get to cleaning those out."

Elena wiped her brow with the back of her hand and leveled her gray-green eyes at her brother. She said nothing.

"*Puñeta!*" he swore at her in Spanish. "I said, 'thanks for helping!'"

"I'm really doing it for myself," she said, without emotion.

His eyes softened. "I know how you feel," he said, "but you don't have to take it out on everyone."

Elena looked away.

"Come here," Dan motioned. "Look at this hen. She's so thin her breastbone feels like a knife. She shouldn't even be laying."

"I don't want to feel her," she said, turning her head away.

Dan thrust the hen into her arms. "Yes, I want you to see for yourself..."

The hen fluttered in Elena's arms as she cupped her hands under the sharp breastbone. The hen settled down and Elena stroked its soft down, feeling the warmth penetrating her hand. Poor thing, she thought. And when she looked up, her eyes were filled with tears.

She returned the hen to Dan, and they both stood in silence for a few moments, then he said, "This hen will be dead soon if she is fed as little as she has been. I really feel criminal taking her eggs to sell at the market. Wobbles would have had the same fate. Did you want that?"

Dan held Elena in an unswerving stare. He continued, "Carl gave you the best choice—selling Wobbles. We didn't have to eat her."

Anger faded from her voice, Elena said, "Thanks, Dan."

What Elena did not know was the extent to which Carl regretted his behavior. He hadn't meant to be so hard on her. Sensing he had hurt her deeply, he suffered remorse; although at the same time, he didn't fully recognize the depth of his emotions. Shortly, he rationalized, the discomfort he felt would lift; then he and his stepdaughter could put the unpleasant incident behind them and get on with their normal relationship.

Several days passed and he found he gained no relief from the oppressive feelings. It was then he realized that the mere passage of time would neither erase his reaction nor improve their relationship.

Two images preyed on his thoughts: The first was of the white-feathered Wobbles, her wings flapping wildly, her red crest flaming, and her marble blue eyes stunned by fear as she struggled frantically to avoid being imprisoned in the basket. The second image was of Elena's green-gray eyes flooded by tears, her sobs caught in great heaves. Angry words resounded in his ears. I hate you! I hate you! I hate you!

One more day passed before something happened to make Carl finally take action. As he went on his customary evening walk, the same uncomfortable weight of guilt and sadness plagued him. Twice around the property, and still the tightness in his chest persisted, the knotted ball of emotion would not soften. He had hurt someone he loved, and he had lost something very valuable in his life—Elena's trust.

Black clouds bellied low. A scurrying breeze quivered in the mango tree, stirring the scent of promised fruit. A crescent moon cut through the inky sky. He stared up at it, allowing his mind to drift. Memory took over and he fell back in time to the winter of his seventh year.

He was drawn back to a snowy afternoon. It was as clear in his mind as if he were experiencing it for the first time: Star-shaped flakes laced the fir trees on the woody path to his country home in Switzerland. Shoulders of snow dwarfed alpine fences, like white giants surrounding him. Powdery flakes fell from mutable clouds, obscuring the dirt path, dusting his boots as he hurried, turning the air a milky blue, so sharp it stung his nostrils with each breath he took.

He tightened his hold on his book strap and ducked his nose into the warmth of the red scarf that snaked around his neck. As he broke into a steady run, he was surprised by a flashing movement in the snow. He narrowed his eyes and saw a ball of grey-white fur flurrying by, its round contour heightened by two floppy ears. Carl squealed, "A rabbit, a rabbit!"

It was a very young rabbit that had strayed from its burrow. Carl took off after it, each step more gleeful, as he tried to close the gap between them.

Taking off his green woolen coat as he ran, Carl held the garment in front of him. The gap between himself and the rabbit began to widen. His breath shortened. I must catch him! he told himself. Then the rolling ball of fur suddenly froze. His coat flopping in front of him, Carl rushed forward for the catch. He dove on the small form and entrapped it in the folds of his coat.

Terrified, the rabbit stiffened. Carl's eyes widened. Had he smothered it? For seconds he stood there, holding the inert prize in his coat. There was no sound, except for his own breathing. Snowflakes whirled, peppering the tiny bundle as he drew it closer to him. He rolled his eyes skyward in supplication—Please don't be dead! Snow wet his lashes.

With suspended breath, Carl worked worried fingers into the folds of the coat. He reached a trembling foot, felt the small sharp claws, then moved up to the furry belly and the warm chest. Pressing his fingers against the quick trigger of the animal's heartbeat, Carl's own pulse tripped with excitement.

He dared to peek through the opening he had made into the folds and stared wide-eyed at the rabbit's shivering form—the tiny grey-white hairs riffling in quick tremors, and the wonderful whiskered face with its accusing glassy blue-black eyes.

Carl's own heart thumped so hard he felt he might lose his grip on his prize. Firing his echo into the white woods, he yelled, "You are alive! You're mine!" At last he had a pet, an animal of his own to care for, something his parents had forbidden him because they considered it both impractical and unimportant.

His boots left hopping holes in the snow as he plowed his way home, clutching the treasured bundle. When he entered the back porch and removed his boots, cap and scarf, the delicious aroma of brewing stew reached his nostrils. He took a deep breath, and without calling out a customary hello, ran up the wide staircase to his room, taking two steps at a time.

Knowing the dinner bell would sound at any time, Carl shuffled in his closet for an empty box. Finding none, he quickly made a bed of his coat in a corner of the closet and gently placed the rabbit into its warm nest. "Stay here," he ordered, "and don't make a single sound."

Grinning through his gaping front gums, he leaned down low and gave the rabbit a squeeze. "I will call you 'Wagner,' bunny," he addressed a glassy eye, "because you are as quiet as Wagner is noisy," he said, recalling the favorite composer his parents played tirelessly on their gramophone.

At dinner, Carl sat and stared with a detachment that caught his father's attention. "Nothing to say this evening, son?" the grey-garbed figure asked.

Carl shook his auburn head, took a bite of stew and chewed it slowly and deliberately.

"How did you perform in school?"

"Good, Pa," Carl answered in Swiss-German. He was relieved when his two older brothers took over the conversation, informing their father of progress on a sled they were building.

As his brothers held their parents' attention, Carl sneaked bread onto his lap and stuffed it in his trouser pocket. He excused himself from the table as soon as the meal was over, raced to his room and stumbled into the closet.

Pulling the chain on the light bulb, his eyes adjusted as the circle of light revealed the rabbit, still huddled in the bed of his coat. Carl broke into a smile. "Ah, Wagner, you will love this!" he breathed as he dropped the crumbs next to the rodent's nose. Wagner sniffed, then furtively began to nibble.

That night the boy and his rabbit slept together. Carl's face was so close to the furry animal that his nose tickled and he sneezed loudly. "I have to hold you very close, Wagner, so you won't leave me," he said as he wrapped a corner end of the sheet around the rabbit, securing him like a mummy. Wagner stiffened and flattened his ears.

Within minutes, Carl's breathing eased into sleep. His fingers loosened their clutch on the captive Wagner. Having had enough of the stifling bed, Wagner quietly wiggled his way out of the sheet, hopped off the bed, pushed past the cracked door and began to wander soundlessly around the house, leaving tiny pellets as he went.

Carl searched for the rabbit the moment he awakened. "Wagner!" he cried, "where are you!"

He looked under the sheets, under the bed, in the closet. "You're gone!" he wailed.

Hearing the call for breakfast, he was forced to abandon his search. Mournfully, he descended the stairs to the dining room, where the Keller family sat in silence, spooning steaming porridge.

The set faces of his father and mother verified Carl's worst fears. He looked at his brothers; they looked away. Yes, they all knew about

Wagner. "Carl," the senior Keller said over his bifocals, lowering his magnified eyes on the boy. Carl could feel the weight of those eyes. He's got my Wagner. I know he has, he told himself, trembling at the thought. "Where is he, Pa?" he cried.

Through tightly pressed lips, his father said, "You are interrupting." Then, "He's in the kitchen."

Carl sobbed. "You haven't killed him for stew, have you? You haven't, have you, Pa?"

There was silence as his parents suspended their verdict. It was still snowing. Flakes drifted like minutes through the window pane. A milky line of fire was barely visible. Carl's father finally responded. "You may not keep the rabbit. He is a wild animal, a rodent. He is not a pet." The judgment was rendered with all but a gavel.

Carl shot a look at his mother, but her eyes offered no sympathy. "But you haven't killed him?" Carl asked again, knowing the family's fondness for rabbit stew.

"No," his father answered.

In one last attempt, Carl pleaded, "Oh, please, let me keep him awhile. Just for today!"

The chair creaked ominously as his father pushed away from the table. "No. I have explained why. Come."

Low and urgent, his mother's voice broke forth. "Do as your father tells you, son."

Together, the three of them walked into the large square kitchen. Carl's brothers waited at the door. The wood stove blazed as the cook stoked it. Carl spotted an open cardboard box by the sink. "Wagner," he cried, reaching his hands into the box to where Wagner cowered in a corner.

"Pick him up, Carl," his father ordered.

"No!" shrieked Carl, suddenly dissolving into tears again. "I found him! He's mine!"

His father's voice boomed above him. "Do as I say!"

His face red with rage, Carl held his breath and reached for the furry animal, grabbed it and clutched it to his chest. As the boy stumbled to the open door of the back porch, his father's tall form blurred through his tears.

Carl buried his face into the warm fur once more, and then let Wagner go. Instantly, the rabbit streaked down the path and was swallowed by whiteness.

Carl felt himself dissolving into the snowy void. He strained his eyes through the whirling blanket of flakes for one last glimpse of Wagner and was met by emptiness.

"Come back in the house, son." His father's voice brought Carl back.

The rage returned. Lowering his head, he raced up the stairs to his room. As he ran, he sputtered, "I...I...hate you...hate you...hate you!"

Now years later, as the childhood memory faded, those words still jarred in Carl's ears. Raindrops splattered on his head and shoulders, bringing him back to the present. The crescent moon was gone. Through the rain, he walked back to the house.

A few moments later, he knocked on Elena's door.

"Who is it?"

"It's Carl, Elena. I want to talk to you."

The door opened. Elena stood in a blue cotton robe, her hand on the bronze doorknob, her face reproachful.

Carl cleared his throat. "About Wobbles," he began. Tiny droplets of rain beaded on his forehead and shone in his auburn hair. His eyes were heavy with sadness.

"Elena," he continued, laying his hand lightly on her shoulder, "I'm sorry about Wobbles."

Elena looked away, but she allowed his hand to rest on her shoulder. Then she turned, faced him squarely and met the emotion in his eyes.

Carl ducked his head slightly. "I really am sorry," he said.

She nodded in tacit acknowledgement. Her look had softened.

With clear relief showing, he nodded back. Then he pressed her shoulder, turned heavily and left her staring thoughtfully after him.

Only a dull ache remained when she climbed into bed. For Carl, remorse followed him into sleep. Unsettling childhood memories plagued his dreams. He called out in his sleep, waking Mila. When she asked him what was troubling him, he turned over and grunted. Somehow by morning, he had worked through some of his feelings and was able to tell himself to put the experience in the past.

At breakfast Carl sat down at the head of the table. He glanced at Elena. She looked up and gave a small smile.

By Christmas, 1944, the Kellers had eaten or sold all but half a dozen hens, two laying ducks, a few pigeons and one turkey hen. Salome had also been spared.

On Christmas Day, Sofía had a quiet visit with Mila, Carl, Tino and the family. She brought some ripe mangos to lay on the Christmas table to complement a dinner that consisted of the usual—rice and mongo beans. "Do you remember the delicious *lechón* we had years ago when you married Carl, Mila?" Sofía said, reminiscing about her daughter's wedding celebration.

Remembering the festivites and the rich roast pork dinner, Mila nodded. Suddenly, Dan laughed. "I remember not eating it because I was afraid the pig's head might come alive and get up off the plate and eat me!" he said.

They all looked amused. "Please pass the mongo, Mom," Dan said, eyeing the large bowl of warm beans.

Mila passed the mongo, which she and Vida had laced with pieces of chicken and tomatoes. "Surprise, this mongo is special today!" she announced. "Enjoy it. We're down to the last sack of mongo, and about a sack and a-half of rice left."

Dan helped himself to two large spoonfuls, hesitated, and then put half the portion back into the bowl, letting the greenish purée fall from the wooden spoon.

From the head of the table, Carl asked, "How are things at Ben's?"

Sofía sighed, "Just about the same as here, only they are quarreling a lot more about little things that grow into big arguments."

Carl shook his head. "I hate to think about this damned war lasting much longer," he said. "We have a small case of corned beef we buried three years ago, for an emergency, and God knows whether the cans are still good."

Tim looked up from his plate. With a mouthful of food, he said, "Some people are eating dogs and cats, did you know? How would you like to eat..."

Elena didn't let him finish, "Don't make us sick, Tim!" she cried. "It's enough to have to eat mongo for Christmas," she said, wiping her mouth and turning over the corner of the napkin that bore traces of orange lipstick, a gift given to her for Christmas—a treasure in a city that sold bare necessities in its dwindling stores, and often not even those kinds of items. Elena now had two lipsticks.

Tino cleared his throat. Shifting Rosie on his lap, he tried to make a joke, "Hey, at least the mongo is green and red, for Christmas," he teased.

Dale shook her head, and Debra peered into her plate. "Red?" she said, twisting her small mouth in a grimace.

"Sure!" Her father laughed, deeper now, "See those pieces of tomato—they're red."

"Daddy!" she exclaimed and rolled her dark eyes at him.

Laughter broke the tension, and the family ate and talked, mostly about pre-war times when gatherings were not clouded by the storm of war, when food was plentiful and nerves were calmer, when the threat of death and starvation was not hovering at their door. Who could have ever told them that the green pellet of the mongo bean and the white grain of rice would become symbols of survival?

However, as deprived as they were by a lack of food, they were not poor of spirit. The family, as a whole, remained bound together in a unity that sprang from the deep-rooted efforts of Sofía and Lorencio Fernandez to create a life together in the Philippines.

Sofía felt she had lived a good part of her life; and with a forthrightness that shocked them, made a comment as they finished their dinner, "Listen, when the Americans land and move in to fight for Manila, I want you to know it's important to save the young ones first. I have lived my life. The young have to carry on. I am getting old, and I don't want you to worry about me."

Tino responded harshly. "Quiet, Mamá! *¿Qué te pasa?* You'll survive, along with the rest of us!"

Her eyes dimmed by cataracts, she squinted. "Tino, I am serious. I'll

probably die from a bullet wound, from concussion, or when fear over-
comes me. I cannot stand these explosions. When the bombs get too
close, all I want to do is run."

They let her talk, outwardly brushing aside her comments. Inwardly,
they worried about her. She had gotten thinner each year of the war, and
was now slightly hunched over. Having survived the Spanish-American
war in the Philippines, her life had been one dramatic incident of survival
after another—ten childbirths, two infants lost; diseases—influenza,
cholera, malaria. Then the death of her husband and the burden of having
to raise seven children by herself. Now another war...

"Why don't you stay overnight, Mamá," Mila said. "It will give you
a change from the confusion at Ben's. That way, you won't have to rush
home before blackout."

Sofía gave everyone at the table a cursory glance. No one spoke,
waiting for her response. "*Gracias*. I'll stay," she said.

Until it was too dark to see, they played cards and visited. A quiet,
brought by the hush of the blackout, settled over the living room. Shortly
afterwards Sofía and Elena said goodnight and went to bed. Sofía slept on
a cot in the master bedroom, shared by Carl, Mila and Elena.

Carl and Mila followed later. Pulling a sleeveless nightgown over her
head, Mila got into bed beside Carl. "Did you ever imagine we'd spend
such a strange Christmas?" she said, moving closer to him and rubbing
her feet against his legs. "It beats anything I'd ever imagined we would
do."

"Incredible," was all he said, moving closer to her. She smoothed back
his wavy hair. It felt soft and thick. "Sometimes I get so frightened," she
whispered. "Thank God for you. I love you."

Carl made a sound that rumbled up from his chest and resembled a
subdued groan. "And you. Thank God, there's you. How I love you..."
he said softly, pressing his body to hers.

"Shh," Mila warned, "Elena may still be awake; Mamá, too."

Carl got up on his elbow. "I'll sacrifice many things, but not this," he
growled. His lips found hers; he gave her a warm and lingering kiss. Then
he said huskily, "Let's go into the garden."

With her hand on his broad chest, she braced herself up to sitting
position. "That's ridiculous, Carl," she said. "Where in the garden?"

"The shelter," he chuckled softly. "Why not?"

Mila couldn't help responding with a hushed laugh. She fingered the
curly hair on his chest for a moment, then said, "Yes...let's go."

As they closed the door of the bedroom, they heard Sofía's soft snore.
Light rain fell. The sky was starless. Their light-clad forms flitted over the
lawn and into the dark opening of the shelter. They ducked in, carefully
avoiding the rafters. On the coffin-like floor, they spread the emergency
blankets. Slowly, as if they were on a luxurious bed, they removed their
nightclothes and lay naked. Pushing against Carl's muscular body, Mila

lay back, her senses open to the surgings of their love. They floated together in the earth-scented darkness.

In semi-sleep, they lay until dawn, their naked bodies renewed by the mystical energy of love. Totally relaxed, they scarcely stirred when a rooster crowed nearby. The light rain had ceased, and the early morning sky, pink with dawn, retained a few large, slow-setting stars.

"Let's stay out awhile," Carl said. The world seemed to be totally theirs in those few moments when the trees turn green at sunrise; when the dew on the grass sparkles, each drop a separate globe—a small universe.

The magic was broken by a loud, invasive cry from the Japanese soldiers, who were lined up behind the wall of the military compound, launching into their early morning exercises.

Later that day, Mila and Elena put away the few Christmas decorations, including a crèche that Elena had received as a gift on her twelfth Christmas. Handpainted in Belgium, the figures of the holy family were made of delicate bisque, each one hollow and almost weightless. Using old yellowed sheets of tissue paper, the two women carefully wrapped each figure and placed it into a lightweight wooden storage box.

The form of the infant Jesus fascinated Elena. She turned it over several times and finally let it rest in the cup of her palm. The baby Jesus, she thought, how fragile you look, yet how mighty they say you grew to be! Faith. How could one prove faith? How could one believe in a deity one had only experienced through religious conviction? Yes, personal prayer had brought answers, she could never deny that; but would God always come through? Would he save her and her family from death just because she prayed? The dilemma made her head spin. Still, she lowered her face to the tiny clay form and brushed her lips against it.

Mila had put away the last of the nativity set and stood gazing at her daughter. How wistful she looks, she thought—her face thinner and lacking in color, her eyes with such a deep, far-away look. She said nothing as she moved away from the table on which they were working, leaving her daughter to drift on her own thoughts. Moments later, Elena looked up and realized she was alone.

On January 9, 1945, American forces landed in Lingayen. Ironically, this was the same location where the Japanese had landed on Luzon three years before. Strategically, the landing on the gulf put U.S. forces within one hundred and fifty miles of Manila.

That same day, Mila and Vida arose at dawn and went into the garden with two buckets. They stooped over periodically and picked up large tortoise-shelled snails that had invaded the garden, leaving long silver trails from slimy, yellow-brown bodies. The snails were vociferous. They consumed the vegetables and stripped the banana leaves.

The family had been fighting the snail invasion for weeks, dousing them with salt, smashing them with shovels. Still they proliferated, eating up the garden as fast as they were exterminated. Then one morning, Mila, had what she thought was a brilliant idea: Eat them! Why not? The French ate snails all the time. True, this variety was tough, but that would prove to be a small obstacle if her plan worked out.

Now, in secret, she and Vida were actually picking them out of the dewy grass. Secretly, before the family got up, they collected two full pails. Mila whispered to Vida as the last of the snails was dropped into the pails, "We'll soak them in salt for two days; then we will boil them."

Hidden in the dark pantry, the snails soaked in brine for forty-eight hours. The buckets were covered with pieces of burlap and placed in a corner behind the precious sacks of rice and mongo beans.

On the third day, they were boiled until they were soft as mushrooms. Shiny tortoise shells were pulled away and thrown into the garbage. Mila and Vida worked rapidly, making up a tasty sauce of tomatoes and onions picked from the garden. They mixed the sauce with the cooked snails, which they had sliced into small strips. Admiring their concoction, the two women stood back and smiled at each other. "They look like black mushrooms," Vida said, stirring the pots, and offering Mila a spoon. "It is time to taste it!" she announced.

"They will never know the difference," Mila said, over a small mouthful.

At that moment, Tim came into the kitchen. "Know the difference about what?" he asked. He peered into the pots of the thick stew.

Mila leveled her eyes at him and lied. Vida looked away. "...the difference between these black mushrooms and the ones we usually buy," she said.

Tim looked into one of the pots again. "Strange. But we haven't eaten mushrooms for so long, I don't remember what they tasted like. These look awfully black to me!"

When his mother said no more, he added, "Sure they aren't cooked lizards, Mom?"

"Do you think I'd feed you cooked lizards?" Mila said, averting her eyes slightly.

"You might!" Tim answered, laughing as he left the kitchen. "Would you tell me?" He didn't wait for a response.

"¡Ay!" Vida cried. "I feel bad..."

Mila wiped her hands on her apron. "I know. I wonder if we shouldn't tell them..." she said in a low voice. Then she added, "No. You and I have eaten some. They haven't poisoned us, and they taste good. Besides, we have gotten rid of some of the snails."

And so the snail stew was presented that night. "Mushrooms cooked in tomato and onion sauce, served over rice," Mila proclaimed as the platters were passed around. Plates were heaped quickly. "Hmm, mushrooms, eh?" Carl mused. "Not bad. Where did you get them?"

"Ahh..." Mila started to respond, but was cut off by Tim. "From the market," he volunteered. "I saw them being cooked this morning. A new kind of mushroom."

Does he know? Mila asked herself, avoiding her son's artless brown eyes.

"A little chewy, but they're good," Tino commented. "I'll have some more."

Everyone ate until the platters were clean. When they cleared the table, Mila had a knot as hard as a fist in her stomach. She walked to the kitchen to get a glass of water. Tim followed her and went down the stairs to the garbage can. He returned, holding three shells. Saying nothing, he held them in front of his mother. "You shouldn't have lied, Mom," he told her.

The accusation brought stinging tears to Mila's eyes. First she turned her head away from him, then she looked back at him with a look of sorrow. "I lied. I'm sorry, but I thought I was doing something positive, and I knew you wouldn't eat the snails if you knew what they were."

Tim shook his head. "I knew what they were, Mom, and I ate them."

Mila's hands were shaking when she reached for Tim and put her arms around him. He hugged her back, his cheek against her forehead.

Neither of them had heard the rest of the family come in quietly behind them. When Mila and Tim looked up, they were all there. Carl stepped in. "We heard, dear. It's all right," he said, touching his wife's shoulder. Mila stood in place. "Come on. It's O.K.," he repeated. Then Tino stepped in and said, "Hey, Mila, why don't we set up a stall in the market and sell those damn things? Look, we've all survived. You didn't poison us!"

That broke the ice. "Say, Dan," Tim broke in, "let's make a business of it! We can call them special black mushrooms. Mom can be our manager."

"Don't tease her," Elena put her arm around her mother.

"What do you mean?" Tim questioned. "Don't tease her? She deserves what she's getting!"

When Vida poked her head around the door from the pantry, where she had been hiding, Tim said, "You, too, Vida, you are a fellow conspirator!"

By that time, tensions were relieved, and Vida was able to roll her eyes and shirk her shoulders in a gesture of innocence.

Before the family went to bed that night, the air raid sirens wailed. Sixteen B-24's droned overhead. Moments later, bombs shook the city, as the planes hit military targets. Japanese anti-aircraft cracked around the bombers, dotting the sky with furious puffs. "Something white is falling," Dan, who was sitting at the entrance of the shelter, shouted. He ran into the yard, the rest of the family behind him. "It's a parachute!" Tino cried.

"Parachute, parachute," Debra chorused, as they rushed to the other end of the garden where they could see it better. Their Chinese-Filipino neighbors, Lee and Rosario Chew and their baby daughter, Trina, joined them by the fence.

"Yes, I see it!" Lee Chew said, pointing to the parachute as it glided down slowly, a dark miniature figure hanging from strings that were not visible.

"Poor bastard," said Tino. "He'll get shot, if he doesn't fall in the bay and drown first."

Lee Chew shook his head. His wife held the baby close. "Let's all go back into the shelter," Mila said. "The raid isn't over."

The next morning they heard that the pilot of a downed B-24 was gunned down by the Japanese before his parachute landed by the Rizal monument off Dewey Boulevard.

Elena's diary spoke of the incident. *"It's the first casualty like that we've ever seen. Though I never knew his name or saw his face, for me, the man who died is a hero. With the Americans so close to the north of us, we will be getting more and more raids."*

A few days later, Elena wrote: *"January 16, 1945: The Japanese local radio announced today that U.S. paratroops landed in Malolos, Bulacan Province! Bulacan is where Carmen Cruz and Ramón are still supposed to be hiding. I wish I could know what is happening to them.*

"Other U.S. landings were made in the Zambales coastal area of Luzon. The U.S. Army, advancing from a forty-five mile bridgehead in Lingayen, is now past the Agno River. That makes them as close as Tarlac, sixty some miles away! If they keep pushing along like that, they'll soon be here.

"They'd better hurry. We are beginning to use up the last of our food supply. We can't buy anything because Carl stopped working about two weeks ago when the insurance business closed for the duration of the emergency. The last item we got with his final paycheck was five kilos of carabao meat for 1,600 inflated pesos. It was a real treat, as we hadn't had meat available in the markets for ages. We set aside two of the five kilos, and dried and salted them for later.

"Our resources are drying up," Elena continued. *"Mom sold the two diamonds she had from a family necklace that belonged to her Spanish great-grandmother. With the money she bought two new blankets for the shelter and items we needed for our first aid kit.*

"I am feeling numb. I can't keep up with what is going on. It's just too much, and I run out of feelings. The shrapnel that flies around us during the raids could hit me, and I don't believe I'd feel it too much! Maybe that's how soldiers feel in battle, as if everything is unreal—numb.

"I want so bad for it to be over. My sense of fear has been dulled by being over-used. I have feared everything, to the extent that I now fear nothing! That's not possible. Perhaps I'm actually so afraid that I'm afraid to be afraid. Crazy!

"Another reaction I have is a feeling of being outside myself—a feeling I remember having as a little kid. It's as if I were floating above myself and experiencing everything from afar, as if it were happening to someone else.

"One thing that keeps me going is I am needed by my family. Uncle Tino asked me to tell Debra a story last night because she couldn't get to sleep. After I got through, she cuddled up to me and said, 'Please don't leave until I am asleep, O.K.?'

"I sat with her until I could hear her breathing deeply. My mind drifted, and I thought about the days ahead. When will the battle for the city begin? Will we have enough food to survive? Will Trish, my Dad, Aunt Luisa and family make it? Jerry? The same feeling keeps coming back about him."

Despite the lassitude she felt, Elena forced herself to write in her diary. On January 24, sitting by a coconut oil lamp in the kitchen, she wrote: *"The U.S. Army is as far as Capas, Tarlac. They seem to be making their way down the highway to Manila, just forty-five miles from us.*

"The Japs are putting tank barricades all over the city. They are building one just meters from our gate. It looks like this." A diagram followed, showing thick cement blocks embedded in the street. They looked like tombstones leaning against a protective barricade fence made of heavy wood and steel beams that added extra support from behind. Between the barricades there was barely enough room for a pedestrian to pass.

Elena concluded the entry, *"I saved a bit of rice for the two baby turkeys that are only a few days old. How can they ever make it? We don't have enough food to even feed the mother."*

Starving and unstrung by fear, Manila waited for the attack.

Chapter Thirteen

Hellship

Rice. South from Batangas, north to the rice terraces, Luzon's fields prospered under monsoon and sun. It was the same on all the islands. Rice meant food. It was also the fuel that energized the Japanese military. As the ring of American might closed in and began to retake the Philippines, cargo ships by the score left the Port Area docks in Manila bound for Japan and other fronts.

Even Filipinos who had had an ear for the Greater East Asia Co-Prosperity Sphere doctrine were enraged to watch the precious grain stolen under their helpless eyes.

American POWs provided much of the labor unloading trucks of rice onto cargo ships. It was bitter gall for starving men. They came from camps around Manila for grueling work on the docks. One of these POW camps was Bilibid Prison, a clearing house for prisoners being transferred to and from camps on Luzon and other islands. It was also the place where they were cleared to be shipped to Japan.

Ironically, the old prison, built at the turn of the century by American occupying forces, Bilibid was considered more humane. Some of the men got to remain there several months. Often they were attached to small work details in and around Manila at military posts, on the Pasig River, and on the Port Area docks. The labor was always heavy; the hours always long.

When Jerry left the brutal environment of Cabanatuan Prison, he was transferred to Bilibid. It was a relief to be assigned to remain at the prison on a small work crew that was sent out into the city, even though he knew it was temporary, for the grapevine, which generally bore authentic news, had it that his crew would eventually be shipped to Japan or Formosa, as had hundreds of POWs in the last year-and-a-half.

In September, 1944, after the first bombs hit Manila, movement of POWs from Bilibid was delayed because the docks at the Port Area had been damaged.

One evening during the first week in October, Jerry sat with his friend Charlie Sullivan, a young soldier from Ohio. Rusty-haired Charlie had a faceful of freckles and a sense of humor Jerry enjoyed. The two men were able to distract each other from the drudgery and depression of prison life.

Jerry felt like a big brother to Charlie. Often, the redhead's temper would get the better of him, particularly when he became frustrated on a work detail, as he had a month earlier while prying up boards in a warehouse. Losing his patience, he had forced a board up and it had snapped in two, striking the soft flesh of his inner left calf. Lacerated to the bone, it was a fertile place for infection to thrive. A small amount of sulfathiazole that had been doled to him by the medics from a Red Cross shipment had recently run out. The wound had become so ulcerated that Charlie could not touch it without wincing.

The two men finished an evening meal consisting of a scant cupful of soupy rice, which had turned a pale shade of celery green from having been boiled with a few, now absent, vegetables. Jerry scraped the half coconut shell he used as a dinner plate. He licked his fingers. "Don't know how I get this putrid stuff down. I'm so hungry I could eat ten more bowls."

"Pretend it's steak—New York—juicy, with onions and mushroom gravy," Charlie teased.

"Shut up!" Jerry growled and gave him a friendly shove.

"And fluffy mashed potatoes!" Charlie laughed, rolling over on his right side, pretending he was hurt, but carefully protecting his sore leg.

His antics made Jerry break into a laugh. "Aw, come on!" He gave him another playful shove, and then his expression became serious. "How is the leg tonight?" Jerry's eyes turned flinty as he scrutinized his friend's swollen leg. The bandages were wet with rings of yellow discharge. "Better clean it up again tonight. Let me have a look."

Charlie untied the contaminated bandages. The infected crater was as big as a silver dollar. The flesh around the deep center was filled with pus. Discolored, the wound was a shade of bruised purple. Jerry caught a strong whiff of decaying flesh.

Both men stared at the injury. Then Charlie quickly rewound the bandages. "It doesn't look good," Jerry said, "I'll find you a new bandage."

The small area where they sat was between two buildings, one of which was the mess hall. One of the POW cooks shouted from the doorway of the mess hall. "K.P.!" Dozens of men, among them Jerry and Charlie, lined up and marched in to work on the clean-up crew.

At roll call that night, the two were summoned to prison headquarters and were told to pick up orders for departure. "Can you beat it?" Jerry was disgusted. "Just like that."

Limping beside him, Charlie shrugged as if he had expected it. They fell into another line and were given Japanese Army winter uniforms several sizes too small. The woolen pants and shirts were a sick shade of olive green. Jerry tried on the uniform while Charlie sat morosely on a dirty mattress on the floor. The trousers and shirt fit around his bony, 120-pound frame, but the arms and legs were six inches too short.

The shoes that were passed out didn't fit either. None of the POWs would be able to wear them unless they re-fashioned them into slip-ons or slippers. For now, Jerry and Charlie preferred to wear *clacks*, shoes they had cut or whittled out of wood. Like *bakias*, straps of leather or canvas were nailed onto the sides of the wooden soles.

The dormitory felt sultry and closed-in. Sweat ran from Jerry's forehead onto his face. The woolen collar of the uniform shirt itched unbearably. Still, he could not resist striking a pose—elbows jutting in the sized-down shirt, and bare feet turned outward. "Where's the organ grinder?" he grinned, his jaw jutting.

Charlie's leg was throbbing too badly for him to crack a smile. "Rats!" Jerry said, pulling off the heavy clothing and tossing it onto his mattress. Without saying more, he went to the latrine, picked up a square bar of hard coconut soap, scrubbed his hands under a single leaky faucet, and soaked a clean rag in a can he saved to doctor his friend's infected leg.

Two days later 1,800 American POWs boarded what they were told was a Japanese transport ship, which was ready to depart from Pier Seven in the Port Area. Jerry and Charlie were among them.

Bearing only numbers on its stack, the ship sailed out of Manila Bay, passed Corregidor's Rock, and went on to an undisclosed southern island, where they stopped to repaint new numbers on the stack, exchanging numbers with a transport accompanying them. There was no explanation given for this, and no visible indication that the transport was carrying prisoners of war. After the repainting, the ship returned to Manila, got provisions, and by the afternoon of October 20, was on its way northward.

If O'Donnell and Cabanatuan had been demonic holes, Jerry and Charlie experienced the tortures of the POW hellship from the moment they were herded, like so many slaves, into two airless holds large enough for only two hundred men. The two prisoners were pushed by bayonet-bearing guards into hold number one. They filed into the tiers like mummies and were so packed they had to stand, as did most of the other men. After several hours, the POWs traded turns standing so that others could sit or lie down. They were given neither food nor water for the first thirty-six hours.

When the ship sailed south on the second day, all the POWs in both of the sub-decks were given half a canteen of water plus a small meal of boiled rice at 9 a.m. and another at 4 p.m.

On the third day, men in both holds received a full canteen of water apiece, plus two scant meals of rice.

Up to ten or more POWs died daily from thirst, heat exhaustion and the effects of almost three years of malnutrition and disease—malaria, dysentery *beriberi*, pellagra... The decks of the hold were saturated with feces, urine and vomit.

Exhausted by the overwhelming heat, most of the men had stripped down and were either naked or wearing Japanese G-strings—long strips of muslin which they wrapped around the waist and up the groin.

Hour by hour, minute by minute, second by second, the ghostly confederation concentrated on staying alive. They focused their physical energy on the crisis of the moment—the need to eat, to drink, to relieve themselves, to sleep, and to reach out to fellow prisoners who were weaker than themselves. Their mental energy was focused on hope and the need for distraction. Inviting one another into the oases of personal memories, they told and retold their life stories; they shared their dreams, their successes, their losses. In detail, they described mothers, fathers, brothers, sisters, sweethearts and wives. Most of all, they focused on liberation, the day they would be free. In this way, they were able to bear being part of a human cargo in the bowels of the filthy ship.

When they finally left Manila on October 20, Jerry's spirits sank. Up to that point, he had not realized how much he had hoped he would remain on Luzon for the liberation. He was sure now he wouldn't see freedom in the Philippines. That dream was dead. Bound for what loomed in his mind as the edge of nowhere, he wouldn't be able to share the liberation with the Kellers—Elena—in the way he'd hoped.

In the 100-degree heat, fear shot icy splinters through his body. He began to shake. Lowering his head in his arms, he suppressed a sob. Someone behind him put a hand on his shoulder and held it there. It was Charlie.

On October 24, the POW ship was off Shoonan, two hundred miles off the coast of China, and still heading north. Just before the evening gruel, two American torpedoes hit the aft section of the transport, damaging the area where the Japanese were quartered. Prisoners in both holds felt the thundering impact of each hit. The ship shuddered, bolted, and momentarily stopped. No one in the holds was injured.

Two more hits followed, rocking the ship violently and mortally wounding her. The Japanese did not discharge the ship's guns. One of the American POW cooks who was working topside shouted, "It's a sub! It's a sub!" and the men below heard him.

Within minutes, the Japanese began to abandon the ship. They escaped in lifeboats after cutting the rope ladder leading into hold number one, and they dropped the booby hatch so there would be no escape for the men in that hold. POWs from the number two hold managed to push out their hatch and drop ropes to those trapped in the first hold. "Get the hell out!" they yelled to their comrades, lowering the ropes as fast as they could.

The men emerged from the hold like an army of blind rats. Stiff-limbed and blinded by the light, they put on life jackets. Gaining their strength, they began to lower dozens of wooden rafts and life buoys. Then as adrenalin charged them, they moved everything that would float—hatch boards, wooden spars, and miscellaneous pieces of wood.

The hellship started to sink, but it would take about four hours for it to fully submerge, first its stern, then its bow. As quickly as they could, Jerry and Charlie climbed on a wooden raft with two other POWs. They hit the waves on a moderately rough sea.

From afar, the POWs looked like specks on an oceanful of debris. Determined to stay close together to facilitate a rescue, they floated within a two-mile radius, and kept up their courage by yelling at one another.

When several Japanese seaplanes flew over and ignored them, their spirits sagged. Following that, the enemy destroyer that rescued the hellship's sailors started up and distanced itself. Hope died when a lifeboat of Japanese rowed after the destroyer, coming close enough to several of the rafts to make the POWs think they were being rescued.

Some of the prisoners dove into the water and swam for the lifeboat. As they approached, the officers and men stood up with swords drawn and jabbed at the POWs. Spurts of blood shot from wounds inflicted on the hands, arms, shoulders and heads of the Americans. A barrage of curses chorused from the hundreds of POWs who watched with horror as their bleeding comrades swam back to their rafts.

Spewing out his anger, Charlie yelled, "Bastards! God-damned yellow bastards!"

Too stunned to speak, Jerry clenched his jaw so hard his teeth ached. Then he jerked his head away to concentrate on paddling the raft with his hands. The other three joined him, and they paddled as if they were in a race, three of them using cupped hands, and one rowing with the only oar they had. They stayed within the two-mile radius, circling and recircling one another's floatation devices, expending their anger, and cheering as the hated hellship dipped slowly into the indigo blue shadows of sunset.

Jerry and Charlie's destinies were now linked to those of the two who shared the raft with them. The four men rocked on the rise and fall of the swells. Inky water frothed with flashes of latent sunset light on the paraphernalia floating around them. Voices joined in an eerie litany, ebbing and flowing like a prayer.

Overcome by pain from his gangrenous leg, Charlie fell into a feverish sleep. Jerry and the other two lay awake, clutching onto the boards of the raft, and linking arms and legs to form a human chain. Temperatures had dropped and they lay pressed together for warmth, grateful now for their woolen clothing.

Stars in the Milky Way chipped into the dome of night, sparking bright jewels on black velvet. Directly above, early stars glowed a soft lantern light.

"We're heading north to northwest," Jerry announced.
The man lying to his left asked, "You, Navy?"
"Naw. I was born on the Colorado range. Just know the stars."
"Beautiful, aren't they? What's your name, buddy?"
"Merrill. Jerry Merrill, radioman, pursuit squadron, Clark Field."
"Angelo Broncocelli, Newark, New Jersey. Infantry, Bataan."
"Broncocelli," Jerry nodded.
"Call me Bronco."
The third man had not spoken since they had scrambled onto the raft. He was so seasick he now lay with his head over the side and vomited.

As darkness coated over the long hours to midnight, Jerry and Bronco agreed to take turns keeping watch over the others. While one snatched a few hours of sleep, the other fought exhaustion to stay awake.

On the dawn of the second day, the sun broke on the waves and shot rosy spangles into the water. Jerry opened his eyes and looked over at Charlie. He was still asleep. Bronco lay on his back and stared at the sky. The fourth man was missing.

Jerry pointed to where the POW had lain. "What happened to...?"
Bronco lowered his eyes. "Don't know. Must have fallen in."
"My God! When?"
"Can't say. Somewhere along the watch. I must have dozed." Pain spoke through his voice.

Jerry coughed. He put his hand to his throat, now so dry and swollen from thirst he couldn't talk without struggling. "Damn!" he managed to husk through.

At that moment, Charlie roused, lifted his head and called out, "Water. Please! Water." His face was fiery red and his eyes so dazed by fever they looked as if they were made of glass.

Jerry reached over and pressed his shoulder. "Take it easy, Charlie. Stay down."

Strands of red hair whipped at Charlie's forehead. "Water!" he croaked.
"Sorry, Mac," Bronco said, "there's no water."

The day before, they had emptied the one canteen they were able to save. Before Charlie cried out again, they were distracted by a misshapen form sloshing by the side of the raft. Facing down, it turned out to be the bloated body of a POW. It was swollen like a grotesque balloon. They stared at it in silence as it passed by, awash on the fluctuating waves.

Throughout the second day, more bodies floated by, and the flotilla of survivors dwindled. There was not much yelling among the POWs now. Those who fought on to stay alive were mostly controlled by the will of the ocean; they were growing weaker and more listless with each hour that passed.

The sun became an enemy. Its merciless rays caused oozing blisters wherever flesh was exposed, and as noon dragged into afternoon, then evening, each man withdrew into inner caverns of his mind, preserving every bit of strength for whatever lay ahead. Without water, each knew he was doomed. How long they could go on depended on whether or not a miracle rescue came. They had learned to survive, and as survivors, the last thing they would give up was hope.

By the evening of the second day, Charlie's fever heightened. He became delirious. They had to hold his hands so he wouldn't tear at his gangrenous leg, putrefied to the point that both Jerry and Bronco covered their noses while they tied him more securely on the raft. All the while, Charlie screamed at them, cursing as if he were fighting his own executioners. Then he would sag back and drift on the seas of his own nightmares, before he wrestled his way up again, in a rage which defied the angriest waves pounding around them.

Just before midnight, they heard the death rattle. Charlie took several agonized breaths and died. Jerry passed his hand over his friend's pale forehead and caressed away strands of unruly hair. Then he pressed his face into Charlie's shoulder. "Thank God, Charlie. It's over," he said.

The two who remained unstrapped their comrade and tenderly rolled him into the sea. Though they bowed their heads, both felt too numb to pray. "Poor bastard," was all Bronco could say, as Charlie's body rode the swells, and was swept into a trough and sucked away.

"Sea's getting rough," Jerry mumbled. The swollen tip of his tongue had split. Every word cost him, sending flashes of searing pain into his mouth and throat.

Then, in what seemed like a miracle, a silver rain of pilot fish fell on and around the raft. The two men scrambled after the fish, slipping and sliding, tipping the raft as they tried to catch them. All but two wriggled free. Bronco had a death grip on these. He swallowed one and gave the other to Jerry. "Don't chew," he said. The fish felt cool in Jerry's parched mouth and he gulped hard to get its wriggling body down. He gagged twice, but was able to keep from vomiting.

For several hours, the small amount of nourishment and moisture had its effect. Acting like a narcotic, it relieved their hunger and thirst. They slept through until morning; then awoke, shielded themselves from the sun with their clothing and returned to sleep, losing all track of time.

Toward evening, Jerry awoke. His mouth and throat were fiercely dry again. He groaned. Concentrate on something, he told himself. Rolling over on his back, he stared at the stars pulsing out of a sky turned heliotrope in a majestic sunset. Suddenly, he felt integrated with the elements—the sky, the sea, the universe. The raft dipped up and down like a heartbeat. He listened to the refrain of the ocean, the thumping cadence of the waves, the whoosh of briny water pulsing under the raft boards, the susurrating wind—light as a flute, deep as a cello, certain as a drum.

As the night air chilled, the stars sharpened and seemed to gaze down at him, impervious as so many eyes. He stared back, but his vision played tricks. Silvery chips blurred, enlarging and recessing. Fascinated, he imagined his eyes were a telescope. He played with the shining images, losing himself as reality fused with fantasy. In and out of the silver haloes, faces appeared. He saw his mother's face. Her pale blue eyes studied him over gold-rimmed reading glasses. He remembered kitchen smells about her—baking bread, creamy butter and thick strawberry jam. His father followed—his familiar open face, intense blue eyes, true-blue, like Jerry's own. He was sure he even detected machine shop grease and stale cigars.

Dozens more faces illuminated, then faded, reminding Jerry of cloud-watching. The images kept changing. Many he recognized as comrades lost on Bataan and the stinking prisons of O'Donnell and Cabanatuan. Then out of a field of stars, Elena's face suddenly flowered. Jerry prolonged her vision, memorizing each detail of her face. She glowed with a unique beauty, reminding him of wild orchids he had seen in the sheltered jungles of Bataan—smooth as virginal satin and creamy as candle wax. Shy blooms, their misty green throats hidden in sun-interrupted shadows, they seemed to be in symbiotic union with mossy trunks of trees.

He felt a stinging joy at the sight of her face and an aching sadness when her vision faded. He wanted so much to see her again, to greet her as a friend, to discover her as a woman.

Overcome with loneliness, he called out, "Bronco!" But Bronco did not answer. He was still too deeply asleep.

Jerry lay back and looked at the stars. At that moment he gave up all the faces he had ever loved. He gifted them to the stars, as if by doing so, he would immortalize them. "Oh, Christ," he pleaded, "oh, Jesus, stay with me."

His weariness felt like a heavy chain that dragged him back to the mercy of sleep. The night passed, and he opened his eyes to see Bronco hunched by the edge of the raft. Water splashed wildly as he drank from cupped hands.

Jerry yelled, "That's poison! The salt will kill you!" Without looking at him, Bronco kept drinking. "Going to die anyway," he sneered, screwing up his face as the salt scoured his innards.

By afternoon, Bronco was out of his head. He tore off his life jacket and pulled away from Jerry's restraining hold. "I'm going to swim for it," he shouted. The raft pitched dangerously. Bronco plunged into a towering breaker.

Jerry turned dead white. "Bronco!" he yelled as his friend's head bobbed up every few seconds in the choppy swells. "Goddammit, Bronco!"

It was no use. Bronco rode the waves like an unstrung puppet, arms and legs tossing aimlessly in the greedy mouth of the sea. He vanished in a little over a minute.

For hours Jerry did not move. He lay spread-eagle on the raft. The sun baked through his clothing. When he finally moved, it was to dip his hand listlessly into the water to try to catch another fish. After awhile, his hand felt dead. Lifting it out of the water cost him all his strength.

When the sun set on the third day, Jerry looked forward to the coolness of evening. Then as night temperatures fell, he pulled his warm shirt tightly over himself—cocoon-like. Absent-mindedly, he strapped himself to the raft, and immediately fell into another exhausted sleep, not realizing that he had neglected to cinch the straps around his body securely.

Sometime around one in the morning, he awoke as if he heard someone call his name. Then the loneliness hit him again. He tried to pray the Lord's Prayer, but could not get past the first line, "Our Father, who art in heaven," before sleep claimed him once more. He struggled through a delirious sequence of dreams—always challenged, always falling short of some goal. Then just before dawn, deep in another world of consciousness, he had one last dream: He was riding a tall brown stallion, a horse with an unruly black mane. He felt sure he had ridden the horse before. They were trotting, going somewhere, though there seemed to be no hurry.

The familiar Rocky Mountains rose up ahead as he and the stallion rode through fields of summer-scorched grass. Shivers of wind ran over the range in a continuous rippling. He loved that undulating motion, and felt it deep within himself as he rocked in the saddle.

Exhilarated, he pulled on the reins and the horse shot forward, headed for the purple-blue mountains, pacing himself into a bouyant trot, lifting Jerry high off the saddle. The aroma of sage spiced the air. The sky was a lucid blue, totally cloudless; and the sun shone so intensely, he jammed down the broad brim of his hat. "Go, Cheyenne!" he cried. Cheyenne? How did he remember that name? That horse? He leaned into the majestic stallion's arched neck and they took off at a full gallop.

Eyes focused, Jerry saw a movement ahead in the sea of grass, mostly wild wheat now, with dancing heads of grain. Two antelopes flashed out of the field and leaped ahead.

"Follow, Cheyenne!" he nudged the horse's side and the stallion flew ahead, its hooves barely touching the ground, its black mane slashing at the wind.

Sweat poured off Jerry's brow and stung his eyes. He wiped it off with his shirt sleeve. A blinding wave of glare crossed his path at that moment. Meteor-like, the light exploded just as he rode into it. Simultaneously, a black hole of darkness comsumed him. He dreamed no more.

Without ever awakening, Jerry had rolled off the raft into the water when his legs worked their way free of the belt straps. Dragon green water roiled around him as a mountainous swell empowered the raft, turning it into a trajectory, sending it full-force into the side of his head, splitting the flesh, and cutting deep into the white bone of his skull.

Blood gushed from the wound, tainting the water crimson. The raft pinned him under long enough for water to shoot into his lungs.

Jerry struggled for one last breath. Then he floated face up, his eyes closed as if he were asleep.

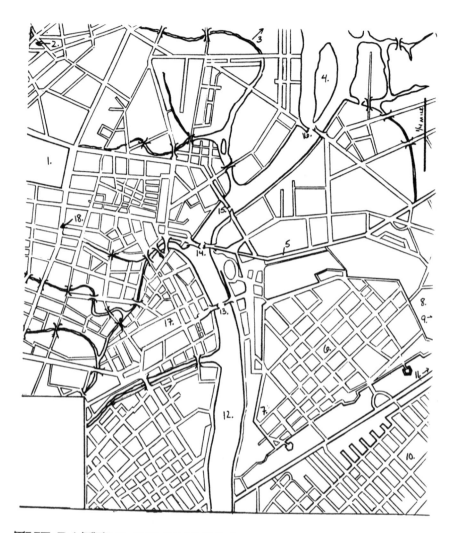

THE BATTLE OF MANILA (80% of the City Demolished)
(Map drawn by Elena and included in her diary)

1. Bilibid Prison—POW camp
2. Santo Tomas Univ. & POW camp
3. Pasig River near Malacanan Palace bridged by 37th Infantry
4. Proviser Island Battle
5. Taft Ave. (aka Daitoa Ave.)
6. Walled City (Intramuros)—last ditch stand by Japanese

7. Fort Santiago
8. Golf course
9. Ermita—devastated by fiery street fighting
10. Port area
11. Dewey Blvd. (aka Heiwa Blvd.)
12. Pasig River
13. Jones Bridge—demolished by Japanese
14. Santa Cruz Bridge—demolished by Japanese

15. Quezon Bridge—demolished by Japanese
16. Ayala Bridge—demolished by Japanese
17. Downtown Manila—ravaged by fiery battle
18. Santa Cruz area—ravaged by fire

Chapter Fourteen

The Fire

"Vida," Mila called, "what are you doing watering the orchids?"
Caught by surprise, Vida jumped back, splashing water over herself.
"I...I know you hate to see the orchids die," she explained, setting the
watering can down.
"I hate to see them die..." Mila felt her eyes moisten, "but we've got
to save the water for drinking and cooking," she said.
Wiping her damp hands on the hem of her faded pink dress, Vida
looked down. "We would die like these flowers without water. *Sayang*—a
pity!" she cried.
Mila fingered the fading surface of a bloom, its purple center an
anemic lavender. She dipped her hand into the watering can, cupped some
water and let it dribble on the thirsty orchid.
"I am sorry," Vida said, touching Mila's arm. In her deep brown eyes,
Mila could see the tears well. "I wanted to water them just one more
time," she said, picking up the watering can. "I will pour the water back
into the storage tub," Vida said, heading for the vat used to save rationed
water, which they used only for necessities.
Elena overheard their conversation from the living room window. She
watched Vida carrying the watering can. Her mother followed, her steps
heavy. Elena thought, She looks so tired; she's beginning to walk like
Belana, with small careful steps. Her heart ached for her, but she did not
want to let Mila know that she knew how she felt. Instead, Elena went
to the piano and began to play a passage from Beethoven's "Appassionata," which she had learned by herself. The piece was full of meaning
for her. The sorrowful notes brought back the scene of Sarita's last recital,
which had become a symbol of resistence to war's oppressive forces. She
played it now, for her mother, hoping that the music would help to
release her sadness.
Mila heard. She leaned against the wall which was opposite to the
piano and closed her eyes. The music was a bridge over which mother
and daughter crossed, to a retreat where they could escape their present
trials—a place where their spirits could find expression.
When she finished playing, Elena turned to look for Mila, but she had

left and was back in the garden, walking around slowly, looking at her plants.

Elena told of the incident in her diary, which had become like a friend in whom she could confide when she felt she could talk to no one else. She added to the entry with an irony: *"Mom's sadness over the dying orchids was overshadowed this afternoon by the strange thing that happened to Dan. Would you believe a Japanese soldier saw Dan in the yard and pounded on the gate for him to let him in. Dan opened the gate, and the soldier just stood there and grinned at him. Dan couldn't figure out what he wanted, so he just stood there. Then the soldier, who looked as if he wasn't much older than Dan, reached into his pocket and pulled out a piece of unwrapped peppermint candy. He motioned for Dan to eat it. Not wanting to test his friendly approach, Dan put the candy into his mouth. When he bit into it—imagine this—he found he had a mouthful of cod liver oil! The soldier laughed as if it was the funniest thing he had ever seen. Dan was mad, but he held the awful tasting stuff in his mouth until the soldier left. Some joke! The only thing Dan said to us was, 'I could have taken him. He was short and skinny.'*

"Carl came out of the closet, where he had been listening to the news. He said that the soldier was probably in his teens. We see a lot of young soldiers. The Japs are using up their manpower fast. Speaking of 'fast,' Carl said the news from New Delhi says the Americans are now just twenty-five miles away. They are surrounding the entire lower half of Luzon with their forces from the north; and on the east, with their landings at Zambales. They are also south of Manila in Batangas. Batangas is the province Vida was born in."

She continued the long entry. *"About five hundred evacuees passed by at sunset. They are from the north, retreating from the fighting. In long, bedraggled files they passed, barefooted, with their bayóng bags hanging at their sides or swinging from bamboo poles on their shoulders. The bayóng bags, made of fiber, are stuffed with their most important possessions. They are dejected and totally exhausted!*

"Coming from the south, hundreds of Japanese soldiers and marines, who have evacuated a hospital nearby, dragged down the street, some of them still wearing hospital pajamas. Many of them acted like they were drugged, which they probably were! Where can they be going?

"It was so strange to see both groups, each heading in a separate direction, trying to get through the maze of tank barricades.

"Dan and Tim are guarding our pens and our dogs because theft is going on everywhere in this starving city. We don't go out anymore, except for occasional trips to try to find emergency items. It's too dangerous to leave the house, and what for? There's nothing one can buy anymore. A chicken costs up to 2,000 pesos, a sack of rice, 30,000; and these items can only be found in the black market.

"Because we don't leave the security of our home, we don't know what

is going on in other parts of the city. In fact, most of the residents are incommunicado like we are."

Incommunicado. For the residents of Manila, it meant their worlds had shrunk to the size of their homes. Because of shortwave radio,they knew more about the advance of the American forces than they knew about their neighbors nearby.

Each day the Kellers and their neighbors, the Chews, exchanged bits of news. They shared precious items they each knew the other might need—a little sugar, coconut oil for the lamps, a ripe banana from their gardens...

The Chews' house was part of a compound. The house next to them was owned by the Japanese Air Force, its original inhabitants having been ousted months before. Most of the time, the house was empty, but several times a month it was used by Japanese Kamikaze pilots, who would spend their last hours in a wailing ritual that sent chills down the spines of those in the neighborhood. The mysterious incantations would begin at sunset and end in the early hours of the morning, when dead silence would follow the departure of the pilots on their final mission.

The Chews, who were closest to the activities of the Kamikazes, would tell the Kellers when to expect the ghostly cries. The Kamikazes were instructed by the Emperor of Japan to "bear the unbearable." They had names like "Thunder Gods," which symbolized their power and blind devotion to Japan.

To the residents of Manila "Kamikaze" meant terror, a fanatic and threatening force. It reflected the extreme in the Japanese military mind— a devotion to country that was so blind, they would do anything to uphold and defend it, including suicide. What else would they be willing to sacrifice? The answer in most minds was—anything!

The first week in February, 1945, the Kellers heard explosions and saw fires mushroom from different parts of the city. Sharp machine-gun and rifle fire and sporadic blasts of artillery sounded nearby. Shortwave radio had said the Americans were eighteen miles from Manila. Was this the beginning of the battle for the city?

Bits of information coming from the street said *guerrillas* were staging a raid against the Japanese in the outskirts of the city at the Cementerio del Norte, for torturing and killing political prisoners there.

The Kellers would not know until later that what they heard was also part of an American frontal attack on Manila. At the same time, the Japanese began their demolition of the city by fire.

On February third, seven or eight large fires raged in Manila. Dan and Tim tended the vegetable garden and watched the flames billowing, leaving suffocating clouds of red and black over them. The sun, sheathed by a film of burning oil, was an orange moon swinging in a flaming, smoke-filled sky.

Dan went to the filter and filled a small bucket of well water, which they had been using to save what they could of the vegetable garden. He leaned over the plants, carefully baling only one can of water for each plant. Tim worked in the row behind him, cutting talinum. Suddenly, the warning whistle of a shell deafened them, as a missile exploded like a huge blinding star some fifty feet away, throwing them into the talinum bed. The shrapnel sprayed everywhere, but miraculously missed Dan and Tim.

Stunned but untouched, the brothers sat up and stared at each other in disbelief. They struggled up, but before they brushed the dirt off themselves, they went to look at the hole in the corner of the garden. The half dozen banana trees that had stood there were ripped apart and lay in shreds; a penca of green bananas had been obliterated. Bits of the fruit were blown into unrecognizable fragments all over the yard.

Tim began to dig back the dirt around the hole to find part of a telling projectile, but it was either buried too deeply or had fragmented.

They wondered what kind of shell it was, but they never found out, nor did they ever know who had fired it. There were more explosions in the area that day. Ammunition stored by the Japanese blew up a block away, cutting off electricity to the neighborhood for good. Later another shell landed on the Kellers' garage, blowing the wooden structure apart. The family decided to go under the house for cover. "Things will get worse," Carl stated. "Under the house we'll have two layers of protection —the floor and the roof."

"O.K.," Tino stepped in, "let's get moving. Debra, you and Rosie go get your pillows. Dale, let's get the mats."

Elena heard the strain in his voice and she reacted by joining her cousins, "Come on girls, I'll get my things, too."

Within minutes, the family had brought their bedding, a supply of water and food—rice, mongo, and the last of the cracked wheat, which they planned to cook up as mush. They spread *petate* mats on the dirt, which made a good ground cover for their bedding. The grass fiber mats were easy to roll out and also served as padding over the earth floor.

Keeping the flame of the coconut oil lamp as low as possible, they got the *kalan* stove from the shelter. Blowing softly on the coals, they took turns getting the fire started. When the rice was done, they cooked some mongo. They saved the cracked wheat for breakfast.

They sat in a circle around the glowing clay stove and ate their dinner in silence, except for Rosie's whimpering. Even Debra was quiet, her dark luminous eyes questioning, as she studied each of the faces around her. It was Elena who sensed her fear and reached for her small hand.

"This is really strange down here, isn't it, Debra? It feels like a silly dream."

Debra leaned against Elena. "I'm afraid," she said, pressing her face into Elena's shoulder.

"I'm afraid, too," Elena nodded, "but we're all together, and that means something."

"What?" Debra asked.

Elena played with Debra's fingers a moment as she calculated her response. "We're together and that means we will take care of each other, no matter what happens."

Debra said nothing more, but for the rest of the evening, while they sat quietly around the *kalan*, reluctant to lie down on their makeshift beds, she stayed by Elena's side.

The night sky, brilliant with fire, shot eerie light through the wooden slats that surrounded the foundation of the Kellers' house. The foundation consisted of tall, heavy wood posts, each one embedded in cement, creating a kind of dirt basement for the house. It offered its temporary security from the tightening ring of battle that was pressing into their neighborhood.

The fire in the *kalan* grew dimmer. Mila put a few more coals in to keep the stove burning until morning. "We must get some sleep," she said, stirring the fire, sending out a bright shower of sparks.

"I think one of us should stand guard," Dan said.

"Good idea," Carl agreed. "Let me be the first. I'll stay up until about one o'clock, then one of you can take over."

Dan and Tim argued about who should follow Carl. Tino broke into the discussion and said, "I'll go after Carl, and then I'll decide who goes after me."

An hour after the family had settled restlessly into their beds, removing sharp stones and clods of dirt from under their mats, Elena lay awake, listening to Debra's nasal breathing in the mat next to her; to the loud bursts of explosions going off; to the occasional soft coo of the pigeons in the pens under the house; to the shifting of the chickens on their roosts. Then she heard Mila clear her throat. "Are you awake, Mom?" she asked.

"I can't sleep," her mother whispered.

"I can't either," Elena said, sitting up. She saw Mila's form in the shadows, a white sheet wrapped tightly around her. "You look like a ghost, Mom," she said, stifling a nervous laugh.

"Shh, you'll wake everyone up."

"I think we're all awake!" grumbled Tim from his mat.

"Yeah," chorused Dan.

The others stirred. Soft whispering began among them. They shared feelings, easing tensions each had been nursing alone. "What are we going to do if our house catches fire?" Elena asked.

"We'll go to the shelter," Mila answered.

"I know, but what about our things?" Elena said.

"We'll save what we can," Carl spoke out from where he sat, against the foundation post, keeping guard.

"We'll try to save the most important things," added Mila, getting up and stirring the coals once more.

"What about the camphor chest with our heirlooms, the desk and the silver?" Elena persisted.

The coals threw a rosy hue onto her mother's face. "I've been thinking about our things, too, Elena. We'll just have to save what we can."

"We'll have to save ourselves first," Dan said, with a sobering conviction that ended the dialogue. One by one, they lay back in their unfamiliar beds and tried to go to sleep, knowing that the next day would add to the crisis that faced them.

Elena sighed and turned on her side. She fell into a dream-filled sleep, awakening with a start several times during the night, aware of the humid smell of the earth on which she lay. It was a reminder that she could no longer count on the familiar security of her own bed.

Cut off from everything, hiding under their house as the walls of fire reached closer and explosions split the air, the Kellers were not aware that on February 3, the American First Cavalry sent a spearhead column from their descending drive to take Santo Tomás Internment Camp by surprise and free several thousand Allied civilian prisoners of war. They did not know that the firing from Cementerio del Norte was also support for the American attack; nor did they know that after they took Santo Tomás, the Americans started exchanging fire with the Japanese across the Pasig River, in an initial attack on the city. Simultaneously, to the east, the 37th Infantry was approaching Manila, while the 11th Airborne paratroops were advancing from the south.

When they awoke the morning of February 4, they only knew the fire was getting closer, the dynamite, shells, and bullets were ear-splitting, and their food supply was quickly shrinking. To venture out now would invite suicide. They had no choice but to stay within their confines and wait.

Though they did not know the extent of the American attack, they sensed that the firing and explosions they were experiencing were far larger than they could see or hear. They felt like rats in a burning cage, forced to wait, to conserve their energy for an ultimate fight for survival or death.

There was an element about being trapped that brought into play the brightest sparks of life. Whether they would die or be freed, the Kellers doggedly planned for their survival, acting as if they were going to survive. They were filled with a tenacious drive that allowed them to work efficiently—side-by-side—bonded, as if they had rehearsed their roles many times: They lit the *kalan*, cooked meals, fetched water, emptied chamber pots into a hole they had dug for sewage, washed tattered underwear in cloudy, reused water, and kept their eyes vigilant on one another. There was a unity among them that each was drawn to like a magnet—a strength in their numbers.

The morning of the fourth, after the family had eaten a scant breakfast of cracked wheat mush, they stood outside, close to the house and watched the city burning. There was deadly beauty to the fire. From east to west, from north to south, a morning sky as a backdrop, the flames were staged in a drama of sight, sound and smell. A rolling mass of colored cotton, the oil and paint-fed flames transformed into a kaleidoscope of pink, yellow and black. No one in Manila would ever see the sky quite that way again.

Eyes riveted on the heavens, the family stared, spellbound by the inferno. Tino spoke first. Shaking his head in disbelief, he exclaimed, "My God, the Japs are burning everything! I've got to go to Ben's and see how they are!"

"Don't be a fool, Tino," cried Carl. "You're asking to be killed!"

Dale rushed up to her husband and held on to his arm. "Tino, don't be crazy!" she yelled.

Debra and Rosie ran up and tugged on their father's free arm. Tino pulled away. "You're all getting hysterical! I'm going to be careful; it's just a few blocks away!"

Elena stepped forward and drew Debra to her. She wiped her cousin's eyes. "Don't cry. It's all right, don't cry." Then she looked over at her uncle and blurted. "We have a right to be upset. Nobody wants to lose you, you know!"

Tino gave her a sober glance. When he spoke, his voice was calmer. "I'm sorry. All of you—I'm sorry. I got carried away. I'm worried about Mamá. I want to go, but I won't do anything rash." He looked at Dale and the girls.

At that moment, Vida told them someone was calling to them from the fence. It was Lee Chew. His hair was uncombed and he had circles under his eyes. "I just talked to some people on the street," he said. "They came from the downtown area. Bad news. The Japs are blowing up the bridges, setting fire to ammunition dumps, burning everything. Civilians who get in the way are being shot." He paused, then cleared his throat and continued, "The Americans are attacking the city from every direction, they say. That's the good news. We'd better all stay right where we are."

"It must be true," cried Carl, "the whole city is going up in flames; the shelling and firing are getting closer by the hour."

A cold chill went through Elena. This was it—the liberation! Suddenly, she was afraid to breathe. She felt as if she were standing on a precipice, as if the slightest movement might send her plunging to oblivion. "Ouch!" Debra cried, pulling her hand away from her cousin's. "You're squeezing my hand too tight!"

"Sorry. I didn't realize."

Got to get hold of myself, Elena thought. She reached for Debra's hand again and held it gently. "Look, Debra," she said, "Baby Trina and her mother are by the fence."

Rosario Chew and her daughter looked as bedraggled as Lee. "We didn't sleep last night," Rosario said. "The house isn't safe and we don't have much of a basement."

"Why not stay with us?" Mila offered.

"Thank you," Rosario nodded; her long hair, usually in a bun, was loose around her shoulders. "We'll go in our shelter tonight, where it will be safer, but, thank you."

When the Chews left the fence and the Kellers went back under the house, Mila said, "Rosario is right, it's safer in our shelters. Let's get our things ready."

Carl joined her. "Let the *kalan* cool, roll up your beds and let's go upstairs and plan what to do."

They gathered in the living room and decided they would each pack an emergency bag of personal essentials—a change of clothes, toothbrushes, and a few other necessary items. All agreed the bags were to be as small as possible so as not to crowd the shelter.

Elena gave a great sigh and headed for the closet that she, her mother and Carl shared. She rummaged around the stacked shelves until she found her old leather hatbox, pulled it off the shelf and laid it on her bed. The smell of mothballs hit her when she opened it. She found a collection of old hats and veils she had forgotten—an old straw hat with a blue satin ribbon she had worn for Easter when she was eleven, her communion veil, several sprigs of artificial flowers, limp and faded...

She emptied the hatbox and wrapped its contents in tissue paper, returning the items to the shelf, where she placed them on top of the box that stored the nativity set. Then she knelt under the bed and pulled out other boxes and *bayóng* bags that held all the things she had taken from her armoire when she gave it up for Tino and family. The first thing she looked for was Jerry's drawings, the pencil he had used and the red ribbon she had worn on his visit. Fingering the drawings, she stared at the one of her, remembering how she had challenged the slight pout he had put into the lines of her mouth. Lifting the paper to her face, she brushed her nose against it, hoping for some remembered scent of him. There was none, only the slight odor of mildew that was typical of items stored in moist tropical heat. Folding the drawings, she placed them at the bottom of the hatbox and laid the pencil and ribbon beside them. Then she found the American flag she had made from an old sheet and placed it over the drawings. Other treasures followed—the small wooden music box from her grandmother, a first communion prayer book, copies of Jerry's letters, two lipsticks, a silver medal of the Virgin Mary, two complete changes of clothing, one of which was the red and white sailor blouse she had worn during Jerry's visit. The material had worn thin and was faded from many washings. She matched a pair of navy blue shorts that had white polka dots, with the blouse, thinking as she put the items into the hatbox that they didn't quite go together. As she clicked the lid of the round black leather bag shut, Mila came into the room. She stood by Elena's bed and said, "Did you remember your toothbrush?"

"I forgot it!" Elena cried, "I'll get it."

Elena brushed past her, and Mila put her arms out to her. The two women fell into an embrace. When they released each other, each saw the sadness in the other's eyes, the deep look of grief that comes with expected loss. "After this is over, *cariño*..." Mila started to say, but could not finish.

Elena caressed her mother's arm. She nodded and slowly walked to the bathroom to get her toothbrush.

The family made several trips to the shelter. When all the bags were lined up on the narrow floor, they peered into both entrances of the trench, one at a time, and came away with amused looks on their faces. "Are you thinking what I'm thinking?" Dan asked.

"Uh huh!" several of them chorused. "There's no room for us!" Debra cried gleefully.

"Right! There's no room for us," Tino patted her on the head. "What next?"

"What about the bamboo clump?" Elena said, pointing to the tall sanctuary of giant bamboo that grew just feet away from the shelter. "Let's put some of our suitcases in there."

"What about the gecko?" Vida grinned at her.

"*Ay!* To heck with the gecko!" Elena shrugged and gave Vida a soft slap on the shoulder.

Vida laughed and walked to the bamboo clump with a bag. The rest of them followed, nestling their small bags and suitcases into the bed of dead leaves that had fallen amongst the dark trunks and provided a sheltered hiding place. The thick trunks grew so close together the bags had to be squeezed in between them.

After they had hidden their personal belongings, the family returned to the house and moved out foodstuffs, including the dwindling sack of rice and mongo beans, which they also hid in the bamboo clump. "Tonight, we'll dig up the corned beef," Carl told them when they had finished hiding the rice and mongo.

When darkness fell, Carl, Tino, Dan and Tim crept to the bamboo. They cast uneven shadows in the glaring night. Carl measured two paces toward the high wall behind the clump and pointed to the spot. "Here. Dig here." His voice sounded low and raspy.

There was a lull in the shell fire coming from the Americans across the Pasig. Rifle fire was sporadic, but sounded several blocks away. "Hurry," Tino said, as he and Carl dug their shovels into the ground.

"Dan, Tim, give us a hand," Carl instructed.

They worked fast, unearthing the half case of corned beef they had buried three years before, when Dan and Tim, now eye level with Carl, had been over a head shorter than their stepfather.

A sudden shot pinged over their heads. They ducked. Two more shots followed. The four of them lay down and rolled over in the grass, until they were under the protection of the bamboo. "It's the Japs at the compound. They must have heard us," Dan said softly.

"Stay down," Carl ordered. "Soon as they quit, take the case right into the shelter."

For several minutes they lay on the cool grass and listened. The shelling had started up again, but the shots from across the wall stopped. "Now!" Carl hissed.

Under the incandescent night, they dragged the wooden box to the mouth of the shelter and lowered it into the trench. Dan carried the lantern, which he lit, dimming the flame to a quivering flicker.

With the shovel blade, Carl pried the lid of the case open. He handed the twelve cans, one by one, to Dan and Tim. Examining them in the low light, the two brothers stacked the cans on the floor. "Old and rusty," commented Dan, "but probably still good."

Using a small attached key, Tino opened one of the rusty cans. He got out his penknife and, with the tip of the blade, he took out a bit of corned beef. Tasting it, he said, "Salty, but it's still OK. Here, you taste." He offered some to the others.

Carl and Dan shook their heads, but Tim reached over and had a taste. "It'll go good with rice and mongo," he smirked.

Motioning to Dan and Tim, Carl said, "Let's get out of here, so we can get back with the rest of the family. Leave a few cans here, and put the rest in the bamboo."

Later that night, the family crowded into the dark womb of the shelter. They leaned against one another and tried to sleep. Debra put her head in Elena's lap. Elena stretched out her legs, until her feet butted up against the wall of shelter. She dropped her head on Vida's shoulder. Mila sat on the lookout stool. "I can't sleep anyway," she said. "I might as well sit here..."

Elena saw the rosary laced in her mother's fingers and whispered to herself, "...and pray."

In the shelter the sound of bursting shells and ripping gunfire were dulled. The air felt close, and their bodies built up heat. Perspiring and stiff, Dan and Tim left the shelter after midnight and lay against the clump of bamboo. A volley of gunfire went off overhead. Opening his eyes, Tim felt a bullet whistle just inches from his face. His eyes were hot and dry when he tried to blink. "God!" he yelled, sitting up.

Dan pushed him back down. "Stay low!" he cried.

Tim rolled over and covered his face. Moments later there was an interval of quiet, and the brothers crawled back into the shelter. "Take a look at Tim," Dan said.

"*Dios!*" exclaimed Mila, holding her son's face. Carl lit the lamp, and together they examined Tim's face. "I don't see anything," Mila said. "Your eyes are very red; that's all. The bullet passed terribly close."

Carl frowned. "Listen. That's a warning. Stay in the shelter!"

Pushed against one another, the family drifted into a fitful sleep. They prayed the light of dawn would come soon. The next few days were spent in the same manner. In and out of the shelter, the family packed a push-cart full of household items, knowing for certain now, that the tidal wave of fire, slowly and deliberately consuming the city, would eventually surround and engulf them.

On the morning of February 9, Tino, wearing an old straw hat and a tattered shirt and carrying a *bayóng* bag, set out for Ben's house. Debra and Rosie were asleep in the shelter when he kissed Dale and said, "I promise I'll be back."

He was gone for three hours. When he returned, he looked as if he had walked twenty miles. Holding Debra and Rosie on his lap in the trench that led to the shelter, he told his story. "I made my way very slowly to San Andreas Street, using side alleys, hiding in bushes and crouching down as I crept along. I saw two dead Filipinos. Shot." He paused and showed them two bullet holes in the *bayóng* bag. "I have this to show for it, but I got there safely." He wiped the sweat off his forehead and went on. "There's an enormous fire at the Rizal Stadium. Ben's compound is so close they may have to leave the house and hide in a ditch they have dug in the field behind them until the fire subsides. I told them to join us here."

"Oh, I hope they come!" Mila cried, her rosary still in her fingers, the crystal beads clinking softly.

Her brother shook his head. His eyelids drooped with fatigue. "Too risky to move now. Ben told me the Japs are burning everything in sight. I saw them myself, shooting at civilians." As proof, he raised the bag with the bullet holes. "They're almost out of food at Ben's. He accepted the *ganta* of rice, but I had to make him take the two cans of corned beef. He didn't want to short us."

Mila broke in. "How is Mamá?" she asked, her eyes bright with worry.

"Pobre Mamá," Tino said, "she's hysterical. The explosions are driving her crazy. She sits in the corner of the makeshift shelter they have under the stairs, with her hands over her ears. She won't eat, and she can't sleep."

"¡Ay, Mamá!" cried Mila.

Elena imagined her grandmother, crouched in fear—Sofía, who had given so much of herself, who had fanned in her granddaughter an inner strength, a proud self-esteem.

His voice heavier with each word, Tino continued. "In the Ermita, civilians are being gunned down as their houses catch fire. There's rape going on..."

"Lise, Isabel, and Chiquita!" Elena said aloud.

Tino sighed, but did not look up. "The truth is, the Japs are taking a suicide stand. Nothing but a flattened, gutted city will be left," he said, perspiration dripping down the sides of his face. "I wish it was all based on rumor, but people escaping from the Ermita are spreading the news all over the city."

"What do the Japs have to lose," Carl added. "They're finished anyway."

On the tenth of February, the walls of fire towered over the Kellers' block. After eating a handful of rice and three spoonfuls of mongo for breakfast, Elena crept to the Chews' fence and gave a short whistle—a signal they had agreed they would use to let one another know it was safe to come to the fence. Suddenly Rosario appeared behind the bushes, where the wall was low, creating a kind of entryway to the compound. Trina was straddled on her hip. They both look so pale, Elena thought, as they approached the fence. "Here, we thought you could use this corned beef," Elena said, handing the two cans she carried to Rosario.

Rosario reached for the cans, then stepped back without taking them. "Just a minute. I've something for you, too."

"Hurry!" Elena said. "The firing is starting up again." She heard the loud whistle of two shells, followed by shattering explosions, as they fell in the blocks nearby. You know they are close, Elena thought, when you hear the whistle first.

Rosario's face popped up over the bushes. "Ssst, Elena!" she hissed. Her heart leaping, Elena, cried, "You scared me!"

Rosario gave a chuckle. "Oh, I'm sorry! Here, quick, take this coconut—fresh milk for the little girls."

"*Eres un cariño*," Elena said. She waved and ducked down, crawling back across the yard and into the shelter. Smoke from the fire made her eyes water. She looked up and saw the towering flames moving in, about ten houses away. In the street, Japanese soldiers yelled. They carried gasoline cans. There was no doubt they were setting fire to the residences. The bloody screams that came just before a volley of gunfire told Elena that civilians were being murdered, just as Tino said.

I've got to stay busy, she said to herself. Must not think about the killing. She grabbed the coconut scraper and a small hatchet from a pile of utensils near the trench and began to hack furiously at the thick green fibrous husk, hitting it repeatedly. "Elena!" Mila's voice broke through. "Why are you hitting so hard? The shell is cracked. You're losing liquid!"

Elena looked at her. Saying nothing, she began the ritual of extracting milk from the fragrant white inner meat. The rhythmic action calmed her turmoil—her hands around the husk, the scraper held between her knees, the coconut meat flaking into a bowl, and, finally, the slow sure squeezing of the pulp... Mesmerized, she was lost in the process. When there was no moisture left in the pulp, she took the bowl of milk to her mother, who was still standing by, watching her, and said, "Look. Some nice coconut milk for the girls for tonight. From Rosario..."

Mila's shoulders relaxed. "She's so thoughtful."

Elena lowered her eyes and nodded. "She thanked us for the corned beef," she sighed. Then staring up at the raging sky, she said, "It's getting closer, Mom."

Mila put her arm around her daughter and gently urged her into the shelter. "Try to rest, Elena. We may not get any sleep tonight."

Elena reversed her steps. "I will, after I take this milk to the pantry, where it's cooler."

"Keep it here," her mother said. "It might not be possible to go back into the house later."

But Elena said, "I've got to go." She crept to the house, the coconut milk swishing whitely in the glass bowl she held tightly in both hands.

By late afternoon, Carl, Tino, Dan and Tim began to move furniture from the house into the yard. Everyone in the family joined them. Mila and Elena each grabbed an end of the narra table. Dale and Debra carried chairs. Dan and Tim hauled Mila's Chinese soapstone desk. Carl and Tino brought down the heavy camphor chest. They crowded the furniture against the *bonga* palm, on the side away from the house. "That's all we can save!" Carl exclaimed. "The fire is getting too close. Let's move the pushcart over by the *bonga*; it's too near to the stairs."

"Let's do that after dinner, Carl," Mila said. "We're all so tired."

Vida, who had had the *kalan* going all afternoon, cooking a thin chicken broth, hailed them toward the shelter. "Starvation soup!" she announced. She stirred the pale liquid, saying to herself, "I put a hen out of misery!" Then she waved the wooden spoon. "Only bones," she cried.

"Come on!" Tino called out. "Let's have some bones."

"Any rice with those bones?" asked Elena.

"No," Vida looked serious suddenly. "Rice again tomorrow...if God allows," she added.

Steam rose from the soup, adding to the moisture in the shelter. As the family drank the hot broth, sweat drenched their clothing. "The baby turkey will have to go hungry tonight," Elena said.

There were no rice scrapings to feed the lone surviving turkey chick hidden in a cardboard box in the bushes about twenty feet from the shelter.

Tim saved a half cup of soup. "Salome will go for this," he said. The pig had been squealing, pulling against the rope that tethered her to a bush a few feet away from where the box with the turkey had been placed.

"Hurry up, Tim!" Tino warned, staring at the tidal wave of fire creeping up against the houses in the Chews' compound. "Let's run back to the house, Carl, to be sure we haven't forgotten anything."

"Jesus, we're next!" cried Carl, as he joined Tino up the stairs for one last trip into the house. Elena ran behind them. Mila called after her, but she paid no attention. As Carl flung open the screen door, he saw Elena running up the stairs behind him. "Go back with the others!" he ordered.

"I'll only be a minute," she yelled. "I have to get the coconut milk I shredded this morning!"

"To hell with the milk!" Carl shouted back, but Elena ran past him toward the pantry. She stopped short of the door, transfixed by an inferno that blazed from the four houses in the compound. She watched the Chews' house flash into flame. She heard screams, followed by the roar of the undulating sheet of fire, growing ever closer. A dragon-like tongue of fire whipped around the mabolo tree and torched it. The tree burned white-hot, like a sacrifice on a funeral pyre, with a beauty so intense, Elena was bewitched by it. Red-gold leaves shimmered, then, freed from branches, flew crazily into the burning night. The ripe mabolos turned to bright brass and plummeted to the ground, each one a small exploding sun.

Suddenly suffocated by a strong mix of fumes from sulphurous fruit and burning leaves, Elena choked and momentarily shut her watering eyes. Quickly, she moved away from the impending flames and into the pantry, which was already so hot she was barely able to handle the door-knob.

She grabbed the glass bowl of coconut milk and ran down the hall, her head lowered and her breath held. Carl's steps thundered through the living room as he and Tino hauled final armloads of their belongings. "For God's sake, Elena, go back with the others!"

In the rumbling of the fire, his voice sounded distant, unreal. Elena paused in the living room and gazed at the outline of her piano shouldered against the wall. She moved toward it quickly and closed the lid over the keys. Then she ran back down the front stairs to where the family was gathered by the *bonga* palm, hiding behind the pushcart which they had moved away from the front stairs.

As she crowded in with the rest of them, Mila grabbed her arm, "That was stupid of you, Elena," she snapped.

"I just didn't want to lose the milk," Elena explained.

"Hmm!" Mila voiced her frustration and turned away, staring at the house, seeing the windows and doors light up in a blinding flash as the fire hissed through the kitchen and pantry walls.

Debra crawled over and tugged at Elena's arm. "I want some milk, please," she said. Her face was bright in the fire's reflection; her eyes were wide, her pupils dilated.

"Here," Elena said, tipping the bowl of milk toward her cousin's small upturned lips.

Debra took a mouthful, then spat it out. "It's sour!" she cried. Elena could smell the rancid milk as it sprayed her arm. "Shh," Carl whispered from where he crouched near the front of the pushcart. "There are some Jap soldiers at the gate!"

All eyes focused on the gate, outside of which three Japanese soldiers stood, their faces lit by fire, the barrels of their guns moving, as they poked at the heavy padlock, which they had placed there months before. One of them stopped, lifted a *nambu* woodpecker machine gun and was about to shoot off the lock, when another soldier pointed to the flames eating the back of the Kellers' house. At that instant, a throaty order was called to them from the street. Shots cracked into the air. The three soldiers turned, answered the fire and bolted away. A clatter of wooden *bakias* echoed sharply. Desperate screams split the fiery night. Ripping machine gun fire followed. Then silence, except for the roar of the avalanching flames.

Crouched like terrified animals, the family moved stealthily behind the *bonga* palm. As suffocating flames ate at their house, they peered through the giant dark fronds of the *bonga*, and stared in shock at the white-hot furnace in front of them. Mila pressed her head against Carl's shoulder and shut her eyes. Dale held Tino's hands.

Vida and Elena clutched the two girls. All of the women were crying, except Elena, who was hypnotized by the burning pyre of their house.

Sheets of flame shot into the air from windows and doors, breathing out an agony of merciless heat. Tongues of flames touched the venetian blinds. One by one, they burned, clicking loose, until they all ripped down, consumed by relentless fire.

Just before the piano fell, a powerful force of fiery gas hissed out the front door and exploded, blinding the view of the house, now a grotesque abstraction of igneous elements. Seconds later, the piano fell, hurtling through the floor, emitting eerie chords—a ghostly discord vibrating through a hell of fire, each agonizing sound striking at Elena's heart like a searing blade of steel.

Her eyes turned to glass, Elena stared, unseeing, hearing only the dying music of her piano. Mila's hands reached gently behind Elena and brought her shoulders around. Drawing her daughter to her, she whispered, "Elena." Sobs broke loose from her breast, but Elena's eyes were dry.

"They're back!" The guttural sound of Tino's voice brought them to attention. Mila looked up, Elena's head still buried against her shoulder.

Two of the soldiers had returned and were gesturing toward the burning house with their rifles. No one breathed. Then without warning they turned and went off down the street, cans of gasoline visible in the flickering shadows.

Mila heaved a deep sigh. "They won't be back. Our house is already burning. Thank God, oh, thank God!"

I am numb, Elena thought. I see nothing. I feel nothing. Her eyes remained dry and she had stopped her tearless sobbing. Dan offered her a towel he had soaked with water from the filter. "Here," he said, "cool off. The fire is like a furnace."

The rest of them soaked whatever clothing they could in the well water and moistened their hot skin. They sat for several hours and watched the house burn, until it collapsed in a loud groan, leaving only twisted metal bars and pieces of tin roofing in a graveyard of crackling, glowing ashes, from which, now and then, a hail of embers leaped in a macabre dance.

"If we don't die like rats, we'll see morning!" Tino exclaimed, lifting Rosie's sleeping form up against his shoulder and heading for the shelter. The rest of them dragged behind him, aware that though the fire was dying, the shelling had not stopped.

Sitting on the lookout stool, Mila took up her rosary. "We won't die like rats," she said. Her lips tightly drawn, her brown eyes ringed by dark circles, her thin fingers played on the crystal beads. "We'll see morning," she stated flatly.

Chapter Fifteen

Cross-fire

Under a red-domed sky, Manila burned and smoldered in a purge of fire—fire from burning buildings, burning flesh, burning gasoline; fire from shells, mortars, and bullets. In this holocaust, people hid like rodents, ducking into shelters, ditches, remains of houses, even into craters made by bombs and shells, to escape the merciless storm of fire.

There was little difference between the sky at dawn and the night sky, except that the morning sky was a lighter hue of red—that, and the occasional presence of the sun, which swung from behind flaming clouds and smoke like a giant orange, its shape mutable, distorted by heat.

It was this kind of sky Elena woke to on the day after the house burned. She had slept for several hours, curled up awkwardly on the floor of the shelter. Her back ached when she tried to straighten up, and she noticed a black-and-blue mark on her leg. Strange I never felt it, she told herself; it's probably from the hard floor, or maybe I was accidentally kicked.

She felt nauseated. Vida offered her a handful of rice. She declined and drank some water instead. The smell of wood ashes coming from the house brought back terror from the night before. She had a sudden urge to see what remained of the house. "I'm going to the bathroom," she mumbled, climbing over Debra and Tim, who sat eating small portions of rice at the entrance of the shelter. She crawled several feet to the bamboo clump and ducked down in a tight space between the trunks before taking down her shorts. She squatted, raising her head to see beyond the shelter to where the house had been. House, trees, bushes— gone! In their place, gray, smoldering piles of ashes, from which an occasional twist of scorched metal protruded.

Steam from her urine brought her attention to herself. She pulled up her shorts and was about to start to crawl to the area of the house, when a barrage of gunfire picked up in tempo. A clash down the street, she thought, though she could see nothing but a gray horizon, where she was sure the street ought to be. She looked over at the Chews'—gone!

She waited. Five minutes later the gunfire died down. Elena half-crawled and half-fish-tailed her way to what had been her home. As she got closer to the ruins, the piles of smoldering slag loomed like a gray dune ahead of her. Getting up on her haunches, she did a sideways dance into the sea of ash. In seconds she was up to her ankles in burned debris. "Ouch!" she cried as her feet brushed by coal-like fragments of wood still burning deep in the ashes. She moved quickly over the area below the living room. A piece of broken china scraped her knee. She lifted the fragment, its design and color so scorched she did not recognize the piece. Finding the china gave her a guide to where she was. She told herself she was probably in the area below where her parents' bedroom had collapsed.

The charred debris still felt hot on her legs and feet, but did not seem as intense now. She avoided areas that were still smoldering and stayed where the ash was shallow and had cooled. She inched her way to the bedroom. Smoke from slag made her eyes burn. For a moment she crouched in place and ran her fingers through the hot, silt-like ash—a lone and solitary figure in an endless sea of gray. Around her, more oceans of debris, every house on the block demolished by the conflagration. Not a human sound anywhere, just the salvoes of artillery, the discharge of mortars, the pinging of gunfire, in a neighborhood turned battlefield.

"Got to get back," she whispered. She dragged her fingers through the ashes once more before turning to crawl back to the shelter. Her fingers struck a small object. Scooping it up, she let it roll into her palm. It was small and roundish and covered with ashes. Opening her palm, she lifted it to the light. Her jaw dropped. "Oh!" she breathed. Blowing a fine dusty cloud from the small faded form, she again cried, "Oh! It's the infant Jesus," she said out loud. "From my crèche, it's the baby Jesus!"

Elena hunched over and closed her hand over the hollow ceramic form of the Christ child. In a chant-like prayer, she sang out, "Out of the ashes! Out of the ashes! I found you out of the ashes!"

She uncurled her hand and looked at the form again. No more than an inch and-a-half wide and two inches long, it was stripped of color, its features blurred by heat. How could it possibly have survived? she asked herself. It looks like it's a thousand years old. In this impossible incinerator, how could I have found such a miracle?

Then because she could not answer except by responding emotionally, she lowered her head and brushed the scorched and faded form of the infant with her lips. "Thank you," she whispered. Tears she had held the night before spilled on her hands and onto the ashes, leaving tiny pits.

The family sweltered in the noon heat. The sun had hit a mid-point in the sky, adding its heat to the the charred ruins of their house, creating an unbearable furnace. Still stunned by the intense experience of early that morning, Elena sat in silence, listening to her brothers. "We lost the pigeons last night," Dan said, his face black with soot. "They flew from their open pens. A couple of chickens went crazy and flew right into the fire."

Tim cut in, "There are two Rhode Island reds that survived, but they're badly burned."

Carl heard them and said, "Next time you see them, be sure to grab them. We need to end their suffering." He threw off his shirt. Perspiration ran through the hair on his chest. "Who is taking care of the baby turkey?"

"I am," Elena said. "I'm going to give it some rice scrapings. There was nothing for it yesterday."

Carl gave his familiar squint and said, "Do the best you can."

That afternoon, the shelling became heavier again. Mortar fire from the compound was constant. It was coming at an angle over the Kellers' yard and landing beyond the street. Two mortars landed short of the street, sending the family back to the shelter.

Debra and Rosie fell asleep. Rosie had wet herself repeatedly. The stench of urine and unwashed bodies forced Elena to move closer to the emergency entrance of the shelter, where Mila sat on the lookout stool. Exhausted from nights of sleeplessness, the hot *kalan* close to her feet, Mila leaned, eyes closed, against the dirt wall behind her. Elena touched her mother's forehead. Mila opened her eyes. Her look was dark and glazed. "Please let me sit there for awhile," Elena said.

Bracing her shoulders, Mila sat up and pulled her blue skirt over her knees. "Look," she said, "I must have torn it."

Elena looked at the faded skirt and smiled faintly, "Come on, Mom, let me sit there. You get some sleep."

"I'm too tired to sleep. Let's talk a little," she said. "Are you all right?"

"Sure—I am really all right. I have something special to show you," she said, her face brightening as she reached into the pocket of her sailor blouse.

Her mother leaned forward and tried to see what Elena held in her half-opened hand. "What is it?"

"It's a miracle," she answered, slowly uncurling her fingers and revealing the miniature Christ child.

"From the fire?" Mila breathed. She touched the blurred, discolored face.

"Yes. From the ashes. I found it this morning."

Mila leaned her head back heavily. Closing her eyes, she gave a low groan. When she opened them, they were welled with tears. "*Un milagro*," she whispered softly, "a miracle..."

"Come here," Elena said. She wrapped her arms around her mother and squeezed her tight. "God must be with us!" she cried.

Mila hugged her back. A light kindled in her eyes when she said, "He's with us."

"I think there's bad news, too." A shadow crossed Elena's face. "When I looked over to where the Chews' house was, I saw nothing but ashes. Not a sound was coming from their compound."

Mila raised her hand to her forehead. "I've been so worried about them," she sighed.

Elena said nothing more. The two fox terriers, who had been crouched in the shelter, came over and nuzzled into Mila's blue skirt. They were trembling, fearful of every blast they heard. For days, they had eaten just a few scraps; in shock, they no longer barked.

Petting the small male on his brown-patched face, Elena said, "We won't be here forever, Max."

Sheba whined. Mila stroked her gently. "They can't understand all this," she said. "I'll take you up on your offer, *cariño*," she added. "I need some sleep."

Elena must have sat on the stool for about an hour, when the intensity of the firing alerted her. She heard her uncle's voice coming from the bamboo clump. "Here," he said, "here by the bamboo. There's no room in the shelter, but you're welcome to stay. We have a little food to share..."

Elena peered over the emergency entrance and saw a huddle of people. She recognized a neighborhood family, Andrés and Juana Gonzalez; Clara, their daughter, son-in-law and their six-year-old girl. They had crawled in through the low wall of the Chews' fence. They had nothing with them except a small black dog. Andrés held on to the ragged end of a short rope tied around the dog's neck. They looked like spectres. The woman kept her chin pressed down, hiding her tearful face. "What happened?" Tino asked as they allowed themselves to be herded to the wall of bamboo.

His red-rimmed eyes half-closed, Andrés murmured as if he were in a dream, "We lost our oldest—Angustia—last night. We ran from the house. A shell exploded. She went up in, in...," he paused, the horror of the scene paralyzing his words. "She went up in little pieces!" he cried. He drew his wife to him. She buried her head in his neck.

For a moment, Tino did not kn)w what to say. Then extending his hand, he said, "I'm so sorry. What can we do to help?"

Their surviving daughter, Clara, her husband and child moved in with the older couple. They pressed together tightly. The little girl said, "I want some water."

Elena was ready with the water jar. She climbed out of the shelter and extended the bottle to the child. "Here, drink," she told her. "What's your name?"

Before she answered, the child drank deeply. Water dribbled down her tattered yellow dress. "Linda," she gasped, getting her breath.

The grandfather kept on talking. "We buried her in an armoire. She's there," he droned, waving aimlessly.

Elena offered the rest of them some water. They all drank. Andrés had stopped talking. Mute, he stared off into space. His son-in-law pushed him gently against a trunk of bamboo. "Rest, father," he said.

"How did you find us?" Tino asked him.

Clara edged over to her husband. "Tell them, Paco."

Paco cleared his throat. We came every-which-way. We got lost. No landmarks. Then we saw the bamboo. Knew it was your place."

Her eyes focused intently on Paco's face, Clara cut in, "We spent hours. Ducked bullets and mortars. The Japs saw us from the military compound. They fired at us. We never saw them. They just fired and fired. Then we came upon the bodies."

"Yes," Clara's look was glazed now. "Yes, bloated bodies of soldiers... many, many civilians. Over there." she pointed to the Chews' compound.

Words sticking in her throat, Elena strained forward. "What did you see there?" she asked, pointing directly to where the Chews' house had been.

"You tell them, Paco," mumbled Clara, the muscles of her face slack.

"There are three bodies in the ruins," Paco said. He heaved a sigh—"a man, woman and a tiny child."

"The Chews!" exclaimed Elena.

"Yes," said Tino. "It must be...the Chews." He held on to Elena's hands.

"How?" he asked Paco.

His words were disconnected when he answered, "They were... shot... all shot to death."

"*Bestias!*" shouted Tino. Then in English, "Beasts!" Tears rolled down Andrés' face. His wife Juana lifted her chin and gave a long wail. The others shared silently in the sorrow.

Coming from the shelter, her eyes bleary from sleep, Mila joined the group. "*¿Qué pasó?*" she asked. They told her.

That night, the night of February 11, they finished the last of the rice and mongo beans. Five cans of corned beef remained to be shared among fifteen people. Each of them knew the cans could feed them for only a day or two.

At noon the next day, the sun once again leveled its veil of radiation, sending a mirage of liquid movement through its heat waves, transforming every object into trembling fluidity. Momentarily, the fusillade of shells, mortars and bullets let up. Elena decided it was time to crawl to where the baby turkey was hidden, twelve feet from the shelter. She carried the last handful of rice crust to the starving chick. On her belly, she inched slowly to the box that lay in the heavy vines. When she reached it, she heard a soft scratching inside the box. She rose to her knees, but the vines were in the way. Without thinking, she stood up half-way to get look at the chick. Yes, it was alive. Seeing its drooping head, she reached over and stroked its speckled feathers. She could feel its fragile breastbone.

Reaching into her pocket, she drew out the handful of rice scrapings and placed it beside the turkey's pale beak. The bird was too weak to eat.

It kept its beak closed when Elena tried to push some firm grains of rice up to it.

Completely engrossed in what she was doing, she did not think about the Japanese at the compound, who were shooting at every movement they saw or sensed. As Elena leaned down to lower the box, the hollow blast of a mortar shell discharged. It exploded less than ten yards behind her, shattering its way into the thick *bonga* palm, sending a spray of shrapnel and a fan of shredded leaves in every direction.

Elena neither saw nor heard the shell burst. The force of the blast lifted her off her feet and threw her into the vines. As the explosion slapped her down, its concussion knocked her out, leaving her without feeling. Momentarily blind, deaf, and without sensation, she did not lose all consciousness; but seemed to float in a void, a black hole of consciousness. Where am I? she asked herself. Where is the light? I can't see anything but darkness. I'm falling...My God, I must be dead! Why can I still think? I can't be dead and still think.

Frantically, she groped for consciousness, like a swimmer lost in the deep, without air, without sensation—drowning. Head first, she floated in the tunnel. Down, down, down...Then like jagged lightning, daylight broke through at the end of the tunnel, blinding her. It was several seconds before she could make out the outline of the shelter. Her mother was calling her.

Adrenalin surging through every cell of her body, Elena jerked herself up and sprinted to the shelter. She left a trail of leaves swirling behind her and the overturned box with the dead turkey. "I'm hit!" she yelled as she ran, slapping her body with her hands. Blood dripped from her left elbow.

Carl jumped out of the shelter entrance and enveloped her in his arms. "You're all right, Elena! You're all right," he repeated.

Mila was there with a wet towel. She pressed it against the shallow shrapnel wound on her daughter's elbow, keeping up the pressure to stop the blood. While she held her fingers on the rag, she ran her other hand over Elena to check for more wounds. The force of the mortar and its deadly spray of flying fragments had been absorbed by the *bonga* palm. "Another miracle!" Mila said, stroking Elena's face and steadying her trembling body.

Carl took her hand. "Thank God!" he said, the words rushing from his mouth. Then he frowned. "From now on, nobody moves unless they absolutely have to!"

Elena did not need to be told. After Mila dressed her wound, she huddled on the floor and covered her face.

February 12 and 13 turned the Kellers' yard into a shooting gallery—shells, bullets, grenades, mortars and rifle and machine-gun fire burst, sprayed and exploded, in a relentless salvo that crashed into eardrums and battered nerves, until all senses seemed to go numb. Squeezed dry of emotion, the family and its refugee neighbors moved like puppets. They pushed on their bellies to get to the bamboo clump to relieve themselves. During lulls they belly-crawled to the filter to fill the jars with precious water. They opened the cans of corned beef and shared them, passing the rationed portions to one another mechanically.

They ate the corned beef slowly. It lasted longer that way, easing some of the hunger pangs, and it tasted less salty when chewed in small mouthfuls. Then they sipped the salty water and remained thirsty for long hours after they had drunk their share.

The hours, the minutes, the seconds dragged by painfully. Caught in a front-line battle for the military compound behind them, and a bigger battle between American forces and the Japanese at Rizal Stadium and Harrison Ball Park down the road from them, they knew they would be sure targets if they exposed themselves.

During the night of the twelfth, they began to see mysterious figures —soldiers crawling in the dark—making their way through the yard. They moved soundlessly, under the screaming of bullets and shells that bolted through the sky and burst in the night above them.

At dawn on February 13th, Elena wrote on a scrap of paper she had managed to find in her hatbox: *"Slept about three hours last night. I kept bumping into heads, arms and legs. There are nine of us sleeping in the shelter. The shells, mortars, hand grenades and bullets fall like rain. Through the shelter opening we feel the concussion badly. The air pushes into our ears and feels like it's trapped, so we think our eardrums will burst. Makes me feel I will never take another breath! Getting out of the shelter is deadly, even to go to the bathroom. A couple of times I think I've wet my pants! When it gets dark, we see weird shadowy figures crossing our yard. It's a no-man's-land. Japanese or American—either way—they would shoot at us."* In another paragraph, she continued, *"Last night we also heard heavy tanks rumbling through the barricades. We're sure they were American! Pray they hurry. We can't go on much longer..."* she ended in a scribble.

The worst was far from over. On the afternoon of the thirteenth, Tino was hit by grenade fragments and gunfire, coming some seven yards away from the military compound. He and Carl had crawled from the shelter to the water filter. Both men had waited for a lull in the firing before going for water.

When he reached the filter, Tino got up on his knees and put a glass jar up to the spigot. He filled it and reached over to Carl, still on his belly, for the other jar. "Get down, Tino!" Carl warned as bullets ripped by them.

Tino ducked. Too late; they'd been seen. A grenade went off behind him. A spray of bullets followed. Tino fell forward. Carl crawled to him and tried to lift him. Semi-conscious, Tino was a dead weight. "Tino!" yelled Carl. "Try to move. Got to get you out of here right now!"

At that moment Dan fish-tailed his way to them. He and Carl rolled Tino over. He gave a deep groan. His torn shirt exposed several shrapnel wounds from which the flesh hung. He had other surface wounds on his arms. His left ankle was drenched in blood, spurting like a miniature fountain from a bullet that had knicked an artery in his instep.

Carl and Dan half-carried and half-dragged Tino to the shelter trench. Mila crouched, ready with the first aid box. Seeing the blood spouting from his instep, she reached for the tourniquet and yelled at Dale, "Hold his leg up!"

Stunned, Dale did not move. "Hold his leg up, Dale!" Mila yelled again.

Still she did not move.

Mila grabbed Tino's foot and placed it on Dale's shoulder. "Hold it up!" she ordered. "He'll bleed to death if you don't!"

Through her tears, Dale stared ahead. She held on to Tino's foot as if her hands were glued to it. Mila applied the tourniquet. "You're O.K., Tino. You are all right," she repeated as she worked the tourniquet.

Losing blood fast, Tino rolled his eyes back. As he fainted, his face a sick green, he breathed out several words so softly they were barely audible, "Save yourselves."

Debra and Rosie crawled next to their father's head. "Daddy!" cried Debra, "don't die, Daddy!"

Elena brought out some clean rags and wiped surface shrapnel wounds on her uncle's arms and chest. She said, "Here, Dan, finish this." She drew her cousins away from their father and went into the shelter entrance, sitting where they could still see him. "Your Daddy isn't going to die," Elena said, her words filled with conviction. "You'll upset him if you cry like that. Just say, 'He's going to be all right!'"

Stroking their heads and wiping their eyes with the back of her hands, Elena soothed them. The loud crying stopped. They sobbed quietly as she talked to them gently. Vida joined them and began a low hum.

Carl relieved Dale. "Go with the girls. I'll do this," he told her, taking Tino's limp foot and holding it up while Mila worked on him. The bleeding had slowed. He could see where the bullet had knicked an artery in his instep. Probably from rifle fire, he thought. He saw his brother-in-law's eyes flicker. "Hold on, Tino," he said.

Mila finally stopped the bleeding. They washed and dressed the other wounds. Then they settled him in the trench, his head just inside the shelter. Mila took a wet rag and cooled his forehead. "You're not going to die, Tino..." she told him.

For the first time, Tino looked up at her as if he heard her. Dale took the rag from Mila and continued to wipe his forehead. She leaned forward and kissed her sister-in-law. "You saved his life!"

Mila knew she had.

When it got dark, Carl, Dan, Tim and Paco pulled Tino as far into the shelter as they could. They placed a large, shallow laundry tub they had saved over his exposed torso. Dale gave him shallow spoonfuls of water. His pallor was gone; he had a feverish flush.

Mila diluted some corned beef and made it into a broth for Tino. She passed the bowl down the line in the shelter. It reached Debra, who was hunched next to her father. She dropped it. Hot salty broth spilled over Tino. "*Puñeta!*" he swore in Spanish.

The rest of them were stunned into silence. Then a slow gutteral laugh emanated from deep in Tino's chest. It traveled up and shook him before bursting out of his throat.

One by one they added to the chorus. They laughed tentatively for several moments. Tino was the last to stop.

He's going to make it, Mila thought.

By morning, some of Tino's wounds had scabs. His fever was down. Sensing the presence of dried blood, red ants had started to sting him. Enraged, he raised up on his elbows and cursed. "You sons of bitches, get off me!"

Then suddenly, he muttered, "Jesus!" He raised himself up higher on his elbows. "I must be hallucinating!"

Debra poked her head out of the shelter. "What do you see, Daddy?"

"Ah-Americans!" the words rang out of his mouth.

"Americans!" Debra shouted. The word traveled rapidly among them. They breathed it out, as if it were holy—"Americans!" Then again—"Americans!" until it reverberated through the shelter.

One by one, the family emerged. They squinted in the sun, adjusting their eyes until they were able to focus clearly on the faces of two American scouts, who were standing by the wall that separated the Kellers from the Japanese military compound. The soldiers stared in shock at the bedraggled group, which now included the Gonzalez family. "What in Christ's name are you doing here?" the tall and blond one of the two exclaimed.

Smiles froze on their grimy faces. No one answered.

The shorter, dark-skinned scout spoke. "We ambushed the compound behind you last night. Helluva battle. It's a damned good thing none of us knew you were here!"

"Someone knew we were here!" cried Tino from the trench.

"Jesus!" the scout cried. "We need to get help for you!"

Still no one in the group spoke. They just stood there as if they had been turned to stone. Debra broke the spell. Gingerly, she touched the darker scout on the arm. He smiled. Patting her matted hair, he said, "You better get back in the shelter, honey. You're in the middle of a battlefield."

Carl squinted. Tears glistened in his eyes. "Damned glad you're here!" he said. "Can you help us?"

The light-haired one shook his head. His battle uniform was soaked in sweat. "We can't. We're scouting the area. You need the medics. Have to crawl back five hundred yards," he pointed south, "to the outpost we set up in the field."

"But there are Japs hiding everywhere," Carl said grimly.

"It's your only chance. You've got to get out now. We're pushing on to Rizal Stadium. Our main force is going right through here!" the soldier warned.

The dark-haired American saw something move. "Heads up!" he cried; and, as if their response was programmed, the two scouts crouched and charged through the rubble and out through a large shell hole that had ripped apart the front wall of the Kellers' fence. They seemed to vaporize into the gutted horizon line.

Carl's face sagged. "I'm going. We don't stand a chance around here," he said.

Chapter Sixteen

Sofía

Ben's house escaped the fire. The family hid in the basement pantry. Their arms and legs overlapping, they crammed together and prayed the cement walls would withstand the bombardment. Listless from lack of air provided by two narrow wall vents, they waited for breaks in the firing so they could crawl to an adjacent basement toilet. Confined in darkness, they were never sure what time of day or night it was. To pass long hours, they told jokes and familiar stories. They recited the rosary together in a dreary chain of voices.

On the third morning each of them scooped out an individual portion of cold rice from a community bowl. It had been hours since Sofía had uttered a word. Past the point of hysteria, she had succumbed to a state of silent depression. Emotional strain and malnutrition had made her physically vulnerable to a recurrence of an old illness—malaria. The fever had sneaked into her life several times since its original onset many years before.

Two-year-old Paz rolled over onto her grandmother's lap. Sofía reached down absently and smoothed the child's curly dark head. "*Preciosa*," she said inaudibly, as scenes shifted in her mind like fast footage in a film strip, taking her back several decades to when she was a young mother.

"Mila, *mi preciosa* Mila..."

Paz pressed closer. "Belana," she whimpered sleepily. The fever kept rising. Sofía trembled. Her skin felt blistering hot. I am suffocating! I must get out of here, she said to herself. Gently, she nudged the sleeping Paz onto a rumped bedspread on the concrete floor. Then she edged toward the door on hands and knees. Ben saw his mother in the crack of light as she opened the door. "*Mamá, qué te pasa?*" he asked.

Sofía mumbled an answer under her breath. In the jumble of words, Ben thought he heard "*nada.*" Assuming she was going to use the toilet, he leaned back against the hard cold wall, half sick himself from lack of food.

It was high noon, but when Sofía stood out in the open, she saw a war-torn world, a strange monochromatic gray world, dull, dark and gloomy. Familiar landmarks had disappeared, replaced by craters and gutted malformations rising grotesquely in a wasteland of blown and burned debris.

Crablike, she ducked down and began to crawl sideways. Her braids had become undone, and long strands of graying hair whipped around her shoulders. Then, looking like an apparition, she half-stood and began to step over the scorched ground and its bizarre forms—a bent and blackened bicycle frame, a wheel-less baby carriage, a dented stove peppered with bullet holes.

A half-mile away from Ben's, she stumbled over a foul-smelling, black-helmeted form. It was the swollen body of a Japanese soldier. The flesh was burned away from his face, revealing parts of his skull. There were indistinct murky holes where eyes, nose and mouth had been. *"Diablo!"* Sofía gasped. Her mind badly jarred, she was certain she must be in hell. *"Diablo!"* exploded from her mouth again. She averted her eyes and turned away from the stink of death. Breaking into an unsteady gait, she took a few more erratic steps and tripped over a fallen window grill. Losing her balance completely, she pitched forward.

The mound of ashes on which she fell felt soft and warm. She curled up in fetal position, tucking her head into her chest. Gunfire began to burst anew. Sofía lost consciousness as delirium thrust her back to fragmented scenes of the past:

She found herself in Valencia, Spain. She was eight years old. It was nighttime. Summer. She lay very quietly in her narrow bed and could hear the waves and smell the sea breeze from the nearby shore. She listened for the special sound of baby chicks that were in a box under her bed, proud her father had entrusted them to her. *"Pollitos!"* she called out to them. "Why don't you 'peep'? You are much too quiet!"

Slipping out of bed, she stood barefoot in her long white cotton nightgown. She lit the candle on her night table, crouched down and set it by her side. Then she reached under the bed for the box. Immediately, the chicks began to peep. In the flickering flame, their yellow fuzz twinkled with light.

Delighted, she picked up one of the balls of fluff. In her haste, she knocked the candle over. Flames flashed around the hem of her nightgown. It caught fire in seconds.

"Papá!" she screamed. Her father, who was in the courtyard outside his daughter's bedroom smoking a bedtime cigar, came running immediately.

The next thing Sofía knew she was cradled in his arms, wrapped tightly in a blanket. "Papá, Papá," she wailed as the pain from badly burned feet and legs became unbearable. In her mind she continued to react to the chaotic scene—the white torch of flame circling around and up her nightgown, the invasive odor of burning flesh—a scene that would be branded in her mind.

She smelled that burning flesh again in the debris of war. Painfully, she opened her eyes. She was lying on a bed of ashes. Back in hell? If not hell, then where? Dramatically, her temperature had dropped. Her mind began to clear, as on a battlefield when the clouds of conflict lift. Her world gradually refocused. As the realization of where she was hit her, a surge of fear returned with its protective shield, and she instinctively froze. Only her eyes moved as they scanned up, down, and around. Then she saw them—a pair of army boots planted right above her head. They were filthy with caked mud and dust. She closed her eyes tightly so she would not see the death blow when it came. When it did not come, she opened her eyes, and without blinking, waited...

"Ma'am?" a deep voice drawled. "Ma'am, are you all right?"

Chapter Seventeen

Liberation

Fear took Carl by the nape of the neck. He dashed across the yard to the Chews'. Gunfire pinged at him from every direction. He was not sure where he was in the mountain of slag. Then he saw them—Lee Chew, face down, his white shirt tattered by machine-gun bullets, his back a piece of bloody flesh. Rosario lay a few feet away. Congealed blood had matted her long black hair over her face. The fingers of her right hand were inches away from Trina. The child's eyes were closed, her mouth slightly open as if she were sleeping. She lay in a small puddle of blood. A bullet had entered her neck, just under the hairline.

A loud groan exploded from Carl's heaving chest. Rage brewed with fear and catapulted him like a living shell. Under mortar, machine-gun, and sniper rifle fire, he was forced intermittently to take cover in the rubble. It was a half-hour before he got to the outpost five hundred yards away. A dozen foxholes sheltered a group of infantry. Brokenly, Carl told them his story.

Within minutes he was heading back to the shelter. Two medics with a stretcher came up behind him. They found the family crouched around the bamboo with their *bayóngs* and bags. The medics carefully lifted Tino onto the stretcher. One of them said, "Listen now. We'll go six feet apart. Stay close to the ground. Don't stop for anything, unless they're firing directly at you," he paused to lift his end of the stretcher. "Then go down. But keep running as soon as you can!" he barked. "Let's go. Who's first?"

"I am," Elena volunteered. She stepped up, hatbox in one hand, and in the other, a short rope to which Max was tied. She felt like a tight spring ready to snap. Something inside her shouted, Run!

The medics rushed away with the stretcher. They were six feet ahead when Elena ran forward. The rest of the group strung out unevenly behind her. She could hear Carl say, "Go!" Mila ran with Debra, followed by Dale with Rose. She could hear Salome squealing as Tim dragged her on the rope. The Gonzalez family were the last to run.

In one long dash for life, Elena kept her place in line behind the medics. She moved in a stumbling run, her heart beating in her mouth, her hair flying. One word shot from her mouth—"Run! Run! Run!"

Gunfire burst around them without let-up. The medic's words burned in her mind. "Don't stop for anything except for a barrage directed at you." Energy surged through her. It seemed to lift her off the ground. "I won't stop at all!" she cried. She was so blind to all but the need to escape that she failed to notice the three bodies of the Chews as she passed—her eyes straight ahead.

She followed the medics to the outpost, the rest of them behind her. Elena was stopped by the body of a Filipino civilian that lay in her path. Dead for several days, it emitted a nauseating stench. She held her nose, side-stepped the corpse and ran a jagged line to the field.

She stumbled right into a foxhole. Jolted, as if from a dream, Elena found herself eye-to-eye with four bearded American soldiers. One of them peered at her wide gray-green eyes and blinked. Under a low helmet and over a curly beard, his eyes were the part of his face that she could see clearly. He stared and asked, "You're real?"

Nothing came out of Elena's mouth. She simply stared back at him.

Another soldier studied her—the torn, dirty clothing, the sooty, bloodstained arms and legs, the straggly hair. He started to chuckle. "Didn't know they had hillbillies here in the Philippines," he said.

Elena stared down at herself. She saw that her legs were covered with grime and dried blood from her shrapnel wound, as well as from her uncle's wounds. She was barefoot. The polka dots on her shorts had turned grimy; the pants hung loose around her waist. Suddenly she felt hunger gnawing at her. She realized she hadn't eaten since last night; and then, had just had bites of corned beef.

Without knowing why, Elena felt a surge of overwhelming emotion. "W-what day is it?" she asked, wiping a dirty palm over her wet eyes.

One of the men leaned forward to touch her, but thought better of it and said, "It's February 14, honey—St. Valentine's Day!" He smiled. Seeing his white teeth and broad smile, she remembered Jerry, and more tears came.

The curly-bearded one said, "Don't cry! Come on now. It's Valentine's Day!"

Valentine's Day? How improper for it to be Valentine's Day! She sat up straight. The irony began to amuse her. She let out a giggle. The soldiers' eyes shone, and they laughed with her, reserved at first, but then boomed, in shared elation.

At that moment, a mortar exploded in a foxhole across the field. The soldiers pushed Elena's head down. She didn't see a body fly into the air, nor did she see the the medics running over. "Shit!" one of them shouted.

Suddenly Dan appeared. "We're leaving, Elena," he said. "Oh!" Elena cried, grabbing her hatbox. Remembering she had let Max loose, she looked around for him and saw that Dan had him by the rope. "Hurry," he said.

One of the soldiers reached for her arm as she got out of the foxhole.

"Goodbye!" he said. Taking his helmet, he placed it on her head. Then playfully he took it back and put it on his own head. "Thanks—all of you!" she cried.

"Bye!" the G.I.'s said in chorus, as she turned with Dan to join Carl and the others.

"Where are we going?" Elena asked Carl, who was herding everyone together when she and Dan reached him.

"Tino is headed for the field hospital. We're going to Hans Benslis' house south of here. The soldiers say there are several homes in that area that are still standing."

They waited for the medics to carry the stretcher away. Dale and the girls cried. Tino waved to them. Color rose back in his face. He's going to make it, Elena told herself. She waved back. Debra whimpered. "Come on," Elena said, taking her by the hand. "Let's get Rosie. We are going to go to a place where I hope there will be food."

Debra stalled. "I want to go with Daddy!" she cried.

"Your Daddy has to go to the hospital, so he'll get well. We're going to Bensli's," Elena said.

"Who's Bensli?" asked Debra.

"He's a Swiss friend of Carl's. Hurry, before the firing starts again."

Once more, they moved six feet apart, crouched low to the ground. Ten blocks later, they were well within the American lines. They found the Bensli house still standing, its green wood frame loomed ahead of them like an oasis.

A block away was the open-air market, where Carmen Cruz had met Vida many months before. It was now liberated. As they passed the rubble of shelled and burned out stalls, it seemed incredible to them that this spot was now a part of their historic past.

When the family entered the Benslis' yard, they met another American encampment. A platoon of men from the First Cavalry were entrenched in foxholes. "Snipers," a corporal said, as the Keller group filed past. "Watch out for them!"

Two hours later, Hilda Bensli ladled out rice and talinum soup to the fourteen refugees lodged in her basement. They had taken turns washing in a shallow laundry tub filled with cold water from a well. Each one used the water until it was so black it had to be thrown out. After washing up, they put their filthy torn clothes back on.

Elena felt cleaner than she had ever felt in her life. She looked at Dan, who sat next to her on the basement floor. "I can see your face again," she said. Then noticing a cut on his arm, she asked, "Where did you get that?"

Spooning his soup, her brother explained. "On the run over, but I don't remember how." She looked at the small wound on her elbow and saw that it had a scab.

The warm broth acted like a sleeping potion. Sitting upright, as they had in the shelter, one by one, they fell asleep.

The next morning, Elena awoke to find herself in the middle of the basement floor. She had rolled over many times during the night, fighting a black anxiety brought on by nightmares—bizarre scenes of fire, shelling, and dead bodies, all descending on her like bats in hell. At dawn she sat up, and realizing where she was, began to sob with relief. The others, lying on the floor around her, continued to sleep soundly. No one stirred when she got up to blow her nose and then go to the hat box in the corner of the bare room. Laying out the items on the floor, she found what she had been looking for—her diary and the only extra outfit she had saved—the dirndl skirt made from drapes and a white blouse. She changed into them quickly, rolling up the sailor blouse and polka dot shorts, filthy from days of wear, and putting them aside for washing.

She went to a pail full of water in the corner of the basement and dipped her hands in. The water felt cool as she splashed it on her face. Then she used the chamber pot in the bathroom. There was no water in the pipes or in the toilet. Looking around, she thought, How amazing that this place survived. The Japs must have cleared out of here to concentrate in our area and downtown for their last fight.

Through the large screened window of the daylight basement she could see the soldiers of the First Cavalry moving around their encampment. They looked tall and lithe to her. Suddenly she felt a surge of elation. We're actually free, she thought.

The familiar smell of a *kalan* fire reached Elena's nostrils. Opening the door, she followed her nose to where Vida fanned the coals of a makeshift *kalan* she had put together from rocks and bricks. Studying her in the early morning light, Elena again felt her chest welling up. It looks so good to see her sitting there with the sun making her hair gleam and the skin on her arms shine. She's so thin, but so alive, Elena thought.

"Good smell?" Vida looked up and smiled.

"Mmm..." Elena voiced her approval. "Is that what I think it is?"

"Rice," she answered, making the smoke waft and the coals glow brilliant red.

Rice, repeated Elena to herself, what would we do without it? The corned beef was becoming a memory at the prospect of eating fresh warm rice again. "I am very hungry!" she said.

Vida's eyes twinkled.

As Elena waited for the rice to cook, she saw a helmeted sergeant coming toward them. He held a rifle in one hand and a paper sack in the other. "Hi!" he said. "This is for you." He extended the sack.

Flustered, Elena took a step back. "Oh," she managed to respond. Vida walked over and accepted the gift.

"Thank you," she said.

The sergeant helped her unload the sack. A dozen cans of food rolled out—spam, string beans, fruit, milk, and margarine. Vida's eyes shone. She pulled Elena forward. "Food!" she cried.

Elena gave a shy smile. Regaining composure, "It's very thoughtful of you," she said. "Thank you."

"You're welcome. We thought you could use it. You're all pretty skinny," he said. Taking off his helmet, he scratched his head. "You need to stay inside. We shot another sniper a few hours ago. They are still around, hiding in the fields."

"We'll be careful," Elena said. She had relaxed and was enjoying the conversation, noticing the young man's bright eyes and ruddy face."

"Things are clearing up in this area. Tanks are coming through. It's downtown that's still bad," he said.

"I know," Elena said. "We just got out of the battlefield."

The sergeant shook his head. Hearing the staccato of machine-gun fire from the encampment, he swung around and was gone before he could say goodbye.

The two women grabbed the pot of rice and went in the house, where everyone feasted on a breakfast of rice and spam. Later they heard another sniper had been killed.

The tanks the soldier said were coming through arrived midmorning. They rumbled over the dirt road by the Bensli property on their way to the battle a mile-and-a-half north. Dozens of Filipinos lined up on both sides of the road and yelled out cheers, waving their arms and making the V-for-Victory sign. The entire group at the Bensli house ran out to join the welcome.

Elena felt a catch in her throat that had been with her since early morning. It was a joy so close to tears, she laughed and cried by turns. Her vision of the soldiers in the tanks attached to the 37th Infantry Division blurred as they rode in the open, waving and throwing candy bars. A half-eaten C-bar flew at Elena. She caught it and waved her thanks. Standing next to her, Mila and Carl were yelling *"Mabuhay!"* with the crowd. *"Mabuhay!"* yelled Elena. Then again and again, *"Mabuhay!"* It seemed to right to use the word in Tagalog, which toasted life.

When she wrote in her diary that evening, it was as if she wrote about the first day in a new life. *"Many times today I had to tell myself that it's really true—we have been liberated. The Americans have taken over this part of the city—its outskirts. They have gun emplacements all around, and they are picking off Jap snipers who are firing from the ruins of burned houses and from trees and bushes in the fields. Heavy guns are blasting at Rizal Stadium. The G.I.'s from the encampment on this block got a sniper this morning. Dan and Tim saw him. They said half his head was blown off. The Filipinos who passed him threw rocks and spat at his corpse."*

She told about the tanks and the food that was given to them by the G.I., then she wrote, *"As soon as the stadium is taken we'll go to find out what happened to Uncle Ben and the rest of the family. Right now, there is furious fighting where our old house was, and at the Ermita and the walled city.*

"A Swiss friend of Mr.Bensli made it across the lines from the Ermita. He said hundreds of people have been massacred and raped there. They even killed the people taking refuge at the Spanish Embassy and at the Philippine General Hospital. There's nothing left of the legislative building or the courthouse. It's street-to-street fighting there. We're so worried about the family and about our friends. What's happening to them all? There's no news except from people who cross the lines..."

Manila was taken street by street, block by block, house by house. The noose made by the First Cavalry, the 37th Infantry and the 11th Airborne tightened by the hour, but it would be after the first of March, 1945, before the fighting ceased. Manila lay in an agony of shelled and blistered rubble, mortally wounded.

Pillaged and raped, the city writhed in the suffocating stench of thousands upon thousands of dead. But the battle for her would be won. Fighting for her life, she made a promise that she would would rise anew from the cratered moonlike wasteland.

The homeless, the displaced, wandered everywhere. Starving and destitute as the Kellers had been, they searched, like birds, for a place to perch, to stay the night, to regain their energies, so they could move on.

After a week at the Benslis', the family awaited news about Tino. They had heard nothing. Then one afternoon he arrived in a jeep and surprised them. Dale and the girls ran up, helped him out and smothered him with hugs and kisses. The others joined in the welcome. "Tino!" Carl hailed. "You're back so soon! Wasn't the food good?"

"You can't kill an old son-of-a-bitch like me!" Tino grunted. He limped as he walked to the house, but his gait was light and his face shone with enthusiasm. "Say," he told them, "had news through the hospital grapevine that Mamá and Ben are in another field hospital in the Santa Ana district. They made it. But there was something about Mamá I didn't understand. Apparently, she nearly died from starvation and exposure. Ben was wounded—a bullet in his shoulder. It's all I know."

"*Gracias a Dios.* But what about Mamá?" Mila cried.

Tino nodded. "We'll know shortly when we get a ride out to see them."

Two days later, they were offered a ride in an army truck. They crossed a pontoon bridge over the Pasig. The Jones Bridge and other bridges crossing the river had been blown up by the Japanese when they cut themselves off in a last-ditch stand for the city.

Street after street, the black grit of war sifted over shattered buildings, headless trees and charred bodies, plus hundreds buried in mountainous debris. Landmarks—the stadium, the legislative building, the courthouse— reduced to desolate ruins, transforming a once-familiar landscape to an ominous scene of destruction.

As the truck crossed the Pasig, Dan, who was on his knees on the wooden seat, called out, "Look at those dead Japs. Burned. Still holding their guns in that pillbox!"

Elena, hands over her face, slid down to the floor of the truck. I won't look, she said to herself. I've seen enough... and that horrible smell!

"Hey, Elena, look what I see," cried Tim, who rode next to his brother.

Then she heard Carl yell, "Stop the truck. Please!" Something is wrong, she thought.

The truck jarred to a stop. Elena heard the excitement coming from voices on the street. She sat up quickly. A group of refugees stood around an old pushcart, top-heavy with bags, boxes and loose items of clothing and bedding. Then she saw a frantic arm waving to her. "Lise!" Elena screamed. Lise was up to the truck when Elena jumped out and fell into her arms. "My God, Lise!" was all she could say.

"We just got out of the Ermita!" Lise cried. "Thought we'd never make it. Piles and piles of dead..."

"Shh, don't tell me," Elena hugged her tight. "We've just been through it ourselves."

Lise began to cry quietly. "Some didn't make it."

Elena didn't want to hear, but the look on her friend's face told her that she must listen. "W-who?" she asked, dreading the answer.

"Remember Madame Rahbi?" Lise began, "She said..."

Elena cut in, "She said, 'You'll be enveloped in flames, like a great oven. Many will die.'" As she finished, Elena suddenly knew. "Isabel!"

"Yes, poor Isabel," Lise nodded. "And Father Kiley—murdered in the church!"

Elena clutched Lise's hand. "Father Kiley!" she cried, tears springing to her eyes. "How?"

"He wouldn't let the Japs search the sacristy. They crucified him," Lise said. She sighed heavily. Her thin shoulders slouched, making her look years older.

The two young women—symbols of civilians caught in a death struggle—bore their pain together. Closed in a tight embrace, their sobs rose as from the depths of their souls.

Carl tapped Elena on the shoulder, "We've got to go, Elena," he said, barely above a whisper.

He held her hand and reached out to touch Lise's elbow. "I'm glad you're all O.K."

Elena turned back. "Did the Japs get Isabel?" she asked suddenly.

"No—a grenade."

Elena breathed a sigh of relief.

The Kellers waved slowly from the truck. "They're on their way to a rescue camp. We'll be going, too," Carl said.

"I thought we were going to see Belana," said Elena.

"Yes," nodded Carl, "but in a few days we'll go to the repatriation center in Santo Tomás."

Elena's heart leaped. I hope I can see Trish, my dad, aunt, and the rest of them, she thought, as the truck swayed on the road to the hospital, avoiding the rubble and the dead.

The field hospital was a converted school house. Its rooms were too small for the narrow cots, its halls too tight for the rush of doctors and nurses caring for the wounded.

A husky medical officer led the Kellers to Sofía's cot. "She's over there," he said, pointing to a corner crowded with beds and I.V. stands. "You asked about Ben Fernandez. We released him yesterday. Shoulder wound," he said, heavy brows drawn, as they reached Sofía's bed.

A bottle dripped into a tube in her arm. To Elena, she looked as if she were made of wax. Two heavy braids spread like gray wings on her pillow. A sheet that covered her rose almost imperceptively. "She's been very ill," the doctor said. We had to give transfusions. She was dehydrated after being lost in the battlefield." His thick brows moved as he talked.

Mila gripped Carl's hand. "Lost?" she questioned.

The doctor gave a slow nod. "The medics said the explosions must have terrified her. She ran off into a field. Had collapsed when they found her. She also had a fever."

Mila's voice trembled. "*La malaria*! Will she live?"

The doctor looked at Sofía's comatose face. "I believe she'll come out of it. She's in and out of consciousness. Don't stay long," he said.

Mila leaned over the bed. "Mamá," she whispered. "*Es Mila*," she said in Spanish. "Mamá?"

Sofía's eyelids raised slightly, then closed. Mila bent over and kissed her white forehead. Again, Sofía's eyelids fluttered for a moment, and closed. Her pale dry lips stuck to her teeth. "I don't think she hears me," Mila said.

Elena reached under the sheet for her grandmother's hand. "Belana?" she called, squeezing the bony fingers gently.

"Ahh," Sofía groaned, her eyes open now.

The doctor stepped forward. "She's coming out of it. Don't tire her."

"M-Mila," Sofía voiced her daughter's name in a hoarse whisper.

"*¡Ay*, Mamá!" Mila cried, pressing her face to her mother's.

Sofía's hollow eyes went from face to face. She studied the doctor. Her look clouded. In a voice that was more of a groan, she rasped, "Major Thompson?"

The doctor glanced at Mila. She stroked her mother's hand. "Major Thompson was someone she knew years ago. You must look like him," Mila explained.

The doctor nodded, "I'm Dr. Robinson, *Señora* Fernandez," he said, patting her arm.

"Thank you, Dr. Robinson," Mila said. When she turned back to Sofía, she saw she had slipped from consciousness.

"Come and see her. It helps," Dr. Robinson told them as they filed back into the hallway.

"We're going to Santo Tomás in a few days," Carl told him. It's closer. We'll be back."

Dan and Tim raced outdoors ahead of the family. An army abulance arrived and began to unload more wounded. Two nurses ran out to assist. As Dan walked to the ambulance, he stared at one of them. He turned back to Mila and started to say, "I think it's..." when Mila pushed ahead of him and called out, "Angela!"

The small dark nurse, her hair clipped short, looked up from beside the stretchers. Her coal-black eyes snapped wide open. "Mila!" she cried. "Wait, Mila!" She hung on to the plasma bottle and looked around. Another nurse rushed in on the scene and took it from her. Crying out, Angela stretched forth her arms and fell into Mila's embrace. They rocked in each other's arms, voicing a chant-like murmur that rose like a prayer. Dan squeezed his sister's hand. "Can't believe it!" he cried.

Elena had no words.

Angela's story came out in fragments. "We were liberated when the First Cavalry came through. Helped them by blowing up a bridge. Sabotaged Jap reinforcements. But lost so many of ours. Marco..."

Not Marco! thought Dan. Angela went on. "A hero. Single-handed, he set up the dynamite. Didn't make it back. The Americans rolled through—finally. What hell...but here I am."

Dan fought tears. When Mila and Elena had finished hugging Angela, he walked up to her. "You're a a hero—Carmen Cruz—you're a hero..."

Angela folded into Dan's arms. Together they wept for Marco.

When the army truck bumped away from the hospital, Angela had disappeared into the group of medics who tended the wounded.

On February 27, the Kellers entered the repatriation center at Santo Tomás. Elena found Trish as she and her family were packing, preparing to board an Army transport plane repatriating them to the United States. Weeks of starvation had reduced Trish to some eighty pounds. But her face bore the spark of freedom, and she gave her old friend a hug that took her breath away. Tears blurred their image of each other's faces.

They sat on the stairs of the main building and talked in familiar whispers, as they had before the war. Still whispering, they left the stairs and walked to the shanty where Luisa and family lived, and had another reunion there.

An hour later, they went through shelled-out portions of the main building. "Jill Wier bled to death there." Trish pointed to where a shell had blasted through a stone wall. "Her jugular was severed."

Elena shuddered.

Motioning her to a large window, Trish said, "I used to sit on this sill at night, Elena, and look at the stars. I thought of you often. I prayed a lot."

Trish's blue eyes looked at her softly. "I don't know why I never lost faith. I knew we'd survive. Even when Jill was killed, something kept me going."

Something kept me going, too, Elena thought. She did not want to question it now. "Some things are a mystery," she said.

"It's all a mystery," Trish smiled. Her teeth looked prominent on her gaunt face. Elena glanced at Trish's thin hands, then at her own. "We look like two old crones, don't we?" she remarked.

"Yeah, but I'm eating like a fool," laughed Trish.

"Me, too!" Elena said.

Arm-in-arm they walked to Trish's shanty to continue packing her belongings for the long flight home. They talked non-stop. After saying goodbye to Trish, Elena went to the administration office to inquire about her father. An officer there told her Stu had left to join MacArthur's headquarters. He handed her a small note. "He knew you would be asking," he said.

Elena opened the folded square of paper and recognized her father's round hand. *"Dearest Elena,"* it began, *"I just heard you are all safe! I'm grateful. I am going back now to finish what I started in Corregidor. Will do my best to see you. But if I can't, you know I love you."* It was signed, *"Your Dad."*

Elena was not to see him before she, Mila, Carl, Dan and Tim were repatriated to the United States. Two weeks after she got the note, the Ferdandez family met at the field hospital to say goodbye to the Kellers.

Sofía had moved back and forth from the door of death. Gradually, the frail thread that held her life strengthened. She regained consciousness; gradually she began to eat. Blood transfusions returned color to her face. On the afternoon the family circled her cot, she no longer looked to them like a corpse.

"Oye," she said, "I am going to America, too, as soon as I get back on my feet. I can go as an American!" she exclaimed, a spark of humor shining in her luminous eyes.

"An American?" several of them questioned.

"Sí! Those transfusions—American blood!" she sat up in bed.

"By golly, Mamá, you're right. You're an American by blood," Tino said. His face showed he had gained weight. Debra and Rosie stood beside him and giggled.

Josefina and Carlos spoke in unison. "No, Mamá," they chorused.

"¿Cómo?" Sofía questioned.

"Manila is home," Josefina said, "you can stay with us."

"Or with us!" Ben stepped forward.

Sofía nodded her head. "We'll see," she said with deliberation, "we'll see..."

"We came to say *'adiós,'*" said Carl, stepping forward from the circle. "We're leaving in a few days for the States. We need a new start."

"¡Qué bien!" several of them cried, but there were tears in their eyes.

Ben tried to make a joke. "Hey, where did you get that dress, Elena? You look like a green parrot!"

Heads focused on Elena's dress. It was bright chartreuse, with glass buttons on the front and a swirling circle skirt. The dress had come from the Red Cross. There had been little choice.

Elena tossed her head. "I like it!" she said.

"*Mi Elena*," Sofía reached for her granddaughter. "Come here, *cariño*." Taking Elena's hands she folded them into her own. "My proud Elena!"

Later that day, they said goodbye to Vida. Carl told her he would send money to Batangas when he got a job in the States. She thanked him. "It will help my family. And maybe one day I can have my *sari-sari* store."

When it was time for Elena to hug her, Vida looked her straight in the eye and said, "Remember me when you think about the gecko, ha?" She slipped a bracelet made of coconut shell into Elena's hand.

Elena stifled a sob. "I'll never forget you!" she said shakily. Then seeing Vida's brave face, she held up the bracelet and said, "Thank you. Good luck on the *sari-sari!*"

The goodbyes were not over. Before the Kellers left Manila, Elena received a short message from the Red Cross. It was a response to an inquiry she had made when they got to the camp, requesting information as to Jerry's whereabouts. The message informed her that "regretfully" Jerry Merrill was missing and presumed drowned. On October 24, 1944, an American submarine torpedoed the Japanese transport on which he was being transferred to Japan with hundreds of other POWs. The Red Cross added that Jerry's parents in Colorado had been notified.

The blow was wounding. Despite the months of grieving she had done, sensing from deep within, where intuition lay that Jerry was dead, the formal announcement made it a final reality. Awash in a flash flood of renewed emotion, her tears flowed in a last goodbye.

In time, the empty place left by grief would heal alongside the other losses. But she would leave part of herself in the broken remains of the Philippines—for her, now holy ground to which she would have allegiance for the rest of her life.

At siesta time on the afternoon before her departure, Elena lay on the bamboo slat bed in the shanty. She traced the path of a black beetle as it went up the thatched wall. The insect meandered, seemingly unstable, uncertain. She observed its roundabout course, its shiny stick-like legs making tedious progress. She talked to it: "You don't know where you are going anymore than I do," she chided. "You are free to do what you want, but you are wandering all over the place."

The beetle knew exactly where it was headed. Circling back and forth, stopping to probe into the thatch, it finally climbed the open window frame; and by slow degrees moved out to the open air.

Elena conceded: "You fooled me. Knew all along where you were going." Then insight sparked—perhaps I will find my direction in the same way. For now, at least I know I am free.

It was bitter-sweet freedom. She knew she was still attached to the umbilicus of war by the fire of survival that continued to burn within—an inner energy that had given her courage to withstand the shocks of war. It was a fire she still held onto, for it had become synonymous with life.

Could she translate its energy to fuel new experience, allow herself to be open to the journey ahead? She turned to her diary: "*I am really not ready, but I have to go. I've packed my hatbox. I have a few new things, but will take some old rags, too.*"

Pen in mid-air, an analogy flashed into her mind—the old and new garments of experience! If she could take these clothes with her, her green dress and the blood-stained shorts and ragged sailor blouse, why not a mix of experiences—past, present, and future?

She could vitalize her life, keep that inner fire, draw from its positive energy to provide continued courage to face a new existence. Eventually, the vacuum left by the holocaust—the killings, the torture, the hunger, the personal loss—would fill with shapes of the future. Even the loss of her first love, Jerry, could lend its embers to light future yearnings.

She wrote one more line before closing the diary, "*I can't quite bear all this change, but tomorrow I am going to try.*"

On March 15, 1945, the LST carrying the Keller family pulled away from Manila. A dawn light cast its innuendos over the dimming shoreline and its ghost army of hunched ruins. Moments later, the sun bannered over the water, touching purple waves with brass, lighting the sunken hulls of dozens of ships in the harbor.

Elena leaned against the side of the landing craft as it made its way to the troop ship. Except for the grind of the motor, it was quiet. No shells, no bombs, no fire. She took a deep breath. The sapphire ring her mother had given her sparked its blue light. On the same hand, she wore Vida's bracelet.

She glanced over at the fixed expressions of her family. Pressed together in a line along the side, their faces were brightened by the sun, but sadness ruled their eyes. Refugees, they were leaving their adopted homeland, their solitary possessions in two *bayóngs*, an old suitcase, and a hatbox. Carl pulled Mila closer. He wore a new army jacket and mismatched old khaki shorts. Dan and Tim had held on to their worn shirts and patched pants. They were young men now, several inches taller than Elena, who had insisted on wearing the parrot green dress rather than the WAC uniform issued to her. She had crammed the uniform into the hatbox. Mila wore her comfortable culottes and had a blue bandana around her hair. Both women wore *bakias* on their bare feet.

Touch replaced talk. Carl gave Dan a pat on the shoulder. In turn,

Dan touched Tim, with eyes that acknowledged their goodbyes to the land of their birth.

Mila reached for her daughter and encircled her by the waist. The gesture made tears spring to Elena's eyes.

In silence, the bond that linked the family together was reaffirmed.

They watched the shore minituarize. A resplendent sun sparkled on the water. The motion of the waves became like music. In the rise and fall, Elena imagined she detected strains from the "Appassionata." She remembered Sarita, now as free as she. Though they would not see each other again, spiritually they were linked by the music. The soul-stirring passages moved inside Elena, fed her spirit, and broadened beyond her, gaining power and momentum toward the future.

One by one, the Kellers turned and faced the towering hull of the ship. It loomed like a monolith.

GLOSSARY

Tagalog
The Phillippine National Language

Atis — A sweet, pulpy tropical fruit filled with seeds.
Bahala-na — What will be, will be.
Bahay kubo — My home (my hut).
Bandurria — A stringed mandolin-like instrument.
Barong Tagalog — Male national dress, featuring a long-sleeved, loose-fitting embroidered shirt.
Bayóng — A sturdy carrying bag made of tough reed or grass fiber.
Betel nut — The seed from the betel palm, which is a mild stimulant when chewed.
Bibingka — A national dessert made with grated coconut and rice flour.
Bonga — A tall, dense tropical palm.
Bulak — Cotton.
Bunút — The process of floor polishing using coconut husks.
Dagmay — A rough dark handwoven fabric.
Dalaga — An unmarried woman.
Ganta — A traditional dry measure equal to two litres.
Hindî! — No!
Isá — One.
Igorot — A Malay tribe of northern Luzon.
Iná — Mother.
Kalan — A coal or wood-burning clay stove used in native cooking.
Kalachuchi (also Frangipani) — A fragrant, flower-bearing, tropical tree.
Lampaso — The process of polishing wooden floors with special rags.
Lanzone — A small tropical fruit with yellow skin and sweet clear meat, somewhat grape-like.
Lepanto — A handwoven fabric with elegant Igorot designs.
Lumpia — Philippine egg rolls.
Mabuhay! — Long life!
Magkano? — How much is it?
Magkano sitaw? — How much are the beans?
Maraming salamat — Thanks.
Masaráp — Delicious.
Mongo — A mung bean which has the consistency of a green pea but is smaller.
Narra — The national hardwood tree used for making furniture.
Nipa — A tropical palm used for thatching and weaving.
Nipa shack — A native hut made of nipa thatching.
Papaya — A melon-like tropical fruit.
Patawarin — Forgive, pardon.

Pay-pay — A stiff fan made of grass fiber.
Putanginamo! — Equal to: son-of-a-bitch!
Ramie — Cloth made from grass fiber.
Rattan — A tough climbing vine used for furniture making.
Salamat po — Thank you.
Sampaguita — A fragrant, star-shaped white blossom. The national flower.
Sari-sari store — A small convenience store.
Sayang — What a waste.
Sitaw — Stringed beans.
Supot — A handy carrying bag made of grass fiber.
Tagalog — The Philippine national language.
Talinum — A spinach-like green vegetable.
Terno — The female national dress of the Philippines.
Tuba — Wine made from fermented coconut sap.
Waláng hiyâ! — To have no shame!
Yanco — A filipino term for Americans, which was used during the Philippine-
    American war of 1898.

Spanish

Adiós — Goodbye.
Aguila — Eagle.
Amiga/o — Friend.
Aquí — Here.
Aves — Prayers to the Virgin Mary.
¡Basta! — Enough!
Bestias — Beasts, animals.
Bien — Fine, good.
Bueno — Good.
Café con leche — Coffee with cream or milk.
Cariño — Dear, love.
Cocodrilo — Crocodile.
¿Cómo? — How?
¿Cómo está/s? — How is/are...?
Corazón — Heart.
Diablo — The devil.
Dios mío — My God.
¿Dónde está? — Where is...?
El amor es poderoso — Love is powerful.
Elegante — Elegant.
Eres un cariño — You are a dear.
Es Mila — It's Mila.
España — Spain.
Está bien — That or he/she/it is fine.
Gracias — Thank you.
Gracias a Dios — Thank God.
Hija/s, hijo/s — Daughter/s, son/s.
¡Hola! — Hello!
Kilo/kilogram — A metric unit of weight measure (.4536 kilograms are equal to one
    pound).
La favorita — The favorite.

Lástima — Too bad.
Linda — Lovely, beautiful.
Los niños — The children.
Mi amiga/o — My friend.
Mi Elena — My Elena.
Mi preciosa Mila — My precious Mila.
Milagro — Miracle.
Muy bonita estás — You look very pretty.
Nada — Nothing.
Niñas — Girls.
Oye — Listen.
Paz — Peace.
Plancha — A flatiron; also used to refer to ironing.
Pobre — Poor thing, poor person.
Pollitos — Chicks.
¿Por qué? — Why?
Preciosa — Precious.
Provinciana/s, provinciano/s — Provincial/s.
Puñeta — A curse to you.
¿Qué? — What?
Qué bien — That's good.
¿Qué pasa? — What's happening? What's the matter?
¿Qué pasó? — What happened?
¿Qué te pasa? — What's the matter with you?
¿Qué te pasó? — What happened to you?
Querida — Dear.
Queridísima — Very dear one.
Qué tonta — How silly, how foolish.
Recuerdo — Souvenir.
Rubia/s, rubio/s — Blonde/s.
Rubita/s, rubito/s — Little blonde/s.
Salud — Health; to your health.
Señora/s, señor/es — Lady/ladies; mistress/mistresses — gentleman/gentlemen,
    mister/s.
Sí — Yes.
También — Too, also.
Tetas — Breasts.
Tonta — Silly, foolish.
Un milagro — A miracle.
Ven a comer — Come and eat.
Verdad — True, truth.

Spanish-Tagalog

Abaca/abaka — Hemp fiber used for weaving and other products.
Adobo/adobo — A national dish featuring a vinegar, garlic and soy sauce. Also a
    style of cooking.
¡Ay!/¡Ay! — Oh, dear!
¡Ay, Dios!/¡Ay, Diyós! — Oh, God!
Bakia/s/bakyâ/s — Wooden-soled, slip-ons.
Banca/banka — A long, narrow paddle boat with outriggers.

Barrio/barrio — A neighborhood community.
Basurero/basurero — Garbage collector.
Bata/bata — A loose-fitting gown or smock worn by women.
Bodega/bodega — Warehouse.
Bougainvillea/bougainvillea — A flowering tropical vine.
Calamansi/kalamansi — A small tropical lime.
Calesa/kalesa — A horse-drawn, two-wheeled carriage designed for several passengers and a driver.
Camiseta/kamiseta — Undershirt.
Camote/kamote — Sweet potato.
Carabao/kalabáw — A domestic water buffalo.
Carretela/karretela — Essentially, the same as a calesa.
Carromata/karromata — A horse-drawn, two-wheeled, enclosed carriage designed for two passengers.
Cassava/kassava — A starchy root often processed as flour.
Centavo/séntimós — Equal to half a U.S. penny.
Cochero/kochero — The driver of a horse-drawn carriage; a coachman.
Cogon/kogon — A tall tough grass, which often grows so thick it becomes impassable.
Hectare/ektarya — A metric unit of area equal to 2.471 acres.
Gecko/gekko — A small tropical lizard with adhesive toes and a distinctive call that mimics its name.
Guerrillera/s — Female guerrilla/s.
Guerrillero/s — Male guerrilla/s.
Lavendera/lavandera — Washerwoman.
Lechón/litsón — A national dish featuring roast suckling pig.
Loco/loko — Crazy.
Mabolo/mabulo — A malodorous, peachlike fruit.
Mango/manggá — A tropical fruit that tastes like a peach with a slight acidic flavor.
Merienda/merienda — Afternoon tea or snack.
Mestizo/mestizo — Offspring of mixed parentage.
Panatela/panatela — A long slender cigar.
Pancit/pansit — A noodle dish.
Pañuelo/pañuelo — Handkerchief or scarf, also panyô.
Penca/penka — The long fruit cluster of the banana tree.
Petate/petate — A sleeping mat made of grass fiber.
Piña/pinyá — Pineapple; also a fine cloth woven from pineapple fiber.
Sala/salas — Living room or parlor.

Special Terms

Amah — Nurse or nanny.
Appassionata — Beethoven Sonata in F Minor, Op. 57.
Atlas moth — Large pale brown moth with gray and black markings.
Battle of Midway — A decisive Naval battle of WW II, fought in June of 1942, resulting in a U.S. victory.
Beriberi — A disease resulting from the absence of vitamin B.
"Clacks" — Slip-ons whittled out of wood by POWs in the concentration camps in the Philippines.
Dengue fever — A tropical virus transmitted by a mosquito and characterized by fever and severe pains in the joints.

Dysentery — A severe inflammation of the large intestine characterized by diarrhea and fever.

Headhunters — Primitive tribes in Northern Luzon who at one time decapitated slain enemies.

Mata Hari — A WW I spy executed by the French.

Mickey Mouse Money — Inflated currency issued by the Japanese occupation forces in the Philippines.

New Guinea — Islands north of Australia from which Allied forces staged a major counterattack against the Japanese in WW II.

Pearl of the Orient — Metaphor for pre-war Manila.

Pushcart — A two or four-wheeled cart pushed by hand.

Typhoon — A tropical cyclone-like storm—"a big wind."

Voice of Freedom — An underground radio station broadcasting in the Philippines during the Japanese Occupation.

ISLANDS IN THE PHILIPPINES, PROVINCES, CITIES, TOWNS, SPECIAL PLACES AND HISTORICAL FACTS AND FIGURES REFERENCED IN *FIRES OF SURVIVAL*

Islands of the Philippines

Cebu — An island known as one of the Visayas, which are a group of islands located between Luzon and Mindanao.

Leyte — Located in the Visayas, Leyte became the first landing site for U.S. forces during the liberation of the Philippines in October, 1944.

Luzon — Comprising a third of the total area of the Philippines, Luzon is a large island located at the northern point of the Philippine Archipelago.

Mindanao — The second largest island in the Philippines and located at the southern point of the island chain.

Provinces, Towns, Cities, Special Locations, Historical Information

Luzon

Manila — Capital of the Philippine Islands and the main commercial center for the country. Eighty percent of the city was destroyed during WW II.

Districts include the Ermita, Intramuros — the Walled City, Pandacan, Pasay and Santa Ana.

Waterways — Manila Bay and the Pasig River.

Streets, Avenues and Boulevards — The Escolta (Main Street), Taft Avenue aka Daitoa Avenue; and Dewey Boulevard aka Heiwa Boulevard during the Japanese Occupation; Mabini, San Andreas and Vito Cruz Streets.

Special Locations — Cementerio del Norte, La Salle College, the legislative and post office buildings; the Philippine General Hospital, the Port Area, Rizal Stadium and Harrison Ball Park, and the following prisons: Bilibid, Fort Santiago and Santo Tomás.

216   *Fires of Survival*

Luzon's Provinces

Albay Province — Located in Southeastern Luzon. Legaspi, the capital, was the site of Japanese landings in 1941; and, subsequently, of U.S. landings in 1945.

Bataan — A peninsulva surrounded by the South China Sea on its western shore and by Manila Bay on its eastern, this history-making province was the site of Philippine/U.S. military resistence against overwhelming Japanese forces. It was also the province from which the Bataan Death March began its 112 kilometer march by POWs to concentration camps in Tarlac. In 1945 American troops landed in the town of Mariveles to recapture the peninsula.

Batangas — Located southwest of Manila, Batangas is the site of ancient Lake Taal and Taal Volcano, which has erupted several times this century.

Benquet — A mountainous province in northeastern Luzon, Benquet surrounds the independent city of Baguio which thrives under a separate administration. The city, known as a mountain retreat, suffered much damage during the war.

Bulacan — Historic Bulacan province was the site of Biak-na-Bato, General Emilio Aguinaldo's headquarters during the Philippine/American war of 1898. Other special locations include Marilao, Balagtas, Malolos, Plaridel, Bahay Paniqui Caves (Bat House Caves), and Mt. Lumot, south of the caves.

Cavite — Sitting on the southern side of Manila Bay, Cavite's role in the defense of the islands was significant. Cavite Naval Base saw action under both the Americans and the Japanese.

Cagayan — Of historic significance in this northern province is the city of Aparri, where the Japanese first landed on Luzon in December, 1941.

Corregidor — An island province located at the mouth of Manila Bay, this island, known as "The Rock," became a fortress in Philippine/U.S. resistance against the Japanese, until its capture in May, 1942.

Ilocos Sur — Located in Northern Luzon, this province was the site of a Japanese landing at Vigan in 1941.

Laguna — Just hours away from the city of Manila, Laguna saw guerrilla action during WW II. Special areas of interest located on Mt. Banahaw include Kuweba ng Dios Ama — Cave of God the Father; the "Hidden Doors" Boulder, Pitong Lihim; and the Place Where the Trees Knelt, an unusual stand of twisted, bent-over trees.

Mindoro — An island province on the southwestern side of Luzon, Mindoro saw military action during the war.

Mt. Province — Situated in mountainous northern Luzon, this province is the site of ancient rice terraces. Bontoc is its capital city.

Nueva Ecija — Located on the eastern side of central Luzon, Nueva Ecija was the location of Cabanatuan Concentration Camp, where American and Filipino POWs suffered torture, starvation and disease.

Pampanga — Situated on Luzon's central plain, Pampanga was the site of Clark Air Force Base during WW II, a strategic base for the defense of the islands.

Pangasinan — Bordered by the South China Sea, this province witnessed two his-toric invasions on Lingayen Gulf: the Japanese in 1941 and the U.S. in 1945.

Tarlac — Located in central Luzon, Tarlac is known for its infamous concentration camps—Capas and O'Donnell—the prisons where thousands of Filipino and American POWs lost their lives.

Zambales — Its western shore facing the south China Sea, Zambales was the location of a U.S. Air Force base in the town of Iba.

Historic Facts and Figures

U.S. Military Leaders:
General Douglas MacArthur (1880-1964) — Commander-in-Chief of the Pacific Theater in WW II.
General Jonathan Wainwright (1883-1953) — U.S. general, commander over military operations in the Philippines, left in charge by General MacArthur when he retreated to Australia.
General King — U.S. general who surrendered to the Japanese on Bataan in April, 1942.

U.S./Philippine Military Units:
The Philippine Scouts, the 11th Airborne, the First Cavalry, the 37th Infantry and others.

Japanese Military:
General Homma — Commander-in-Chief of the Japanese Imperial Army in the Philippines.
Sigemori Kuroda — One of the generals in charge of the Japanese occupation army in Manila.

Special Terms:
Banzai — Battle cry or victory cheer.
Greater East Asia Co-Prosperity Sphere — A doctrine of cooperation among Asian people espoused by the Japanese Imperial Forces in WW II.
Kamikaze — A suicidal airplane attack practiced by the Japanese air force.
Kempetai (also kempeitai) — Japanese military police.
Nambu Woodpecker Machine Gun — The name of a machine gun used by the Japanese.

World Leaders:
Franklin Delano Roosevelt (1882-1945) — 32nd U.S. President, Commander-in-Chief of the nation's forces during WW II.
Winston Churchill (1874-1965) — British Prime Minister, statesman and author.

Filipino Patriots, Artists and Poets:
Emilio Aguinaldo (1869-1964) — Revolutionary leader during the Philippine/American War in 1898 and leader of the revolutionary army in 1896 against the Spaniards. He was president of the first Philippine Repubic, which he founded in Biak-na-Bato, Bulacan Province.
Fernando Amorsolo (1892-1972) — Celebrated Filipino painter of Philippine scenes and subjects.
Francisco Baltazar (1789-1862) — Poet from Bulacan Province who wrote on national issues.
José Rizal (1861-1896) — Philippine patriot and writer who was martyred by the Spaniards. Rizal Park (Luneta) in Manila is a shrine dedicated to him.

BIBLIOGRAPHY

Atlases:
Census Atlas of the Philippines - 1939, Vol. V; Commonwealth of the Philippines, Commission of the Census-Manila; Manila Bureau of Printing, 1939.

Dictionaries:
The American Heritage Larousse Spanish Dictionary, 1987, by Houghton Mifflin and Librairie Larousse, Boston, Mass.
Basic Tagalog by Paraluma S. Aspillera, 1968, by Charles E. Tuttle Co., Inc.; 19th printing, 1988.
Concise English-Tagalog Dictionary by Jose Villa Panganiban, Ph.D., 1969, by Charles E. Tuttle Co., Inc., Rutland, Vermont & Tokyo, Japan; 20th printing, 1992.
Pilipino/English-English/Pilipino by Sam & Angelina Bickford; 1985, 1988 by Hippocrene Books, Inc., New York, N.Y.
The Reader's Digest Great Encyclopedic Dictionary, Including Funk & Wagnall's Standard College Dictionary, 1966, by The Reader's Digest Association, Inc., Pleasantville, N.Y.

Encyclopedias:
Funk & Wagnall's Standard Reference Encyclopedia, Vol. 19, 1965, by Wilfred Funk, Inc.; published by Standard Reference Works Publishing, Inc., N.Y.; including updated year books of same.

Other Reference Books:
Aguinaldo-A Narrative of Filipino Ambitions by Edwin Wildman; 1901, by Lothrop Publishing Co., Boston-Norwood Press.
I Saw the Fall of the Philippines by Colonel Carlos P. Romulo; 1943, by George G. Harrap & Co., Ltd. — In association with B.U.E. Ltd., London.
Manila, Goodbye by Robin Prising; 1975, by Houghton Mifflin Co., Boston.
Our Islands and Their People as Seen with Camera and Pencil by Maj.Gen. Joseph Wheeler & Jose De Oliveras; 1899, by N.D. Publishing Co.
Outside the Walls by Gladys Savary; 1954, by Gladys Savary; printed by Vantage Press, Inc., N.Y.
The Philippine Cookbook by Reynaldo Alejandro; 1982, 1985, by Perigree Books published by the Putnam Publishing Group, N.Y., N.Y.
Philippines Handbook by Peter Harper & Evelyn Sebastian Pedlow; 1991, by Moon Publications, Inc., Chico, California.
Pinoy: The First Wave (1898-1941) by Roberto Vallangca; 1977 by Strawberry Hill Press, Portland, Oregon.
The Second Wave: Pinay & Pinoy (1945-1960) by Caridad Concepcion Vallangca; 1987, by Strawberry Hill Press, Portland, Oregon.

Yesterdays in the Philippines by Joseph Earle Stevens; 1899, by Charles Scribner's Sons, N.Y.

Magazines:
Ex-POW Bulletin published by American Ex-Prisoners of War, 700 Wabash, Olathe, KS 66061.
"Japanese Hellships" report by AXPOW Jack R. Williamson, 9/91.
"Follow-up to Japanese Hellships" report by Ted L. Pleuger, 11/91.
National Geographic Society, Washington, D.C.
"The Philippines-Freedom's Pacific Frontier" by Robert De Ross, 9/66.
"The Philippines-Better Days Still Elude An Old Friend" by Don Moser, 3/77.

Articles, Pamphlets, and Newspapers:
From the National Archives:
"Cabanatuan, Camp I." report on American Prisoners of War by the Japanese in the Philippines, prepared by the Office of the Provost Marshall General, Nov. 19, 1945.
"Cabanatuan, May 27, 1942" report...same as above.
"Camp O'Donnell" report...same as above.
"October Ship" statement of Boatswain Martin Binder, Liaison and Research Branch American Prisoners of War, July 31, 1946.
"Old Bilbid Prison" prepared by the Office of the Provost Marshall General, Nov. 19, 1945.

The San Francisco Examiner
"This is My Story" by Jonathan W. Wainwright; copyright 1945 by King Features Syndicate, Inc.